Lynne Graham was born in Northern Ireland and has been a keen romance reader since her teens. She is very happily married, to an understanding husband who has learned to cook since she started to write! Her five children keep her on her toes. She has a very large dog who knocks everything over, a very small terrier who barks a lot, and two cats. When time allows, Lynne is a keen gardener.

After spending three years as a die-hard New Yorker, **Kate Hewitt** now lives in a small village in the English Lake District, with her husband, their five children and a golden retriever. In addition to writing intensely emotional stories, she loves reading, baking and playing chess with her son—she has yet to win against him, but she continues to try. Learn more about Kate at kate-hewitt.com.

D1639321

THE SHEIKH CROWNS HIS VIRGIN

LYNNE GRAHAM

GREEK'S BABY OF REDEMPTION

KATE HEWITT

MILLS & BOON

First Published in Great Britain 2019
by Mills & Boon, an imprint of HarperCollins*Publishers*
1 London Bridge Street, London, SE1 9GF

The Sheikh Crowns His Virgin © 2019 by Lynne Graham

Greek's Baby of Redemption © 2019 by Kate Hewitt

ISBN: 978-0-263-27343-4

MIX
Paper from
responsible sources
FSC C007454

FSC
www.fsc.org

This book is produced from independently certified FSC™ paper
to ensure responsible forest management.
For more information visit www.harpercollins.co.uk/green.

Printed and bound in Spain
by CPI, Barcelona

THE SHEIKH CROWNS HIS VIRGIN

LYNNE GRAHAM

CHAPTER ONE

ZOE DESCENDED THE steps of her grandfather's private jet and as the sunlight of Maraban enveloped her she smiled happily. It was spring and the heat was bearable but, best of all, she was taking the very first brave step into her new life.

On her own, on her own *at last*, free of the restrictions that her sisters would have attached to her but, most importantly of all, free of the *low* expectations they had of her. Winnie and Vivi had been amazed when Zoe had agreed to move to a foreign country for a few months without freaking out at the prospect. They had been equally amazed when she'd agreed to marry a much older man to fulfil her part of their agreement with their grandfather, Stamboulas Fotakis. Why not? It wasn't as though it was going to be a *real* marriage, merely a pretend marriage in which her future husband made political use of the fact that she was the granddaughter of a former princess of a country called Bania, which no longer existed.

Long before Zoe was even born the two tiny realms of Bania and Mara had joined to become Maraban and apparently her late grandmother, the Princess Azra, had been hugely popular in both countries. Prince Hakem wanted to marry Zoe literally for her ancestry and she would become an Arabian princess and live in the royal palace for several months. There she would enjoy glorious solitude with nobody bothering her, nobody asking how she felt or worriedly enquiring if she thought she should have more therapy to help her cope with ordinary life. Even though she hadn't had a panic attack in months, her siblings had always been on edge around her, awaiting another one.

Zoe adored her older sisters but their constant care and concern had held her back from the independence she needed to rebuild her self-esteem and forge her own path. And taking part in this silly pretend marriage was all she had to do to finally obtain that freedom.

All three sisters had agreed to marry men of their grandfather's choosing to gain his financial help for their foster parents, John and Liz Brooke. Winnie and Vivi had already fulfilled that bargain. But in Zoe's case, no pressure whatsoever had been placed on her and, indeed, John and Liz's mortgage arrears had been paid off shortly after her sister Vivi's marriage had taken place. Yes, she thought wryly, even her extremely ruthless grandfather had shrunk from taking the risk of putting pressure on his youngest granddaughter, having taken on board her siblings' conviction that she was hopelessly fragile and emotionally vulnerable. Nobody had faith in her ability to be strong, Zoe reflected ruefully, which was why it was so very important that she proved for her own benefit that she *could* be strong.

Like her sisters, Zoe had grown up in foster care, and a terrifying incident when she was twelve years old had traumatised her. But she had buried all that hurt and fear, seemingly flourishing in John and Liz's happy home, only for those frightening insecurities to come back and engulf her while she was studying botany at university. Having to freely mix with men, having to deal with friends asking why she didn't want a boyfriend, had put her under severe strain. Her panic attacks had grown worse and worse and, although she had contrived to hide her extreme anxiety from her sisters, she had, ultimately, been unable to deal with her problems alone. Weeks before she sat her final degree exams, she had suffered a nervous breakdown, which had meant that she had had to take time out from her course to recover.

Although she had subsequently completed her degree and worked through the therapy required to put her back on an even track where crippling anxiety no longer ruled her every thought and action, her sisters had continued to treat her as if she could shatter again at any moment. While she understood that their protectiveness came from love, she also saw that their attitude had made her weaker than she need have been and that she badly needed the chance to stand on her own feet. With her sisters now married, one living in Greece and the other in Italy, coming to Maraban was Zoe's opportunity to prove that she had overcome her unhappy past.

Zoe stepped into the limousine awaiting her, grateful for the reality that her arrival in Maraban was completely low-key. Prince Hakem had insisted that no public appearances or indeed anything of that nature would be required from her. He might be the brother

of the current King but he had no official standing in
Maraban. Zoe's grandfather should have been travelling
with her but a pressing business matter had led to him
asking if she could manage alone if he put off his arrival
until the following day. Of course, she could manage,
she thought cheerfully, gazing out with lively interest
at the busy streets of the capital city, Tasit, which was
an intriguing mix of old and new. She saw old buildings and elaborate mosques with quaint colourful tur-
rets nudging shoulders with redeveloped areas boasting
soaring skyscrapers and office blocks. Maraban was
evidently right in the middle of the process of mod-
ernisation.

Oil and gas wealth had transformed the country. Zoe
had read everything she could find on Maraban and had
rolled her eyes at the discovery that nobody appeared to
know why her grandmother, Princess Azra, had failed
to marry the current King, Tahir, as she had been expected to do. The bald truth was that Azra had run
off with Stamboulas Fotakis sooner than marry a man
who'd already had three wives. Presumably that story
had been suppressed to conserve the monarch's dignity.
Luckily, Stam had told her everything she needed to
know about his late wife's background.

Darkness was falling fast when the limo driver
turned off the road and steered between imposingly
large gates guarded by soldiers. Zoe strained to see the
enormous property that lay ahead but the limo travelled
slowly right on past it, threading a path through a vast
complex of buildings and finally drawing up beside
one. She was ushered out and indoors before she could
even catch her breath and was a little disappointed to

find herself standing in a contemporary house. A very *large* contemporary house, she conceded wryly, with aggressively gilded fancy furniture and nothing whatsoever historic about it. A female servant in a long kaftan bowed to her and showed her up a brilliantly lit staircase into an entire suite of rooms.

Her disappointment that she wasn't going to be living in the ancient royal palace slowly ebbed as she scanned her comfortable and well-furnished surroundings. It wasn't ideal that none of the staff spoke her language and that she didn't speak theirs but miming could accomplish a lot, she told herself bracingly as her companion mimicked eating to let her know that a meal was being brought. And long before she went home again, she should have picked up at least a few useful phrases to enable her to communicate more effectively, she told herself soothingly.

A maid had already arrived to unpack her suitcases when a knock sounded on the door. Zoe made it to the door first.

A slimly built young man and a uniformed nurse hovered outside. 'I am Dr Wazd,' the man told her stiffly. 'I have been instructed to give you a vaccination shot. The nurse will assist.'

Zoe winced because she hated needles and she was surprised because she had had all the required shots for Maraban. But then what she did know that a medical doctor would not know better? She rolled up her sleeve and then frowned as she saw the doctor's hand on the syringe was shaking. Glancing up at him in surprise, noting the perspiration beading his brow, she wondered if he was a very newly qualified doctor to be so nervous and she was relieved when the nurse silently filched the syringe from him and gave her the injection without further ado. It stung and she gritted her teeth.

No sooner was that done than a tray of food arrived and she sat down at the table to eat, noting that she was feeling dizzy and woolly-headed and surmising that she was already suffering the effects of jet lag. But while she was eating, she began feeling as though the world around her were slowing down and her body felt as heavy as lead. Feeling dizzy even seated, she rose to go to the bathroom and had to grip the back of a chair to balance. As she wobbled on her heels, blinking rapidly, a suffocating blackness folded in and she dropped down into it with a gasp of dismay…

His Royal Highness, Prince Faraj al-Basara, was in a very high-powered meeting in London dealing with his country's oil and gas production when his private mobile thrummed a warning in his pocket. Few people had that number and it only ever rang if it was very, *very* important. Excusing himself immediately, Raj stepped outside, his brain awash with sudden apprehension. Had his father taken ill? Or had some other calamity occurred back home in Maraban?

Maraban was a tiny Gulf state but it was also one of the richest countries in the world. A terrorist incident, however, would bring the home of his birth to a screeching halt because the security forces were equally tiny and these days Maraban relied on wealth and diplomacy to stay safe. When Raj thought nostalgically of home, it was always of a place of stark black and white contrasts where four-wheel-drive vehicles and helicopters

startled livestock in the desert and where a conservative Middle Eastern ethos struggled to cope with the
very different mores and the sheer speed of change in
the modern world.

It was eight years, however, since Raj had last visited
his home because his father, the King, had removed him
from his position as Crown Prince and sent him into
exile for refusing to go into the army and for refusing
even more vehemently to marry the bride his parent had
chosen for him. No, he had not been a dutiful or obedient son, Raj acknowledged with grim self-honesty, he
had been a stubborn, rebellious one and, unfortunately
for him, there was no greater sin in his culture.

That said, however, Raj had, since, moved on from
that less than stellar beginning to carve his own path
in the business world and there his shrewd brain, in-
tuition and ability to spot trends had ensured mete-
oric success in that sphere. He had also learned how
to steer Maraban into the future from beyond its bor-
ders, making allies, attracting foreign businesses and
investment while constantly encouraging growth in the
public infrastructure required to keep his country up
to speed with the latest technology. And his reward for
that tireless focus and resolve? Maraban, the home that
he loved, was positively booming.

He was pleasantly surprised when he answered his
phone and recognised his cousin, Omar's voice. Omar
had pretty much been his best friend since the dark days
of the military school they had both been forced to attend as adolescents, an unforgettable era of relentless
bullying and abuse that Raj still winced to recall. As
Crown Prince he had had a target painted on his back

and his father had told the staff to turn a blind eye, believing that it would be beneficial for his only child to be toughened up in such a severe environment.

'Omar…what can I do for you?' he asked almost cheerfully, relieved of the anxiety that his elderly father had taken ill because Omar would not have been chosen as messenger for that development. *That* call would only have come from a member of his father's staff. After all, his mother had died while he was still a boy. The memory made him tense for his mother had died in a manner that he would never forget: she had taken her own life. It had taken a very long time for Raj to accept that her unhappiness had surpassed her love for her nine-year-old son and he had never forgotten his sense of abandonment because, once she was gone, everything soft and loving and caring had vanished from his childish world.

'I'm in a real fix, Raj, and I think you are the only person with sufficient knowledge to approach with this,' Omar declared, his habitually upbeat voice unusually flat in tone. 'I've been dragged into something I don't want to be involved in and it's serious. You know I'm a royalist and very loyal to my country but there are some things I *can't*—'

'Cut to the chase,' Raj sliced in with a bemused frown. 'What have you been dragged into?'

'Early this morning I received a call from someone at the palace who asked if I would look after a "package" and keep it safe until further notice. And that's the problem, Raj… I didn't get delivered a package, I got a woman.'

'A *woman*?' Raj repeated in disbelief. 'Are you joking me?'

'I wish I was. All the women in the tribe are outraged and I've been thrown out of my tent to accommodate her,' Omar lamented. 'My wife thinks I'm getting involved in sex trafficking.'

'It could *not* be that,' Raj pronounced with assurance because the penalty for such a crime was death and his father was most assiduous in ensuring that neither drugs nor prostitution gained ground in Maraban.

'No, of course it couldn't be,' Omar agreed. 'But even though the order came from the very highest level of the palace I should not be asked by *anyone* to imprison a woman against her will.'

'How do you know the order came from the very highest level?' Raj demanded.

His cousin mentioned a name and Raj gritted his teeth. Bahadur Abdi was the most trusted military adviser in his father's inner circle and could only be acting at the King's command. That shocking truth shed an entirely different light on the kidnapping because it meant that Raj's father was personally involved. 'Who the hell *is* this woman?'

'You're not going to like the suspicion I'm developing any more than I do,' his cousin warned him heavily. 'But I contacted the palace as soon as I appreciated I was being asked to deal with a *live* package and I was told that she was the last descendant of the al-Mishaal family, which was a shock. Thought they were all dead and buried long ago! Were you even aware that *my* father divorced my mother two months ago?'

Raj was shocked enough by both those revelations

to listen keenly as Omar described his mother's refusal to discuss the divorce and the oddity of her continuing calm over the termination of a marriage that had lasted almost fifty years and had spawned four children and at least a dozen grandchildren. Prince Hakem, Raj's uncle and Omar's father, however, was an embittered and ambitious man, who ever since Raj's exile had been striving to become the recognised heir to the throne in Raj's place. Ironically, Raj didn't even really feel that he could blame his uncle for his ambition because, as the King's younger brother, Hakem had spent his whole life close to the throne but virtually ignored and powerless, his royal brother refusing to grant him any form of responsibility in the kingdom. Furthermore, only the King could name his heir and Hakem had long desired a role of power and the rise in status it would accord him.

'So, what's the connection with this woman?'

Omar shared his suspicions and Raj paled and experienced a spontaneous surge of rage at such a manipulative plot being played out in virtual secret behind the palace walls. 'Surely that is *not* possible?'

'It may not be. I must admit that the woman doesn't look remotely as if she carries Marabanian blood. She's got white-blonde hair…looks like something out of that fairy tale… *The Sleeping Beauty*,' Omar revealed heavily.

Raj parted compressed lips. 'Princess Azra of Bania was the daughter of a Danish explorer, who was blond,' he murmured flatly. 'I don't know much about Azra's elopement with her Greek tycoon, who was working in Maraban when the two countries joined, but I do know her flight with another man created a *huge* scandal.

She was supposed to become my father's fourth wife and instead, she ran off with Fotakis and married him.'

'Didn't know that…but then it's not really my slice of history in the same way as it's yours.' Omar sighed heavily. 'Just give me some diplomatic advice about what to do next because I'm at a standstill. This woman has *obviously* been kidnapped. Our doctor says she's been drugged, so she's unconscious and she arrived with no means of identification. But even if she *is* one of the al-Mishaal family's next generation from that marriage all those years ago I still can't believe that any *young* woman would agree to marry a man as old as my father—'

'It would shock you what some Western women would be willing to do to become an Arabian princess with unlimited wealth at their disposal. Suggest that a crown could also be on offer and there would be many takers of that particular bargain,' Raj breathed with cynical derision, his lean, darkly handsome features clenching hard as he reflected on his own experiences and the shattering betrayal he had endured…and worst of all, only *after* he had destroyed his standing with his father for ever. Even years after that youthful disillusionment, he was grimly aware of the pulling power of his status and wealth in the West. In his radius even seemingly intelligent women frothed and gushed like champagne, desperate to attract and bed him. Sadly for them, he didn't find being chased, flattered or potentially seduced remotely attractive because he preferred to do his own hunting in that field. And, almost inevitably, that shattering act of infidelity following on from his mother's suicide had underlined his growing conviction that women were not to be trusted.

'Possibly not...shocked,' Omar clarified as tactfully as he knew how because he too was probably thinking about that old and demeaning history that still scarred Raj's pride. 'But I *can* tell you that if that is my father's game, very few of our people would like or accept such a marriage. My father is unpopular: he's as old school as your father. I don't know anyone who would be willing to accept him as the heir in place of you, *no*, not even if he *has* somehow contrived to bring back the ghost of the al-Mishaal royal family as a potential bride!'

Raj had been away from palace politics for a very long time but he had not forgotten the scheming games of one-upmanship involved. In the role of Hakem's bride, Princess Azra's granddaughter would be a priceless figurehead, Raj acknowledged grimly. Half the population of Maraban came from Banian roots and all had been seriously dissatisfied forty-odd years ago when the joining of the two states was not matched as had been promised by a marital alliance between Bania's only Princess and Mara's King. All those people had felt cheated by the absence of Banian blood in the royal family tree of Maraban. It would be a triumph for his uncle to marry Azra's descendant and it definitely would increase his popularity, which was precisely why Raj's father would never have allowed such a marriage to take place: King Tahir did not tolerate competition or, for that matter, a little brother he deemed to be getting too big for his boots. After such a publicity-grabbing stunt, Hakem could only have been hoping to be named the King's heir and step into Raj's former position as Crown Prince in his nephew's stead.

Omar broke into Raj's racing thoughts. 'Tell me, what am I to do with her?' he demanded, infuriated that an innocent woman had been kidnapped to prevent a marriage he believed to be wholly inappropriate. 'How do I safely *and* decently rid myself of this appalling responsibility? '

And Raj told him with a succinctness that shook both of them before he powered back into his meeting to apologise and explain that a family crisis demanded his immediate attention. He contacted an investigation firm, who had done excellent work for him in the past, to request an immediate file on his uncle's putative bride. He needed information and he needed it fast yet he was aware that he was struggling to concentrate.

Why?

For the first time in eight years, Raj would be returning to the country of his birth and, although anger was driving him at the prospect of being forced to deal with another unscrupulous and mercenary woman, on another much more basic level he was quietly exhilarated at the prospect of seeing his homeland again...

Zoe surfaced from an uneasy, woozy dream to find someone helping her to lift a glass of water to her lips. Her eyes refused to focus and her body felt limp but she knew she needed the bathroom and said so. Someone helped her rise and supported her—more than one someone, she registered dimly, because her limbs were too weak to carry her. She tried to scan her surroundings but the walls being weirdly bendy spooked her and

momentarily she shut her eyes as she was helped back
to bed. She had been drugged, taken somewhere, she
registered fearfully, fighting without success to stay
conscious and focus. She had to protect herself, *had* to
protect herself! That self-saving litany rang through her
brain like a wake-up call…but even that panic couldn't
prevent her from sliding down into oblivion again.

When Raj received the info on Zoe Mardas, he was
forced to rapidly rearrange his expectations. Why on
earth would such a woman be willing to marry a man
almost as old as her grandfather? Clearly, financial
greed would be a most unlikely motive for a woman
with the billionaire Stamboulas Fotakis at her back.
Fotakis was her grandfather and, by all accounts, an
extremely protective relative. Other more stressful con-
cerns then started dawning on Raj. The Greek tycoon
would scarcely take the kidnapping of his granddaughter lying down. He would not allow it to be hushed up
either. Yet, even more strangely, it did look as though
Fotakis had been the prime mover and shaker behind the
proposed marriage between Hakem and Zoe. What was
Stam Fotakis getting out of it? Some lucrative business
deal? Or a title for his granddaughter? Raj pondered
those unknowns and decided to contact Fotakis direct…

Someone was brushing Zoe's hair when she next woke
up, someone murmuring softly in a foreign language.
She opened her eyes and saw an older woman, who
smiled down at her from her kneeling stance by her side
while she brushed Zoe's long mane of pale blonde hair
with admiring care. She did not seem hostile or threat-

ening in any way and Zoe forced a smile, her innate
survival instincts kicking in. Until she knew what was
happening she would be a good little prisoner, playing
along until such time as her grandfather came to rescue her; because one thing she *did* know: Stamboulas
Fotakis would not be long in putting in an appearance.
He would create a huge fuss the instant he realised that
Zoe had gone missing and no rock would be left un-
turned in his search for her, she reflected with a strong
sense of relief.

Gently detaching her hair from the woman's light
hold, she sat up and the woman stood up and helpfully
showed her straight to the bathroom. Even by that stage,
Zoe was recognising that she had not been disorientated
the night before when she had thought the walls surrounding her looked rather odd. Evidently, she was no
longer at the villa in the palace complex, she was in a
tent, a very large and very luxurious tent decorated with
rich hangings and opulent seating but, when all was said
and done, it was *still* a tent! And the connecting bathroom was also under canvas. Zoe felt hot and sweaty
and looked longingly at the shower, but she didn't want
to risk the vulnerability of getting naked. She freshened
up with cold water, dried her face and frowned down at
the unfamiliar long white fine cotton shift she now wore
in place of the skirt and top she had travelled in. That
creepy nervous doctor and his sidekick, she thought in
disgust. She would never trust a doctor again!

Why had she been taken from Prince Hakem's villa?
Although no one had ever told her that it was *his* villa,
she had simply assumed it was. Presumably somebody
didn't want this marriage of his to take place, she rea-

soned reflectively. No problem, she thought ruefully,
there had been no need to assault her with a syringe,
send her to sleep and ship her out to a tent because she
would quite happily go home again without any argument. Furthermore, she rather thought that would be her
grandfather's reaction as well because he had demanded
very strong assurances from her bridegroom-to-be that
she would be safe and secure in Maraban and he would
be appalled at what had happened to her. Surely her becoming a princess to follow in the footsteps of her for-
merly royal grandmother, Princess Azra, would not still
be so important to Stam Fotakis that he would expect
his granddaughter to risk life and limb in the process?

Two women were setting out a meal when she returned to the main tent and she roamed as casually
as she could in the direction of the doorway that had
been left uncovered. What she glimpsed froze her in
her tracks in instant denial. She saw a circle of tents and
beyond them sand dunes that ran off into the horizon.
She was in the desert, so escaping would be more of a
challenge than she felt equal to because she would need
transport and a map at the very least for such a venture.
The discovery that she had been plunged into such an
alien environment sent her nervous tension climbing
higher and she swallowed hard. Where else had she expected a tent to be pitched but in the desert? she asked
herself irritably.

Above one of the tents she espied the rotor blades of a
helicopter. Was that how she had arrived? Had she been
flown in? She shuddered as another far more frightening thought suddenly occurred to her.

Why was she assuming that she had been kidnapped to prevent the wedding taking place in forty-eight hours? Her grandfather was an extremely rich man. It was equally possible that she had been taken so that a ransom demand could be made for her release. That scenario meant that someone laying violent hands on her was a much more likely development, she decided sickly, her tummy hollowing out. As one of the women carefully threaded her stiff arms into a concealing wrap and even tied it for her, Zoe could feel all the hallmarks of an impending panic attack assailing her and she was already zoning out as her thoughts raged out of her control.

She saw a mental image of herself beaten up in a photo for her grandfather's benefit. Her heart raced and she turned rapidly away from the view of the encampment, incapable of even noticing that the two women with her were hastily bowing and backing out of the tent again or that a male figure now stood silhouetted in the doorway. Her throat was tight, making it hard for her to catch her breath. She was shivering in spite of the heat, cold, then hot, dizziness making her sway as panic threatened.

I'm fine, I'm strong, I can cope, she chanted inwardly. But the mantra that usually worked to steady her failed because for several unbearable seconds she was simply overpowered by fear.

A male voice sounded directly behind her and a hand brushed her shoulder. Startled, terrified, Zoe reacted automatically with the self-defence tactics she had spent months learning so that she had the skills she needed to ensure her personal safety.

She spun at speed, her elbow travelling up for a chest

blow and her clenched fist heading for a throat strike while her knee lifted to aim at the groin. Raj was so disconcerted by a woman the size of a child attacking him that he almost fell over in sheer shock and then his own training kicked in and, light as dancer on his feet, he twisted and blocked her before bringing her down on the rug beneath their feet with careful hands.

'Let go of me, you bastard!' she railed at him, clawing, biting and scratching and in the act contriving to dislodge the white *keffiyeh* that covered his head.

Still reeling with disconcertion, Raj backed off several steps because he couldn't subdue her without hurting her and he refused to take that risk. She squirmed frantically away and the sheer terror in her face savaged his view of himself. Her eyes were glassy, her face white as snow.

'You are quite safe here. Nobody is going to hurt you.' Raj crouched down to her level while she wriggled back against a carved wooden chest like a trapped animal and hugged her knees, rocking back and forth. She was tiny and his every instinct was to protect her. 'On my honour, I *swear* that you are safe...' he intoned with as much conviction as he could get into the assurance, because she wasn't listening to him and she wasn't looking at him.

He was annoyed that his cousin had not sent his English-speaking wife, Farida, in to Zoe immediately to explain that there was no threat of any kind against her. But most of all, he cursed his father and the omnipotence he wielded in Maraban, for Raj was convinced that his wily father had ordered the kidnapping of Hakem's youthful bride-to-be. Would his father have

counted the cost to the woman involved? Would he even
have foreseen that he was unleashing the kind of explo-
sively damaging scandal that no self-respecting country could withstand? No, his father, Tahir, would not
have looked at that bigger picture of cause and effect.
He would simply have set out to ensure that his ambitious brother's plot to raise his status was foiled while
steadfastly refusing to acknowledge the likelihood of
unexpected consequences.

In a fierce temper at that frustrating knowledge, Raj
sank down beside Zoe Mardas on his knees and began
to coax her into attempting a breathing exercise, aimed
at calming her down. Extraordinary green eyes, clear
as emeralds, skimmed over him and she blinked, long
feathery lashes dipping. For a split second he was frozen in place by her ice-cool Scandinavian beauty. He
coached her in breathing in, holding her breath and
then very slowly breathing out again. She did so and
then shot him an exasperated look, *not* the kind of look
Raj was accustomed to receiving from young women.

'Yes, I do know how to do that for myself!' Zoe told
him sharply as soon as she was breathing normally
again. 'Why do you know how?'

'For a while in my teens, I suffered similar episodes,'
Raj admitted, startling himself with that candour as
much as he startled her; for the severe bullying he had
endured at military school had for years afterwards
left him damaged. He could only think his candour
had been unwisely drawn from him by his glimpse of
her at her most vulnerable and a natural need to put
her at her ease.

In receipt of that surprising admission, Zoe stared

back at him in wonderment because in her experience men were much less willing to admit to suffering such a condition. But before she could question him further to satisfy her curiosity, he vaulted gracefully upright again. She watched him smooth down his rumpled white buttoned tunic and snatch up the white head cloth she had dislodged in their tussle. And then, strikingly, for the first time in her life Zoe looked at a man with interest because there was no denying it: whoever he was, he was without question the most beautiful creature she had ever seen. Dense silky blue-black curls covered his well-shaped skull while high cheekbones and hollows fed into a truly spectacular bone structure sheathed in olive skin. Dark-as-the-devil eyes glittered below straight ebony brows. A faint shadow of stubble surrounded his wide sensual mouth, his full soft lower lip tensing as he noticed her lingering scrutiny.

Turning pink, Zoe hurriedly glanced away while scolding herself for staring but, really, with looks of that quality, he had to be accustomed to being stared at by women, she reasoned defensively, uneasy with her speeded-up heartbeat and the sudden tightening of her nipples.

She wasn't *that* sort of woman, she reminded herself resolutely. Sex didn't interest her. Basically, men didn't interest her. She had been thrown off the path of normal development at the age of twelve when an attempted rape had devastated her. Ever since then she had held herself apart, avoiding mixed company unless it was family-orientated. She was perfectly happy around her brothers-in-law, Eros and Raffaele, and she hadn't been nervous either when dealing with the male parents at the childcare nursery where she had worked for months immediately after her recovery from her breakdown. Back then a full-time job in her own field of botany had seemed too challenging as a first step back into the real world.

'Who are you?' she asked baldly.

'You may call me Raj. I am no one of importance here,' he intoned in smooth dismissal, for he intended to fly back out of Maraban within the hour because he could not risk discovery and possible arrest. 'But this nomadic base camp is where my cousin, Sheikh Omar, lives at this time of year.'

Zoe bridled as she scrambled upright, wishing for about the thousandth time that she was even a few inches taller, for being only four feet eleven inches tall was not an advantage when it came to persuading people to take her seriously. Unsurprisingly, Raj towered over her but he wasn't quite as tall as her brothers-in-law, both of whom put her in mind of giants when she was around them. 'Is he the man responsible for bringing me here…*against my will*?' she stressed acidly.

'No, he is not,' Raj told her emphatically. 'Nor would he harm a hair on your head but he has kept his distance because he does not speak English.'

'Then who *is* responsible for bringing me here?' Zoe demanded, standing her ground, tensing her spine to keep her back and shoulders straight and her head high. Her favourite self-help book urged that even if you didn't *feel* confident, it was still possible to fake confidence and by so doing actually acquire it.

'I'm afraid I can't tell you that,' Raj countered flatly.

Zoe's green eyes flared as if he had slapped her. *'Why not?'* she demanded.

'It would serve no useful purpose.'

Zoe breathed in very deeply to contain the temper she hadn't known she had until that moment. He was so incredibly patronising, so superior and his attitude affected her like a chalk scraping down a blackboard, setting her teeth on edge. 'That's my decision to make, *not* yours,' she said succinctly.

Engaged in replacing his *keffiyeh*, Raj looked heavenward, involuntarily amused by that argument. She was like a doll with that tiny stature of hers and her phenomenally long blonde hair and she barely reached his chest.

'You're not taking me seriously,' she condemned.

'I'm afraid not,' Raj conceded grudgingly. 'I arrived here to sort this unfortunate mess out and that is what I intend to do.'

'Is it indeed?' Zoe snapped, incredulous that he had simply admitted his inability to treat her like an intelligent individual because, in her experience, most people lied on that score, denying that her diminutive size coloured their attitude towards her.

Raj paced several steps away from her, having discovered that proximity was unwise. His attention kept on dropping to that soft full pink mouth, that shimmering fall of pale hair, the barely noticeable little feminine curves hinting at her physical shape beneath the robe. He shifted, a kick of lust at his groin exasperating him for it was inappropriate and Raj was *always* very appropriate in his reactions to women. He controlled his responses, he did not allow them to control him and he had never understood the intoxicating lust that he had heard other men talk about, because only one woman had ever tested his control and, even then, it had not overwhelmed him.

'I intend to have you conveyed home as soon as it is possible…unless you are unwilling to give up the possibility of marrying my uncle, Prince Hakem, and becoming a princess,' Raj murmured bluntly. 'I suspect my aunt, his wife of many years, whom he recently divorced, would be relieved to have the ingrate back by default, little though he deserves her forgiveness and understanding…'

CHAPTER TWO

'ARE YOU TELLING me that Prince Hakem was already married at the time he agreed to marry me?' Zoe gasped in astonished disbelief, her triangular face tightening and losing colour at that horrendous concept.

'Of course, you were *already* aware of that reality,' Raj informed her with considerable scorn in his tone. 'After all, he has been married for many years. He has four children and a very large number of grandchildren... However, I assume that your grandfather was unwilling to accept a polygamous marriage, so my uncle *had* to divorce his wife before he could be allowed to marry you...'

Zoe was stunned by what she was learning. She wondered if her grandfather had been aware of those same unpleasant facts and then she told herself off for shying away from the unlovely truth that Stam Fotakis had wanted his granddaughter to become a princess regardless of what it would take to achieve that end. Prince Hakem had *had* to divorce his wife to take Princess Azra's granddaughter as a bride! Zoe was appalled and mortified and guilt-stricken, feeling that she should've done her homework better and shouldn't be in the position of finding out such a crucial fact when it was too late to change anything. Hakem's poor wife! Raj was definitely correct in his conviction that her grandfather would never have accepted a polygamous marriage and would only ever have settled for his grandchild becoming the Prince's sole wife.

'I didn't know... I *swear* I didn't know that he was a married man!' Zoe protested vehemently, a guilty flush driving off her previous pallor. 'In spite of what you seem to think, I would never have agreed if I had known that he was getting rid of his real wife just to marry me for a few months.'

Raj had no idea why she was bothering to defend her behaviour by pleading ignorance of the reality that his uncle had been a perfectly happy married man before her availability had ignited his ambition. Zoe Mardas might look convincingly like a storybook princess or a heavenly angel, but Raj had an innate distrust of that level of physical beauty and a cynical view of humanity. Beautiful on the outside but what less than presentable motives were she striving to conceal from him? He had discovered for himself that beautiful on the outside too often meant ugly on the inside.

In any case, Zoe could not possibly be as naïve as she was pretending to be. She *had* to know her own worth in Marabanian terms. Thousands of delighted Banians would flood the streets to celebrate an alliance between a royal Prince and Princess Azra's grandchild. His uncle had come very close to pulling off a spectacular coup in the popularity stakes.

'I assume you are willing to go home now?' Raj queried, marvelling at his own restraint in asking her that question because, frankly, he was determined to get her out of Maraban by any means within his power.

'Of course, I'm willing to go home!' Zoe shot back at him in reproach. 'Good grief, I'm not wanting to marry a man I've never even met, who divorced his wife just to become my bridegroom! Do I look that desperate?'

'I don't know you. I have no idea what your motivations are or, indeed, *were*,' Raj parried with the intrinsic hauteur that came as naturally to him as breathing, his exotically high cheekbones taut, his arrogant nose lifted, his hard jaw clenched.

Zoe's colour heightened, her eyes brightening with anger, for in a couple of sentences, he had cut her down to size, enforcing the distance between them while also underlining his indifference to her feelings about anything. He looked different with that headdress covering his riot of coal-black curls. While the *keffiyeh* framed and accentuated his superb bone structure and those dark deep-set eyes set below slashing ebony brows, it also made him look older and off-puttingly sombre.

'I confess that I am surprised, however, that you have not even met Prince Hakem. While such traditional matches still occasionally occur in Maraban, they are no longer the norm and I would not have thought a woman from your background would have been prepared to accept a husband sight unseen,' he admitted smoothly, dark eyes glittering back at her in cool challenge.

A wild surge of temper rocked Zoe where she stood, thoroughly disconcerting her, and her small hands coiled into tight fists by her side. The derision lacing his intonation and his appraisal was like a slap in the face. He might say that he didn't know her but she could

see that, regardless of that reality, he had still made un-
savoury assumptions about her character.

'Who the hell do you think you are to talk to me like
this?' Zoe suddenly hissed at him, out of all patience
and restraint because the way he was looking at her, as
though she were some sort of lesser being, infuriated
her. 'I came to this wretched country in good faith and
my trust has been betrayed. I was drugged, *kidnapped*
and subjected to a terrifying experience! Now you start
judging me even though you don't know the facts.'

'I agree that I don't know the facts, nor do I need to
know them,' Raj countered, disconcerted by the passion etched in her heart-shaped face as she answered
him back. He wasn't used to that—he wasn't used to
that kind of treatment at all.

He had been reserved from childhood, discouraged
from letting his guard down with anyone, continually
reminded about *who* he was and *what* he was and exactly what his rank demanded. After his mother's tragic
death, he had had to learn to conceal his feelings and
his insecurities, had had to accept that such personal
responses were out of step with his status. An accident
of birth had imprisoned him in a separate category,
denying him the relaxation of true friends or freedom.
When he had finally broken out of that prison, he had
discovered to his consternation that that often icy reserve of his, which kept people at a distance, was as
much a natural part of him as his face.

'Well, you're going to hear the facts, whether you
want to or not!' Zoe snapped back at him curtly. 'Prince
Hakem approached my grandfather to suggest the marriage, *not* the other way round. I didn't meet him be-

forehand because there was no need for me to meet him when it was never intended to be a normal marriage. I was to go through the ceremony and live quietly afterwards in the Prince's home. He swore that he would treat me like a daughter and that no demands would be made of me. Then after several months I was to go home and get a divorce…'

Raj's spectacular eyes gleamed as darkly bright as polar stars while he absorbed that surprising information. He understood now why his aunt had agreed to the divorce without making a fuss. Hakem must have promised to remarry her once he was free again and, in support of her husband's royal ambitions, Raj's aunt had been willing to make that sacrifice. 'But what was in this peculiar arrangement for you?' Raj persisted with a frown of bewilderment. 'It cannot surely have been enriching yourself when your grandfather is such a wealthy man…'

'Status!' Zoe almost spat out the word as if it physically hurt her and, indeed, it did. 'I would've become a princess and, while that doesn't matter much to me, it means a great deal to my grandfather and I wanted to please him. He's done a lot for me and my sisters.'

'Being a princess wouldn't have been much of a consolation while you were living in Hakem's home,' Raj informed her very drily. 'Hakem's wife and children are well known and well liked and everyone who knew them would have been ready to loathe you on sight.'

'Well, the marriage is not going to take place now, is it?' Zoe cut in thinly, turning away from him to wander across to the far side of the tent. 'After all that's happened, *nothing* short of handcuffs and chains would persuade me to stay in Maraban!'

Raj was disconcerted to find his brain sketching an erotic mental image of her chained to a bed, all flyaway blonde hair, passionate green eyes and little heaving pale pink curves for his private delectation. He stiffened and shifted restlessly while he fought to kill that untimely vision stone dead. But, sadly for him, there was nothing politically correct about his body and within seconds he was filled with desire.

'You know, I don't want to be rude or melodramatic,' Zoe began shakily.

'You may not want to be but you can't help behaving that way?' Raj incised hoarsely, knocked off balance now by his libido, that intimate imagery of her strengthening rather than fading and exercising the most extraordinary power over him.

Zoe spun. 'You're the one being rude!' she condemned, challenged to catch her breath when she clashed involuntarily with his intense gaze. 'Acting like being kidnapped is normal and refusing to tell me who orchestrated this whole stupid charade!'

'I am withholding that information because there is *no* possibility of the man involved being punished,' Raj admitted hoarsely.

What was it about that jet-dark gaze that made goose bumps rise on her exposed skin and sent little shivers running down her taut spine? Why did she suddenly feel so ridiculously overheated? Why did her tummy feel as though butterflies were fluttering through it? Instinctively she pressed her thighs together on the ache low in her core and she blinked in bewilderment and growing self-consciousness, her colour heightening as the explanation for her reaction dawned on her and shot through her like a lightning bolt. It was attraction, simple sexual attraction, and she was experiencing it for the first time *ever*. It made her feel all jumpy and twitchy, like a cat trying to walk across hot burning coals. Sheer shock crashed through her slender frame as she endeavoured to rise above her inner turmoil and focus on the conversation.

'And why is there no possibility of punishment?' Zoe demanded boldly.

'I will not discuss that with you. Please get dressed and we will leave.'

'To go where?' Zoe demanded in surprise.

'We are flying first to Dubai and then on to London, where you will be reunited with your grandfather,' Raj explained. 'As that arrangement is acceptable to him, I assume it is equally acceptable to you.'

'Acceptable?' Zoe echoed and she moved forward with a frown, her astonishment unhidden. 'Are you telling me that you have actually *spoken* to Grandad?'

'Of course.' Raj's intonation was clipped and businesslike. 'He was very angry about your disappearance and I had to reassure him that you were safe and that I would personally ensure that you are restored to his protection as soon as possible.'

But Zoe was still struggling to come to terms with the startling reality that he had already discussed the entire episode with her grandfather because that he should have boldly taken that step was utterly unexpected. Most people avoided Stam Fotakis in a temper and tried to wriggle out of accepting responsibility for anything that annoyed the older man. In fact, the only person she knew who ever stood toe to toe with her grandfather when he was in a bad mood was her sister, Vivi, whose temper matched his. Whoever Raj was, he was fearless, she decided enviously, for when her grandfather started roaring like an angry bull, Zoe simply wanted to keep her head down and take cover.

'I'm in a hurry. We will leave as soon as you are ready. My time here is limited,' Raj admitted flatly, tension tightening his smooth bronzed features. 'I would be obliged if you would be quick.'

'Well, I would need my clothes back to be quick, and I don't know where they are,' Zoe told him thinly, lifting her chin.

With an exclamation, he strode to the doorway and, a moment later, a little woman in tribal dress came running to do his bidding. Zoe's garments were located and laid in her arms, freshly laundered and fragrant. She stalked into the bathroom to look longingly at the shower and then she thought defiantly, What the hell? I'm not putting on clean clothes unless I'm clean as well!

As Zoe stepped beneath the flowing water with a deep sigh of relief, Raj strode out of the main tent, the old rules of polite conduct kicking in even though it felt like a lifetime since he had had to pay attention to such outdated beliefs. She was a single woman and he was a single man and he was in a very old-fashioned place where only his rank had granted him the right to speak to her alone. Even so, he had noted that the females in Omar's family were hovering nearby to ensure that the proprieties were observed. He was relieved that her attack on him had gone unnoticed for that would have very much shocked the tribe, none of whom would have recognised the need for a woman to learn the skills to protect herself. Male relatives were supposed to protect the women in the family.

Evidently, however, Zoe Mardas had not been protected, Raj reckoned thoughtfully, wondering what had happened to her, wondering why she had been so terrified and acknowledging that he would never know. He didn't get into deep conversations of that nature with women. His relationships, if they could be called that, were superficial and consisted of lots of sex and not much else. He doubted that he would ever want anything more from a woman. Why would he? Love had once made him stupid. He had given up everything for love and had ended up with nothing but the crushing awareness that he had made a serious mistake.

'Raj!' Omar gasped as he surged up to him, red-faced from the effort and winded, a small, rather tubby man, who rarely hurried at anything he did. 'You need to leave. One of the camel traders phoned to tell me…a bunch of military helicopters are flying in.'

'Soldiers love to rehearse disasters. It'll be some war game or something,' Raj forecast, refusing to panic. 'I told Zoe to hurry as politely as I could but you know what women are…'

'Raj, if you're caught on Marabanian soil, you could be arrested, *imprisoned*!' Omar emphasised in frustration. 'Grab that stupid woman and get in that helicopter and go!'

The racket of rotor blades approaching made both men throw their heads back and peer into the sky.

'Do you see those colours? That is the royal fleet, which means your father is on board!' Omar groaned in horror.

'It's too late to run. I'll have to tough it out.'

'No, *run*!' Omar urged abruptly. 'Right now...leave the woman here. I think this was a trap. I think she was dumped with me because they knew I was sure to ask you for your help. In the name of Allah, Raj, I will never forgive myself if you come to harm because of my thoughtlessness!'

A trap? Raj pondered the idea and as quickly discarded it. Why would his father, who had considered him a disappointment practically from the day of his birth, seek to trap him in Maraban? Sending Raj into exile, finally freeing himself from a son and heir who enraged him, had been the best solution for both of them, Raj reasoned ruefully.

'My father always warned me that Tahir was very devious, *very* calculating,' Omar breathed worriedly.

'He is,' Raj agreed. 'But he has no reason to *want* to find his son breaking the terms of his exile. Why would he? That would only embarrass him. I'll stay out of sight. Ten to one, he's taken one of his notions to call a tribal meeting and hash over boundaries and camel disputes. He revels in that kind of stuff...it takes him back to his youth.'

'The army craft are encircling the camp to land in advance,' Omar informed him.

'Standard security with the monarch on board,' Raj dismissed.

'No, I'm telling you,' Omar declared in growing frustration at his friend's lack of concern. 'This was a trap and I don't know how you're going to get out of it...'

CHAPTER THREE

THE RACKET OF the helicopters nearby unnerved Zoe and she dressed in haste, flinching from the cling of her clothes to her still-damp skin. When a woman entered the bathroom to fetch her, she was grateful she had hurried and she walked out through the main tent, glad to be embarking on her journey home.

It was a surprise, however, when she was not escorted to the stationary helicopter she had espied earlier and was instead led into another tent, where a group of women were seated round a campfire.

'The King is visiting,' the woman opposite her explained to her in perfect English. 'My husband, Omar, can only receive the King in his tent, which is, unfortunately, the one you have been using, which means that you will have to wait here with us.'

'Your husband?' Zoe studied the attractive brunette, who wore more gold jewellery than she had ever seen on one woman at the same time.

'Sheikh Omar. The King is his uncle. I am called Farida…and you?'

'Zoe,' Zoe proffered, accepting the tiny cup of black

coffee and the plate of sliced fruit she was given with a grateful smile. 'Thank you.'

Hopefully she would be on her way home within the hour, she reasoned, munching on a slice of apple with appetite. 'Where's Raj?' she asked curiously. 'I thought he was in a hurry to leave.'

'Prince Faraj is greeting his father,' Farida framed with slightly raised brows.

Zoe coloured, wondering if her familiar use of Raj's name had offended. 'I didn't know he was a prince,' she said ruefully. 'He said he was nobody of any importance.'

Farida startled her by loosing a spontaneous giggle and turned, clearly translating Zoe's statement for the benefit of their companions. Much laughter ensued.

'The Prince was teasing you. He is the son of our King.'

Zoe's eyes widened to their fullest extent and she gulped. '*He's* the bad-boy Prince?' she exclaimed before she could think better of utilising that label.

'The bad boy?' Farida winced at that definition. 'No, I don't think so. He is my husband's best friend and he took a dangerous risk coming here to see us. '

'Oh…' Zoe noticed that Farida didn't risk translating her comment about Raj being a bad boy and resolved to be much more careful about what she said. According to Raj these people had had nothing to do with her kidnapping and they had looked after her well while she was unable to look after herself. She didn't want to slight them.

After all, she knew next to nothing about Raj, had

merely read that tag for him on a website she had visited, which had contained the information that he had been sent into exile years ago for displeasing his father, the King.

'Risk?' she found herself pressing, taut with curiosity. 'What did he risk?'

'That is for his telling—*if* he has the opportunity,' Farida said evasively. 'But do not forget that the Prince is the King's *only* son, his only child in fact. He was born to the King's third wife when he had almost given up hope of having an heir.'

Zoe nodded circumspectly, unwilling to invite another polite snub and swallowing back questions that she was certain no one, least of all Farida, would wish to answer. Stupid man, she thought in exasperation. Why on earth hadn't he told her who he really was? It was not as though she could have guessed that he was of royal blood. She felt wrong-footed, however, and, recalling how she had assaulted him, gritted her teeth. It was his own fault though: he shouldn't have crept up on her like that.

An adorable toddler nudged her elbow in pursuit of a piece of apple and Zoe handed it over, waving her hand soothingly at Farida, who rebuked the little girl.

'No, my daughter must learn good manners,' Farida asserted.

'What's her name?' Zoe asked as the toddler planted herself in her lap and looked up at her with eyes like milk-chocolate buttons, set beneath a wealth of wavy black hair.

Farida relaxed a little then, and talked about her three children.

* * *

Accompanied by Omar, Raj strode into his cousin's tent where his father awaited him, seated by the fire.

'I thought I would find you here,' his father informed him with a look of considerable satisfaction. 'You are grown tall, my son. You have become a man while you have been away. Omar, you may leave. We will talk later.'

Raj's appraisal of the older man was slower and filled with concern because he could see that Tahir had aged. It was eight years since he had seen his father in the flesh. His parent had been in his fifties when Raj was born twenty-eight years earlier and the agility that had distinguished Tahir then had melted away. From a distance, Raj had watched his father's slow, painful passage to the tent, recognising that the rheumatoid arthritis, which had struck his parent in his sixties, now gripped him hard in spite of the many medical interventions that had been staged. He was still spry but very thin and stiff, the lines on his bearded face more deeply indented, but his dark eyes remained as bright and full of snapping intelligence as ever.

'Sit down, Raj,' the King instructed. 'We have much to discuss but little time in which to do it.'

Raj folded lithely down opposite and waited patiently while the server ritually prepared the coffee from a graceful metal pot with a very long spout. He took the tiny cup in his right hand, his long brown fingers rigid as he waited for one of his father's characteristic tirades to break over his head. Tahir was an authoritarian parent and had become even more abrasive and critical after the death of his third wife, Raj's mother. Sadly, that had been the period when Raj had been most in need of comfort and understanding and, instead of receiving that support, Raj had been sent to a military school where he was unmercifully bullied and beaten up. From the instant Raj had left school, he and his father had had a difficult relationship.

'I knew that Omar would run to you for help. He never had a thought in his head that you didn't put there first,' Tahir remarked fondly. 'We will not discuss the past, Raj. That would lead us back to dissension.'

'I'm sorry, but this woman…' Raj began even though he knew the interruption was rude, because he was so keen to find out why his father had acted as he had and had risked an enormous scandal simply to take his brother down a peg or two.

'You never did have a patient bone in your body.' Tahir sighed. 'Have sufficient respect to listen first. I want you home, Raj, back where you belong, as my heir.'

Raj was stunned. For a split second he actually gaped at the older man, his brilliant dark eyes shimmering with astonishment and consternation.

His father moved a hand in a commanding gesture to demand his continuing silence. 'I will admit no regrets. I will make no apologies. But had I not sent you away, my foolish brother would never have plotted to take your place,' he pointed out grimly. 'For eight years I have watched you from afar, working for Maraban, loyally doing your best to advance our country's best interests. Your heart is still with our people, which is as it should be.'

Raj compressed his lips and gazed down into his

coffee, dumbfounded by the very first accolade he had ever received from his strict and demanding parent.

'Do you want to come home? Do you wish to stand as the Crown Prince of Maraban again?'

A great wash of longing surged through Raj and his shoulders went stiff with the force of having to hold back those seething emotions. He swallowed hard. 'I do,' he breathed hoarsely.

'Of course, my generosity must come at a price,' the King assured him stiffly.

Unsurprised by that stricture, Raj breathed in deep and slow. 'I don't care who I marry now,' he declared in a driven undertone, hoping that that was the price his father planned to offer him. 'That element of my life is no longer of such overriding importance to me.'

'So, no longer a romantic,' his father remarked with visible relief. 'That is good. A romantic king would be too soft for the throne. And it is too late to turn you into a soldier. But your marriage... On that score I cannot compromise.'

'I understand,' Raj conceded flatly, shaking his hand to indicate that he did not want another cup of coffee, for any appetite for it had vanished. Sight unseen, some bride of good birth would be chosen for him and he and his bride would have to make a practical marriage. It would be a compromise, a challenge. Well, he was used to challenges even if he wasn't very good at compromises, he acknowledged grimly. But he would have to learn, and fast, because it was unlikely he would have much in common with the bride chosen for him.

'I should thank Hakem for bringing the Fotakis girl to my attention because I didn't even know she existed,' the King mused with unconcealed satisfaction. 'I was outraged when I realised what my brother was planning to do. I was even more outraged when I realised that I had no choice but to approach Fotakis himself... the man who stole the beautiful Azra from me. But he has given his permission.'

Only then registering what the older man was proposing, Raj threw his head back in shock. 'You're expecting me to marry *Zoe*?'

'And to do it right now, today. I brought the palace *imam* with me,' his father told him bluntly. 'This marriage would be your sign of good faith, your pledge to me that from now on you will act as a sensible son. Marry her and I promise you that nothing will stand in your path.'

'Zoe wants to go home!' Raj pointed out incredulously. 'She will not want to marry me.'

'Her grandfather has given his permission,' the King pointed out with a frown of bewilderment. 'A prince for a prince and a bridegroom less than half Hakem's age, you make an acceptable substitute in Fotakis's eyes. You have no choice in this, Raj. The girl is too great a prize to surrender, a huge gift to our people. No more popular bride than Azra's granddaughter could be found for you. We will have a big state wedding to follow. I believe she is as beautiful as her grandmother. You should be pleased.'

Raj compressed his lips on the reality that his father was insane. He talked as though women still dutifully and happily married the husbands picked by their most senior male relative. But even in Maraban those days were long gone. It was now only men of his father's venerable age who still expected the right to tell their offspring who they should marry.

'Zoe wants to go home,' he repeated steadily.

'You have two hours to persuade her otherwise. I have already prepared an announcement to be made from the palace,' the King told him solemnly. 'Their Prince has come home and done his duty at last.'

'Zoe was expecting to divorce Hakem within a few months,' Raj reminded his parent tautly.

'Yes, you can let her go once the fuss has died down. You can choose your own second wife,' Tahir informed him with the lofty air of a man bestowing a gift on the undeserving. 'I won't interfere, although there is one exception to that rule. That whore, Nabila...you cannot bring her into the family under any circumstances.'

At the mention of that name accompanied by that offensive term, Raj lost every scrap of colour, his eyes lowering, his expression cloaked by his spiky black lashes, for he had just learned that his father *knew* what had happened eight years earlier between his son and his first love. Discomfiture filled him to overflowing but the meeting, Raj recognised by that final warning, was over. He vaulted upright with something less than his usual grace. 'There is no risk of that development. I've not seen her in many years,' he revealed stiffly.

'Go and get ready for your wedding,' his father urged, clearly not accepting the possibility that Zoe might refuse to marry him. 'And send Omar in!'

Having had her breakfast, Zoe was ushered into another tent and left there alone. She checked her watch, shifted her feet, frustrated that she didn't know what the cause of the hold-up was. When Raj entered, she spun fully round to face him and then she froze, remembering uneasily that he was a prince and that she had not treated him as she should've done. But then that was *his* fault, she reminded herself, lifting her chin again. He looked tense, the smooth chiselled bones of his face taut beneath his bronzed skin, his dark deep-set eyes curiously intent on her.

'I thought you were in a hurry to leave,' she reminded him, wondering why even that scrutiny could heat her up inside her skin as if she were being slowly roasted. He made her feel hot and bothered and uncomfortable and if that was sexual attraction, well, then she wanted no part of it. Those physical reactions were affecting her ability to behave like a rational being.

'My father spoke to me *and*...our situation has changed,' Raj admitted, half turning towards the open doorway, avoiding a more direct look at her, lest he lose his concentration.

Any man would've looked though, he assured himself. Her beautiful hair was restrained in a long braid but he still remembered that silken veil unbound. Her shapely legs were exposed by a short skirt. The matching top in soft pastels moulded to her rounded breasts, and on her feet were the most ridiculously impractical heels he had ever seen a woman wear in the desert. Of course, she hadn't known that she would be waking up in the desert, but those towering heels, which still only contrived to lift her a couple of inches in height, were downright dangerous. At the same time, there was something absurdly feminine and cute about those tiny glittery sandals with their plethora of straps. He dragged in a deep breath, gritted his white even teeth. *Cute?* What was he thinking?

That it was safer to look at her feet than her breasts or her legs when his body was behaving as though it belonged to a sex-starved teenager. Since when had he been unable to control his libido? He could not recall ever having that problem before.

Zoe was very stiff, picking up on the undertones in the atmosphere while reading the physical tension he was putting out in waves. *'Our* situation?' she queried, surprised by that designation.

'Ours,' Raj emphasised. 'I don't know how much you know about me.'

'Well, you told me that you were nobody of any importance but Farida told me the truth—that you are the King's son,' Zoe countered in a tone of reproof. 'I also know that you were sent into exile.'

'Eight years ago,' Raj clarified sombrely. 'I refused to marry the woman my father chose for me because I was in love with someone else. There were other factors but essentially that is what caused my long estrangement from my father. You may not be aware of it but in my world a son is expected to be obedient and, to be fair to my father, I was a rebel from day one.'

More than a little disconcerted by that very personal explanation of his troubled relationship with his parent, Zoe coloured, her green eyes clinging to his brooding dark features and the fluctuating emotions he was striving to hide; only those expressive eyes of his continually gave him away, glimmering and glittering, alive with all the passion he struggled to contain. Unwilling fascination gripped her and she gave way to her curiosity. 'What happened with the woman you loved? Did you marry her?'

'No, she cheated on me,' Raj admitted flatly.

'I'm sorry,' she muttered automatically, wishing she hadn't asked.

'You don't need to apologise. It happened a long time ago when I was still young, trusting and naïve. I am not the same man now,' Raj parried wryly.

Because that woman had broken his heart, Zoe registered, recalling her sister, Winnie's heartbreak when she had had to leave the man she loved, after discovering that he was married. Zoe had never experienced anything that intense and she wasn't sure she wanted to either. But then she had never had a boyfriend. After the attempted rape she had fortunately escaped, she had feared and avoided men. She had had one or two male friends at university who had stayed close to her for a while to test her boundaries, hoping she would warm up to them but it hadn't happened. She had stayed apart and untouched and was much inclined to think that that was the best way to live. Without risk, without hurt, without disappointed hopes and unrealistic dreams of some fantasy happy future.

'You said "our" situation,' she reminded him, keen to steer the conversation out of deep waters. 'What did you mean by that?'

'My father has offered me a most unexpected suggestion,' Raj framed with care, brilliant dark eyes locked to her heart-shaped face and the eyes bright as emeralds against her porcelain pale skin. The contrast was breathtaking. 'He has asked me to come home and take my place as his heir again.'

'My goodness, that's wonderful news! I mean...' Zoe hesitated '...if *that* is what you want?'

'I want to come home with my whole heart. This is the first time I have been home in eight years,' Raj admitted harshly, his sincerity bitingly obvious. 'But unfortunately, the King's proposition came with a key stipulation attached. My father has asked me to take Hakem's place as your bridegroom and marry you.'

Zoe blinked several times and continued to stare at him, her heart thumping rapidly enough that it seemed to thunder in her ears. 'But...but why? That's a crazy suggestion!'

'Not if you consider who you are,' Raj pointed out with a wry twist of his wide sensual mouth. 'Half our population are originally from your grandmother's country and they were most resentful when my father and their Banian Princess failed to marry at the same time as the two states allied to become one. As a result, the royal family does not reflect the origins of both countries. If the King's son were to marry Princess Azra's granddaughter, it would be very popular with our people. Principally, *that* is why my father wants us to marry.'

'But I never even met Azra. She died before I was born,' Zoe argued. 'It's just an accident of birth.'

'No, it is your heritage and a vital and proud heritage to those who remember the Princess and a country that now only exists as part of Maraban,' Raj contradicted. 'I should also mention that your grandfather and my father have been in touch—I should imagine only through an intermediary—and this suggestion that you remain here to marry me instead has been discussed by them.'

'Good heavens… Grandad *knows* about all this?' Zoe gasped, already shaken by Raj's serious respect for her ancestry, which was, she realised finally, far more valued in Maraban than it would ever be anywhere else.

'Your grandfather is agreeable to the exchange of bridegrooms,' Raj delivered.

Zoe turned slowly pale with anger. 'But what about me? What about what *I* want?' she demanded starkly.

'That is why I am here…*asking*,' Raj stressed sardonically. 'Your grandfather and my father are quite happy to believe that only their consent is required. I am not that foolish.'

Her anger drained away again. 'Thank goodness, someone here has some sense,' she mumbled.

'You were willing to marry Hakem sight unseen,' Raj reminded her.

Zoe's knees felt weak and she flopped down on a cushioned seat as if her breath had been stolen from her. She was at a crossroads. 'That's different, that was before all this happened and I realised Hakem had abandoned his wife for me and stuff like that,' she argued uncomfortably. 'It was a mistake to agree. Now I just want to forget all this nonsense and go home again.'

'But I am asking you to stay here and marry me,' Raj stated with precision. 'And it is an entirely selfish request.'

Taken aback at that confession, Zoe tilted her head back to look up at him. 'Is it?'

'Yes. It would mean the end of my exile and my estrangement from my father,' Raj pointed out grittily. 'And not only that, my marriage to Azra's granddaughter would delight my people as well. What is in it for you other than the acquisition of an entirely use-less title, I don't know, but it would at least be as much as you would have received from my uncle. I can also promise to treat you as well as he would have. He is a decent man, regrettably poisoned by his pointless need to compete with my father.'

What is in it for you? Zoe appreciated his honesty with regard to the advantages to him should he marry her. Even so, her understanding of his position did nothing to stop her brain from whirling with wild indecision. She had been ready to go home and give up on her quest for greater independence but now Raj was offering her another option. Yet somehow marrying him struck her as a far more intimidating prospect than marrying a much older man, who had sworn he would treat her like a daughter. Raj was so much younger, more aggressive, more virile… Her brain ran out of descriptive words as she glanced warily at him.

He was so poised in his long white buttoned tunic, a black cloak folded back over his broad shoulders, his lean, darkly handsome face grave and cool while he awaited her answer, those glorious dark-as-the-devil eyes gleaming with an impatience he was too polite and intelligent to voice. A positive reply would mean a lot to him. She understood that, she really did. She also still yearned for the opportunity to live an independent life, unfettered by the expectations of her family. But most of all, she wanted to prove herself to herself and she wanted to be strong without leaning on anyone else for support. Even less did she want to run home with her tail between her legs and disappoint her grandfather as well.

'What would it take to win your agreement?' Raj pressed, the skilled negotiator that he was breaking cover.

Zoe coloured as if he had turned a spotlight on her and dropped her head. 'Well, I don't know what your expectations would be but I can assure you now that I wouldn't want sex. I'm not into sex. It's something I can live without, but *you*?'

That he couldn't even look at her without thinking about sex was a truth Raj decided he needed to keep to himself. Overpowering curiosity assailed him at the same time. What had put her off sex? One bad experience? An assault? Those were not questions he could ask and he suppressed the urge to probe deeper even as he winced inwardly from the upfront immediate rejection she was handing him. She didn't want sex with *him*. He had never met with that kind of rejection before and he pushed away that awareness, deeming it arrogant and ultimately unimportant in the greater scheme of events.

'I can offer you the exact same marital agreement that persuaded you that you could marry my uncle,' Raj broke in to insist with measured cool.

Zoe tossed her head back in surprise. Little tendrils of white-blonde hair were beginning to cling to her damp brow because she was feeling too warm even in the shade of the tent. Probably because even talking about sex set her cheeks on fire with self-consciousness, but she knew that she had to be frank with him. There was no other way and no room for any misunderstandings if she was candid from the outset. It shook her to acknowledge that she was seriously considering the marriage he was suggesting, for it was unlike her to take a risk. And Raj, her sixth sense warned, would be a risk.

'Unfortunately, you're not old enough to treat me like a daughter!' she told him ruefully.

'But I am old enough not to put pressure on a woman, who doesn't want me, for sex,' Raj retorted without hesitation. 'I appreciate that you would have to take that guarantee on trust but it *is* the truth. I have never had to put that kind of pressure on a woman and I never will.'

'OK,' Zoe mumbled, feeling that they had done the topic of sex and not having it to death. 'I admit that I would like to stay in Maraban and explore a little of my heritage.'

'I could make that possible,' Raj told her.

'Where would we live?'

'In the palace, which is, I must admit, a little dated,' Raj acknowledged, choosing to understate the case because he himself considered his surroundings immaterial as long as the basics were in place.

His father, unhappily, had a great reverence for history and it had proved a major battle to persuade Tahir to allow even modern bathrooms and cooking facilities to be constructed in the ancient building. Guests were lodged in one of the very contemporary villas built within the palace compound to provide convenient accommodation for visitors while preserving his father's privacy.

'I could live with dated,' Zoe muttered uneasily. 'I'm really not very fussy. My sisters and I lived in some real dives before we met our grandfather a couple of years ago and he invited us to move into a property that he owns in London.'

'The palace is not a dive,' Raj murmured with reluctant amusement. 'To sum up, you are prepared to consider my proposal?'

'Thinking about it, wondering if I can trust you.' That admission slid off the end of Zoe's tongue before she could snatch it back and her face flamed with guilt.

'I keep my word...*always*,' Raj proclaimed with pride, dark eyes aglow with conviction. 'You have nothing to fear from me. You would be doing me a very great favour. The last thing I would do is harm you. In fact, if you do this for me, I will protect you from anything and anyone who would seek to harm you.'

He was gorgeous, she thought helplessly, standing there so straight and tall and emotional, *so* very *emotional*. She had never met a man who teemed with so much emotion that he couldn't hide it. She had never met a man she could read so clearly. Reluctant hope, growing excitement and the first seeds of satisfaction brimmed in his volatile gaze. She couldn't take her eyes off his, could still hear the faint echo of his fervent promise to protect her from all threats.

'We would still be able to get a divorce after a few months?' Zoe checked anxiously.

'Of course. We would not want to find ourselves stuck with each other for ever!' Raj quipped with sudden amusement.

And for the very first time in a man's presence, Zoe felt slighted by honesty. She scolded herself for being oversensitive. Naturally, he wouldn't want to stay married for good to a woman he didn't love and neither would she wish to stay with him, would she? He was simply voicing the facts of their agreement.

'Then…' Zoe rose to her feet, suddenly pale with the stress of the occasion and the big decision she was making for herself without consulting her sisters, who probably would've voiced very loud objections '… I will agree to marry you and I can only hope that it brings you the advantages that you believe it will.'

Raj took a sudden step forward and raised his arms and then let them fall again as he stepped back. 'Forgive me, I almost touched you but I am sure you prefer not to be touched.'

'I do.' But Zoe was lying. He had been about to sweep her up in his arms and hug her and she was disappointed that he had recalled her rules and gone back into retreat. He was passionate, a little impulsive, she suspected, the sort of guy who occasionally in the grip of strong feeling would act first, think later. She would have liked the hug, the physical non-sexual contact, the very warmth and reassurance of it, but it was better that he respected her boundaries, she told herself urgently. 'So when will this marriage take place?'

'Today.'

'Today?' she exclaimed in soaring disbelief.

'My father does not trust me enough to allow me to return to the palace without immediate proof that I have changed my ways,' Raj told her grimly. 'This marriage will provide that proof. He brought the palace *imam* here with him.'

'We're getting married here…*now*?' she prompted incredulously. 'What on earth am I going to wear?'

'My father leaves nothing to chance. I would suspect that his wife has brought appropriate clothing for you.'

'Which wife?' she prompted curiously.

'He only has one wife still living. My mother died when I was nine and her predecessor died about ten years ago. The Queen, his first wife, is called Ayshah,' Raj proffered. 'She is pleasant enough.'

Zoe breathed in deep and slow. She was going to marry Raj and make a go of her life all on her own. She would stay in Maraban for several months and there would be no more panic attacks. She would pick up some of the language, learn the history and find out about her grandmother's culture. It would be an adventure, a glorious adventure, she told herself firmly while watching Raj stand by the doorway, quite unconscious of her appraisal. He smiled with sudden brilliance. And gorgeous wasn't quite a strong enough word for him at that moment...

CHAPTER FOUR

'MY FATHER TELLS me that the King is arranging a state wedding to take place in two weeks' time and for that you can wear a Western wedding gown,' Farida informed Zoe in a discreet whisper. 'The King wants to make the most of your entry into the family.'

Apprehensive enough about the wedding about to take place, Zoe could have done without the news that there was to be a second, which would be a public spectacle. Such an event lay so far outside her comfort zone that even thinking about it made her feel dizzy. But she squashed that sensation. Baby steps, she told herself soothingly. She would cope by dealing with one thing at a time, and fretting about the future would only wind her up. Right at that moment it was sufficient to accept that she was about to legally marry a man she had only met for the first time that day.

Marrying Raj's uncle, however, she would have been doing the same, she reminded herself wryly, and at least Raj came without previous attachments such as wives, children and grandchildren. Yes, she had definitely dodged a bullet in not marrying Hakem. Raj was single and refreshingly honest. He had admitted that he had once suffered panic attacks too. He had even admitted to defying his father over the woman he loved and subsequently discovering that she had cheated on him, which must have been a huge disillusionment. Most men that Zoe came across would have concealed such unhappy and revealing facts. That Raj had been so frank had impressed her.

Surrounded by fussing tribeswomen presided over by the elderly Queen Ayshah, who sat in the corner, entirely dressed in black, barking out instructions, Zoe studied her reflection in the tall mirror. She was so heavily clothed in layers and jewellery that she was amazed she could move. A beaten gold headdress covered her brow, a veil covering most of her hair, weighty gold earrings dangling from her ears, hung there by thread. She had very narrowly sidestepped having her ear lobes pierced there and then and she had Farida to thank for tactfully suggesting thread be used to attach the earrings instead. More primitive gold necklaces clanked and shifted round her neck with every movement while rich and elaborate henna swirls adorned her hands and her feet. What remained of her was enveloped in a white kaftan covered in richly beaded and colourful embroidery. Below that were several gossamer-fine silk layers, all of which rejoiced in buttons running down the back. Getting undressed again promised to be a challenge, she thought ruefully.

She had insisted on doing her own make-up though, having run her eyes over her companions, already festooned in their glad rags and best jewellery for the wedding, their faces over-rouged, their eyelids bright blue. Only Farida had gone for the subtle approach. Zoe had used more cosmetics than she normally did and had gone heavy on the eye liner when urged to do so but at least there was nothing theatrical about the end result.

'My wedding celebrations lasted a week,' Farida told her.

'A *week*?' Zoe gasped.

'But yours will only last the afternoon. The King does not wish to spend the night here. The state wedding celebration parties will go on longer, I expect,' Omar's wife chattered. 'Everyone loves these events because they get to see family and friends, but this has been arranged so quickly that it is a very small and quiet wedding—but the jewellery Raj has given you is magnificent.'

'What jewellery?' Zoe whispered.

'Everything you're wearing comes from the royal house. Traditionally, the jewellery is your wedding gift.'

'The King must've brought that with him as well,' Zoe muttered.

'Yes, you were getting married today whether you wanted to or not!' Farida laughed. 'But who could say no to Raj?'

Zoe could feel her face heat and was grateful when the sound of music outside the tent sent all the women to the doorway. She followed them and glanced out to see some sort of ceremonial dance being performed with much waving of swords and cracking of whips. Men leapt over the campfire, competing in feats of daring that made her flinch and at one point close her eyes. A moment later, she was ushered out in an excited procession into another larger tent filled with people. She was led up to the front where a venerable older man appeared to bestow some sort of blessing on her and gave a long speech before handing her a ring. Farida showed her which finger to put it on. In the middle of the speech, she finally glimpsed Raj, resplendent in a sapphire-blue silk tunic, tied with a sash, his lean, darkly handsome features very serious. She tried and failed to catch his eye.

Another, even older man spoke more briefly and then moved forward to flourish a pen over a long piece of parchment, which he duly signed. In fact, several people signed the parchment and then she in turn was urged forward to sign as well, before being led away again without a word or a look exchanged with Raj.

'And now we party!' Farida whispered teasingly in her ear.

'You mean…that's it *done*? We're married now?' Zoe exclaimed in wonderment.

'As soon as you signed the marriage contract, it was done. I would've translated for you but I didn't want to risk offending the King by speaking during the ceremony,' the lithe brunette confided. 'You are now the Crown Princess of Maraban.'

'And I don't feel the slightest bit different!' Zoe confided with amusement, reckoning that her grandfather would be sorry to have missed the ceremony but she assumed he would be attending the state wedding, which was to follow. Her sisters would have to come as well and she smiled at the prospect as Farida guided her into yet another tent full of chattering women where music was starting up in the background.

Introduction after introduction was made and plate after plate of food was brought. There were no men present. Farida explained that the reception after the state wedding would not be segregated but that rural weddings were of a more conservative ilk. Zoe sipped mint tea and watched the festivities as the dancing began. Married, she kept on thinking; she couldn't believe it. But she wasn't really married, she reminded herself wryly, not truly married because she and Raj were not going to live together as a married couple. She wondered how he was feeling. Was he wishing she were his ex-love, who had let him down? Or did the significance of the actual marriage escape him because he was not in love with his bride? Or, more likely, was he simply happy that he was back in Maraban and accepted by his father again?

At one point, Zoe drifted off in spite of the noise and liveliness surrounding her and wakened only when Farida discreetly pressed her hand. She blinked in bemusement, for an instant not even knowing where she was. Darkness had fallen beyond the tent and it was quieter now, only a couple of women dancing, the rest gathered in chattering groups. Slowly her brain fell back into step and she suppressed a sigh, murmuring an apology to Farida for her drowsiness.

'Your body is probably still working on ridding you of the sleeping drug you were given at the palace. Our doctor said it would be a couple of days before you fully recovered from that. I am so sorry that that happened to you,' the other woman said sincerely.

'You were involved in it against your will...not your responsibility,' Zoe pointed out gently.

'And sadly, the instigator will only be celebrating

the reality that he has regained his son,' Farida murmured ruefully.

The last piece of the puzzle fell into place for Zoe and her eyebrows shot up in surprise as she finally appreciated that only Raj's father could have had her kidnapped and remained safe from punishment of any kind. That was why Raj had remained silent about the identity of the perpetrator; that was why he had seemed to feel partially responsible for her ordeal. Clearly the King had been determined to prevent his brother, Hakem, from marrying her.

'It is time for you to retire,' Farida told her, reacting to a signal from Queen Ayshah, who raised her hand and gave her a meaningful look.

That the old lady was still going strong while she felt weary embarrassed Zoe. She lumbered upright, feeling like an elephant in her cumbersome layers of clothing, hoping it was cooler outside than it was inside. But that was a false hope, she recognised when the humid air beyond the tent closed in around her and she was forced to trek across the sand in her wildly unsuitable shoes that dug in at every step. A camel was led in front of her and made to lie down. Farida instructed her to climb into the saddle, which, weighted down as she was by fabric and jewellery, was no easy task, but at last the deed was accomplished and the animal scrambled up again and swayed across the sands in the moonlight, accompanied by whoops from the women crowded round her and with the aid of the herdsman with his very modern torch.

'It is symbolic,' Farida explained. 'Queen Ayshah stands in your mother's place and she is sending you to your bridegroom.'

Zoe rather thought it was more as if she were a parcel to be delivered, although thank heaven, she reflected with a choked giggle, Raj wouldn't be expecting to *unwrap* the parcel. She slid more than she dismounted from the camel and picked herself up off the sand, thinking fondly that she was having an even more exciting wedding day than either of her sisters had enjoyed while wondering when her mobile phone would be returned to her so that she could bring her siblings up to date with events.

She almost staggered into the tent lit by lanterns that awaited her and there she froze in consternation. A large bed confronted her and it dawned on her at last that this was her wedding night, which she was expected to spend in close proximity to her new husband. She wasn't going to get her own tent this time or even her own bed because she was supposed to *share* the bed. In silence she pulled a face because she hadn't anticipated that, although she knew that she should've done.

After all, her agreement with Raj that their marriage would be platonic was a private matter that neither of them was likely to discuss with anyone beyond their immediate family. Grateful when the women retreated again she sank down on the bottom of the low divan and breathed in deep while she waited for Raj to arrive. My goodness, she was getting so hot. She straightened and walked into the primitive bathroom that had been erected alongside and clearly in haste for their comfort. A mirror sat propped up on a chest and piece by piece she removed the heavy gold jewellery and set it on the chest along with the veil.

At that point she heard shouts and catcalls outside and she scrambled up to return to the main tent just in time to see Raj striding in and covering the door again with obvious relief. 'Everyone gets overexcited at weddings,' he said wryly, studying her with fixed intensity.

Colour mantled her cheeks, self-consciousness reclaiming her as she hovered. 'Perhaps they're also celebrating the fact that their Prince is home again,' she suggested.

'It is possible,' Raj fielded with quiet assurance.

He wore confidence like invisible armour and she envied him that gift, wondering how he could ever have suffered the ignominy of panic attacks. He had the innate calm of a man comfortable in his own skin yet, from what little she had already learned, his past was littered with drama and disappointment. Yet he had overcome those realities and moved on, much as she wished to do.

'Do you know where my clothes are? Are they still back at the house I was taken from?' she asked uncomfortably.

'I will enquire for you in the morning,' Raj murmured smoothly.

'I don't even have a toothbrush!' Zoe protested, falling back on trivialities rather than dealing with her insecurities over the situation she was in.

'I will give you one,' Raj informed her in a tone of finality.

Zoe swallowed hard on a burst of angry exasperation. Was she supposed to go to bed naked with all her make-up on? It wasn't his fault that she had been separated from her luggage, she told herself urgently, and she shouldn't take her ire out on him. Deal with it, she instructed herself, and she went back into the bathroom and removed the ornate kaftan before beginning to undo the buttons of the layers beneath. Arms aching, perspiration dampening her face, she stalked back uneasily into the bedroom. Raj was on his phone, black eyes skimming to her instantly. He cast the phone down and studied her enquiringly.

'I'm afraid I need your help with all these buttons,' she framed in considerable embarrassment. 'I don't want to tear anything...'

'No, that would indeed be embarrassing,' Raj conceded. 'It would look as though I ripped the shifts off you.'

Breathing fast, Zoe spun round, presenting him with her slender back. 'I just don't get why it has all those buttons in an absolutely inaccessible place!'

'Because you are not supposed to take it off by yourself,' Raj informed her softly, a faint tremor racking her as she felt the gentle pressure of his fingers against her back as he undid the buttons, because a man had never got quite that close to her before and that he should be undressing her, even though it was at her request, was still a challenge. 'Your bridegroom is supposed to remove the three shifts slowly and seductively. It is a cultural tradition.'

'Oh...' Zoe gasped and then as the ramifications set in, *'Oh,'* she said again.

'You will have Ayshah to thank for the shifts because I don't think most brides bother with this particular tradition these days,' Raj told her huskily, skimming the first shift down her arms and letting it drop to the rug beneath her bare feet before embarking on the next set of buttons. 'That is a shame.'

'Is it? A bridal version of the dance of the seven veils…or whatever?' Zoe heard herself wittering on nervously, cringing even as the words escaped her.

Raj rolled his eyes and gritted his even white teeth because peeling her out of the silk shifts was testing his self-control. Her skin glimmered through the gossamer-fine tissue like the most lustrous of pearls and that close the sweet scent of her, of roses and almonds, was unbelievably feminine and alluring. Raj tugged down the second shift and let it fall before stepping away, carefully not looking at what would now be an enhanced view of her body because he did not require that encouragement.

Bemused, Zoe spun round, registering that he had stopped and walked away. 'I don't want to sleep in this one,' she muttered uncomfortably. 'These shifts are precious to your stepmother. They were put on me with a care that implied they were made of solid gold.'

'She is not my stepmother,' Raj incised curtly. 'She is my father's first wife.'

'Right… OK,' Zoe framed, registering that she had hit a tender spot with that designation, but very much out of her depth when it came to labelling or understanding the doubtless complex relations created in a family consisting of more than one wife. 'But what am I to sleep in?'

Raj was forced to look at her and the image locked him in place. She was so clueless he swallowed hard on impatient words. She might as well have been standing there naked for the thin material hid very little.

The pert little swells of her small breasts were obvious, not to mention the intriguing tea-rose colour of her prominent nipples and the pale curls at the apex of her thighs. Raj sucked in a sustaining breath, hot and hard as hell. 'I will get you something of mine,' he asserted, rather hoarse in tone, his dark deep voice roughening the vowel sounds.

'I'm sorry I'm being such a pain,' Zoe mumbled uneasily as Raj dragged out a leather holdall and opened it to rummage through it.

'I didn't bring much because I didn't think I'd be staying long.' Raj sighed, finally extracting a T-shirt and a pair of boxers for her use.

Zoe grabbed the garments with alacrity and spun round beside him. 'Just undo the last ones, please, and I'll be out of your hair,' she promised.

Raj suppressed a groan, his attention locking on the sweet curvaceous swell of her bottom. Presented with the delights of her in reality his imagination could take flight with ease and he ached with arousal. He grappled with the buttons, no longer deft, indeed all fingers and thumbs as he thought of laying her down on the bed and teaching her the consequences of teasing a man. But even as he thought of such a thing, he was grimly amused by it because he knew she was quite unaware of the effect she was having on him and that he would never touch a woman who had stated so clearly that she did not want to be touched. In fact, he had never been with a woman less aware of her seductive power over a man and, while at first he had found that absence of flirtation and flattery refreshing, now, suddenly, he was finding that innocence of hers a huge challenge.

'Now you can go and take it off and get changed,' Raj informed her thickly.

Zoe turned back to him, catching the harsh edge to his voice and looking up at him to see the dark glow of his eyes accentuated by the flare of colour over his high cheekbones. 'Raj…what's wrong?' she questioned helplessly.

'How honest can I be?' Raj asked.

'I want you to feel that you can always be honest with me. In fact, that's very important to me.'

'Even if it embarrasses you?' Raj prompted.

'Even if it embarrasses me,' Zoe confirmed without hesitation.

'You are half naked and very beautiful,' Raj breathed huskily. 'I have sworn not to touch you but I am still a man and you tempt me. You can still trust me to keep my word but I would be grateful if you…' He fell silent because Zoe had already backed into the bathroom, her face as startled and as red as fire.

Only ten feet from him, separated only by tent walls, Zoe looked at herself in the last shift and she burned all over with mortification. She'd had no idea quite how sheer the shifts were because at no stage had she seen her reflection in them in the mirror. Half naked seemed like an understatement when she was showing everything she had got! Shame and chagrin enveloped her. He had said she tempted him. Dear heaven, did he think her display had been deliberate? No, surely not. She peeled off the last shift, laid it carefully to one side and stepped into the shower, hoping it would cool her off. She didn't want to go back into the bedroom and look him in the eye again.

Cold water drenched her and she stood there as long as she could bear it, before, shivering, she got out and grabbed a towel off the pile. He had been frank with her and she was glad of that, she reflected ruefully. If they were to live in close proximity, she would have to be more careful, more *aware* in a way she had never had to be before. His T-shirt fell past her knees and she put on the boxers, although they struck her as overkill.

'Zoe?' Raj murmured quietly.

She peered into the bedroom and he handed her a toiletries bag.

When even her teeth were clean, she *had* to return to the bedroom but she looked nowhere near him as she crossed to the bed and climbed in straight away.

Raj went for a long cooling shower and tried to remember when he had last had sex. It had been weeks and weeks. He should make more effort in that department, he told himself firmly. Had he formed the habit of regular sex, he was convinced he wouldn't have been so tempted by Zoe. But then, it had been years since he had enjoyed regular sex, he acknowledged ruefully. These days he had occasional one-night stands and he never spent the night because he had discovered that spending too long with the same woman only encouraged the kind of entanglements and expectations that made him feel trapped. 'One and done', he called his routine. He didn't do relationships, he didn't do girlfriends, he didn't do dates. Nabila had sent him flying off such a conventional path.

But Zoe, the wife he could not touch, he was learning to his cost, was a whole new ball game...

Zoe peered out from under the sheet as Raj strode

across the tent, his long, lean, powerful body clad only in boxers. Her eyes widened, drawn by the flex of steel-hard muscle across his bronzed torso. He was a work of art, she thought numbly, barely able to accept that such a thought could be hers and that for the first time ever she was admiring the male body, which had until that moment inspired her only with fear. But then Raj was something else, Raj somehow fell into a totally different category and she didn't understand how that was or even why. Yet he was one of the most masculine men she had ever met. Everything about Raj from his innate poise to the rough stubble now darkening his jaw line and the well-honed strength of his physique screamed male. She closed her eyes tight, blanked her mind and slowly, inexorably fell asleep.

The nightmare that assailed her was an old familiar one. She was sprawled on the floor of an old hut, sneering thugs surrounding her while another cut off her clothes with a terrifyingly sharp knife. She was trapped. Shouting or screaming only earned her another punch and she was already in a great deal of pain because one arm and a leg were broken and, she believed, several ribs. She could barely see out of her swollen eyes but there was nothing wrong with her ears and she could hear every one of the filthy, perverted things they were threatening to do to her. She was petrified, lapsing in and out of consciousness, fighting the sickening effects of concussion…and outside a thunderstorm was crashing and banging like extra evidence that she had been plunged into a living hell.

'It's OK…it's OK,' a vaguely familiar voice was assuring her and she clung to that voice like a drowning swimmer, letting it pull her fully out of the bad dream.

'No,' she croaked in a shaken whisper. 'I'll never be OK again.'

Outside the thunder crashed deafeningly loud and she flinched and gasped, registering that there really was a storm outside, just as there had been the night she had almost been gang-raped. 'I don't like storms,' she muttered, clutching at his warm, solid body for support.

'You were having a nightmare, moaning, shouting for help. I tried to wake you up,' Raj admitted. 'But it took a long time to bring you out of it.'

'The storm confused me, probably woke me in the end... There was a storm in the nightmare too...except it wasn't really a nightmare, it was something that happened to me...but it's been years since I dreamt about it,' Zoe framed shakily. 'I'm sorry.'

'You don't need to apologise. We can't police our dreams,' Raj dismissed, leaning away from her to light the lantern by the bed.

Her anxious eyes widened at the sight of him because being in bed with a half-naked man felt so very alien to her. And Raj was all male as he stretched, that fantasy V-shape flexing across his lower rock-hard abdomen as he shifted to reach for a glass of water and handed it to her.

Colour rising, Zoe gulped down water as if she were suffering from dehydration. She didn't like the way her brain was spewing random sexual thoughts at her. It was scary being that close to Raj and wanting to touch him. *Touch* him? What insanity was attacking her? Since when had she wanted to touch a man? Yet all of a sudden she could imagine *touching* Raj, smoothing a hand over that satin-smooth golden skin laid down over muscle. She sat up and put the glass down just before another deafening crash of thunder boomed and it sent her careening into the shelter and security he offered like a homing pigeon.

Raj had never before found it a problem to have an armful of fragrant woman in his arms. But when the woman was Zoe, it was a major problem. He had heard her shouting for help and saying, 'No, *please*...' over and over again and a kind of unholy rage had gripped him that someone so small and defenceless had been driven to begging, her fear and desperation palpable. Only it became complicated when she got too close to him and his body reacted against his will. He was so hard he dared not leave the bed for fear that she would notice and get scared that he couldn't be trusted. But he was not made of stone.

He closed his arms round her, murmuring soothing things in his own language, doing his best to resist urges that he felt should shame him. 'Were you raped?' he asked in a roughened undertone.

Zoe flinched, her slender body trembling in his hold, and she looked up at him. 'No. I was lucky. I was beaten up but I was rescued before it got that far.'

Raj's level black brows lifted. *'Lucky?'* he derided, not only stunned by what she had told him, but also feeling honoured that she had trustingly bestowed such a terrifying secret on him.

And Zoe laughed and spontaneously smiled. 'Yes, very lucky. I'm a survivor.'

That glorious, utterly unexpected smile was more

than Raj could withstand. Zoe looked up into eyes as bright as liquid starlight and marvelled at the beauty of them. He lowered his head and claimed her soft pink mouth with his.

The thunder boomed beyond the tent. Lightning strafed the ground, lighting up the walls, but Zoe didn't hear or notice any of that because there was a kind of magic in Raj's kiss and it was like no kiss she had ever had before. And yes, she had had kisses before, had tried several times at university to get into the spirit without succumbing to the terror of getting out of her depth with some guy who might then get angry and refuse to listen to her protests. When Raj slid his tongue between her parted lips, an insistent heat she had never felt before flared between her thighs. His hands stroked through her hair and she felt her breasts swell and her nipples tighten and tingle. The warmth of his skin and the weight of him against her led to the discovery that her body liked those masculine aspects of him. Even more did she appreciate the aromatic smell of him, an insanely attractive combination of musky male and designer cologne, which tugged at something very basic inside her. His tongue brushed hers and withdrew, leaving her aching for more, every nerve ending on fire.

And then he set her back from him and dragged in a shuddering breath while still looking at her as though she were the only woman in the universe, a gift of his that yanked at her heart strings. 'I'm sorry,' he breathed in a raw undertone. 'I broke my promise not to touch you.'

'Do you see me running or screaming?' Zoe demanded, shaken by his sudden withdrawal while her body was still humming and pulsing like an unfamiliar entity.

Raj's slightly swollen and very sensual mouth compressed, dark eyes glittering with angry regret. 'I will not make excuses for myself but I assure you that *this* will not happen again. Go to sleep, Zoe. You are safe.'

Since she didn't have much choice, Zoe turned away and snaked back to her own side of the bed, defensively turning her back to him. She had only herself to blame for the way she felt, she thought unhappily. She had told him she wasn't interested in sex, had shown him her fear and, in return, he had sworn not to touch her. Naturally he was angry that he had broken that pledge. Sixth sense told her that Raj didn't usually break promises and probably didn't think much of those who did. But he had warned her earlier that he found her attractive and their current circumstances of false intimacy and mutual dependence only made resistance more difficult.

But for the first time in her life, Zoe had *wanted* a man and she knew that she wasn't likely to forget the crazy buzz of excitement that he had unleashed inside her. She, she reflected in mortification, had been more tempted than he was because he had quickly called a halt.

And what had she wanted to do?

To her eternal shame, she had wanted to snatch him back and *make* him keep on kissing her and, not only that, in the back of her mind she had been well aware that she craved more than that. Somehow, and she really didn't know how or when it had happened, she was finally ready to *try* sex, to experiment, but there was no room for sex in their agreement, particularly in a marriage destined to last only a few months.

When she wakened in the morning, Raj was gone, but one of her suitcases sat in a prominent position near the bed. With a smile of relief, she got up and went to open it before going to freshen up. Clad in light cotton trousers and a pink top, teamed with glittery sandals, she found breakfast awaiting her on her return. She was really hungry and tucked in with appetite, although she was no fan of the yogurt drink included, reckoning it was probably one of those healthy options that she rarely enjoyed.

She walked out of the tent and an explosion of utterly unexpected colour greeted her. A field of flowers stretched before her and she walked in amongst the colourful blooms in wonderment at such a floral display in so seemingly inhospitable a landscape.

'Zoe...stay where you are!' Raj shouted at her, incensed to see her outside and unprotected and wandering with a toddler's absence of caution.

'What on earth—?' she began, glancing up from the pink, purple and mauve blooms she was studying as she crouched.

But Raj, black curls shining, was sheathed in jeans and a T-shirt and already striding towards her, careless of the flowers he crushed beneath his feet, clearly untouched by the beauty of the scene. He scooped her up bodily in his arms, exclaiming in Arabic. 'And what the hell are you wearing on your feet?' he then demanded incredulously.

'Sandals!' she snapped. 'You stood on the flowers

of an *asphodelus fistulosus* and it was the only *one* in this mass of bugloss.'

'There are scorpions and snakes, lying in the shade below the flowers!' Raj bit out, startling her. 'Here you wear only proper footwear that protects you.'

'Oh… OK.' Zoe nodded, recognising concern and superior knowledge when she saw it. 'I didn't know… but the flowers were so beautiful.'

Raj carried her back to the tent, thinking that he would never forget that first glimpse of her in that sea of flowers, white-blonde hair falling to her waist and glittering like highly polished platinum in the sunlight, and those huge green eyes blinking dazedly up at him as he lifted her, full of shock and incomprehension of the risk she had taken. He had trod on pretty flowers and it had bothered her. She was sensitive, also possibly a little ditzy to walk out thoughtlessly into what could be a very hostile environment. But it was his duty to take care of her, watch over her, his job to protect. And the enormity of such a responsibility sat heavy on his shoulders for an instant because he had never been responsible for another human being before.

Nor did he want to be responsible, he told himself staunchly. He would take care of her to the best of his ability without ever forgetting that she was not *truly* his wife and he refused to think of her as such. Zoe was a short-term prospect, not a keeper. He would be ice, he would remain impervious to her charms. He was not about to complicate things by getting too involved with her. He had hard limits and he would observe them, retaining softer feelings, if he could even experience such emotions again, for his future *real* wife. There would be none to waste on Zoe, even if she looked adorable posed amidst flowers. What an asinine thought that was! He surely had more sense than that, enough intelligence to keep his distance, he instructed himself bitterly; he had learned his lesson with Nabila.

Innocent didn't mean she was a virgin. He would never believe a woman's word on that score again! Cute didn't mean trustworthy. Nabila had lied like a trooper and he had not recognised her deceit. Adorable definitely didn't mean loveable. Cute and adorable were words that should never feature in his vocabulary because caring about the wrong woman hurt like hell and he wasn't revisiting that mistake for anybody!

CHAPTER FIVE

WITHIN AN HOUR a brief flight in the helicopter returned them to the palace.

Zoe walked through an ancient porticoed entrance and instantly felt as though she had been transported into another world and another time. An awe-inspiring giant hallway full of pillars and elaborately tiled walls greeted her as well as a wealth of fawning servants, some of whom were in actual tears welcoming Raj back to his home. Brushing off their blandishments with palpable embarrassment, Raj hurried her on into the building while a cohort of attentive staff fell in behind them.

'My father has placed us in the oldest part of the palace, which is…unfortunate,' he told her in a clipped undertone. 'It is, however, where the Crown Prince always has his apartments, so I cannot fault him for following tradition.'

'Why's it unfortunate, then?' she queried uneasily, even while her eyes fled continually to her surroundings. She was enthralled by the exotic quality of the internal courtyard gardens she espied from the stairs and the fabulous views out over the desert, not to mention the stonework, the domed roofs and the stern palace guards, dressed as though they had stepped out of a medieval painting, armed with swords and great curved knives. The palace was everything she had dreamt of when first coming to Maraban but far more grand and mysterious than she had naïvely expected.

'Only one bedroom has been prepared for us,' Raj breathed curtly, his strong jaw line clenching. 'It will be difficult to give you privacy.'

'We'll manage,' Zoe told him with an insouciance she could not have contemplated before meeting him in the flesh. She knew in her very bones that she could trust Raj, believed that he would never try to force her into anything, but when she pondered that conviction, she was challenged to understand why she had such faith in him. He'd shown her empathy, tenderness, kindness the night before, she reminded herself ruefully.

'That is very generous of you but not strictly within our agreement,' Raj pointed out, refusing to be soothed.

'Can't be helped,' Zoe murmured, breathless from trying to keep up with his long stride as he traversed long corridors at speed and mounted flights of stone stairs with lithe ease. 'This is a very large building.'

'But *not* modernised,' Raj retorted grimly, throwing wide a door before a hovering servant could reach for it and guiding her into a simply vast room in which a bed hunched apologetically in one corner.

'Plenty of space though!' Zoe carolled like Job's comforter.

The remainder of her cases were already parked along with the one that had travelled out to the desert encampment. A maid glided up and tilted one suggestively, looking eager to unpack, while Raj stalked across the huge Persian rug, like a jungle predator at bay looking for something else to complain about.

A connecting room, she quickly learned, contained cavernous wardrobes.

'This suite was last occupied by my father fifty-odd years ago,' Raj informed her grimly. 'You can tell.'

'You didn't use these rooms when you were younger?'

'No. Before my marriage I was expected to live in my father's household.'

Zoe passed on into a ridiculously gigantic bathroom with a great domed roof studded with star tiles. The bathroom fittings huddled somewhat pathetically against the walls. 'It just needs more furniture,' she told Raj with determined cheer. 'We could have one of those fainting couches in the middle and I could lie there like Cleopatra eating grapes.'

His starlit eyes focused on her without warning, an intensity within that look that made something quiver and burn low in her pelvis. *'Naked?'*

'Whatever turns you on,' Zoe mumbled, face burning, outclassed in her attempt to be light-hearted and dropping her head even while she pictured herself lying there naked for Raj's enjoyment. A ridiculous fantasy, she scolded herself, for there would be nothing particularly sexy or seductive about her very small curves on display.

'I have staff to introduce you to now,' Raj announced, biting back the comment that seeing her naked in any circumstances would work a treat for him. There would be no flirtation between them, he instructed himself harshly, no foolishness.

'*Staff?*' she exclaimed in dismay.

'Principally my PR team, but you will have your own PA to keep you well informed of events. My father has made certain requests. He would like you to give an interview to our leading newspaper.'

Zoe had frozen. 'An...*interview*?' she yelped in dismay.

'Saying how you feel about arriving in your grandmother's country and being on the brink of a state wedding. My team will advise you and remain with you during it. There is also a fashion stylist, who will recommend a suitable wedding dress and new clothes.'

'I brought a wedding dress and an entire wardrobe with me,' she informed him helpfully.

'It would be distasteful to me were you to wear the dress you purchased for the marriage you planned to make to my uncle,' Raj delivered succinctly. 'You will wear nothing bought for that purpose.'

Zoe just couldn't see why it should matter what she wore. 'Don't you think you're being too particular?'

Raj settled hard black eyes on her, startling her. 'No. I know what I like. I know what I *don't* like. The concept of you wearing anything chosen with another man in mind offends me.'

Zoe sucked in a sustaining breath, deciding that he was more sensitive to her past history than she had appreciated. She returned to supervising the maid hanging her clothes because it seemed safer to keep her head down.

'You will be kept very busy over the next few days

choosing wedding apparel,' Raj informed her from the doorway.

'Can I use your phone for a few minutes?' Zoe asked abruptly. 'Mine needs charging and I want to catch up with my sisters and my grandfather.'

'Of course.' Raj dug out his phone, cleared the password and handed it to her. 'I will see you later.'

And then, just like that, he was gone and she was staring at the space where he had been, all black silky curls with his dark, devastatingly beautiful face taut and uninformative. She had wanted him to stay with her, had wanted *more*. For a charged moment, she couldn't cope with seeing that large gap between reasonable expectation and sheer idiocy for, naturally, Raj wasn't planning to hover over her like a protective and loving spouse because he wasn't really her husband in the truest sense of the word. No, he was genuinely offering her what she had told herself she needed and craved: an independent life in which they would live separate in mind and body. So why did that sensible arrangement now seem much less inviting? Why did his attitude currently feel like something of a rejection? She shook off that strange notion and told herself to stop overthinking everything before she drove herself mad.

Her grandfather was delighted to hear from her and eager to be assured that Raj was treating her properly, while adding that he would be arriving for the wedding, the fierce pride in his voice as he mentioned 'state' wedding so strong that it made her roll her eyes and swallow back a sigh. Winnie and Vivi were far less accepting of the change of bridegroom.

'He's a lot younger than the oldie,' Vivi warned her

worriedly. 'Make sure he doesn't try to get too friendly because he may have a different agenda.'

And when Zoe protested about how kind and considerate Raj had been so far, Winnie snorted. 'He's a prince, a future king—obviously he'll be full of himself. And I looked him up online…he's incredibly good-looking. Watch out for him trying to change the terms of your agreement.'

But when Zoe went to bed that night there was no sign of Raj being full of himself or looking to change the terms of anything. He had joined her earlier for dinner out in their private courtyard, a space shaded by towering and somewhat neglected trees and shrubs, and he had then excused himself to work. She had been measured up for a new wardrobe, had looked at length at designer dresses on a screen and had stated her preferences. By the end of the day she was too exhausted to stay awake, wondering where Raj was.

Raj worked late into the night before bedding down on the sofa in his office. It was the safe option. A vision of Zoe naked troubled his rest and at four in the morning he was on his phone trying to find out what a fainting couch was; for some reason he was determined to buy one regardless of cost. He groaned out loud at the conflict tearing at him. He didn't want to get involved. He didn't want to have sex with her…except when his resistance was at a low ebb. Why the hell would he buy a fainting couch for her to pose on? He found a purple velvet one hung with tassels and pictured her with a driven exhalation of breath before he thumped the cushion beneath his head. No couch, no flirtation, no sex, no intimacy whatsoever, he reminded himself grimly.

* * *

'Well, I couldn't say much for the accommodation,' Vivi remarked with a decided sniff.

Zoe bit back a tart response because her sister had been making critical comments ever since she had arrived the night before and it was starting to annoy her. 'It's very comfortable and Raj says I can take furniture from any of the unused rooms in the palace or buy new stuff, but contemporary wouldn't really work in surroundings like these. I haven't had time yet to change anything with all this wedding craziness going on.'

'That monster bathroom is just ridiculous,' Vivi opined snarkily.

'Raj's father wouldn't agree to any structural alterations when the bathrooms first went in. As far as he can, the King wants to preserve the palace as it was when he took the throne and I can understand that. It's a very old and historic building and he feels more like the custodian for future generations than the owner who has a free hand,' Zoe pointed out.

'You've got more confident…that's clear and I definitely approve of that,' her eldest sister, Winnie, said warmly. 'Here you are giving interviews and the like. I never thought I'd see the day.'

'Oh, the interview was easy,' Zoe carolled. 'Raj's PR team headed off any too personal questions for me and advised me on what to wear and all the rest of it.'

'But you picked your own wedding gown,' Winnie said knowingly, scrutinising the tiny glittering figure of her youngest sister. The dress was an elegant sleeved sheath with a modest neckline. Elaborate embroidery sewn with crystals and pearls adorned the lightweight tulle and it was the perfect fit for her petite frame. 'It's very chic.'

'Oh, stop changing the subject, Winnie,' Vivi cut in curtly, keen to cut through the chit-chat to what she believed was truly important, which was *protecting* Zoe. 'You know that you're as worried as I am. We *talked* about it last night.'

'And we're not going to talk about it any more,' Winnie declared, throwing her fiery sibling a pleading look. 'It was Zoe's decision to do this and the deed is done. They're already married.'

'With *one* bedroom in a palace the size of a small city!' Vivi interrupted worriedly, seriously suspicious of that development. 'How's she going to fight off a guy twice her size?'

Zoe paled at the tenor of the conversation. 'I won't have to fight him off. Raj sleeps elsewhere. We haven't had to share a bed since that first night I told you about, and that was kind of unavoidable and he apologised for it.'

'Raj is smooth, sophisticated, *predatory*,' Vivi outlined in condemnation, finally speaking her mind, for she had taken one look at Raj in all his good-looking, silkily soft-spoken glory and seen him as a major threat to the terrifyingly innocent and fragile little sister she loved. How could such a very handsome and wealthy man *not* be predatory? Zoe's near rape had almost destroyed her and Vivi didn't want her sister plunged into any situation that could threaten her peace of mind. 'I would imagine he is never stuck for the right word in a difficult situation.'

'He's not predatory,' Zoe argued with distaste. 'He's been kind. He's courteous and considerate and that's all we need right now.'

'Leave it, Vivi,' Winnie said ruefully. 'All you're doing is putting more pressure on her.'

Zoe's hand shook a little as she reapplied her lipstick. She was furious that Vivi had called Raj predatory after only meeting him for an hour over the formal dinner that had been staged the night before. Stam Fotakis, her grandfather, had been grudgingly impressed by Raj, pointing out to her with satisfaction that, unlike her sisters' husbands, Raj had never been tagged a womaniser.

Diamonds flashed with every movement of her body. Raj had sent her jewel cases containing a tiara, a necklace and earrings. She didn't know whether they were family heirlooms or bought specially for her use and she hadn't had the chance to ask him because she had barely seen Raj since their move to the palace two weeks earlier. He joined her for dinner every evening but his manner was formal and distant and she didn't know how to break through that façade.

And although she had tried to penetrate that barrier to establish a friendlier vibe, Raj remained resolutely detached and very, *very* polite. His attitude frustrated the hell out of her. She didn't know what the matter with him was or what was travelling through his brain. The warmer, milder, more approachable side of Raj had vanished as though it had never been.

Although she could have had no suspicion of the fact, Raj's attitude was frustrating his royal parent even more.

'Any normal man would want to *keep* her!' King Tahir was proclaiming to his stony-faced son.

'I have no intention of keeping Zoe as a wife,' Raj asserted quietly. 'You knew that going into this.'

'She's a beautiful, gentle girl. Everyone who has met her has talked highly of her. She could be a tremendous asset to you with her personality and ancestry,' his father fumed. '*Why* are you sleeping in your office with a beautiful wife in your bed? Have you forgotten how to woo a woman?'

The obstinacy that ran through Raj like a steel backbone flared and he gritted his teeth. 'She agreed to a fake marriage and I will abide by that agreement as I will abide by the one I made with you.'

The King paced the floor and silence fell. It was the silence of unresolved differences and residual bitterness that most often distinguished meetings between father and son. It took effort for the older man to persist. 'I loved your mother. I *know* she was unhappy as my wife but I loved her very much and the mode of her death devastated me,' he bit out harshly. 'I have to live with my regrets and my mistakes but I still remain grateful for the time I had with her.'

Raj swallowed hard, unable even to look at his father and utterly taken aback by that confession. He had never realised that his father actually loved his mother but he did recall that, after her passing, the older man had lived like a hermit for over a year. Not guilt so much as grief, Raj adjusted now, his view of the past softening the trauma of loss just a little.

Ironically, even appreciating that could not lift his gloom because there was nothing to celebrate when marrying a very beautiful woman who appealed to him on every level but who would ultimately leave him. His mother had left him by taking her own life, Nabila had left him through betrayal of all that he held dear. But then, hadn't he *agreed* that Zoe would ultimately leave him? Hard cheekbones colouring at that timely recollection, he reminded himself that he was in control of events and walking the path he had chosen. By the time Zoe walked out of his life again, he would surely be glad to reclaim his freedom.

The state wedding was so official and serious that Zoe's face ached with her set and determined smile. Being the cynosure of all eyes was taxing for her, but she wouldn't let herself dwell on that reality because she was well aware that all brides were subject to close scrutiny. Instead she reminded herself that she was lucky enough to have her grandfather, her sisters and their husbands with her for support. Sadly, the formality of the event had persuaded her sisters that their young children were better left at home and she suppressed a sigh. Winnie's son, Teddy, was a very lively little boy and her toddler daughter was full of mischief while as for Vivi's twin boys, sitting still for any length of time was a massive challenge for them, but Zoe was still disappointed not to have had some time with her nephews and niece because she had always adored children and had grieved over the truth that she was unlikely to have any of her own.

Yet her recognition of her attraction to Raj and her enjoyment of that amazing kiss had made her think that just maybe there was hope for her in the future. Maybe some day, after all, she would be able to have a relationship with a man like any normal woman, and if that happened then she just might have children of her own to love and care for eventually. More than anything else, what she had learned about herself since arriving in Maraban had convinced her that staying in her grandmother's country was the very best thing she could do to steer herself back into the land of the living. There was a whole world out there waiting to be discovered and for the first time in years she was filled with hope and optimism.

In the short term, however, she acknowledged wryly, there was the marrying, the constant smiling and the solemn bridegroom to contend with at their reception. If a smile had cracked Raj's face once she must not have been around to see it. A half-smile would play about the corner of his full sensual lips in the most infuriatingly tantalising way and she would watch and watch those lean, darkly beautiful features of his, but the real thing never quite made it, even for the authorised wedding photographs, which had proved to be an exercise in rigid formality.

Yet everywhere in Raj's radius, a virtual party was in swing, his return to being Crown Prince clearly a development that was celebrated by the many important guests attending, who ranged from visiting royal connections to business tycoons, top diplomats and local VIPs. His popularity was undeniable, although he was quick to dampen comments that tactlessly suggested that some day he would take Maraban forward in a different way from his father. Zoe sat through a lot of business talk before escaping back in the direction of her sisters.

She had already done her stint with Queen Ayshah, who had employed Farida as a translator and had embarrassed the other young woman greatly by insisting on passing on her convictions of what it took to be a good royal wife. A feminist would have had a field day with those rules, Zoe reflected with strong amusement, but then the elderly Queen had grown up in a different world where a woman's happiness and even her life could be utterly dependent on retaining her husband's favour. Thankfully, Raj would have no such power over her, Zoe thought fondly as she took a detour towards the cloakroom before approaching Winnie and Vivi.

In the big anteroom surrounding the cloakroom, a tall, slender woman rose from a chair and addressed her. 'Your Royal Highness?' she murmured with modestly evasive eyes. 'May I have a word?'

Zoe looked up into one of the most beautiful faces she had ever seen: a flawless oval graced by almond-shaped brown eyes with remarkable lashes, a classic slim nose and a pouty full mouth. The woman wore a sophisticated silk suit, tailored with precision to show off her well-formed figure and falling to her ankles while still toeing the line of local mores on modest dress. The pale golden hue of the outfit set off her glowing olive colouring and her wealth of tumbling black wavy hair to perfection.

'I am Nabila Sulaman,' she revealed in a very quiet voice. 'I was Raj's first girlfriend and, as I'm sure you're aware, it ended badly between us.'

Thoroughly disconcerted by that introduction, Zoe merely gave an uncertain nod while her mind raced to understand why the wretched woman would want to approach her.

'I run one of your grandfather's construction firms and he brought me here with his party of business people. I would definitely not have received an invite on my own behalf,' Nabila admitted, startling Zoe even more with that freely offered information. 'I'm very much a career woman and I don't want past mistakes to taint my future now that I've returned to Maraban to work. My parents suffered a great deal over my short-lived relationship with Raj. My father is a diplomat but he has been continually passed over for promotion since I blotted my copybook with the royal family. I am speaking to you now because a lot of time has passed since then and I was *hoping* that you could persuade Raj to bury the hatchet.'

Zoe winced at that bold suggestion. 'I'm sorry but I don't think I'm the right person to intercede for you. I don't interfere with Raj's life and he doesn't interfere with mine.'

'How very modern he must have become,' Nabila remarked with a dismissive toss of her beautiful head and an amused smile. 'Well, I think you should know that I'm in charge of the Josias project as CEO of Major Holdings, and that Raj and I will be working together in the near future. Please make him aware of that. I'm leaving now.'

'But Raj is here. You could speak to him yourself,' Zoe pointed out.

'No. I don't want to put him in an awkward position and surprise him in front of an audience,' Nabila declared with assurance. 'We haven't seen each other since we broke up.'

'Oh...' Bemused, Zoe watched the poised brunette walk away again and she entered the cloakroom with a lot on her mind. Nabila was gorgeous, clever and successful and had once been the woman Raj loved and wanted to marry, Zoe reflected ruefully. Loved and wanted to marry *a long time ago*. Eight years back, she reminded herself, practically pre-history in date. But even though that was her mindset she still headed straight for her grandfather to check out his opinion of the brunette.

'Nabila Sulaman? She's one tough cookie, a real go-getter,' Stam opined. 'Had to be to get so far in the construction field. She's Raj's ex?' Her grandfather grimaced. 'I wouldn't have included her in my party if I'd been aware of that.'

'Oh, it doesn't bother me,' Zoe hastened to proclaim just as her sisters joined them and then, of course, the entirety of her short conversation with Nabila had to be recounted.

'She's got some brass neck!' Vivi declared. 'I wish I'd been with you. Didn't you learn anything from us growing up?'

Zoe blinked and studied her sibling's exasperated expression. 'What do you mean?'

'You don't tangle with an ex. You certainly don't give her any information... I mean, what you were thinking of, telling her that you and Raj don't interfere in each other's lives?' Vivi demanded ruefully. 'How normal does that sound? You *want* the ex to think you're the love match of the century.'

'Put a sock in it, Vivi,' Winnie cut in. 'Zoe doesn't have to pretend if she doesn't want to. It's a marriage of convenience and both of them know and accept that. It's not personal for them the way it was for you and me.'

Zoe had lost colour. No, it was *not* personal, she repeated staunchly to herself, because, unlike her sisters and their husbands, Zoe had had no prior relationship with Raj before their marriage. Yet even in acknowledging that truth she was taken aback by the revelation that she would have liked to have scratched Nabila's beautiful eyes out because Nabila had *hurt* Raj. A long time ago, she reminded herself afresh, and he was perfectly capable of looking out for himself.

When the festivities were almost at an end, Zoe went to change into more comfortable clothing for their journey. They were to be out of the public eye for two weeks and she couldn't wait to reclaim some privacy. Apparently, the royal family owned a very comfortable villa by the Gulf on the Banian side of Maraban, and Raj had already promised to show her the beauties of her grandmother's birthplace, which was greener and less arid in landscape. She pulled on a light skirt and T-shirt, teaming them with a pair of glitzy high sandals, one of the many, many pairs she harboured in her wardrobe but had never previously worn. She had a serious shoe fetish and knew it.

'We're fortunate to be making so early an escape,' Raj remarked, sliding into the limo beside her, a lean, lithe figure in jeans and a shirt, his black curls tousled as though he had changed out of his wedding finery in as much of a hurry as her. 'If my father wasn't so eager to pack us off on a honeymoon, the celebrations would have lasted all week.'

'Farida mentioned that weddings usually last for days here, but then it was our *second* time round the block,' she pointed out before pressing on, doing what her conscience told her she had to do, which was to warn Raj that he would be working with his ex on some project that she didn't recall the name of. 'I met your ex-girlfriend, Nabila, at the reception.'

Raj's arrogant head turned, a frown building, his lean, darkly handsome face forbidding. 'That is not possible. She would not have been invited. Nabila is a common name in Maraban.'

'Apparently she came in my grandfather's party of guests,' Zoe persisted. 'She's the CEO of some company called Major Holdings and she asked me to warn you that you would be working with her on some project.'

'The Josias hospital project.' Raj's intense dark eyes shimmered almost silver in the fading light. 'But I need no warning. I am not so sensitive,' he breathed with roughened emphasis.

And then he didn't say another word for what remained of the fairly lengthy journey that took them to the airport and a flight and, finally, a bumpy trip in a SUV. And, unfortunately that brooding silence told Zoe everything she didn't want to know or surmise about the exact level of Raj's sensitivity. He was like a pot of oil simmering on a fire but all emotion and reaction was rigidly suppressed by very strong self-control that acted like a lid. But knowing that, accepting that she hadn't a clue what he was thinking, didn't make Zoe feel any happier. For the first time with Raj, she felt very alone and isolated...

CHAPTER SIX

WITH DIFFICULTY, RAJ emerged from circuitous thoughts laced with outrage at the prospect of being exposed to Nabila's deceitful charm again and stepped out of the SUV. He expected to see the sprawling nineteen-twenties villa that his family had used as a holiday home since his childhood. He blinked in disbelief at the very much smaller new property that now stood in its place and signalled the army major in charge of their security to seek clarification of the mystery. A couple of minutes later he returned to Zoe's side.

'Apparently, my father had the old villa demolished several years ago because it was falling into disrepair and he thought it was too large to renovate,' Raj explained. 'It was built by your great-grandparents at a time when the Banian royal family had half a dozen daughters. My family used it rarely after your mother's father died. My father likes the sea but the Queen does not.'

Relieved that Raj was talking again, Zoe murmured, 'Did you come here much as a boy?'

'Often when I was very young with my parents. My mother loved it here.' His lean strong face tightened, his perfect bone structure pulling taut beneath his bronzed skin. 'I remember her skipping through the surf and laughing. No worries about etiquette or protocol or who might be watching and criticising her behaviour. She could be an ordinary woman here again and she loved it.'

'An *ordinary* woman?' Zoe queried, puzzled by that label.

Momentarily, Raj turned away to evade the question because he disliked talking about past traumas. In his experience a trouble shared was not a trouble halved and he preferred to gloss over such issues. Without skipping a beat, he deftly changed the subject. 'My father should have told me that there was a smaller property here now,' Raj breathed. 'As he only comes here alone, there may only be one bedroom.'

'Oh, let's not get into *that* debate again!' Zoe carolled with a comically exaggerated shudder that locked his eyes to her animated face. 'We're adults, we'll get by, even if you make me sleep on the floor!'

Her green eyes could dance like emeralds tumbling in sunlight, Raj noted abstractedly, settling a hand to her spine to guide her down the path because it was dark and she could hardly move in her high heels without stumbling on the stony surface beneath their feet. He had watched her throughout the day, had been forced to watch her teeter and sway and steady herself on furniture every time she lost her balance. She might continually wear high heels but had evidently not yet learned how to comfortably walk in them. The idea of her falling and hurting herself made him want to go into her wardrobe and *burn* every one of those preposterous shoes. It was an odd thought to have and he tagged it as such and frowned in bemusement.

'You know, I wouldn't do that.'

'You're not sleeping on the floor either!' Zoe warned him as they approached the well-lit front door. A lovely wrap-around veranda fronted the building and their protection team surged ahead of them to check that the house was safe. 'Where have you been spending the night since we got married?'

'My office.'

'Is there a bed there?'

Raj shrugged a broad shoulder. 'A sofa,' he admitted grudgingly.

Zoe gritted her teeth in annoyance. 'Are you *that* scared of me?'

Dark colour scored the hard, slanted lines of Raj's spectacular cheekbones and his stunning eyes flashed gold with angry disbelief. At that optimum moment the protection team reappeared to usher them inside. It didn't take long to explore the interior of the beach house. There was a surprisingly large contemporary ground-floor living area and a winding staircase led upstairs to a spacious bedroom and bathroom.

'There's no kitchen!' Zoe exclaimed abruptly, glancing out at the walled swimming pool beyond the patio doors. 'How are we supposed to eat here?'

'The staff stay in a new accommodation block built behind the hill and cater to our needs from there,' Raj told her. 'Meals will be delivered. It's not a very practical arrangement but my father enjoys his solitude.'

'I'm starving,' Zoe admitted.

'I will order a meal.'

'I'll go for a shower and change into something more comfortable,' Zoe said cheerfully.

She was halfway up the stairs when Raj spoke again. 'I am not scared of you, nor was I implying that you would choose to tempt me into breaking my promise,' he assured her levelly. 'But it annoys me that my father is making it so difficult for me to offer you the privacy I swore to give you.'

'And why *is* he doing that?' Zoe prompted, tipping her head to gaze down at him, her cheeks warm from his misapprehensions about her. No, she wouldn't ever set out to deliberately tempt him but she was painfully conscious that she wanted him to make some kind of move on her because she was keen to explore the way he made her feel. It was just sex, she told herself guiltily, sexual urges tugging at her hormones, and there was nothing more normal than that, she told herself in urgent addition, nothing to be ashamed of in such fantasies. It was simply her bad luck that she was married to an honourable male who believed in keeping his promises and not taking advantage. Luckily for her, she could not even imagine a scenario where she would tell him honestly how she felt and, for that reason, the humiliation of making a total fool of herself over him was unlikely.

In the meantime, all she could freely do was glory in the sheer physical beauty of Raj, his wonderful broad-shouldered, lean-hipped and long-legged physique that magnetically glued her attention to him, the dark deep-set eyes that were silver starlight when he stared up at her, his perfect golden features taut. Heaven knew, he was gorgeous and it was little wonder she was obsessed, she conceded ruefully. He had broken through her barriers, made her experience feelings she had never known she could feel, but he hadn't intended to do that and now she was stuck with the rules according to Raj, which had about as much give in them as steel bars.

'My father believes you could be my perfect *for ever* wife. He's hoping for more than a pretend marriage from us and obviously he's doomed to disappointment,' Raj extended drily.

'Oh…' Deprived of speech by that piece of bluntness and stung by the assurance that she was safe for ever from being asked to entertain the idea of something *other* than a pretend marriage, Zoe sped on into the bedroom.

There was so much she didn't know about Raj, she reflected. All she had were the bare bones of his background and the fact that his first love had cheated on him. At least, she was assuming that Nabila had been his first love but, really, what did she know? Little more than was available on the Marabanian website about the royal family. And ignorance was *not* bliss. Raj had frozen and backed off the instant she'd asked about his mother. Nabila wasn't the only no-go zone; his mother clearly was as well. Zoe heaved a sigh as she showered, wondering what had made Raj quite so complex and reserved.

Raj glanced up from his laptop as Zoe reappeared downstairs, clad in some kind of pastel floaty dress that bared most of her shoulders and a slender length of shapely leg. Not even the most severe critic could have deemed the outfit provocative, but her pert little breasts shifted as she completed the last step and he went instantly hard, cursing his libido and the fierce desire he was holding back that was becoming harder and harder to contain. Most probably he would need her covered from head to toe not to be affected, he conceded wryly, and what good would that do when he had already seen her virtually naked and could summon up that mental image even faster? He clenched his teeth together, hating the sense of weakness she inflicted. It was weak to want what he knew he shouldn't have. He prided himself on being stronger and more intelligent than that.

Nabila had been enough of a mistake to scar a man for life, a warning that his judgement wasn't infallible, that people lied and cheated to get what they wanted or merely to make a good impression and cover up the less presentable parts of their character. But, at least, he no longer carried resentment where Nabila was concerned, he reflected absently. Time had healed his bitterness and maturity had taught him more about human nature. Even so, the very prospect of having to deal with Nabila in any form, most particularly in a professional capacity in the company of others, was deeply distasteful to him. It was even more offensive to him that Nabila had dared to approach his wife and introduce herself. That had been brazen and, although he knew that Nabila could be utterly brazen and calculating, he could not begin to understand why she had made such an inappropriate move.

'Wow…look at the food!' Zoe whispered in wonderment as she glimpsed the array of dishes spread across the low table in front of him. 'You should've started without me.'

'I do have *some* manners,' Raj told her huskily, amusement glimmering in his shrewd gaze.

'I never said you didn't,' she muttered in some embarrassment, lifting a plate to serve herself and watching him follow suit. 'But I did take ages in the shower.'

Raj could have done without that visual of her tiny, delicately curved body streaming with water. 'I had a shower before we left the palace.'

'I didn't have time and it was so warm in that car even with the air conditioning.' She sighed. 'So, I'm about to ask you to be straight with me on certain issues because if you aren't I could slip up and say something embarrassing to the wrong person,' she pointed out, trotting out the excuse she had come up with in the shower to make Raj talk about what he didn't want to talk about. 'Who was your mother?'

Raj tensed and swallowed hard. 'She was a nobody in the eyes of most. Ayshah and my father's second wife, Fairoz, were both royal princesses from neighbouring kingdoms and my father married them to make political alliances when he was in his early twenties. Since *he* did *his* duty in the marital line you can understand why he expected me to be willing to do the same eight years ago.'

'Yes, but he grew up during a very unsettled period of Maraban's history when there was constant war and strife. It was different for you because you didn't live through any of those wars or periods of deprivation,' Zoe told him calmly, her retentive memory of what she had read about Maraban's history ensuring that she had a clear picture of past events. 'Now tell me about your mother and why she was nobody in the eyes of others.'

'She was a commoner, a nurse. My father had heart surgery in his fifties and she looked after him in hospital.'

Zoe smiled in approval. 'So, it was a romance?'

'Well, no, for most of my life I assumed he simply took my mother as a third wife in the last-ditch hope that a much younger woman could give him a child,' Raj confided with a twist of his full sensual mouth. 'That was the perceived reality. It never occurred to me that he had fallen in love with her until he admitted that to me only a few days ago. Now I am shamed by my prejudice but, in my own defence, my mother was a very unhappy wife and I remember that too well.'

'Why was she unhappy?' Zoe pressed.

'Picture the situation, Zoe,' Raj urged with rueful emphasis. 'Two childless older wives of many years were suddenly challenged by a much younger new arrival and they didn't like it. They didn't think my mother was fit to breathe the same air as their husband and when she quickly fell pregnant, as they had failed to do, their resentment and jealousy turned to loathing. They bullied her cruelly and treated her like dirt. My father likes a quiet life in his household and he did not interfere between his wives. He ignored the problems.'

'I'm *so* sorry,' she murmured, registering that Raj must have been old enough to understand how his mother was being abused and that his troubled relationship with his father and Ayshah probably dated from that period.

'By the time I was nine years old, she was so depressed that she took her own life with an overdose. It happened here in the old original house. Perhaps that is also why my father had it demolished,' he admitted in a driven undertone. 'There, now you know the whole unhappy story of my childhood.'

Zoe reached for him, her small fingers spreading to grip his much larger hand in a natural gesture of sympathy, finger pads smoothing over the sleek brown skin. 'Thank you for telling me,' she whispered. 'I wouldn't have pushed so hard if I'd known it was a tragedy.'

'She was a wonderful, loving mother but it was many years before I could forgive her for leaving me,' Raj confessed in a rueful undertone.

'I have no memory of either of my parents. I was only a baby when they died in a car crash,' Zoe told him with regret. 'Cherish the memories you have, try and build a bridge with your father. Everybody needs family, Raj.'

'I prefer not to need *anyone*. Independence, in so far as it is possible, is safer. Do you want something sweet to finish?' Raj enquired in casual addition. 'There is a fridge hidden in that cupboard over there. The maid filled it with desserts.'

Listening to him, Zoe had lost much of her appetite, but she scrambled upright and fetched the desserts to serve, knowing that Raj would welcome that distraction. It seemed that she always, *always* put her foot in it with him. She should have been more patient, should have waited until he was willing to talk, instead of forcing the issue. Beating herself up for her nosiness soon led to her faking a yawn and saying she was going up to bed.

Raj worked on his laptop for an hour, giving Zoe time to fall asleep. He mounted the stairs as quietly as he knew how and then he saw her, lying on the bed in something diaphanous, the pool of light surrounding her veiling her entire body in soft gold. She looked up from her book, green eyes wide, little shoulders tensing, petite breasts pushing against the finest cotton to define the pointed tips and that was the moment that Raj finally lost the battle. Hunger surged through him with such power it virtually wiped out conscious thought. She was there, she was where he wanted her to be and, in that moment, she *was* irresistible.

Zoe was fiercely disconcerted when Raj simply stalked like a prowling jungle cat across the room and bent down to snatch her up into his arms. 'Raj?' she exclaimed uncertainly, all the breath from her body stolen by that action.

'I want you... I *burn* for you,' he breathed rawly. 'Tell me to put you down and I will walk away. I will not try to railroad you into anything you don't want.'

Zoe stared up into his silvered eyes and her entire body clenched while her heart pounded in her ears. 'I want you too,' she admitted breathlessly, barely able to credit that she had the nerve to admit that and yet if he could admit it, why shouldn't she?

As he cradled her in his arms, a faint shudder of relief racked his lean, powerful frame and he claimed her parted lips with so much passion he took her by storm. Head swimming, mouth swollen, she plunged her fingers into his silky black hair, revelling in the crisp luxuriance of his curls and holding him to her. There was no sense of fear, no sense of threat and she rejoiced in that freedom, pushing up into the heat of him as he brought her down on the bed. She yanked at his shirt as he reached for her nightdress, their combined movements ending up in a tangle.

'We're behaving like teenagers!' Raj rasped in disbelief, gazing down, nonetheless, at her flushed and lovely face with ferocious satisfaction. He had never craved anything as much as he craved her hands on his body and he leant back from her to pull his shirt up over his head and discard it.

Zoe looked up at him, secretly thinking that she was behaving like a teenager because her experience of men was probably about that level. She truly was a case of arrested development, cut off from normality at the age of twelve when everything to do with men and sex had frightened her into closing down that side of her nature. Now she wondered if she should warn him that she was a virgin, but wasn't there a strong chance that her inexperience would turn him off? Or, at least, make him pause to consider whether they should be having sex in the first place? She didn't want Raj to stop and ESP warned her that if cautious, logical Raj got in charge again, her desire to have sex for the first time could be thwarted.

Raj, however, chased away all her apprehensive thoughts simply by taking his shirt off. As he leant back over her to toss it away, his abdominal muscles flexed like steel girders and she gazed up at his superb bronzed torso with helpless appreciation. Heat flowered low in her pelvis, making her press her thighs together on the resulting ache. Exhilaration flooded her at the knowledge that she was finally feeling what other women felt when they desired intimacy with a man.

'I thought you didn't like sex,' Raj breathed in a driven undertone.

And then I met you.

But she wasn't going to frighten him off by telling him *that*, was she?

'It's time I tried again,' she muttered obliquely.

'I will endeavour not to disappoint you,' Raj growled, his lips ghosting in a whisper of a caress across her collarbone that made her shiver, lean brown hands tugging up the nightdress inch by inch, fingertips lightly glossing over her slender thighs and finally her narrow ribcage. The butterflies fluttering in her belly took flight.

The nightdress fell away and Zoe sat up to embark on his jeans. It might be her first time but she wasn't about to lie there like some petrified Victorian virgin and let him do everything, she told herself squarely. Her hands were shaking so much though that she could hardly get the zip down and he closed a steadying hand over hers, pressing her fingers against him before arching his hips to snake lithely out of his jeans. His boxers went with them and she stared at the evidence of his arousal and then, dry-mouthed, reached out to stroke him, her heart already racing as though she had run a marathon.

The instant she touched him, Raj tugged her up against him with a hungry groan and crushed her mouth under his again, his tongue prying apart her lips and skating across the roof of her mouth before colliding with hers. Another burst of heat shot through her, tightening her muscles, and she shifted closer still, wanting the hard heat of him plastered to every inch of her. He was so passionate and she loved that passion, could feel it surging through his lean, powerful body to meet her own.

He laid her back and shaped her breasts with sensuous hands, smoothing, massaging, moulding, before dipping his head to catch a straining pink nipple in his mouth and swirl his tongue round the throbbing peak until her spine arched and a stifled gasp was torn from her. She was much more sensitive there than she had ever realised and little tingling thrills began to dart through her, trickling down into her pelvis to create a hot liquid pool between her thighs.

Her hips arched up of their own volition, her body controlling her responses, and all the time the nagging craving at the heart of her was building to an unbearable level and she was making little impatient sounds she couldn't quell. When he finally touched her where she most needed to be touched, her body jackknifed and a wild flood of sensation seized hold of her, provoking a cry from her lips. It was her very first climax and the sheer intensity of it took her by surprise.

Raj smiled down at her and kissed her even more hungrily. 'You are so receptive,' he husked.

Lying there dazed by the experience, Zoe reached up to explore him, palms spreading across his chest, captivated by the strength and heat of him before sliding lower to encounter a restraining hand.

'Not now,' Raj grated out. 'I'm too aroused and I need to be inside you. Are you protected?'

For a split second she didn't know what he was talking about and then comprehension sank in and she shook her head in an urgent negative. With a groan, Raj sprang off the bed naked and dug into his luggage, spilling out everything on the floor in wild disarray and then leafing through the tumbled garments to retrieve a wallet and extract a foil packet.

'I only have a few. I will need to buy more. I have not been with anyone recently and we must be careful.'

Warmed by his admission that he had had no recent lovers, Zoe frowned.

'Careful?' she queried.

Surprised by the question, Raj glanced at her. 'In our situation, a pregnancy would be a disaster...not that it's very likely. Look how many years it took my father to produce a child!' he urged wryly. 'For all I know a low sperm count runs in the royal genes.'

'But contraception is pretty much foolproof these days...surely?' Zoe pressed.

'Nothing's foolproof in that line. Accidents and surprises still happen,' Raj pointed out, coming back down on the bed with a smouldering look of hungry urgency silvering his stunning eyes. 'But it will *not* happen to us.'

Zoe reddened, disconcerted to find herself in the very act of picturing a little boy or girl with his spectacular dark eyes. Some day in the future, she promised herself, and most definitely she would become a mother with someone she had yet to meet. Raj would just be an experience she recalled with warmth, she told herself; nothing more, nothing less was due to the man who had rescued her from her fears.

She stretched up, winding her arms round his neck to draw him down to her and she kissed him, enjoying that freedom and that new confidence to do as she liked, and it all came from the reassuring, delightful discovery that Raj appeared to want her every bit as much as she wanted him.

He tugged at her lower lip with the edge of his teeth, sent his mouth travelling down the elegant line of her slender neck and that fast conversation was forgotten as another cycle of arousal claimed her. Her temperature rose, a fevered energy gripping her limbs as her heart-beat quickened and her breathing fractured.

Excitement quivered up from her pelvis when she felt him surge between her thighs, sliding into her inch by inch, sending the most exquisitely unexpected sensations sizzling through her.

'You're very small and tight,' Raj ground out breath-lessly.

And then with a final shift of his lean hips he forged his passage and her whole body jerked with the pain of it and she cried out.

Raj stilled. 'What's wrong?'

Mortified that she had made a fuss, Zoe grimaced. 'It hurt more than I was expecting. It's my first time.'

As shock clenched Raj's lean, darkly handsome features and he began to withdraw from her, Zoe grabbed his shoulders. 'No, don't you dare stop now!' she told him. 'I've been waiting such a long time to experience this.'

The deed was already done, Raj rationalised, but anger was roaring through his taut body and it was only with difficulty that he swallowed it back because he didn't want to risk hurting her any more…even if she had chosen to have sex with him as though he was an adventurous new experience much like a day out behind the wheel of a supercar, he reflected wrathfully.

'Raj, please…don't make a fuss,' Zoe urged, studying him with huge green eyes that pleaded.

And Raj did what every nerve ending in his body urged him to do and surged deeper into the welcome of her, a low growl of sensual pleasure wrenched from him. And from that point on, no further encouragement was required. A wondrous warmth began to rise low in her pelvis, building on the visceral ache for fulfilment, making her fingernails dig into his long smooth back as excitement seized her and held her fast. The feel of him over her, inside her, all around her sent rippling tremors of joy spiralling through her and when she hit the heights again, it was explosive.

In the aftermath she felt as though she were melting into the bed in a boneless state and the very last thing she needed then was Raj freeing himself from their entangled limbs and springing off the bed to breathe rawly, 'You've got some explaining to do. You *lied* to me!'

CHAPTER SEVEN

GRABBING THE SHEET to cover herself, Zoe hauled herself up against the tumbled pillows, watching Raj yank on his jeans. Going commando, she noticed, colour flaring in her face. It was as if her mind weren't her own any more. She couldn't take her eyes off his lithe bronzed body, couldn't concentrate.

'I didn't lie,' she reasoned stiffly.

'You *lied*,' Raj repeated wrathfully. 'You said it was time you tried sex *again* when clearly you had never had sex before—'

'Well, I may have blurred the edges of the truth a bit,' Zoe mumbled defensively.

'You lied and I detest dishonesty!' Raj shot back at her fiercely.

'So what?' Zoe fired back, her temper sparking in answer to his.' It was *my* decision to make—'

'And mine. I wouldn't have touched you had I known I would be the first!' Raj bit out curtly. 'But you chose to withhold that knowledge, which was unfair—'

'Oh, for goodness' sake…' Zoe thrust the blonde hair falling round her hot face back off her damp brow. 'It was just sex. Why are you making such a production out of it? We're consenting adults, neither of us is in another relationship.'

Raj skimmed scorching dark eyes to her. 'I don't do relationships.'

'Well, I'm afraid you're *stuck* in this one,' Zoe told him with unashamed satisfaction. 'You can't have it both ways, Raj. If you don't do relationships, then you should be quite happy to have had no-strings-attached sex.'

Dark colour scoring his superb cheekbones, Raj shot her a blistering look of derision and strode out of the room. She listened to his bare feet thumping down the wooden stairs and then the slam of the front door signifying his exit from the house. Switching out the lights, she got out of bed to walk over to the window and finally picked him out striding down onto the beach. Moonlight glimmered along the hard line of his broad shoulders and danced over his curls.

Mortification gripped Zoe, who was conscious she had said stuff she didn't actually believe to hit back at him because she had felt humiliated by his annoyance. It *had* been her decision to have him as her first lover, hadn't it? But she wasn't liberal enough to plan to have casual sex with anyone, even if she had made it sound as though she were. She had simply wanted that experience, had wanted *him*. Was that so bad? But it also felt wonderful to no longer fear the act of sex, to no longer feel that she was somehow less than other women and missing out on an experience that others enjoyed.

Uneasily aware then of the ache at the heart of her from that first experience, she went into the bathroom and ran herself a bath to soak in. She had messed up, brought sex into their platonic relationship…but, hey, hadn't Raj been the one to make the first move? Why hadn't she thrown that at him? It was *his* fault they had ended up in bed. Why, in his eyes, would it have been acceptable to become intimate if she had had more experience? How had it somehow become wrong because she had been inexperienced?

Throwing on a cotton wrap and stuffing her feet into flip-flops, Zoe left the house and trudged across the sand to where Raj was walking through the whispering surf.

Raj heard her approach. There was nothing stealthy about Zoe crossing sand. He breathed in deep and slow, rising above his angry discomfiture and the guilt she had inflicted him with.

'All right, I'm sorry I didn't tell you beforehand, but you're the one who dragged *me* into bed,' Zoe reminded him flatly, her face burning. 'Regrets now are a bit late in the day and they're not going to change anything.'

'In my culture a woman's purity is highly valued and respected. That may seem outdated to you—'

'Very much so. Why should a woman be any more restricted with what she does with her body than a man is?' Zoe slung back at him half beneath her breath.

'I feel guilty that I took that innocence from you,' Raj admitted harshly.

'Even if it's what I wanted? It's not like I'm still a teenager in need of protection,' Zoe argued vehemently, surprised herself to realise how strongly she felt about the decision she had made. 'I just wanted to be like everyone else and know what it was all about instead of feeling…feeling odd,' she framed grudgingly.

'You deserved more than I gave you. It wasn't special…it *should* have been special,' he asserted with conviction.

'Was your first time special for you?' Zoe demanded, cutting in.

Disconcerted by that unexpectedly bold question, Raj gritted his teeth and opted for honesty. 'No.'

'Well, there you are, then, once again you didn't practise what you preach.'

A reluctant laugh was torn from Raj and he turned to look at her, so tiny she barely reached the centre of his chest and yet in so many ways she was absolutely fearless in her outlook, happy to express her views even when they conflicted with his. She was also too stubborn and independent to even acknowledge his point that if she had valued herself more she would not have entertained surrendering her innocence to him. People rarely confronted Raj with his mistakes or criticised him but Zoe had no such filter. She was quite correct: *he* had dragged *her* into bed.

'And I'm sorry if you don't feel the same way,' she added stiffly, 'but what we shared *did* feel special to me.'

Disconcerted, Raj sent her a gleaming glance and then his lashes dropped low. 'I'm sorry if I upset you but I do hate lies,' he murmured grimly.

'I'm usually very honest but I didn't want you to back off,' Zoe completed unevenly.

'You were curious,' Raj commented, wondering if he had ever had such an extraordinary conversation with a woman before, a conversation in which he was painfully honest and she was as well. He didn't think so

and there was something remarkably refreshing about
the experience.

'Yes, sorry if that makes you feel a bit like an experiment…but I suppose you were, rather, a new experience, I mean,' she mumbled apologetically.

Exactly like having a day out behind the wheel of
a supercar, Raj thought again with relish, and he burst
out laughing. No, no woman had ever dared to tell him
before that he was an experiment, but then none had
ever used that word, special, for what they had shared
with him either. 'Am I allowed to ask how I scored?'

'No. That would be bad for your ego…' Zoe gazed
up at him, encountering moonlit dark eyes that shimmered, and her heart skipped a beat.

'You were amazing…and special,' Raj murmured,
lifting his hands to gently comb her tousled mane of
hair back from her cheekbones, the pads of his fingers
brushing the petal-soft skin of her face, sending a quiver
of awareness arrowing through her. 'But I shouldn't
have touched you. I had no right.'

'We're married.'

'In name only,' he reminded her with scrupulous ac-
curacy, and for some reason she wanted to kick him.
'It's not meant to be real but it's starting to feel very
real, which is worrying.'

'Why worrying?' she prompted.

'It wasn't supposed to be like this. We were supposed
to live separate lives and make a few public appearances
together and that was to be that.'

'So, we departed from the set script. But we're not
hurting anyone,' she whispered, her hands settling to
his lean waist, her fingers rubbing over smooth, hot

skin, feeling the ripple of the muscles of his abdomen pull taut at even that slight touch.

'I don't do relationships,' he reminded her stubbornly even as he leant down to her, drawn by the ripe pink swell of her mouth.

'You're right in the middle of a relationship with me...stop kidding yourself!' Zoe countered. 'Do you think you're about to wake up some morning and find yourself handcuffed to the bed and trapped?'

Raj scooped her slight body up into his arms as if it were the most natural thing in the world to carry her and trudged back up the beach towards the house. 'If it was you cuffing me to the bed, I wouldn't fight and I wouldn't feel trapped,' he muttered huskily.

'That's probably the nicest thing you've ever said to me, but I've got to tell you that cuffing you to the bed looms nowhere on my horizon. If you don't want to be there, you can sleep on the floor,' she told him roundly.

'You said you weren't up for that option.'

'Guess I lied again,' Zoe trilled. 'I could happily consign you to the floor now.'

'And if I *want* to share the bed?' Raj left the question hanging as her lashes opened to their fullest extent, revealing emerald-green enquiry.

'You're welcome,' she said gruffly as he set her down and she kicked off her flip-flops. 'I think sex makes me hungry... I'm starving again!'

And Raj threw back his head and laughed, stalking over to the concealed fridge, discovering it was packed with prepared food in readiness for such an occasion. Zoe stiffened, marvelling at how relaxed she now felt with Raj. Barriers had come crashing down when they had shared that bed, she acknowledged, but now that she felt closer to him and no longer separate, she was more likely to get hurt. What had happened to her defences? What had happened to her belief that she was only in Maraban to become stronger and more independent? Now she was involved with Raj on a level she had never expected to be and her emotions were all over the place and making her feel insecure.

Zoe froze, frowning as she surveyed the room. 'All the dinner dishes have been cleared away.'

'The staff have been in. Our protection team probably let them know the coast was clear. The bed's probably been changed as well,' Raj forecast.

Zoe gulped. 'It's after midnight, Raj. Don't the staff sleep?'

'They work rotation shifts. Invisible service is a matter of pride to them.'

They ate snacks and she went up to bed first, the exhaustion of the long day crashing down on her all at once. She pillowed her cheek on her hand and watched Raj strip off his jeans and go for a shower, enviably indifferent to any form of self-consciousness. But then maybe had her body been as flawlessly beautiful as his she would've been equally blasé, she thought sleepily. Instead she was blessed with short legs, tiny boobs and a bottom that was a little big for the rest of her.

'What are we doing tomorrow?' she whispered when he joined her.

'It is already tomorrow,' he pointed out. 'I'm taking you to the old palace where your grandmother grew up and afterwards there'll be an informal meet-and-greet session with the locals and official photographs. My father is making as much possible use of your time in the family as he can.'

'I suppose that was the deal,' she muttered drowsily. 'It'll be interesting seeing where Azra grew up... It was almost as interesting watching your father and my grandfather politely avoid each other at the wedding, and then I was steering clear of your uncle Hakem and he was staying well away from me as well.'

Her brow furrowed at that recollection. Prince Hakem had proved to be a rather colourless little old man and she had been astonished that such a seemingly nondescript personality could be burning underneath with thwarted royal ambitions.

A husky laugh fell from Raj, his breath warming her shoulder. 'My father made a fuss about having your grandfather at the wedding but I talked him round. Stam is, after all, the man who ran off with the Banian princess my father was supposed to marry.'

'But my grandmother, Azra, and your father hadn't even met when she met Stam and fell for him,' Zoe whispered.

'My father still felt it was an insult and it rankled. Go to sleep,' Raj urged. 'This will be another long day but, after the palace visit, we are off the official schedule for the rest of our stay.'

And Zoe thought tiredly of how anxious she had been about having to make any public appearances when she'd first arrived in Maraban and of how inexplicably Raj's presence by her side, or even in the same room, soothed her apprehensions. Somehow, he made her feel safe, protected, as if nothing bad could happen while he was around. It was so silly to endow him with that much importance, she conceded ruefully, and then she slept.

What they had *was* a relationship, Raj recognised with considerable unease. It had become one the minute he married her and intimacy had only deepened the ties and made it more complex. Truly it had been naïve of him not to foresee that development, given the level of attraction they shared Zoe had said it was 'just' sex. Could he believe that, accept that? Was she really sophisticated enough to make that distinction? And could they keep it at that casual level? And in time go their separate ways without regret? It would be like a very long one-night stand, he reasoned while even his brain told him that that was a foolish misconception. He didn't want to treat Zoe the same way he treated his occasional lovers, being distant, keeping it impersonal, always hiding his true self. He felt much more comfortable with Zoe. He wanted to make her happy. For the first time ever with a woman, he would just go with the flow…

Zoe wakened in the morning in Raj's arms. 'Hey, your only body temperature seems to be hot as the fires of hell,' she complained, striving to slide away to cool off.

Raj pulled her back to him with ease and the thrust of his arousal against her stomach made her eyes widen. She looked up at him, all bronzed and in need of a shave, with blue black curls, and he was to die for and there was no denying that she was willing. 'Oh…' she said in entirely another voice.

'If it would be uncomfortable for you…?' he husked, hitching a perfect ebony brow in enquiry.

It probably would be a little bit, she acknowledged,

but there was a hungry tingle of awareness heating up between her thighs that made her hips shift with longing. 'No, it wouldn't be,' she lied shamelessly. 'But I need to clean my teeth.'

'No, you don't…you smell like strawberries and woman,' Raj framed thickly, cupping her cheekbones and devouring her mouth as though his life depended on it.

And that was that for Zoe, her heart thumping fit to burst from her chest as her body ratcheted up the scale of arousal as though it had been doing it all her life. When he kissed her, he set her on fire, when he touched her, exploring her urgently sensitive nipples and the tender flesh between her thighs with those long skilful fingers of his, the fire began to blaze out of control and she was turning and twisting, downright writhing with tormented pleasure. By the time he hooked one of her legs over his hips and plunged into her, Zoe was surging towards a climax at an unstoppable pace and the raw, hot excitement of that passionate invasion sent her flying with a choked gasp into the horizon.

'Let's see if you can do that again,' Raj growled as she thrashed under him and he surged into her afresh in a timely change of pace, aiming for long and slow rather than fast and furious.

And she caught her breath again and barely with a quivery little inhale, blonde hair lying in a mad tangle around her head as he rose over and looked down at her, black starlit eyes intent and riveting, her body still singing and pulsing from his last onslaught. His rhythm was sensual, calculated, letting the erotic tension build again and inexorably she shifted from melting to craving. His passion compelled her, and her hands slid over his back, rejoicing in the hard, smooth strength of him as rippling waves began to clench at her pelvis. A wildness took hold of her and she wrapped her legs round him and that final thrust made her soar in an excess of pleasure to the heights again.

Afterwards, he brushed her hair off her damp face and kissed her. 'I hate to hurry you when I've made you late in the first place, but we have to be out of here in an hour if you want to see the palace before we have to face the official welcome...'

'An hour?' she gasped incredulously.

'I'll call your maid and get out of here,' Raj told her helpfully. 'Am I allowed to say that you make a great friend with benefits?'

Was *that* what she was? Zoe thought about that in the shower and pulled a face. It sounded a lot bolder and a lot more laid-back than she believed she was, but who was to say she couldn't change? Wasn't that what her stay in Maraban was aimed at? Finding out who she really was without her sisters and her grandfather wrapping her in cotton wool and watching over her all the time? She was in a brave new world, she reminded herself, and aspects of it were likely to be unfamiliar and scary. Or *sobering*, she conceded ruefully, because her gut instinct was that she didn't want to be a friend with benefits for any man...even Raj.

Her maid had apparently accompanied her from the palace and already had an outfit laid out for her when she reappeared from the bathroom. Zoe cast an eye over the pale green tailored dress and decided it would do very well. At her request her hair was braided, which was cooler in the heat, and when she descended the stairs dead on time, she was smiling, thinking that a maid with hairstyling skills was an invaluable asset and a luxury she had better not become too accustomed to having. It was *all* temporary, she reminded herself, like a winning prize ticket that took her off on an extravagant holiday. Raj was, also, simply a temporary presence in her life. Maybe that was what made the 'friends with benefits' concept meaningless and possibly a little slutty. She winced at that self-judgement.

'You can't wear those shoes trekking round an old building!' Raj exclaimed, engaged in staring at her feet in what appeared to be disbelief.

Zoe sent him a dirty look. 'I'm crazy about shoes, but I'll bring a pair of flats and change into these later,' she conceded reluctantly. 'But don't you get the idea that you have the right to tell me what I should and shouldn't wear... I'm not having that!'

An unholy grin slashed Raj's often serious features as he awaited her reappearance.

The one-time home of the former Banian royal family was huge and sprawling and, although the building had been carefully conserved, it was not used for any purpose other than to house a small museum on the history of Bania and provide the public with the chance to tour Princess Azra's former apartments.

'I wish she hadn't died before I was born.' Zoe sighed, studying old black and white photos of a youthful blonde in local dress. 'Grandad showed me pictures of her. He totally adored her, you know,' she told Raj cheerfully. 'He cast off my father for refusing to do a degree in business and come and work for him. My grandmother told him he was doing the wrong thing and that he should let my dad make his own path but Grandad was too proud and stubborn to listen.'

'It is a challenge for one generation to understand what drives the next. It was years before I could appreciate that in demanding that I marry a woman he chose my father was only asking me to do what he had done himself.'

'But you were in love with someone else,' Zoe reminded him. 'You couldn't possibly have married another woman and made a success of it. You would've been full of bitterness and resentment.'

'My father believes that in our privileged position emotions cannot be allowed to make our decisions for us. I learned the hard way that he was correct,' Raj completed with a harsh edge to his voice.

'You still have to tell me about you and Nabila,' Zoe told him.

'I thought women didn't like a man to talk about previous affairs,' Raj countered in surprise, shooting her a disconcerted glance.

'I'd have to be in love with you to mind that sort of thing and all jealous and possessive and I'm *not*,' Zoe pointed out calmly. 'I'm just being nosy.'

Raj nodded, although the concept shook him because he was unconsciously accustomed to women wanting more from him than he was willing to give, which was why his sensual past consisted of more fleeting encounters than anything else. 'I studied business at one of the Gulf state universities. That's where I met her. Have you ever been in love?' he heard himself ask with astonishing abruptness, but he was, without warning, equally curious.

'No, not even close,' Zoe admitted tightly. 'What happened to me at twelve put me off trying to have a relationship with a man, and then I watched my sisters fall in love and didn't fancy it for myself. There seems to be a lot of angst and drama involved and I'm not into either. So you met Nabila at uni?'

'We were together for two years. I fell hard for her,' Raj bit out grudgingly, while wondering what superhuman qualities it would take to make Zoe fall in love with a man, and then his thoughts became even more tangled because he questioned why he was even thinking along that line. Was it exposure to Zoe? His cousin, Omar, had confided that following his marriage he'd found himself thinking weird thoughts, more like a woman, and that constant female company had that effect on the average man. Raj had to shake his head to clear it and he couldn't grasp how such random ruminations were arising in his usually logical brain.

'Obviously,' Zoe conceded. 'I mean, you weren't likely to defy your father's command for anything less...so you lived together for two years?'

'No, such intimacy was out of the question. If I expected my father to take my wish to marry Nabila seriously, it had to be non-sexual,' Raj proffered curtly. 'He would not have respected anything else.'

Zoe stopped dead and gazed up at him in wonderment. 'Are you saying you didn't sleep with her?'

'Of course, I didn't. My bride had to have an unsullied reputation. It would've been disrespectful to ask my father to countenance any other kind of relationship. He is from a different generation. He does not understand female liberation. In his day a woman's main claim to fame was her purity and a decent woman didn't give it up for anything less than a wedding ring.'

'Gosh, I was cheap,' his bride chipped in, her face suddenly on fire. 'Because as you pointed out, we're not really married in the truest sense of the word.'

'You weren't cheap,' Raj breathed as the museum custodian nervously watched their progress round the exhibits from the other side of the room. Long fingers stroked down her face and lingered below her chin to lift it. 'You were totally incredible and I was unworthy of the gift.'

'That's just flannel,' Zoe informed him, her face warming even more as she connected with brilliant dark eyes that sent butterflies fluttering in her tummy. 'We did what we did because we wanted to.'

'And every time I look at you,' Raj confided thickly, 'I want to do it again.'

'You were telling me about Nabila,' Zoe reminded him doggedly, tiny tingles of arousal coursing through her slight taut length while she fought to suppress those untimely urges. 'Not trying to turn me into a sex maniac.'

'Could I?' Raj asked in a roughened undertone, those gorgeous eyes pinned to her with a feverish intensity that scorched.

'It's possible,' she downplayed in haste. 'Nabila?'

'She told me she was a virgin because she probably assumed that that was what I wanted to hear. But it wasn't, I wouldn't have cared,' Raj admitted ruefully. 'So naturally I respected what she told me and I was prepared to wait until we were man and wife, but she got bored.'

'Hard to be set on a pedestal and to pretend to be something you're not,' Zoe put in thoughtfully.

'Yes, I did have her on a pedestal.' Raj grimaced. 'I was very idealistic at the age of twenty.'

'You were too young for that size of a commitment,' Zoe commented. 'What happened?'

'I refused to give her up and my father exiled me. It was my final visit and I left Maraban in a hurry. Nabila had given me a key to her apartment and my sudden return was unexpected. That was when I found her in bed with one of her so-called friends. It was clearly a long-standing arrangement and what an idiot I felt!' Raj relived, his superb cheekbones rigid. 'I had surrendered everything for her and there she was, the absolute antithesis of the woman I believed her to be—a shameless cheat and a liar, who only wanted me for my status!'

'And your body, probably,' Zoe told him abstractedly, winning a startled sidewise scrutiny. 'You must've been devastated. I'm lucky. I've never been hurt like that, don't want to be either.'

Raj stared down into her beautiful expressive face and wondered why it was so very easy to talk to her about Nabila, whom he had never discussed with anyone before. It was because she didn't have a personal stake in their marriage, at least not one that he understood, because from what he had observed her new royal status and the awe it inspired meant precious little to her. 'The meet and greet downstairs starts in thirty minutes. You can put on the skyscraper heels if you must.'

'If I *must*?' Zoe queried, slinging him a look of annoyance.

'You struggle to walk in very high heels,' Raj pointed out bluntly.

'Because I never went out anywhere until I came to Maraban. I had this fabulous collection of gorgeous shoes and my sisters borrowed them and I never got to wear them until now,' Zoe told him hotly. 'I'll *learn* to walk in them!'

'Obviously,' Raj countered, realising that he had been tactless in the extreme. 'But why didn't you go out anywhere?'

'I panicked if men came onto me, couldn't handle it,' she confided reluctantly. 'But you don't do that to me for some reason.'

'Maybe because you're not falling for me,' Raj suggested glibly, while cherishing the obvious fact that she felt safer and more protected in his company.

'Yes, that could well be it,' Zoe responded cheerfully as she slid her feet into her high heels while leaning on both his arm and a door handle to balance. 'You wouldn't believe how much more confident I feel standing a few inches taller.'

Watching her sip coffee and smilingly chat by his side only minutes later, Raj decided it had nothing to do with the stupid shoes. He remembered their first meeting and her panic attack and marvelled at how much she had already changed. He had merely met her at a bad moment in a scenario that would have frightened any woman, he recognised. His fingers splayed across her spine and he concealed a grin, thinking about the scratches on his back, badges of pride for a man who knew he had satisfied his woman. Not *his* woman, he immediately corrected himself. Well, she sort of *was* his for the present, an acceptance that somehow lightened the cloud threatening his mood.

It seemed no time at all to Zoe before they were being posed in the palace's grand reception room for the photographs and then they were done, and it was a relief to not be on show any more and know that they had only a holiday ahead of them, she reflected sunnily. They were walking back to the car when a photographer popped out from behind some trees and shouted at them. Half of Raj's security team took off in pursuit of him. At the same time Raj's phone started shrilling and one of the diplomats she had met at the reception emerged with a grim face and moved in their direction with something clutched in his hand.

'What the hell?' Raj groused only half under his breath, pulling out his phone while ensuring that Zoe was safely tucked into the car awaiting them.

She watched as the diplomat proffered the magazine to Raj, saw him glance at it with patent incredulity and then compress his lips so flat they went bloodless. After that he strode back and forth in front of the car talking on his phone, his lean brown hands making angry gestures, his whole stance telegraphing his tense, dissatisfied mood.

'What's happened?' Zoe asked anxiously when he finally came off the phone and climbed in beside her.

CHAPTER EIGHT

'A STORM IN a teacup but it's put my father in a real rage.' Raj expelled a stark breath, impatience and exasperation lacing his intonation. 'Last year my father drove Maraban's only gossip magazine out of the country. Now they're based in Dubai and what they publish about us has steadily become more shocking. He should've left them alone. He has to accept that these days everything we do is watched and reported on and our family cannot hope to keep secrets the way we did when he was a boy.'

'I guess he's a bit behind the times. The press are more disrespectful of institutions nowadays. So, what's in that magazine?' she prompted, thoroughly puzzled. 'Some forgotten scandal?'

'Not even a scandal, merely an intrusion.' He had crushed the magazine between his hands and now he smoothed it out with difficulty and handed it to her. 'Of course, you can't read it but the photos are self-explanatory and this article coming out the same week as our wedding, suggesting that I wasn't allowed to marry the woman I loved because she was a commoner, may be embarrassing for my father but it is also an absurd allegation.'

Dry-mouthed now, Zoe stared down at the splash of photographs, depicting Raj with Nabila. *Old* photos, of course. She could see that they were younger but what she had not been prepared to see was the look of adoration in Raj's face as he gazed down at the other woman. He was studying Nabila as if she'd hung the moon for him and for some reason, Zoe registered, seeing those youthful carefree photos of them holding hands, larking about beside a fountain and smiling at each other *hurt*. She couldn't explain why those photos hurt but the instant she scrutinised them in detail she felt as though someone had punched her hard in the stomach because the pain was almost physical in its intensity.

What the heck was wrong with her? Was she starting to care for Raj? Was she suffering from jealousy, despite her earlier reassurance to him that she felt no such emotion concerning him? Those questions made her feel as shaky as if the ground had suddenly disappeared from under her feet. Yes, she was starting to care in the way you did begin to care more for someone when you got closer to them, she reasoned frantically and, yes, she had been jealous when she saw those photos. But none of that meant that she was necessarily falling for him.

'She was my first love and that was all,' Raj continued, wonderfully impervious to his bride's pallor and her silence. 'Very few people marry their first love and what does it matter anyway what I was doing *eight* years ago? It's a really stupid article but it *is* revealing a relationship that only our families knew about to the public. What I can't understand is how they got a hold of such private photos. I had copies but I destroyed them

after we parted and the friend who took the photos—
Omar—would never have shared them with anyone.'

'You said it was an absurd allegation,' Zoe recalled
dully. 'How so when it's true? Your father wouldn't
agree to you marrying her.'

'Not because of her parentage but because I suspect
he had had her checked out and knew a great deal more
about her than I knew at the time,' Raj admitted wryly.
'At least he had the consideration not to throw what he
had found out in my face.'

'As you said…a storm in a teacup,' Zoe remarked
rather stiffly, because all of a sudden she was tired of
hearing about anything that related to Nabila and she
could only marvel at her previous curiosity. Just then
she thought she would be happier if she never heard
the wretched woman's name spoken out loud again. As
for seeing those stupid photos of her with Raj regarding her as if he had been poleaxed, well, that had been
anything but a pleasure for a woman already labelled
as a friend with benefits. No doubt that was why she
had felt envious of the other woman.

No doubt, right at this very moment Raj was thinking
about Nabila, remembering how much he had loved and
wanted her, positively *wallowing* in sentimental memories! And on that note, Zoe decided that she would be
very, very tired that night, in fact throughout the day, so
that Raj would not dare to think she was in the mood to
provide any of those benefits he had mentioned!

'You still haven't told me how it happened,' Raj reminded Zoe stubbornly.

Raj was like a dog with a bone when he wanted information, he just kept on landing back on that same avoidance spot of hers, an area of memory where she never ever travelled if she could help it. She breathed in deep, a little bit of a challenge when he was still flattening her to the wall of the shower. Shower sex? Yes, she had gained a lot of experience she had never expected to have over the past two weeks. Resolving to keep her paws off Raj hadn't worked when he was behaving like lover of the year. It was the only analogy she could make when she refused to let herself think of him as a husband.

But there it was: her watch broke, so a new one studded with diamonds arrived within the hour; phone kept on running out of charge, and a new phone was there by bedtime so that she could talk to her sisters as usual. She preferred flowers growing in the ground to those cut off in their prime and stuffed for a short shelf life into vases, and so he took her into the hills of Bania to stage a luxury picnic beside a glorious field of wild flowers. That had been only one of the blinders Raj had played over the past fortnight. He hated her high heels, seemed to be convinced she was going to plunge down steps and, at the very least, break her neck, *but* he had still bought her shoes, the dreamiest, absolutely over-the-top jewel-studded sandals with soaring heels. She had worn them out to dinner last night in a little mountainside inn, where everyone around them had pretended—not very well—not to know who they were to give them their privacy.

The only problem for Zoe, who was blossoming in receipt of such treatment, was that it was a constant battle not to start caring too much about Raj. She kept on reminding herself that none of this was real. Yes, he was her husband, but this was a convenient arrangement that they'd both agreed to. At best, he was just a friend, an intimate friend certainly, but beyond that she knew she dared not go. She was terrified of falling for him and if she made that mistake, she would be rejected and her heart would be broken.

'*Zoe...*' Raj growled, nipping a teasing trail across the soft skin of her nape to her shoulder with his lips and his teeth, sending a shudder of response through her that even very recent fulfilment could not suppress. 'I want to know how it happened.'

'And I don't want to revisit it.'

'It would be healthier for you to talk about it,' Raj told her doggedly.

'Like you talk about being bullied at military school!' Zoe flung even as she wriggled back into his lean, powerful body, registering that he was ready to go again while conceding that there was nothing new about that because Raj appeared to be insatiable. 'I practically had to cut the story out of you with a knife at your throat,' she reminded him with spirit. 'And by the way, Raj, it wasn't bullying. What you and Omar went through was abuse of the worst kind!'

'If I talked you can talk too,' Raj traded, running a long-fingered hand down over her spine, setting her alight without hesitation.

'This is sexual torture,' she told him shakily.

'All you have to do is say no,' Raj whispered, nipping at the soft lobe of her ear, flipping her long hair over his shoulder as he had learned to do, lost in the magic of her and her response for, as he had learned, it was enthralling to have that much power over a woman, as long as he never ever looked at the other side of the coin and acknowledged the reality that it was mutual.

Zoe straightened her shoulders and breathed, 'Right... I'm saying no...but you're not allowed to look at me like that!'

'Like what?' Raj prompted.

Those stunning dark silvered eyes of his shimmered with hunger and a tiny hint of hurt, and even a hint of hurt on show grabbed Zoe's heart hard and squeezed the breath out of her. She wanted him; every time she looked at him she wanted him.

But that was fine, absolutely fine, she told herself soothingly. It was just sex. She'd had a friend at university who went on a girls' holiday once purely to have sex with a lot of different men. That had been Claire's idea of fun: Raj was Zoe's idea of fun. And the world of sensual freedom she had learned to explore with Raj was the best reward of all. After the shocking attack she had survived as an adolescent, she had never dreamt that she could aspire to such freedom in her own body. Now she could only look back with a sigh when she recalled the frightened, broken young woman she had still been when she'd first met Raj.

'OK... I'll tell you,' she conceded, stepping out of the shower, surrendering to his demand but unable to do so when he was still touching her, something in her shying away in revulsion at any association between making love with Raj and what had happened to traumatise her when she was still a complete innocent.

Zoe settled down on the side of the vast bed, still

wet and dripping and not noticing. But Raj noticed, pale beneath his bronzed skin, his sculpted bone structure rigid because he was worried that he had pushed too hard for her confidences. Lifting her up, he carefully wound her like a doll into a giant fleecy towel, but when he tried to keep a soothing hold on her body, she broke away from him and dropped down into a bedside chair instead.

'There was an older boy, well, not much older, he was fourteen and I was twelve,' she trotted out shakily. 'In the same foster home. We used to play video games together... I thought he was a friend. There was a film I wanted to see, a stupid romantic comedy, and my foster mum said he could go with me, look out for me...but he didn't take me to the cinema.'

'You don't have to tell me if you don't want to,' Raj incised in a hoarse undertone.

'No, my sisters used to say I needed to talk about it, which is why I went to therapy. He didn't take me to the cinema. He took me what he said was a shortcut across wasteland and there was this old hut...and I was complaining because there was a storm and I was getting soaked.'

Her breathing was sawing noisily in and out of her struggling lungs.

'In the hut all these boys were waiting. They were a gang and the price of his entry into the gang was to bring a virgin, any virgin. They beat me up when I tried to get away and I was so badly hurt I couldn't move. They cut off my clothes with a kn-knife...and I had nothing even for them to see b-because I was a l-late developer,' she muttered brokenly, almost back there, reliving the terror, the pain and the shame of that public exposure.

Raj grasped both her trembling hands to pull her back into the present. 'It's in the past, and it can't hurt you now unless you let it... And, as you've already told me, you were lucky—you're a survivor.'

'Yes...' Her voice was stronger when she encountered shimmering dark-as-night eyes that seemed full of all the strength and calm she herself so often lacked. 'Yes, you're right. You have to be wondering how I escaped being raped. The police forced their way in to arrest one of the gang and I was rescued. But now you know why I suffer the panic attacks and why I eventually had the nervous breakdown at university—because I hadn't really dealt with what had happened to me. That was when I went for therapy and it helped enormously.'

Raj lifted her fingers to his mouth and kissed them. His hands were unsteady. All his emotions were swimming dangerously close to the surface and he was fighting to suppress them with every breath in his body. Hers was a distressing story and he now more than understood her fear of men, but there was no need for the rage inside him at those who had been ready to prey on a child for a few moments of vicious entertainment. She had been saved and they had been punished by the law. Only it wasn't enough, he thought fiercely, nowhere nearly enough punishment for the damage that had been inflicted on Zoe. In Maraban, the punishment would have been the death penalty.

As they travelled back to the palace, their honeymoon, as such, at an end, Zoe could see that telling Raj what had happened to her had made him settle back in behind his former reserve. Her small face tightened and her hands gripped together hard. She was questioning why she had shared all her secrets with him and anxious about why she was allowing herself to feel so close to him. Wasn't she acting foolishly? Wasn't it unwise in the circumstances to let every barrier between them drop?

'A surprise awaits you on your return to the palace,' Raj announced, trying to sound upbeat about what he was about to reveal, but failing miserably because he was no idiot and Vivi's cold reaction to him at the wedding had told him all he needed to know about how *he* was viewed by Zoe's family.

'A surprise?' Zoe queried.

He would have to hope that his own surprise went unnoticed while her sister was present. Dark blood highlighted Raj's exotic cheekbones as he thought about the fainting couch he had succumbed to buying and he had to wonder how he had drifted so far from his original intentions. Logic, good judgement and self-control had gone out of the proverbial window the minute he'd laid eyes on Zoe. It was that simple, that *basic*, he acknowledged grimly.

'Raffaele, Vivi's husband, is apparently attending a business meeting in Tasit and your sister accompanied him to visit you.'

To his surprise, Zoe's mouth down-curved and her chin came up, scarcely the display of uninhibited delight he had expected to see in receipt of such news. After all, she was in daily contact with her siblings, revealing a very close bond with them.

* * *

Zoe's rarely stirred temper was humming at the prospect of seeing Vivi. Vivi was only coming to visit to check up on her.

'This is a lovely surprise,' Zoe said, smiling and lying through her teeth as she hugged her older sister, wondering when her redheaded sibling would finally accept that she was a grown woman but, by nature, Vivi, a forceful personality, was very protective of those she considered weaker. It stung Zoe's pride to see herself as weak and breakable in Vivi's eyes.

'I wanted to see how you were managing.'

'My phone calls should've reassured you on that score,' Zoe pointed out as a maid brought in coffee and tiny cakes.

Vivi winced. 'Well, to be frank, they had the opposite effect because you sound so gosh-darned happy all the time.'

'My goodness, when did being happy become a sign that there was something to worry about?'

'It's a sign because I've never really heard you this happy before,' Vivi admitted ruefully. 'You can smile and laugh and seem happy on the surface but it's usually very brief and *now*, all of a sudden, when nobody's expecting it…'

'Have you noticed all the changes I've made around here?' Zoe interrupted abruptly, setting down her cup and springing up to indicate all the additional furniture in the room. 'The staff took photos of the unused rooms and sent them while we were away and I made selections. It's a big improvement, don't you think?'

'If medieval makes you hot to trot,' Vivi remarked with a sniff, strolling across the room to flick a heavily carved piece that in her opinion would have looked fabulous in a horror movie of some creepy old house.

'Let me show you around,' Zoe urged, willing to do anything to evade Vivi's curiosity, because in truth she *was* happy and she didn't really want to think too deeply about why.

Vivi glanced into the bedroom, her attention locking straight onto the male and female apparel currently being unpacked by staff. 'So, what happened to the—?'

In haste, Zoe thrust open the bathroom door, although she hadn't yet added anything to its décor, and then froze at the sight of the very opulent tasselled purple fainting couch in the centre.

'Oh, I like *that*…it's sort of sexy and decadent!' Vivi carolled, walking over to smooth a hand across the rich buttoned upholstery and flick a braided gold tassel.

Zoe was recalling her conversation with Raj and her face was burning hot as hellfire even while a little flicker of heat at her core flamed at the gesture… the *challenge*. Would she or wouldn't she? He would be wondering all day about that, she knew he would be, and a dreamy smile at the knowledge of that erotic prospect removed the tension that Vivi's arrival and awkward questions had induced.

'You know, I don't even need to ask you any more.' Vivi sighed as she returned to her coffee. 'Obviously, the separate bedroom deal crashed very quickly and you're sleeping with him. Whose idea was that? I hardly think it was yours! If you get too involved with Raj, Zoe…there will be consequences, because what you have together isn't supposed to last…and where will you be when the marriage ends?'

'It doesn't matter whose idea it was,' Zoe argued quietly. 'All that matters is that there isn't a problem of any kind with Raj and I, and our present arrangements are our private business.'

Vivi groaned out loud. 'You're besotted with him. It's written all over you,' she condemned, her concern palpable. 'That smooth bastard took advantage of you just as I feared he would!'

'Vivi!' Zoe blistered across the room in a furious voice her sister had never heard from her before. 'You do *not* talk about Raj like that!'

'I'm not saying anything I wouldn't say to his face!' Vivi shot back at her defensively. 'I'm trying to protect you but it looks like I got here a little too late for that. Damn Grandad, this is all his fault, his wretched snobbery pushing you into this marriage, and now you're going to get *hurt*.'

Zoe drew herself up to her full unimpressive height. 'There is no reason why I should get hurt.'

'I know what I saw in your face…you're in love with this guy, who only married you to please his father and use our fancy-schmancy grandmother's ancestry to enhance his standing.'

'I'm *not* in love with him,' Zoe argued fiercely. 'It sounds slutty but we're just having sex for the sake of it!'

Vivi unleashed a pained and unimpressed sigh. 'And what would you know about a relationship like that?'

Zoe lifted her head high. 'I'm learning as I go along, just like every other woman has to. I need that freedom, even if I make mistakes… It's part of growing up,' she reasoned.

'You're definitely growing up,' Vivi conceded ruefully. 'I never thought there would come a day when *you* would fight with *me*.'

'Even Winnie fights with you!' Zoe laughed and gave her much taller sister a hug, relieved the unnervingly intimate dispute was over.

After Vivi had been picked up an hour later, Zoe walked thoughtfully back to her suite with Raj. *Not. In. Love. With. Him.* She was simply happy and there was nothing wrong with being happy, was there? Zoe hadn't enjoyed much happiness in her life and she was determined to make the most of every moment.

She studied the fainting couch set out like a statement, an invitation, and she smiled before she wandered down the steps to the private courtyard around which their rooms ranged, which allowed them complete privacy.

And all around her she could see the proof of Raj's desire to please her and make her happy, for the once dark courtyard had been replanted during their absence into a spectacular jungle of greenery amongst which exotic flowers bloomed. Even the fountain she had admired, which had long since fallen out of use, was now working again, clean water sparkling down into the brightly tiled basin below. He hadn't mentioned a word about his intentions, but then he never did. He never looked for thanks either. Gifts simply appeared without fanfare, gifts like the wonderful transformation of an outdated, neglected courtyard garden.

She didn't need him to love her as he had loved

Nabila, she only needed the proof that he *cared*, Zoe reflected fiercely. And care he did with amazing efficiency and resolve. How could she expect any more than that in a pretend marriage? After all, he was already giving her much more than she had expected to receive. It wasn't going to last, she knew that, *accepted* that and that was her choice, her choice to live for today and worry about tomorrow only when it arrived...

CHAPTER NINE

ZOE SAT UP in bed and her head swam and her tummy rolled.

Worry gripped her. She had believed she had caught a virus when the symptoms first started but weeks had passed since then and the unwell feeling was lingering, despite the careful diet she had observed. Raj had wanted to get the palace doctor in but she had stalled him once a greater concern began to nag at her nerves.

Zoe grimaced at her pallid reflection in the bathroom mirror. She had lost weight and her eyes looked too big for her face. As soon as the dizziness had evaporated, she went for a shower, striving not to agonise *again* over the reality that she had not had a period since she'd arrived in Maraban. After all, she couldn't possibly be pregnant even if the light head, the nausea and her tender breasts reminded her of what her sisters had experienced during pregnancy. How could she be pregnant when Raj had not once run the risk of getting her pregnant? But, she did recall once, weeks ago in the shower when he had overlooked the necessity and she had meant to mention it but hadn't been worried enough to do so.Now she wished she had pointed out that oversight.

Of course no method of birth control was infallible, another little voice nagged at the back of her head. And how on earth was she to put her worries to rest when the acquisition of a pregnancy test in secret had so far proved beyond her capabilities. She never got the opportunity to leave the palace alone. She was surrounded by security and all too many helpful people when she went out. Let's face it, Zoe, she thought forlornly, the Crown Princess of Maraban cannot be seen buying a pregnancy test without causing a furore. It was ironic that what would have thrilled the population filled Zoe with sick apprehension because she couldn't forget Raj saying that such a development would be a disaster in their situation.

Of course, it would be when it was only a pretend marriage and if she had a boy, he would be next in line to the throne. If she was pregnant and it was a boy, she would have to live in Maraban for at least the next twenty years as Raj's ex-wife and she certainly didn't fancy that option as a future. She would have to sit on the outskirts of his life, watching him marry another woman and have a family with her. Naturally, Raj would move on after their marriage ended but she certainly didn't want to sit around nearby to actually *watch* him doing it.

When she emerged from her bedroom, dressed in a pastel-blue dress with her hair in a braid and her make-up immaculate, Bahar, her PA—or social secretary, as Zoe preferred to think of the young attractive brunette—awaited her with a list of her appointments. It pleased her tremendously that after three months away from home she had now acquired the confidence to handle visiting schools and such places without having to drag Raj everywhere with her for support. Coming to Maraban and marrying Raj had been the best decision she had ever made when it came to getting stronger and moving forward with her life.

As her breakfast was brought to the table, Zoe's stomach lurched even as she looked at it and she pushed the plate away and settled for a cup of tea. After all, she couldn't afford to eat if she was going out to an official engagement where her succumbing to a bout of sickness in public would be a serious embarrassment, she reflected with an inner shudder at the prospect. She would catch a snack later, by which time hopefully the nausea would have subsided.

Walking down the last flight of stairs, she was wondering whether or not to call in on Raj in his office when she broke out in a cold sweat. Her legs wobbled under her and she snatched at the stone balustrade to stay upright but the sick dizziness engulfing her was unstoppable and as she lurched to one side, dimly conscious that someone was seizing hold of her from behind, she passed out.

When Zoe came around slowly, she winced at the sensation of a needle in her arm and gripped the hand that was holding hers in dismay. Her eyes fluttered open as Raj leant down to her saying, 'Don't try to get up in case you faint again. Dr Fadel decided a blood test would be a good idea…sorry about that.'

The very quietness of his voice made her scan the room behind him, which seemed to be filled to the brim with anxious-looking people. Mortification made her close her eyes again and do as she was told because she had a clear recollection of almost tumbling down that last flight of stairs.

'I'll be late for my appointment,' she protested.

'You will not be leaving the palace today.'

'But...'

'Not until the doctor has diagnosed what is wrong with you,' Raj spelt out more harshly, in a tone she wasn't accustomed to hearing from him.

In shock at that attitude, she glanced up at him, but he had already moved away to speak to the older man closing a doctor's bag on the desk. She registered that she was in Raj's office on the sofa he had slept on when they were first married, and very slowly and carefully she began to inch up into a sitting position.

Raj stalked back to her. 'Stay flat and lie still,' he told her wrathfully.

He was furious with her, Zoe realised in consternation, wondering why. Possibly the uproar her faint had caused, she reflected unhappily, because the room was still crammed with staff all trying to speak to Raj at once in his own language, so she could only follow one word in three that she was hearing and those were the simple ones. Her ambition to learn Arabic was advancing only slowly. Finally, the room cleared and they were alone again.

'May I sit up now or are you going to get angry again?' Zoe murmured.

Raj gazed across the office at her and then moved forward before hovering several feet from her as though an invisible wall had suddenly come down between them. 'I apologise. I was not angry with you, I was angry with myself for neglecting your health,' he admitted tautly. 'I knew you were unwell but I listened to you when you refused to let me call the doctor in. I *shouldn't* have listened!'

'Raj, that was *my* fault, this stupid virus, and I'm not awfully fond of medics.'

'You will want to express thanks to your bodyguard, Carim. He saved your life when he prevented you from falling down the stairs. At the very least you would have been badly hurt with broken limbs,' Raj framed jaggedly, his hands clenching into fists by his side. 'But such a fall could definitely also have killed you and nothing is worth that risk.'

'Of course, it isn't,' Zoe agreed soothingly because she was shaken as well by the accident that she had so narrowly escaped. 'OK, you were right and I was wrong.'

'I swore to look after you and I have failed in my duty,' Raj informed her hoarsely.

Zoe paled. 'It's not your duty, Raj. I'm a fully grown adult and I made an unwise decision when I chose not to consult a doctor. Please don't blame yourself for my mistake.'

'How can I do anything else?' Raj shot back to her with seeming incredulity. 'You are my wife and you are in a country foreign to you. Who else should stand responsible for your well-being?'

I'm not your *real* wife. The declaration sprang to her lips but she didn't voice it, belatedly recognising that whether Raj viewed her as his real wife or otherwise he would still feel that it was his duty to ensure

her well-being. Three months ago she would happily
have flung that declaration of independence at him but
now she knew him a little better, knew the crushing
weight of responsibility he took on without complaint.
As his father, the King, suffered increasing ill health
and days he was unable to leave his quarters, more of
his obligations were falling on Raj's shoulders. Unsurprisingly, Raj didn't have an irresponsible bone in his
lean, beautiful body and he was infuriatingly good at
blaming himself for any mishap or oversight.

'I'm sorry if I seemed to speak rudely and angrily,'
Raj breathed tautly, silvered dark eyes locked to her
lovely face. 'But I was very concerned.'

'I understand that and I'm fine. In fact I think I'm
recovered enough now to make that appointment.'

'No, they will have to settle for me doing it in your
place,' Raj sliced in forcefully. 'You're not going out
anywhere until we have heard from the doctor—'

'Raj, for goodness' sake, I'm fine,' she told him
again, swinging her feet down onto the floor to punc-
tuate the statement.

'We'll see,' Raj asserted with tact as he reached for
her hand to help her upright, tugging her close to him,
his stunning dark deep-set eyes below his straight black
brows roaming over her delicate face. 'But we will not
see today…however, I am free this evening, and if you
were to feel strong enough to welcome me home on that
couch, I would be extraordinarily pleased.'

Zoe gurgled with laughter and stretched up on tiptoe
to taste his wide sensual mouth with her own. And that
was that, he was magically distracted from his overwhelming anxiety about her welfare. Her heart ham-

mered and her fingers closed into his shirtfront because she wanted to rip it off him. Against her, she could feel him hard and ready and hunger coursed through her, turning her wanton with need.

With an enormous effort, Raj set her back from him. 'We *can't*. People are waiting for my arrival,' he reminded her raggedly. 'But it is one of those occasions when I wish I had the freedom to tell everyone but you to go to hell!'

Zoe flushed, censuring herself for tempting him merely to distract him because it had been a selfish move and he was never selfish, which made her feel bad. On the other hand, the couch invitation was welcome, she acknowledged with a tiny shiver of anticipation, wondering what had happened to the genuinely shy young woman she had been mere months earlier. She wasn't shy with Raj. In fact, she was doing stuff with Raj she had never dreamt she would ever do with any man, once alien things like purchasing very fancy lingerie and posing in it, revelling in the rush of powerful femininity his fierce desire for her and his equally audacious appreciation gave her every time. She had discovered a whole new self to explore and secretly it thrilled her.

Outside the office door, she thanked the guard who had saved her from falling and he grinned at her, telling her in broken English that he would have died sooner than let anything happen to her on his watch. His undeniable sincerity shook her and she climbed the stairs, thinking that until now she hadn't quite grasped how the people around her and those she met during engagements viewed her as Raj's wife, certainly hadn't taken that level of care and concern as seriously as they did. It struck her that many of those same people would be disappointed when she and Raj split up. But then there was nothing she could do about that, was there? She was a sham wife but *they* didn't know that, didn't know that she was nothing more than a glossy convenient lie foisted on the public, she ruminated unhappily.

She was having lunch when the middle-aged doctor she had glimpsed in Raj's office called to see her. Dr Fadel was King Tahir's doctor and resident in the palace and, fortunately for her, he had qualified in London and spoke excellent English.

After the usual polite pleasantries, he asked if he could dismiss the hovering staff and she nodded acquiescence with a slight frown, her tension rising. Of course, he was about to tell her that her hormones were all out of kilter, which was the most likely diagnosis, and she didn't want to discuss her absent menstrual cycle with an audience either.

'I am blessed to be the doctor to break such momentous news,' he then informed her with a beaming smile. 'You have conceived, Your Royal Highness...'

'Conceived...?' Zoe repeated as if she had never heard the word before, and she tottered back down into the seat she had vacated to greet him, so great was the shock of that announcement. That her deepest fear had been confirmed rocked her world to its foundations.

'The blood test was positive. Of course, it is impossible for me to tell you anything more without a further examination.' He looked at her enquiringly. 'Would that be in order? Or would you prefer another doctor, perhaps a specialist, to give you further information? I'm not inexperienced. I do have many female patients in the royal household.'

Zoe was in a daze. She pushed her hands down on the table to rise again. *Pregnant?* she was screaming inside her head, still wondering if it could be a mistake and willing to subject herself to any check-up that could possibly reveal his diagnosis *was* a mistake, she reasoned fearfully as she followed him from the room and he lamented the lack of lifts in the palace. A lift would have to be installed immediately, the doctor began telling her, particularly when her near accident earlier was taken into consideration. A pregnant woman couldn't be expected to run up and down flights and flights of stairs, particularly not a woman carrying a child he described as 'so precious a child for Maraban'.

It wouldn't be precious to Raj, Zoe thought miserably, not to a man who had frankly referred to such an unlikely event as a *disaster*. Suddenly she was in total conflict with herself and split into two opposing halves. On the one hand she adored children and she very much wanted her baby if she did prove to be pregnant, but on the other, she was sort of guiltily hoping that the doctor's verdict was wrong because of the way Raj would feel about it and that felt even more wrong.

A glimpse of the trim and determined little nurse who had jabbed her with a syringe the night she was kidnapped was not a vote winner in the troubled mood she was in, but Zoe refused to react, deeming her potential pregnancy more important as she lay down on an examination couch and an ultrasound machine was wheeled in. An instant later she heard the whirring sound of her baby's fast heartbeat and she paled, feeling foolish for thinking that the doctor could have been in error. It was an even greater surprise to discover that she was already three months along and almost into the second trimester, which meant that she had conceived very early in their marriage.

The doctor happily dispensed vitamin tablets and congratulated her on her fertility, studying her literally as if she were a walking miracle. She supposed in comparison to the last generation of the royal family, she did strike him that way because it had taken over thirty years and three wives to produce Raj.

'The King will be overjoyed,' he told her cheerfully.

'Oh, but...' Zoe hesitated, questioning if it was even possible to keep a lid on such a revelation within the palace.

'The King needs this good news, with his health as precarious as it has been,' his doctor assured her with gravity.

'Then my husband can tell him after I have *first* told *him*,' Zoe countered firmly.

But on one level she thought she was probably wasting her breath because the cat was out of the bag and there was nothing she could do about that: the doctor, the nurse and whoever had done the blood test already knew of her condition. Just how fast the news had spread was borne out only minutes later when she returned to her room and was ushered into the bedroom where tea, a ginger biscuit and the book she had been reading awaited her by the bed like a heartfelt invitation to rest as pregnant women were so often advised to do. Smothering a groan, she lay down, ironically worn out by the day she had had. Off came her shoes and then her dress and she lay back, confronted by the daunting evening lying ahead of her because she had no choice other than to tell Raj immediately. Would it sound better if she did the couch thing first? Or would that look manipulative?

In the event, she didn't get to make that decision because she slept through most of the afternoon, only wakening when the sound of a door closing jolted her awake. She opened her eyes on Raj striding towards the bed and the slumberous expression in his shimmering dark scrutiny as he looked at her lying there in her flimsy underwear. He sank down on the edge of the bed. 'How are you feeling now?'

'OK—hungry now that the sickness has taken a break. Dr Fadel said that with a little luck that should start fading soon,' she told him tightly. 'You see, I'm *not* ill as such. I'm pregnant...'

As she hesitated, her nerves getting the better of her for a moment, she studied Raj; his lean, darkly handsome features had locked tight, his jaw line clenching hard.

'I think it must've been that time in the shower just after the wedding. You forgot to use anything. I should've said something then but I really didn't think anything would come of it,' she acknowledged uncomfortably, wishing he would say something.

Raj blinked because for an instant his surroundings had vanished; what she had told him had to be the very last development he had expected, but it also led to a revelation that hit him even harder. He turned pale, in the matter of a moment recognising the situation he was in.

'We've barely got out of bed to eat for three months,' Raj breathed in a rueful undertone. 'What can I say? I was in charge of contraception and I forgot. So, we are going to become parents…forgive me, I am stunned by the concept of something so surprising.'

'You said it would be a disaster if I became pregnant,' Zoe reminded him uncertainly, still unable to read his mood, particularly when he sprang upright again and started pacing across the floor, clearly too restless to stay seated.

'A disaster more from your point of view than from mine,' Raj qualified with level clarity. 'We agreed to part but I cannot agree to let you leave me carrying our child and I do not want our child raised without either one of us. Surely we are doing well enough together for you to stay in our marriage for some time to come?' A straight ebony brow lifted enquiringly, intense dark eyes scanning her triangular face for an answer. 'Could you accept that? If we remain married, we can raise our child together.'

A quivery little breath ran up through Zoe, allowing her lungs to function again. The backs of her eyes prickled and stung. Until Raj had asked her to *stay* married to him, she had not realised how horribly tense she had become and the painful tension slowly ebbed out of her stiff muscles.

'So, we just go on as normal?' Zoe checked.

'Why not? Are we not both content as we are?' Raj prompted tautly.

Zoe nodded but couldn't help wishing he could be a little more emotional about staying married to her. There she went again, wanting what she couldn't have, she scolded herself, because she knew herself better now. She could look back and recognise the raging jealousy that had assailed her after seeing those photos of Raj with Nabila that had so clearly depicted his love for the beautiful brunette. There was nothing she could do about such feelings except keep them under control and hidden. And considering the circumstances in which they had married, each for their own very practical reasons, it was illogical and pathetic to long for Raj to fall in love with her as well.

'You said…"stay in our marriage for *some time to come*",' Zoe recited tightly. 'What sort of time frame were you considering?'

At that question for further clarification, Raj stiffened and raked long brown fingers through his tousled black curls. 'Must we be so precise?'

Zoe swallowed hard at the edge of reproof in his tone. 'Well, it would be easier for me to know how *you* see the future.'

'With you and our child together. I would impose no limits. I would like to throw away *all* the boundaries we agreed and make this a normal marriage,' Raj spelt out without hesitation. 'I still can't believe that you're pregnant.'

'Neither can I,' Zoe revealed, scrambling off the bed only to be immediately caught up into his strong arms.

'I didn't think it could happen that easily…it is a brilliant accident,' Raj murmured with husky conviction as he came down on the bed with her. 'Are we still allowed to share this bed?'

'Of course, we are. I've been fully checked out.' A kind of sick relief combined with dizzy happiness was filtering through Zoe as she dimly acknowledged that he was giving her what she most wanted. She wasn't going to have to give him up like the salted caramel ice cream she had recently become addicted to, she was going to get to *keep* him. Of course, it wasn't perfect, she conceded reluctantly, not when he only wanted her to stay married to him because she was pregnant. Even so, being accepted as a normal wife was a huge upgrade on being labelled a friend with benefits.

'What are you thinking about?' Raj chided, lying back on the bed with his gorgeous dark eyes fiercely welded to her reflective face.

'Nothing remotely important,' she told him, and she meant it when she said it even if she dimly understood even then that sooner or later she would once again fall into the trap of craving more than he had to give her.

He toyed with her mouth, soft and gentle, and then nipped wickedly at her bottom lip with the edge of his teeth. Her hands lifted and her fingers speared into his black curls, liquid heat pooling in her pelvis as he deliberately snaked his lean hips into the junction of her thighs, the thrust of his arousal unmistakeable. He was always so hot for her. It was enough, it was more than enough to be desired, cared for, appreciated. Even if she felt as though she was keeping him by default? She crushed the thought, burying it deep. She already had more with him than she had ever thought she would have, so craving anything else would be greedy.

'I want you so much,' Raj confided rawly, sitting up over her to wrench off his shirt, yank roughly at his tie. 'Knowing my baby is inside you is so sexy...'

Zoe blinked. It *was*? He was lifting her to deftly undo

her bra, groaning with satisfaction when her small pouting breasts came free to hungrily claim an engorged nipple with his mouth. A gasp was wrenched from her as he teased the other with his fingers. 'You're more sensitive there than ever,' he husked. 'I love your body.'

She knew he did: he never left it alone. He couldn't walk past her without touching her in some way and if they were alone, it almost always concluded in their bed, although they had succumbed to christening his office sofa a time or two and they had once had sex in a limousine on a long drive. He had an astonishingly strong sexual appetite. Anyone watching him could have been forgiven for thinking he hadn't had the freedom to enjoy her for a couple of days at least but that was not the case.

He tugged off her panties and yanked down the zip in his trousers, shedding his clothing with an impatience that never failed to add to her excitement. There he was, all sleek and golden and beautiful, and he was finally hers to keep like a precious possession she had been fighting for without even appreciating what she was doing or even what was happening inside her own head. She had wanted love but then what woman didn't? If *he* could settle for less, she could settle, she reasoned as he snaked down her body with darting little kisses and caresses that set her on fire, ultimately settling between her spread thighs to pleasure her in the way he enjoyed the most.

As a rippling spasm of pleasure gathered low in her body, she clutched at his hair, writhed, squirmed, begged until at last she climaxed in an explosive surge that certainly didn't feel in any way as though she were settling for less. Raj shifted over her then, hungrily kissing her, and the excitement began to rocket again as he sank into her with delicious force, pushing her legs back to deepen his penetration. Definitely not less, she told herself as she rose breathlessly to meet his every thrust, every move instinctive and raw with the excitement she could barely contain. There was more and then even more of that insanely thrilling pleasure before he sent her flying into a wild breathless climax that shattered her senses and her control, leaving her slumped in a wreck of heavy, satiated limbs in the aftermath.

She hadn't heard a phone ring, had been too far gone, but she surfaced when she realised that Raj wasn't holding her close as he usually did. She turned over, saw him talking urgently on his phone while he strode about, naked and bronzed and muscular, and she propped her chin on the heel of her hand, enjoying watching him. That enjoyment gradually faded when he went on to make several other quick calls in succession, alerting her to the knowledge that something must have happened, and because his expression changed from smiling to grim she couldn't tell whether what had happened was a good or bad thing.

'I'm afraid I'm going to have to leave you for the night,' Raj told her with a frown. 'The construction workers have stumbled on archaeological remains at the Josias site.'

'The hospital project in the capital of Maraban?'

'It's potentially a very exciting discovery but it means that the site has to close until we can get an official inspection done tomorrow, and that throws the whole project and the work crews into limbo. I'm flying out there now to meet with the managers and look at contingency plans. It is possible that we won't be able to build there at all,' he concluded gravely. 'And the hospital is very much needed in that area.'

Recalling that Nabila was the CEO of the construction firm involved, Zoe sat up, her pale hair falling round her flushed face, because she knew he was undoubtedly about to meet the other woman again for the first time in eight years and she very much wanted to be in the vicinity. 'I could come with you!' she said in sudden interruption.

'No, not this time. What would be the point? I'm likely to be in meetings most of the night and certainly all of tomorrow, sorting this out,' he told her dismissively as he strode into the bathroom.

'I would still like to have gone,' Zoe confided in a small voice to an empty room.

But did she really need to cling to him like glue? she reproved herself. There were few things more distasteful to a man than a clingy, needy and jealous woman and Raj would quickly get tired of her if she started acting paranoid and suspicious purely because he was mixing with his ex-girlfriend in a business environment. She had to grow up, she told herself urgently, not react to her stabbing insecurity with adolescent immaturity. After all, nothing was likely to change in the short term. She was pregnant and *really* married now.

And how did Raj truly feel about that development? It shocked Zoe to accept that she had not the smallest idea of how *he* felt, and the instant she registered that worrying truth, another little brick of security tumbled down from her inner wall of defences. Sadly, there was no ignoring the truth that the closest Raj had actually come to expressing his personal feelings was the assurance that he regarded her being pregnant with his child as…sexy. Although he had labelled her conception a brilliant accident, which did suggest he was pleased.

Zoe grimaced. Why couldn't he simply have said so, openly? In reality, now that she was recalling that conversation, she realised that Raj had not expressed a single emotion, which for an emotionally intense man of his ilk was not reassuring, she reflected worriedly.

Were duty and a sense of responsibility for his child all that had driven Raj's request that she stay married to him?

And if that *was* the case, what could she possibly do about it?

CHAPTER TEN

Raj's phone rang constantly right up until he left the palace. He was feeling guilty because Zoe had been very quiet when he left. But there was no way he would have considered dragging her across country late at night, especially now that she was pregnant and he had no idea where he would be staying. Zoe looked frail for all her lack of complaint. She had lost her appetite, dropped in weight. Yet even though he had noticed he had said and done nothing because it had not even occurred to him that she could be pregnant. What kind of husband was he? Not a very good one, he decided grimly.

And now he was to become a father. A dazzling smile flashed across his lean dark features. That was a marvellous development, a near miracle in their circumstances.

His phone rang again as he awaited his limo in the forecourt of the palace and he dug it out, only to freeze in surprise as the caller identified himself for, although he had met the man, his royal status ensured that he wasn't especially friendly with anyone in that profession, and the warning the journalist gave Raj astonished him. He immediately called Omar and passed it on to him and Omar announced that he would be travelling to the hospital site as well.

In the early hours of the following morning, having dealt with a torch-lit visit to the site and with wildly excited archaeologists, who were hopeful that the legendary lost city built by Alexander the Great had been discovered on Marabanian soil, Raj was more than ready for his bed. He walked into the comparatively small hotel closest to the site. He was relieved that he hadn't succumbed to the temptation of bringing Zoe because he did not think the level of comfort on offer sufficient for a pregnant woman. As his father had remarked in wonderment when he had phoned him earlier to break their news, Zoe would have to be treated from now on like the Queen she would one day be.

Raj was smiling at the memory and sharing it with his cousin, Omar, who was beside him as he pushed open the door of his room. And then quite forcibly the warning he had received, and begun to discount because he had yet to even *see* Nabila, was revived because Nabila sat up in the bed that should've been his, the sheet tumbling to reveal her bare breasts. Filled with angry distaste at her brazen display, Raj averted his eyes, unimpressed by the expression of seemingly embarrassed innocence she had put on when she glimpsed Omar by his side.

'For goodness' sake, tell Omar to *leave*,' Nabila urged Raj.

'I'm staying,' Omar delivered with satisfaction, never having liked the brunette even when Raj had been in love with her. 'But it is gratifying to discover that you can sink even lower than I expected.'

Raj strode to the foot of the bed. 'What the hell are you playing at?' he demanded.

Deciding to ignore Omar, Nabila focused her eyes on Raj with blatant hunger. 'I want you and I really don't care what I have to do to get you this time around. Isn't that enough?' She treated him to a look of languorous enticement. 'Don't tell me you're not still curious about what it would be like between us.'

Raj's mouth curled with disgust and he swung round to stalk back to the door and address his protection team in the corridor. 'Get her out of here…and find me another room,' he ordered impatiently.

'I'm not asking for marriage this time around,' Nabila crooned behind him. 'I would be your mistress…your every secret fantasy.'

'My *wife* is my every secret fantasy,' Raj countered drily as he strode out.

At dawn, Raj was enjoying a working breakfast on the terrace at his hotel with Omar and the management team of Major Holdings, including the CEO, Nabila, who had contrived to take a seat opposite him. He ignored her to the best of his ability, barely even turning his head when she spoke.

'*Raj!*' she exclaimed, startling him while simultaneously reaching for his hand.

For a split second, he was so disconcerted by that unanticipated over-familiarity and the pleading expression she wore on her face that he did nothing and then he freed his fingers with a sudden jerk and leant back in his chair, cursing himself for not having reacted more immediately to the threat. For Nabila *was* a threat, he acknowledged in a sudden black fury, a threat to his marriage. At that moment, he had not the slightest doubt that a photographer was hiding somewhere in the vicinity, most probably one with a telephoto lens, and had captured that image of them holding hands and that that stolen photo was intended for publication with the presence of their companions eradicated.

A couple of hours later, because she was sleeping in, Zoe turned over in bed, drowsily wondering what had wakened her and failing to notice that her mobile phone was flashing on the cabinet to one side of her. She stole her hand across to the other side of the bed and then remembered that Raj was gone for the night. With a dissatisfied sigh, she dragged her fingers back from that emptiness and reminded herself that it was mortifyingly clingy to want him there *every* night. She could be perfectly happy without him, of course she could be! With no suspicion of just how soon that assumption was to be tested, Zoe went back to sleep.

Zoe wakened in astonishment to find her sisters beside her bed and blinked in disbelief. 'What are you two doing here at this hour of the day?' she demanded.

'We were shopping in Dubai so we didn't have far to come,' Winnie explained stiffly. 'We want you to come home with us. Grandad agrees.'

Zoe sat up. 'Why on earth would you want me to come home with you?'

'*Because*,' Vivi said bluntly, 'Raj is playing away behind your back and you're in love with the rat!'

Zoe frowned. 'No. Raj wouldn't do that to me,' she

said with perfect assurance because, in that line, she trusted him absolutely.

Winnie shoved a mobile phone in front of her gaze. Her lashes fluttered in bewilderment and then she focused and saw Raj with the *one* woman in the world she wouldn't trust him with. Raj in a photo holding hands with Nabila, his lean, darkly handsome features very serious, her face beseeching. Beseeching *what* from him? Zoe broke out in a sudden sweat and then just as quickly, as familiar queasiness assailed her, was forced to leap out of bed and push past her sisters to make it to the bathroom in time to be sick.

'Where did you see that photo? Raj only left last night,' she reasoned when she was able to respond, wondering exactly *when* that photo had been taken and then questioning whether the timing even mattered.

'That photo was offered to Grandad for sale first thing this morning,' Winnie told her in disgust. 'I imagine it was taken by some greedy paparazzo, who worked out what that picture would be worth on the open market.'

As Zoe drooped over the vanity unit brushing her teeth, still weak with nausea and dizziness, Vivi tugged her gently away and settled her down on the fainting couch. 'Take a deep breath and keep your head down. What's the matter with you? Are you ill?'

'Pregnant,' Zoe whispered, still in shock at that photo, fighting to withstand the great tide of pain threatening to engulf her. Raj had refused to take her with him the night before...*no wonder*! Had he known even then that he wanted the freedom to be with his ex-girlfriend?

'*Pregnant?*' Vivi gasped and her sisters engaged in a lively argument above her head, which Zoe was content to ignore because infinitely more important decisions loomed ahead of her, she grasped dully.

How could she remain married to a man in love with another woman and already seeing her behind her back? Holding hands with her? Although that was the least that had probably gone on between them, she recognised sickly, for it was unlikely that Raj and Nabila would not finally have taken the opportunity to have sex. Particularly not when, in that photo, they were staring at each other like long-lost lovers reunited.

'I'll be frank,' Vivi murmured with surprising quietness. 'You're in love with Raj and he's hurting you and we love you enough that we can't just stand back and allow that.'

'I'm *not* in love with him,' Zoe lied, her eyes watering in a last-ditch effort to save face with her sisters.

But there it was: the truth she had suppressed and refused to face except in the secret depths of her heart. She had fallen madly in love with her fake husband and for all the wrong reasons. Reasons like his smile and the sound of his voice and the raw power of his body over hers in bed. Reasons like the English breakfast tea he had ordered on her behalf and the glorious shoes he'd bought her and had put in the dressing room without even mentioning the purchases. Reasons that encompassed a hundred and one different things and many that she would have found hard to put into words.

Winnie's eyes were also brimming with tears. 'Come back with us to Athens…*please*!'

And Zoe's first reaction was to say no, until she considered the alternatives. She could confront Raj and he would probably admit the truth, which would not be a comfort to her. She could pretend she hadn't seen the photograph and silently agonise over it and that prospect had even less appeal. Or she could take advantage of a breathing space in which to decide what she would do next, she reasoned bravely. It wouldn't be running away, she ruminated, it would be giving herself the time to control her emotional reaction and behave like an adult and deal with the situation. If she stayed, she might cry and let him see that she had been hurt, and what was the point of that?

But what if Raj had not actually cheated on her? Raj was not by nature a cheat, she reasoned, wondering if she was clutching at straws when she thought along such lines. Naturally she didn't want to think he could've been unfaithful, but Nabila was different, Nabila was in a class of her own because once Raj had *loved* her. Could he have resisted the chance to finally be with the woman he had once loved? And wasn't hoping he might have resisted only proof that Zoe was weakly willing to make excuses for him? Shame drenched her pale cheeks with hot pink and she decided to listen to her sisters, who had much more experience than she did with men. If Winnie and Vivi both believed that Raj had succumbed to Nabila's wiles, they were probably right. She trusted their judgement more than she trusted her own because she was all too well aware that her feelings for Raj coloured her every conviction and that she wasn't capable of standing back and making an independent call.

Zoe had her maid pack only one suitcase, because

there was no advantage in advertising the fact that she was leaving and would probably never return to the royal palace. She would send for the rest of her stuff later but when she thought about that, thought about the wardrobe Raj had bought her, thought about his favourite outfits, she as quickly decided that she wanted nothing that would only serve to keep unfortunate memories alive.

Her protection team accompanied her to the airport and flatly refused to leave her there. Suppressing a sigh, she let them board her grandfather's private jet with her, knowing that Raj would recall them later after he had read her note and had seen the photo she had sent to his phone. He wouldn't require any other explanation for her departure because he was definitely not stupid.

When that photo came up on his phone, forwarded by Zoe, Raj succumbed to a rage that almost burned him alive and it took Omar stepping in to prevent him from telling Nabila in front of an audience what he thought of her filthy tactics. Omar's intervention ensured that he did what he had to do at the site, which was his duty, and went home as soon as he possibly could to talk to his wife. A single-line note informing him that she would never 'share' a man greeted his return.

The discovery that she had been removed by her siblings and flown to her grandfather's home in Greece came as a complete shock. It was closely followed by a terse phone call from Stamboulas Fotakis, who accused him of disrespecting his grandchild in a grossly offensive public disregard of his marital status. And as if those punishments were not sufficient, he was summoned by his father, who in his ineffable highly efficient way knew exactly what was happening in his son's marriage and pointed out that his son only had himself to thank for allowing a harpy like Nabila within a hundred yards of him.

'When you bring your wife home again, I will have Nabila thrown out of the country,' the King pronounced with satisfaction.

'Let us hope I can bring Zoe home,' Raj breathed with difficulty, mastering his temper but only just in the face of that provocation, for throwing Nabila out of Maraban would only create a scandal that Nabila would relish.

His arrival in Greece late that night was punctuated by further unwelcome attacks. Zoe was in bed and not to be disturbed, according to Stam Fotakis. 'She's fragile,' he told Raj in condemnation. 'She needs protection from those who would use her soft heart against her.'

'I would not use…'

Her sister, Vivi, walked into her grandfather's office and proceeded to try and tear strips off Raj but Raj wasn't taking that from anyone, least of all Zoe's fiery sibling, and an almighty row broke out before Stam ran out of patience and demanded that both of them go to bed. 'If you must, you may speak to Zoe in the morning,' he informed Raj in a ringing tone of finality.

But Raj wasn't about to be steered in a direction he didn't want to go. He let himself be shown to a guest room without any intention of *waiting* until he could see *his* wife. As soon as he was alone, he learned where her room was by the simple measure of contacting her protection team.

Zoe was curled up on a lounger on the balcony beyond her room, watching the sea silver and darken in the moonlight. Misery felt like a shroud tightly wrapped round her, denying her the air she needed to breathe. She had still to accept the concept of a life empty of Raj. Every time she contemplated that terrifying prospect, she felt as though someone were flaying the skin from her bones, only the pain was internalised. How had one man become so important to her survival that her entire world had begun to revolve around him? It both shocked and incensed her that she could have been weak and foolish enough to fall in love with a man she had known from the outset would never be hers on any permanent basis.

When the patio doors behind her slid open, she flinched, expecting it to be one of her sisters, come yet again to offer depressing advice. She didn't want the assurance that she would get over Raj. She didn't want to be told that there would eventually be another man worthier of her love in her future when just then, and against all reason and logic, all her body and her brain cried out for *was* Raj.

'Zoe…?'

In astonished recognition of that dark deep accented intonation, Zoe was startled and she leapt off the lounger and spun round. *'Raj?'* she gasped incredulously.

'Hush…' Raj put a finger to his lips in warning. 'I wouldn't put it past your family to try and drag me out physically and I don't want a fight breaking out between my protection team and your grandfather's. But I will allow no man on earth to tell me *when* I can see my wife.'

'But I'm not your wife—not really your wife,' Zoe protested. 'And I *never* was.'

Raj studied the pale triangle of her face in the moonlight and guilt cut through him because it was *his* fault that she had been hurt and upset. 'I have to explain what happened with Nabila.'

'No, you don't owe me any explanations!' Zoe cut in hastily. 'But you can't expect me to live with you and turn a blind eye to an affair either!'

'Why would I have an affair with Nabila? Have you asked yourself that?' Raj demanded, moving forward to scoop her gently up into his arms and return her with care to the lounger before stepping back to lean back lithely against the balcony wall.

'Because you still love her…' Zoe muttered ruefully.

'Why would I still love a woman who slept with another man behind my back?' Raj asked gently. 'Do you honestly believe I am so stupid that I would still blindly love a woman who was unworthy of my love and respect?'

Zoe reddened and her eyes evaded his. 'I'm not saying you're stupid, just that sometimes people can't control their feelings even when they *know* they should,' she framed uncomfortably.

'But that is not the case with Nabila. My love died the instant I realised how poorly I had judged her character. She was my first love,' Raj admitted grittily. 'At the age of twenty I also believed she would be my last love but I was very young and I was wrong. I couldn't continue to love a woman who lied and cheated once I saw her for what she was. I couldn't love a woman who only wanted me because I am wealthy and one day I will be King.'

'Well, if that's all true what were you doing holding hands with her?' Zoe demanded baldly, influenced against her will by the obvious sincerity of his self-defence.

'Before I left the palace yesterday, I received a phone call from a journalist and it was most illuminating... yes, I *know* you are impatient for an explanation but please bear with me to enable me to tell you the whole story,' Raj urged when she made a frustrated gesture with one tiny expressive hand. 'I learned from that call that Nabila had personally contacted him and given him the photos that proved the existence of our youthful romance.'

'*She* was behind the release of those photos to the gossip magazine?' Zoe exclaimed in surprise.

'Yes. I assume she wanted that information publicised as a first move in her desire to come back into my life. Evidently she assumed there would still be a place for her in my heart.' Raj's wide sensual mouth compressed. 'The journalist involved called to warn me yesterday that she was planning to wreck my marriage and had a photographer lined up in readiness.'

'Journalists love scandal. Why would he have warned you?' Zoe pressed suspiciously.

'Zoe...' Raj murmured softly. 'The gossip magazine was quite happy to publish old photos of a romance few people knew about but the owner, the journalist I mentioned, is a loyal Marabanian and he refused to get involved in framing me with Nabila in a seedy scheme likely to damage my marriage. That was a step too far for him and, instead of playing along, he warned me of her ambition to cause trouble.'

'Well, it doesn't look like the warning did you much good,' Zoe said drily.

'It put me on my guard and I took Omar with me on the trip. When I went to my hotel room that night, she was waiting for me in the bed and I had her removed. We didn't have a conversation either because I have nothing to say to Nabila,' Raj told her doggedly.

'Nothing?' Again, Zoe looked unimpressed by his claim but she was already thinking of the stunning brunette waiting in his bed for him. 'Was she undressed?'

Raj nodded.

'And you weren't even tempted?' Zoe prompted helplessly.

'No, but I think my protection team were,' he remarked wryly. 'Omar can confirm that nothing happened. He was also present at the table when she grabbed my hand.'

'Grabbed?' Zoe queried with a frown. 'But how could Omar have been there when you were alone with her?'

'I wasn't alone with her. The photo is deceptive. Three of Nabila's colleagues were also at that table with us.' Raj dug out his phone and brought up the photo for her appraisal. 'And if you look…*there*…you can just about see the sleeve of the man sitting beside me.'

Her heart thumping hard at getting that close to him again, Zoe stared down at the photo and squinted until she too registered that there was indeed a tiny glimpse of what could only have been another arm at the very edge of the picture.

'Nabila arranged for her photographer to take that photo to suggest an intimacy that does not exist between us. When she grabbed my hand, I was so disconcerted I didn't react fast enough to evade the photographer. I was too *polite* to say what I wanted to say in front of other people,' he derided with sudden visible annoyance. 'I believed I had dealt with her in the hotel room the night before and that she would leave me alone, resenting the fact that I had rejected her invitation... I was wrong, for which I am heartily sorry. But I have *nothing else* to apologise for.'

'So you say...' Zoe muttered, fixedly studying his lean, darkly beautiful face while her brain sped over everything that he had explained, seeking a crack or a hole in his account of events. 'And how do you feel about her now?'

'What would I feel but heartfelt relief that she showed me what she was before I made the mistake of marrying her?' Raj countered wryly. 'Omar is downstairs waiting to act as my witness.'

Zoe swallowed hard on that assurance before an involuntary giggle was wrenched from her. 'Raj, if you killed someone, Omar would bury the body for you! You two are *that* close. Omar in the guise of a reliable witness is a joke!'

Raj dropped fluidly down on his knees beside the lounger and studied her with raw frustration. 'Then I will produce the other people at that table for your examination,' he swore with fierce determination.

Zoe adored him in that moment because she believed him, believed that he would go to any embarrassing length to prove his innocence. He had been warned about Nabila's plans and had assumed that he had taken sufficient precautions to protect himself but the devious brunette had still contrived to catch him out. He simply wasn't sly enough to deal with a woman that shameless, he was too honourable, too loyal, too honest, and that Nabila had attempted to use his very decency against him infuriated Zoe.

'No, that won't be necessary,' Zoe told him tenderly. 'You don't need to embarrass yourself that way.'

'It wouldn't embarrass me if it gave *you* peace of mind,' Raj argued. 'That is all that matters here—'

'No, what really matters,' Zoe murmured with a new strength in her quiet voice, 'is that I *believe* you.'

'But you said Omar is no good as a witness,' he reminded her in bewilderment.

'I was sort of joking,' Zoe muttered in rueful apology. 'I *do* believe that you have told me the truth.'

'Allah be praised,' Raj breathed in his own language.

'How long did it take you to get over Nabila?' Zoe asked then with helpless curiosity.

'Not very long once what I realised what an idiot I had been!' Raj confessed in a driven undertone. 'But the whole experience damaged me, and even before I met her I was already damaged by my mother's suicide. That made it difficult for me to trust *any* woman.'

Zoe ran soothing fingertips down from a high masculine cheekbone to the hard angle of his taut jaw. 'Of course, it did,' she whispered sympathetically. 'You were badly hurt when you were still a child and then hurt and humiliated by what happened with Nabila. I can understand that.'

'But you will probably *not* understand that I never

had another relationship with a woman until I met you,' Raj admitted harshly. 'All I allowed myself was a succession of grubby one-night stands.'

'Grubby?' She questioned his wording.

'It *was* grubby when I compare those encounters to what I have found with you,' Raj confessed.

'And what have you found with me?' she whispered, her gaze held fast by the silvered darkness of his, heart pounding with anticipation, because in those eloquent eyes of his she saw what she had long dreamt of seeing but barely credited could be real.

'Love,' he said simply. 'Love like I never felt for anyone, certainly not for Nabila. That was a boy's love, this is a man's and you mean the whole world to me. I don't know how else to describe how very important you are to me...'

'You're doing great,' she mumbled encouragingly when he hesitated.

'I hate being away from you. I missed you when I went to bed last night and when I woke up this morning. Wherever you are feels like home. Whenever you smile, my heart lifts. At the beginning,' he breathed hoarsely, 'I believed it was only sexual attraction and I tried incredibly hard to resist you...but I couldn't. What I've learned since is that you are the very best thing that has ever happened to me and you make me amazingly happy.'

Zoe breathed in slow and deep and it was a challenge when her lungs were struggling for oxygen. He had just made all her dreams come true. He had just blown her every insecurity out of the water but she still had some questions. 'So why, when I told you that I was pregnant, didn't you tell me then how you felt?'

'Because I didn't know how you felt about me,' Raj responded as though that were an obvious explanation. 'And I had messed everything up with you from the start. I was worrying about you wanting to leave me and going back to the UK to get the divorce I had stupidly promised you, and wondering how I could possibly prevent that from happening. I have never been more relieved than when our unexpected but very much welcome baby gave us the excuse to stay together.'

'I didn't need an excuse,' she told him then. 'I didn't want to leave you...well, probably since the honeymoon, maybe even sooner, I'm ashamed to admit. I fell in love with you weeks and weeks ago and knew it but I wasn't going to tell you that *ever*.'

Raj sprang gracefully upright and lifted her up into his arms to sit back down on the lounger holding her tight, as if he feared she might make a sudden leap for freedom. 'I denied my feelings for a long time and tried to hold back but you give me so much joy it is hard to hide it from you,' he confided huskily. 'That you return my love is almost more than I could ever have hoped for because I love you so much it burns in me like a fire...'

A knock sounded on the patio doors. Raj rose with her in his arms as the door opened.

'What the hell—?' Vivi began in shock when she saw them.

'Bad timing, Vivi,' Zoe interrupted sharply. 'My husband loves me and I'll see you at breakfast.'

Behind her Winnie laughed and tugged Vivi back. 'Yes, breakfast promises to be fun, Raj...with Grandad grouching and Vivi giving you suspicious looks, but if Zoe trusts you, you have my trust too.'

'You turncoat!' Vivi gasped but Winnie was inexorably dragging her out of the room.

'So, where were we?' Zoe prompted as Raj deposited her on the bed and went straight across the room to lock the bedroom door in a sensible move that delighted her. 'Ah, yes, you were saying that your love is like a fire.'

'More of an eternal flame,' Raj assured her poetically. 'You've got me for life.'

'Thank goodness for that. You see, I'm not a changeable woman,' she murmured softly, eyes gliding possessively over his lean, powerful length. 'I expect and demand for ever and ever, like in all the best fairy tales.'

'Perfect,' Raj murmured hoarsely, framing her flushed face with reverent hands as he stared down at her with unashamed adoration before claiming her pink pouting lips with passionate hunger.

And it was perfect for both of them as they left behind their doubts and fears and rejoiced in their newly discovered closeness and trust. Passion united them as much as love, every sense heightened for them both by the fear that they could have lost each other.

'I love you so much,' he breathed in a hoarse groan in the aftermath.

'I love you too,' she whispered, both arms wrapped possessively round him, a glorious sense of peaceful happiness powering her with a new surge of confidence.

EPILOGUE

EIGHTEEN MONTHS LATER Zoe laughed as she watched her year-old son lurch like a tiny drunk across the floor to greet his father, because he had only begun walking for the first time the day before. Raj had been really disappointed to miss those very first steps because he had been in Moscow on business and the video Zoe had sent had only partially consoled him. Now, he swept the toddler up into his arms with noisy sounds of admiration so that Karim's little face literally shone with his sense of achievement and his delight in his father's appreciation.

Raj was a great father, keen that his son would grow up with few of the royal restrictions and traditions that had held him back during his often lonely childhood. Karim was encouraged to play with other children and he was fortunate that his many cousins on both sides of the family were regular visitors. Even King Tahir unbent in Karim's energetic and sunny presence, but then the whole of Maraban was still reacting to Karim's birth as though he were an absolute miracle. That level of interest was a big weight for one little boy to carry on his shoulders and Zoe did everything she could to

ensure that his upbringing was as normal and as un-
starry as she could make it, even though they lived in
a royal palace. Karim also had a pair of grandfathers,
who sought to outdo each other with the very lavish-
ness of their gifts.

Zoe was blissfully happy in her marriage. Raj made
every day they were together worth celebrating. He
loved her as she had never dreamt she would ever be
loved and he gave her amazing support with everything
she did. He had even made an effort to strengthen his
relationships with her occasionally challenging family
and was now her grandfather's favourite grandson-in-
law, while Vivi had apologised for her initial doubts
about Raj's suitability as a husband and fully accepted
him, so that Zoe could relax and mix freely with her
sisters and their husbands.

Zoe's fingers slid down to press gently against the
very slight swelling beneath her sundress that signified
that in a few months Karim would have company in the
royal nursery. She had had an easy pregnancy and an
easy birth with her son and was keen to have her children close together and complete their family while she
was still in her twenties. Raj had wanted her to wait a
little longer but she had persuaded him because Zoe
adored babies and she hadn't wanted to wait when there
was no good medical reason to do so.

'You look like a splash of sunlight when you wear
yellow,' Raj murmured huskily as Karim was borne off
by his nanny for his bath and he intercepted his wife
before she could follow them. 'Our little Prince will
manage without his parents for one bathtime.'

'But—' Zoe began.

'My son has to *share* you with me,' Raj pointed out, appraising her beautiful smiling face with all-male hunger. 'And this evening when your sisters arrive to celebrate your birthday with you, it'll be giggles and girl talk and I won't get a look-in.'

'Well, if you would just wait until bedtime that wouldn't be the case,' Zoe teased.

'I waited for bedtime the last time!' Raj groaned as he bent her back over one strong arm to engage in kissing a trail across her delicate collarbone that sent a highly responsive quiver through her slight body and flushed her cheeks. 'And you didn't come to bed until *three* in the morning!'

Zoe grinned. 'That'll teach you patience!'

'I'm no good at waiting for you,' Raj confessed, bundling her up into his arms with ease and heading for their bedroom. 'I'm not any better at not missing you when I'm away and I'm even worse at getting by without you in my bed.'

'You've only been away two days, but I missed you too,' Zoe confided with a helpless sigh of contentment as he brought her down on the bed. A little ripple of positively wanton anticipation gripped her as he began to remove his business suit, revealing that long bronzed, lithe and powerful physique she adored.

'I wonder if it's normal to have sex as often as we do,' she muttered abstractedly.

'It's a great healthy workout,' Raj assured her with unholy amusement. 'And wonderfully rewarding if done right.'

'No wonder I love you,' Zoe teased him back with dancing eyes. 'You always do it right!'

'But only with you.' Raj groaned with pleasure as she skimmed her hands over him, and kissed her with a raw, passionate love that made further discussion impossible.

* * * * *

GREEK'S BABY
OF REDEMPTION

KATE HEWITT

CHAPTER ONE

'STAY.'

Milly James stilled, shock racing through her at the sound of that single word, uttered in a husky voice by a man she'd never actually seen in person. Her employer.

'Pardon…?' She turned around slowly, blinking into the dim gloom of the wood-panelled study, the curtains drawn against the Aegean's azure sky, the tiniest sliver of lemony sunlight peeking through the heavy material. It was a beautiful summer's day, but in the gloomy shroud of the study it could have been the depths of a dark winter's night, the thick stone walls of the villa keeping out the island's baking heat.

'Stay.'

It was clearly a command, uttered with brusque authority, and so slowly she closed the door, the final-sounding click echoing in through the room.

She hadn't even realised he was in the study when she'd opened the door to do her usual dusting, only to stumble back at the sight of him sitting in the shadows, barely visible.

Alexandro Santos' instructions had been clear—he was not to be disturbed. Ever. And now she'd unwittingly done just that, because she'd heard the car motor starting and she'd thought he'd gone out. Her heart climbed its way to her throat as she tried to make him out through the gloom. Was he angry? How could she have been so careless? 'I'm sorry, Kyrie Santos. I didn't realise you were here. Is…is there something you need?' she asked in as steady a voice as she could.

In the nearly six months since she'd been hired as house-keeper by Alexandro Santos, she'd never spoken to him, save for the first, rather abrupt conversation on the tele-phone when he'd offered her employment. This was the first time he'd been back to his luxurious retreat on the Greek island of Naxos since she'd started work, and she'd been tiptoeing around the villa for the last two days, try-ing to avoid him since he'd made it so clear he didn't want to be bothered. At *all*. And now she might have messed it up completely.

'I'm very sorry,' she blurted, wishing he would say something to break the taut silence. 'I won't disturb you again…'

'Never mind that.' He dismissed her words with a flick of his fingers; she sensed the movement rather than saw it. 'You asked if I needed something, Miss James.' He spoke in a cold drawl, more than a hint of darkness in his tone. She wished she could see his face; the room was so very dark, and the sliver of light barely touched the top of his midnight-dark head.

She blinked, her eyes straining to see more, and, as if he sensed her scrutiny, he moved from where he'd been sitting behind his desk, walking to the window so his back was to her, the light gilding his outline in gold—all six feet three of powerfully built man, his crisp white shirt stretch-ing tautly across his back and broad shoulders.

'Yes,' he answered his own question. 'I do need some-thing.'

'Then how can I help you?' Milly asked, glad that

there might be something she could do. 'Would you like a meal…or the room tidied…?' She trailed off, because she had the sudden, inexplicable sense that he didn't want either of those things, and she felt foolish for offering them.

Alexandro Santos didn't answer her. He hadn't moved, and she still couldn't see his face. She knew what he looked like from the Internet search she'd done when she'd first been hired: dark hair, sculpted cheekbones, cold, blue eyes, a body of leashed and lethal power.

Ridiculously handsome, but in a way that had trailed a chilly finger of unease along her spine. He'd looked both intent and remote, a fierce determination in those blue, blue eyes, a sense of distance about him so even in a crowd he stood out, apart. Now she couldn't see him at all, and that wasn't any better.

'How long have you been working for me, Miss James?' he asked after another endless moment.

'Nearly six months.' Milly shifted where she stood, trying not to fidget. He had no reason to fire her, surely? No cause for complaint. For the last five and a half months she'd kept the villa clean, helped in the garden, and paid all the household bills. As housekeeper for a house that was empty most of the time, she knew she had an easy job, but she loved the villa and the island of Naxos, and she'd been very glad for the work—and the pay.

Although some might have found her life lonely, it suited Milly perfectly. After too many years on the fringes of her parents' chaotic social scene, bounced from boarding school to boarding school, with an endless round of vapid and dissipated parties in between, she'd been looking forward to some solitude…as well as the extremely generous salary Alexandro had offered. He couldn't take it away now, not when she was getting closer to saving the kind of money she needed to make Anna safe and happy, for ever.

'Six months.' Alexandro turned slightly so she could make out his profile—the close-cut dark hair, the straight nose, the angled cheekbone and full lip. He looked like a statue—a dark, dangerous and beautiful block of marble, perfect and so very cold. Even in the dim room, she sensed a remoteness about him, a certain distance in the way he held his body, angled his head. 'Are you happy here?'

'Happy?' The question, the *idea*, startled her. Why should he care for her happiness? 'Yes. Very.'

'It must be rather lonely, though.'

'I don't mind my own company.' She relaxed a fraction, because it seemed as if he were merely concerned for her welfare. And yet…that didn't seem like her employer at all, a man who, according to the Internet, at least, was a cold, driven workaholic, with whispers of ruthlessness towards his competitors. A man who was photographed at various social scenes looking hard and unsmiling; sometimes there would be an elegant woman draped on his arm, but he rarely paid them any attention, at least in the photos and videos she'd looked at. It was almost as if they weren't there at all.

'Still, you're quite young.' He paused, and Milly waited. 'How old…?'

'Twenty-four.' Which he must have known from her rather brief and unremarkable CV.

'And you went to university…'

'Yes, in England.' Four years studying modern languages, and she was fluent in Italian and French as well as her native English, and now she had a smattering of Greek, as well. But Alexandro Santos knew all this.

'Surely you have more ambition, then?' he asked. 'Than cleaning rooms…?'

'I'm perfectly happy as I am, Kyrie Santos.'

'Please, call me Alex.' She remained silent. 'You haven't

considered moving back to Paris? You were working as a translator, I believe, before you came here?'

'Yes.' And being paid peanuts compared to her salary now. She thought of her days in a drab office, translating dreary business letters. Then she thought of Philippe, with his golden hair and gleaming smile, his oh-so-honeyed words, and her insides shuddered. 'I have no desire to go back to Paris, Kyrie—'

'Alex.'

She said nothing, uncertain and again on edge, wondering where this unsettling line of inquiry was meant to lead.

'What about romance?' he asked abruptly, shocking her. 'A husband, children...? Do you want those things, eventually?'

Milly hesitated, unsure how to respond. Surely the question was inappropriate, coming from an employer? And yet how could she not answer?

'I ask because I prefer continuity,' Alex resumed, almost as if he'd been able to read her thoughts. 'If you're going to leave after a year to follow some man...'

'I am not going to *follow some man*,' Milly retorted with stiff dignity. Once upon a time, she would have followed Philippe. She would have followed him anywhere, until she'd found out the truth. Until he'd told her. Even now she could recall the mocking glint in his eyes, the cruel twist to his mouth. She forced the image away and focused on Alex Santos, even though she could barely see him. 'The question is offensive.'

'Is it?' Alex continued to gaze out through the crack between the curtains. It was impossible to tell what he was thinking. She felt like a prop in a play, something he could almost forget was there. And yet he was asking her such personal questions...*why*? 'And what of children?' he asked after another long moment.

Milly tried not to gape. 'I haven't thought about that,' she said at last. 'I'm not interested in having children now, at any rate.'

'Not now? Or not ever?'

Milly shrugged helplessly. 'Certainly not now. And perhaps not ever. Not any time soon.' She knew how fractured and fraught families could be, and while on some level she might have the maternal instinct most women possessed, she had no desire to kick-start it. Anna was her primary concern.

'So you do not wish to have children?'

Milly felt herself flush. Why was he trying to pin her down on this? 'Maybe one day,' she half muttered. 'I haven't thought that far ahead. But really, I can't see how it is any concern of yours.'

'Perhaps you will.'

'I'm sorry…?' He didn't answer and she released the pent-up breath that had bottled inside her lungs. 'Is that all, Kyrie… Alex?' she finally asked. 'If so, I'll go now…'

'That's not all.' His words stopped her in her tracks. 'I have a proposition for you, Miss James.'

'A proposition?' She didn't like the sound of *that*. The word was loaded with meaning, laced with innuendo, even when spoken in Alexandro Santos' curt tone. 'I'm not sure I…'

'A perfectly respectable one. As respectable as one could possibly be, in fact.' A note of rather bleak humour that she didn't understand had entered his voice, and so she simply waited, having no idea how to respond. 'A business offer,' Alex clarified. 'A very generous one. You accepted this position because of the salary, did you not?'

'Yes…' And to get away from Paris and the mocking eyes of Philippe and his crowd, but she wasn't about to go into that.

'Money is an incentive to you?'

'Financial stability is.' And saving money for Anna, but that was something else she had no intention of explaining. It was all too complicated, too sad and too sordid, and her employer did not need to know her personal details.

'And my business proposition will certainly give you financial stability. In fact, that might be considered its chief benefit. But I admit, it might seem, at first glance, a rather unconventional idea.' He let out a humourless rasp of laughter that would have chilled her if it hadn't seemed so despairing. 'Although perhaps not, considering how sensible and level-headed you seem. I think you might well see the practical advantages.'

'Thank you, I think?' Milly gazed at him uneasily, completely out of her depth. 'But I really have no idea what you're talking about. What is this…business proposition?'

Although she wasn't sure she really wanted to know. Whatever it was, it didn't sound like something expected or normal. What could he possibly want from her, in exchange for *money*?

She wasn't naïve; neither was she, sadly, that innocent. She had an inkling of what he might want, and yet she could hardly credit such a possibility. She knew she wasn't pretty—mousy-brown hair, same coloured eyes, a slight, unassuming figure. She wasn't the sort to incite impassioned desire in any man, never mind what she'd once foolishly, so foolishly, let herself believe, with stars in her eyes and fairy tales in her heart. But she wasn't going to think about Philippe.

And it would be just as foolish now to imagine that a man like Alexandro Santos, a handsome billionaire who could probably have any woman he wanted, was interested in her in that way. It was laughable, utterly so, and she would do well to remember that. Just looking at him now, shrouded in darkness, emanating a dark and innate authority as well as an undeniable charisma, made her realise how far apart they were in their experiences. Even when she couldn't see him, she *felt* him, like an electric pulse in the air—dangerous and exciting, and definitely off-limits.

Yet what *could* he want? What else did she *have*? Her mind darted into possible corners, disliking what she imagined there. What if he was into something...well, *strange*? Some kind of fetish or weird kink he wouldn't dare suggest to anyone he considered respectable...but no, she was being really fanciful now. Maybe he simply wanted her housekeeping services.

Perhaps he wanted to fly her to Athens to clean his penthouse there. But Milly knew she was fooling herself. Dusting and sweeping were hardly the most marketable or desirable skills, and it was obvious whatever Alex Santos was about to suggest was something out of the ordinary.

'Kyrie Santos...'

'Alex.'

'Alex.' She made herself repeat his name, the syllables sounding sharp as they came out of her mouth, like the pins turning in a lock. He still hadn't turned, hadn't spoken. 'Are you going to tell me what this proposition of yours is?'

He didn't turn from the window as he answered, his voice flat, toneless, without any warmth. 'I want you to marry me.'

Although Alex remained staring out of the window so Milly couldn't see his full face, he felt her shock. It rippled through the room like an electric current, pulsing between them with a dangerous charge. He angled his head so he could glance back at her, his eyes straining in the darkness. Her own almond-brown eyes widened, her pink lips parting.

She wasn't a beautiful woman by any means, but there was something compelling about her slender frame, the innate dignity in the proud set of her shoulders, the tilt of her chin. To his surprise, Alex felt a shaft of interest slice through him—desire, something he hadn't felt in years. That was rather inconvenient.

'You're…you're not serious,' she finally stammered.

'I assure you, I am.'

'Why would you want to marry *me*?'

It was, of course, an excellent question, and one Alex intended to answer truthfully. There would be no games in their marriage, no pretence in what he intended to be an extremely straightforward transaction. 'Because I don't have the time to find a more suitable and willing woman—'

'Wow, thanks.' The words burst out of her, full of hurt bitterness.

'And,' he continued implacably, 'I need an heir as soon as possible.'

Milly reeled back, hitting the door, her hand fumbling for the knob. 'Don't be alarmed,' Alex said. 'I'm trying to be truthful. It would be foolish for either of us to pretend, even for a moment, that a marriage between us would be anything more than a business arrangement, one involving courtesy and respect on both sides, of course.'

'And yet you said an *heir*…'

'This would not be a marriage in name only, obviously.' He still spoke calmly, but images danced through his mind all the same. Skin burnished gold by candlelight, light brown hair loose on bare, freckled shoulders. Absurd, because their marriage would never be like *that*, and he didn't even know if she had freckles.

'Obviously…' Milly repeated faintly, still looking stunned.

'And time is rather of the essence, although we can discuss the particulars—assuming you are agreeable.'

'*Agreeable*—' The word came out in a squeak. He'd shocked her, clearly, and she hadn't even seen his face yet. The thought almost made Alex laugh, except he hadn't actually found anything funny in months. Twenty-two months, to be precise. 'Kyrie Santos,' she said firmly, once she'd recovered her composure. 'I am *not* agreeable.'

'You haven't even heard the terms.'

'I don't need to hear the terms. I'm not in the habit of selling myself.'

'We'd be married,' Alex pointed out reasonably. 'It would hardly be classified as that.'

'It would be to me.' She shook her head, a shudder running through her whole body, a visceral reaction of something close to disgust, which caught him on the raw. She hadn't even *seen* him yet. 'I'm sorry, but no. Never.' She spoke with such vehemence that he was intrigued as well as irritated. It was exceedingly inconvenient for her to refuse.

'You almost sound as if you've had such an offer before,' he remarked. 'The way you're reacting, as if you're remembering something offensive. As if my proposition recalls another.'

'Of course it doesn't!'

'Of course?' he queried, arching an eyebrow, the one she could see.

'Most men are not in the habit of making such propositions,' Milly said in that same chilly voice of maidenly affront. She donned that voice like a dress—something that could be taken off as needed, a bit of flimsy armour. It made him wonder what she was protecting underneath.

'Aren't they?' he queried. 'Most marriages are business

deals of some kind, Miss James. A negotiation of sorts, no matter what emotional underpinnings they possess.'

'And yet our marriage would have no *emotional under-pinning*,' she returned. 'I don't even know you. I've never met you before today.'

'That is not out of the ordinary, for situations such as this.'

'What makes you think I want to get married?'

'Nothing. Like I said, this would be a business arrangement. And the financial stability is what I think you will find attractive about this proposition.' He let out a huff of laughter. 'Nothing else.'

She stayed silent, and Alex turned slightly, wanting to see her face, able to make it out in the dim room only a little. Her eyes were wide, her lips pressed together.

She looked uneasy, but she also looked…torn. Her hand had slipped from the doorknob, and now her fingers were knotted together. As he gazed at her, she nibbled her lip, her eyes darting this way and that. She looked, he realised, as if part of her was tempted or at least intrigued by his offer, but she didn't want to admit it.

'Financial stability,' she finally said. 'What do you mean by that?'

'I would make marriage worth your while.' He waited, to see if she asked more, but she shook her head.

'Now *that* sounds like selling myself, and to a stranger. I think any marriage should have some kind of emotional foundation, if not love.'

He cocked his head. 'You almost sound cynical.'

'Cynical—?'

'As if you don't really believe what you're saying,' he clarified. 'You want to, but you don't.'

'What I believe or don't believe is of no concern to you,

and of no relevance to this conversation,' she returned sharply. 'The answer is still no.'

'Why?' Alex asked, letting his voice loosen into a lazy drawl. 'Out of interest?'

'Why?' She looked and sounded incredulous, but also up against a wall. Figuratively as well as literally, her back pressed to the door, her chest heaving so he could see the rise and fall of her small breasts. A few wisps of light brown hair had escaped from her normally neat ponytail, framing her heart-shaped face. She was, he decided with some surprise, quite lovely. When he'd made the decision to marry her, her looks had not been part of the equation. She was convenient, suitable, and her lowly position meant he would be able to manage her. That was all he required.

'Yes, why?' he reiterated. 'Why are you not willing even to consider my offer? Not even a single question as to the nature of our arrangement?'

'You've already made the *nature* quite clear—'

'You mean sex?'

'Well, yes,' she nearly spluttered.

'You object to having sex with your husband?'

'I object to marrying someone I don't feel anything for, someone I don't even *know*—'

'Yet people have been doing that for centuries. Millennia.'

'Even so...'

'You told me you weren't interested in romance.'

'Not at this point in my life, no.'

'Or perhaps ever, I believe your words were. So...?'

'That doesn't mean I want to marry *you*.' She sounded exasperated now. Alex allowed himself a cold little smile.

'Would five million euros change your thinking?'

Her mouth opened. Closed. And then again. Her eyes

wide and as brown and soft as pansies. 'That's a lot of money,' she finally said, her voice faint.

'Indeed.' He cocked his head. 'Would you like to hear the particulars now?'

She bit her lip. 'You think I'll change my mind simply because of money? That's insulting.'

'Financial stability,' he reminded her. 'It's a powerful incentive.'

'I'm not some gold-digger.' The words burst out of her, like an old wound breaking open. Alex wondered at it.

'I know you're not.'

'I won't sell myself.'

'So you keep saying, but to think of it that way is distasteful. We are talking marriage, remember. Not being a mistress.'

'Yet it's true nevertheless.'

'Not necessarily. It's a deal, Miss James. We both get something out of it.'

She shook her head slowly, her eyes still wide. 'Considering the nature of our conversation, perhaps you should call me Milly.'

Victory loomed closer, elusive but possible. Probable, even. She hadn't stormed out of the room. She hadn't slapped his face. She hadn't seen it, either. They would get to that all in good time. 'Very well, Milly. Why don't you take a seat?'

'All right.' Milly walked with careful, deliberate steps to one of the leather club chairs in front of his desk and sank into it, ankles neatly crossed, hands linked at her waist like a respectable matron. 'Can we turn the light on?' she asked. 'I can barely make you out, and I've never actually seen you in person, which seems ridiculous considering the nature of our discussion.'

He tensed, and then made himself relax. 'I'm averse to light.'

'You're not a vampire, are you?' It was obviously a joke, but she still sounded uncertain.

'No, most certainly not.' He turned to face her, angling his head in a way he knew would hide the worst. 'I'll turn it on in a moment, perhaps, after we've discussed some of the details.'

'Why me?' Milly asked bluntly. 'Why not someone far more suitable?'

'Because you're here,' Alex answered just as bluntly. 'And you're happy to remain on this island. And in the six months you've been in my employ, you've seemed trustworthy and hardworking, or so my man here, Yiannis, tells me.'

'Yiannis has been reporting on me?'

'Merely relaying his approval of you.'

'Oh.' She sounded surprised. 'He and his wife are very kind. They've been welcoming to me.'

'I'm glad to hear it,' he returned smoothly. It was all seeming very promising. She clearly liked living here, and she wanted the money. All that remained was whether she could stomach looking at him—and sharing his bed.

'And those are your only qualifications for a wife?' Milly asked.

'Yes.'

'Really?' She sounded cynical again. 'You don't care about your wife's likes or dislikes? Her sense of humour, or her sense of honour? What about what kind of mother she'll be?'

Alex's mouth compressed. 'I don't have the luxury to care about those things.' Ezio's latest escapade had provoked a knee-jerk reaction in him to sort this, and quickly.

Milly was silent, and Alex watched her, noticing the

emotions that crossed her face like ripples in water. Indecision, fear, but something else, as well. Something darker… guilt, perhaps, or grief. His proposition had struck a painful chord inside her. He was almost certain of it. 'And why an heir?' she asked at last. 'Isn't that rather an outdated concept?'

'It's a biological one.'

'Still.'

'I want to pass my business on to my child.'

'A son?'

'Or a daughter. It doesn't matter.'

She cocked her head, her eyes narrowing as she tried to make him out. 'Why?'

'Because if I don't,' Alex answered tersely, 'it passes to my stepbrother, who is likely to run it into the ground in a matter of months.'

'It's not like an aristocratic title, is it? Why should it pass to him?'

He drew a quick breath, forcing himself to relax as the memories bombarded him. Christos, looking so pale and weak, one claw-like hand extended towards him. *Begging* him. And Ezio, drunk in some nightclub, not even bothering to show up, to say goodbye to his flesh-and-blood father. 'Because my stepfather stipulated it in his will. The business was originally his, and he bequeathed it to me when he died. But he made a provision that if I should die without issue, it passes to my stepbrother.'

'That all sounds rather archaic.'

Alex inclined his head. 'Family ties are strong in this country.'

'Yet it's your stepfather,' Milly pointed out. 'This isn't about flesh and blood.'

'He was a father to me more than any other man was,' Alex answered gruffly. Emotion clutched at his throat, made it hard to speak. 'And the will is watertight. This is my only option.'

'What about adoption? Surrogacy?'

'As I said, time is of the essence. I'm thirty-six, and I want my child to be an adult when I pass the business on. Also, I believe a child should have a mother as well as a father. Family is important to me.' The words ignited a blaze of pain inside him, and he snuffed it out quickly. Coldly. The only way he knew how, to keep on living.

'What if I can't get pregnant?' Milly asked baldly. 'There are no guarantees.'

'You'd need to have a full medical check before we wed.' He shrugged one shoulder. 'The rest is up to God.'

'Would you want other children?'

He almost laughed at that. He knew she certainly wouldn't, not once she saw him. 'No, one will suffice. After that I will leave you alone.'

'Would I have to live on this island for the rest of my life?'

'You wouldn't be a prisoner, if that's what you are implying.'

'Would we have any kind of…relationship?' She spoke the word hesitantly, as if probing a sore tooth.

'We would treat each other with courteous respect, I should hope.'

'But beyond that?'

He couldn't keep from recoiling just a little, just as he knew she would once she saw him. 'Is that something you want?'

'I… I don't know.' She shook her head, her teeth worrying away at her lower lip. 'This is all so unexpected. I can't even think straight.'

'Yet you are considering it?'

'I shouldn't.' She shook her head, expelling her breath

in a gusty sigh. 'I don't even know why I am, if just a little. The *tiniest* bit.' It came out like a warning.

'The five million, perhaps.' He kept his voice light, inviting her to see the humour. To share it with him.

She shot him a look of wry amusement, and something small and warm bloomed inside him, something unexpected. When had he last shared a look with another person, even in the dark? 'Yes, that might have something to do with it.'

'I don't hold it against you.'

'And so you shouldn't, since you're the one who offered it. But perhaps I hold it against myself.' Her words came out sharply; the moment was broken, that small bit of warmth snuffed out.

Alex watched as Milly rose from the chair, pacing the room, rubbing her hands together as if she were cold. 'No, this can't work,' she muttered, mostly to herself. 'I can't let myself, not like—' She broke off, shaking her head. 'No, I'm sorry. I can't. I won't.' She turned to him resolutely, her look one of both apology and determination. 'The answer is no, Kyrie Santos,' she said firmly. 'I'm sorry. I hope this won't affect our working relationship.'

Alex stared at her, refusing to betray his irritation and, yes, his disappointment, with so much as a flicker. And he did feel disappointed—more even than he'd expected. He could find someone else. He knew that. Yet her rejection stung, because that was what it was. It felt personal, even though he knew it shouldn't. And the laughable part was, he hadn't even turned the light on.

CHAPTER TWO

MILLY COULDN'T SLEEP. She lay tangled in her sheets, staring at the ceiling as moonlight slanted through the shutters of her window and silvered the tile floor of her bedroom. Since the abrupt ending of her conversation with Alexandro Santos this afternoon, when he'd more or less dismissed her from his study after she'd turned down his proposal, her mind had been reeling as she went over every surreal second of the bizarre interview.

I want you to marry me.

How could he have suggested such a thing? And how could she have been so treacherously tempted, even for a moment?

Milly turned over, thumping her pillow in a futile effort to find peace, or at least comfort. Her mind had not stopped zooming off in a dozen different directions since she'd left Alex; she'd kept herself busy, finishing the moussaka she'd been prepping for supper, sweeping the pool area, and paying a few bills, all the while wondering why he'd asked, what would happen now.

Would everything be awkward? Would he find a reason to fire her? She didn't want to lose this job. She was making three times as much money as she had been translating business documents back in Paris, and she liked the spacious villa with its beautiful flower-filled garden, the infinity pool, Yiannis and his wife, Marina, stopping by on occasion, the friendly village of Halki a short distance away.

She liked shopping among the quaint market stalls, a wicker basket looped over her arm as she examined lumps of feta cheese floating in brine, plump, red tomatoes, juicy olives.

She liked the little café with its rickety tables overlooking a dusty square where she sometimes sat and had a coffee after doing her shopping. She liked the quiet, starry evenings, the only sound the distant lapping of the waves. She liked the solitude, and feeling safe. She didn't want to leave here.

So why had she said no to Alex Santos' marriage proposal?

With a groan of frustration Milly rose from her bed. She wouldn't sleep now. She slipped on her thin dressing gown and padded softly downstairs to the living area, opening the French windows as quietly as she could. Alex's bedroom was in the other wing of the house, one she only visited to clean, but she definitely did not want to disturb him now.

Outside the air was pleasantly cool, scented with bougainvillea and orange blossom. Moonlight glinted off the placid surface of the pool, giving it a ghostly feel. Milly wandered over to a wooden chaise and curled up on it, drawing her knees to her chest as she gazed out at the moonlit gardens. She let out a gusty sigh, tension that had been knotting her shoulders since Alex had said stay easing just a little.

She loved the peaceful solitude of this place—after a lifetime of the party or boarding-school scene, the quiet of her own company was a soothing balm, and the villa felt like a home, the first real one she'd ever had.

Five million euros. She couldn't stop thinking about it, about what she could do with that money. Pay for Anna's school fees. Pay for her university, buy her a house, keep her safe for ever. Money might not buy happiness, but it certainly helped…and the thought of finally having financial security, for her and for the one person she loved… well, after a lifetime of chaotic uncertainty, it was tempting indeed.

And so what if she married a man she barely knew? In her life, romantic love had been at best a joke, at worst a lie. She'd seen both her parents fall in and out of it with devastating ease, and her own brush with it had left her feeling more jaded than ever, still cringing in shame.

She didn't want that kind of relationship. She wouldn't take that kind of risk. At least Alex was honest about his feelings. That was more than she could say for Philippe.

So why not marry someone for the practical reasons? Alex's mention of an heir had sent a surprising ache of longing through her. A child of her own…someone to love, who couldn't be taken away from her. *Family.* She hadn't realised she was maternal in that way until Alex had spoken of it, but now, her knees tucked to her chest, she could almost imagine a baby nestled in her arms, the kiss she'd drop on its soft forehead. She'd be *such* a better mother than her own.

A sound from the house had Milly stilling, and then pressing against the back of the chaise, trying to make herself invisible. From the corner of her eye she saw Alex Santos make his way to the pool; he was wearing nothing but a pair of loose pyjama bottoms and moonlight bathed the sculpted muscles of his chest in lambent silver, making her realise just how impressive they were.

Milly's gaze rose from his chest to his face and as if he

could sense, not just her presence, but her stare, he angled his head away from her, his body going still.

'Couldn't sleep?' His voice was husky, somehow sensual, winding around her in the sultry darkness. Milly's arms clenched around her knees.

'How did you know I was here?'

'You left the doors open, and I have good eyesight.' He moved closer to her chaise, the fabric of his pyjama bottoms whispering together as he moved, the muscles of his chest rippling as the moonlight caught them. When he was only a few feet away, his body still swathed in darkness and his face angled away, he spoke again. 'So why can't you sleep, Milly?' He lingered on her name. 'Were you thinking about my offer?'

'Yes,' she admitted, because it seemed obvious. 'How could I not be thinking about it? It's the only marriage proposal I've ever received.'

'I'm sorry it wasn't more romantic,' he returned dryly. 'But I'm sure there will be others…that is, if you don't reconsider…?' He trailed off deliberately, and Milly swallowed hard.

'I shouldn't reconsider…'

'But you are.'

He sounded so certain, and why wouldn't he be? A handsome, powerful, wealthy man. And she was a plain little nobody. He'd probably expected her to jump at the chance. 'It's a lot of money,' Milly said on a shuddery sigh. 'And it would make a difference to me…and to someone I love.'

'Ah. Perhaps the most powerful reason of all.' Alex settled on the chaise opposite her, his face turned away, his gaze on the pool. 'And who is this person you love?'

'My sister. Well, stepsister, but she's as good as a sister to me. Better. The most important person in the world, the only person…' Milly's throat closed up at the thought of Anna and she blinked hard. 'I'd do anything for her.'

'Except marry me?'

'That's why I'm thinking about it.'

'It wouldn't have to be such torture, you know,' Alex said after a moment. 'I wouldn't bother you any more than I had to.'

Bother her? Was that really how he saw their potential relationship? And yet Milly felt reassured that her life wouldn't have to change too much.

'Most people want more from their marriage than that,' she said after a moment, and Alex arched an eyebrow.

'Most people,' he acknowledged, 'but not you, I think.' He turned so he could look her in the eye, although the darkness still hid much of his face. 'Am I wrong?'

Milly swallowed again, her throat dry as she struggled for words. 'I haven't thought about it all that much,' she hedged. 'I haven't…' She trailed off, her gaze on the silvery surface of the pool. 'I haven't had much experience,' she stated at last, determined to be frank. 'Of romance or romantic love. That kind of thing. And the experience I've had has put me off.'

'So here is the ideal solution.'

'Why don't you want romance or love in a marriage?' she asked hesitantly. 'I assume that's the reason for your business proposal?'

Alex shrugged. 'I don't see the point of it.'

'Of romance?'

'Or of love.' He paused. 'That kind of love. And neither, I think, do you.'

It was unsettling, how he seemed to reach right into her mind and pluck out her thoughts. What could he see in her face, even out here in the dark? What was she revealing without realising?

'I've seen it abused,' she answered at last, her tone careful. 'And I suppose I don't trust it very much. I'm not willing to take that kind of risk.'

'Good. Then I think we'd be an excellent match.'

She shook her head, an instinctive movement. 'It's not that simple…'

'Of course not. We can iron out the details as soon as you've agreed. I'm a reasonable man, Milly.'

The way he said her name made her shiver, although perhaps it was simply the cooling night air. 'None of this seems particularly reasonable, you know. We're talking about marriage. Having a *child* together…'

'It's eminently reasonable. Love is the outrageous thing, the ridiculous emotion that's meant to drive all our reason and ambition when it's so flimsy and ephemeral. The whole concept is absurd, insanity. Why would you trust your life to a fleeting feeling?'

'Yet people do.'

'But you're smarter than that, aren't you? As am I.'

She almost laughed at his arrogance, except she knew he was right. She *was* smarter than that. She'd wised up. 'See?' He smiled at her, the corner of his mouth curving upwards, his eyes—at least the one she could see—gleaming. 'We're a perfect match.'

'I haven't even seen your face,' Milly blurted, and although he didn't move, it felt as if he had. As if he'd gone even more still than he already was, every muscle taut and waiting, put on alert. 'Properly, I mean,' Milly clarified. 'We've only spoken in the dark. It's a bit…odd, you know. Clearly you're a private man, but…' Shouldn't she at least *see* the man she might marry?

'Yes, I am.' Alex was silent for a few seconds, seeming to draw into himself. 'Well, there is a reason for the dark.'

Milly gazed at him in confusion, squinting to make

out his expression but it remained shadowed, unfathomable. 'Is there?'

'Yes, there is, but you might as well know it now. See what you might be agreeing to.' He walked quickly back to the French windows and in one quick movement he flicked on the outdoor lights. The terrace was bathed in a bright electric glow, and Milly blinked in the brilliance. Then Alex turned to face her, and a gasp rushed from her throat.

His face...

One side of his mouth quirked upwards. 'Perhaps now you understand a bit more of my reasoning for a convenient marriage?'

Milly sat transfixed, unsure whether to look away or keep staring. Would that be insulting? Unkind? In any case, she found she couldn't move her gaze. What had *happened* to him, since the photos she'd seen on the Internet had been taken?

'It's a shock, I know.' Alex spoke dispassionately, as if he didn't much care that half his face was ravaged in pink and white scar tissue, while the other half was entirely perfect, the coldly handsome man she recognised from his photos, made even more so by the damage on the other side. It was like looking in a cracked mirror, half crystal clear, half warped and broken.

'How...?'

'Fire.' The single word was clipped, dismissive. Milly knew instinctively he wouldn't say more, and she wouldn't ask. 'It puts off many a prospective bride, or so I imagine. I haven't deigned to find out. Perhaps it puts you off.'

'Your scars would have nothing to do with whether I agreed or not,' Milly said when she'd found her voice, but she feared she didn't sound convincing. It was just she was so *shocked*. Even with his insistence on privacy, the rooms shrouded in darkness, she hadn't suspected. Never guessed.

There hadn't been a whisper about it online, or even in the village, where most people knew him, or at least of him. Yiannis and Marina hadn't said a word.

'Very well, then.' Alex straightened where he stood, levelling her with a look. 'Will you marry me?'

Alex knew he should have given her time to adjust to the reality of his scars, but he felt too raw. He hated being looked at, despised the flicker of pity that inevitably crossed every person's face when they saw him in the light. So he made sure very few people did.

In the nearly two years since the fire, only a few trusted business advisors and staff had been able to look him in the eye. He didn't give anyone else the chance, not if he could help it. He entered his office from a private entrance, and, while there, he rarely left. Everything he could do from his office by phone or email, he did, and when he wasn't doing business he was keeping to himself, either in Athens or here, travelling by private jet or yacht to avoid the inevitable whispers and stares.

He had a few trusted staff who had seen his face and wouldn't talk, but he'd never had many friends and so he had even fewer now. As for lovers? What a joke. All in all, it was a lonely life, but it was the only one he could bear to live.

And yet he'd known this moment would come, when the woman who would be his wife would look on his face and shudder. He hated it with an intensity that made his fists clench before he made the choice, very deliberately, to flatten them out. He would not be that kind of man. Not like his father. It was a choice he made every day, deliberately, calmly, because he had to.

'I… I have to think,' Milly stammered, her gaze still tellingly transfixed by the scars that crisscrossed his entire right cheek, starting in his hairline and coming down to the corner of his mouth and quirking his lip upwards in a horrible half-smile he couldn't ever change. There were other scars too, ones she might not have noticed yet, cording the side of his neck and making a patchwork of white lines across his shoulder. 'It's such a big step…'

'Well, don't think too long,' Alex returned in a deliberate drawl, making sure to keep her gaze even though everything in him demanded he turn away. Hide. 'Because if you refuse, I'll have to ask someone else, and as quickly as possible.'

'Do you have an alternative?' She sounded more curious than offended—or relieved.

He didn't, not yet, but he just shrugged. 'I have some possibilities.' None of the women of his acquaintance would agree to marry him looking like this, and he wouldn't want them anyway. Shallow, vapid creatures, caring only for appearances and wealth, and he had only one of those attributes.

No, he realised he wanted *her*, because she seemed sensible and trustworthy, and he had a feeling they could get along tolerably well, which was all he could ask for. All he would ever let himself want.

'Why me, though?' Milly pressed.

Looking at her, Alex knew he was fooling himself if he thought he wanted her just for those modest qualities. No, there was more to it than that. He wanted her, wanted her in the way a man wanted a woman. Desire was dangerous and foolish, and it made him feel exposed in a way he hated.

'You're here. You're suitable. You need the money.' He bit each word off and spat it out. She flinched a little, but then she nodded.

'At least you're honest. I…appreciate that.' She sighed, turning away from him to stare out at the water. 'I love it here,' she said softly, and he tensed.

'That's a good beginning.'

'Is it? It doesn't seem nearly enough.'

'But if you don't want love in your marriage, why not this?'

'I feel as if I'm signing my life away.'

'You'd have every freedom.'

'Except the freedom to marry someone else.'

'True.' He paused. 'I would not countenance divorce. A child needs both parents.'

'Nor would I,' Milly returned sharply, with more force than even his tone had possessed. 'My parents are on their third and fourth marriages. I would *never* get divorced.'

Alex inclined his head. 'Yet another point upon which we agree.'

'I still don't know you. I don't know if you're kind, or trustworthy, or *good*.' Her voice throbbed with emotion. 'Shouldn't I know those things?'

Yes, of course she should, and he knew he couldn't promise her any of it. He wasn't kind. He hadn't been trustworthy. As for *good*… 'I suppose you'll have to take my word for it.'

'And if we marry, and I discover your word is worthless? You…mistreat me…or lock me away…'

'Mistreat you?' He couldn't keep the offence from his tone, or a deep-seated conviction from shuddering through him. It was as if she were looking into his soul, and yet not seeing anything at all. 'I would *never* hurt a woman.' He'd never meant anything more, and yet she still seemed uncertain as she turned back to face him.

'I don't want to think you could do something like that, of course, but I don't know you, Alex. I don't know you at all.'

'Then ask me,' he bit out. 'Ask me whatever you want.' He stood there, bracing himself for whatever questions she fired at him, but she remained silent, gazing at him in helpless frustration.

'You make it sound like a job interview.'

'Of a sort.'

Another sigh and she nibbled her lip as she started to shake her head. He could feel her slipping away from him, like an ebbing tide. The scars had tilted the odds against him. Of course they had.

'I just don't think I can do this,' she said softly, her gaze sliding away from his. Her shoulders hunched; she looked guilty. 'I watched my mother marry for money, time and time again, and the results were disastrous...for her as well as for me and my sister. I can't be like her in that way. I won't let myself.' She paused, her shoulders hunched, her gaze averted as if she couldn't bear to look him in the face. 'I'm sorry.'

'Really, there is no need to apologise,' Alex returned stiffly. He wasn't going to argue with her; he certainly wasn't going to beg. 'Consider the matter closed,' he said, and then he turned and walked back inside the villa, staring blindly ahead all the while.

CHAPTER THREE

WHEN MILLY AWOKE the next morning, she knew Alex had gone. It was only a little past six, lemony sunshine banishing the last of the pearly grey light of dawn, but she knew all the same. She could almost hear the echo of the whirr of the helicopter blades signifying his departure; perhaps that was what had woken her up.

Quietly she slid out of bed and went to the window, opening the shutters fully to take in the breathtaking view of sun and sand, sea and sky. The blue-green waters of the Aegean Sea shimmered under the azure perfection of another summer's day. Inside Milly felt strangely hollow.

As soon as Alex had walked back into the villa last night, his body and gait both stiff with dignity and affront, Milly had questioned her decision—and not just because of the money. Yes, she could use the money, especially for Anna's sake, but what if this was the only marriage proposal she ever received? More importantly, what if it was the best?

As Alex had sussed out, she was cynical and wary of such fanciful feelings as love and romance. If her parents hadn't put her off, her dalliance with Philippe certainly had.

Even now she could remember the mocking twist of his lips as he'd gazed at her. *'Do you honestly think I'd fall for a little mouse like you?'*

No, she wasn't going to go down that route again. So why not this? She wouldn't get duped or hurt, and she'd have financial stability, companionship of a sort, and even a child. After the financial and emotional turbulence of her entire childhood, who was she to scoff at those things?

Standing at the window, letting the sunlight stream over her, she wondered why she'd refused—even as she acknowledged why. Because her mother had married for money rather than love, and she never, ever wanted to be like her mother.

But this would be different, a little voice inside her persisted.

Would it? Another insidious voice mocked back. *Would it really?*

Turning away from the window, Milly went to shower and dress. She had a full day of housework ahead of her, and she needed to stop thinking for a little while. Blot out all the what-ifs and just *be*. Still, she wondered when Alex would return…and what it would be like when he did.

The house felt emptier than usual as she went about her work, sweeping and mopping and dusting. She put off doing the inevitable—cleaning Alex's bedroom, stripping the bed and washing his sheets. It had felt like any other room just days before, but now it was different. Perhaps she was.

After a solitary lunch reading at the kitchen table, she decided to put it off no longer, and in truth she was curious. Upstairs, down a separate corridor that held only his master suite and two guest bedrooms, she tiptoed towards his door, holding her breath, half expecting someone to pop out, something to *happen*. Of course, nothing did.

Milly pushed open his bedroom door and then stepped into the sparsely furnished room—a king-sized bed on a low dais with rumpled sheets and duvet, the indentation where his head had lain still visible on his pillow. There were no ornaments or knick-knacks, no photos or mementoes. There never had been, in her six months there.

The room was luxurious and as impersonal as could be, like something found in a high-end hotel. Milly began to strip the bed, her methodical movements belying the sudden thud of her heart, her dry mouth. Why was she being affected this way?

Unthinkingly she slipped off the pillowcase he'd used and pressed it to her face, inhaling an unfamiliar musky and very male scent. She was still holding it when her mobile phone began to vibrate, and she jumped like a scalded cat, dropping the pillowcase.

Her hands near to shaking, Milly slid her phone from the pocket of her jeans and glanced down at the screen. *Anna.* All thoughts of pillowcases and the head that had lain on them vanished as she swiped to take the call.

'Anna? Are you okay?' As ever Milly couldn't keep the anxiety from her voice as soon as she spoke with her sister. Her situation was so precarious, and she was so very young.

'I'm fine, Milly.' Anna's voice was quiet, a little sad. Milly knew she hated living with her father, Milly's stepfather—one of them, anyway—and Milly couldn't blame her. The situation was dire, and there was nothing she'd been able to do about it. Carlos Bentano kept custody of his only child more out of a cruel whim than any love or affection on his part.

'Good.' Milly walked away from Alex's bed, gazing out at the sparkling sea. 'I was hoping you could come visit here at the end of the summer,' she said, trying to inject a positive note into her voice, as if what she was suggesting could really happen. 'For a few weeks at least...'

'If he lets me,' Anna said quietly, her voice filled with

doubt, and Milly sighed. Carlos Bentano and Milly's mother had married when she was fourteen and Anna just four. While their parents had been partying up with the last of their money, both penniless, minor aristocrats, Milly had been like a mother to Anna, only to be wrenched away from her four years later, after the inevitable and acrimonious divorce. In the intervening years, her contact with her stepsister had been all too fleeting; she'd seen her once or twice a year, if that, although not for lack of trying.

Carlos was just as likely to turn Milly away at the door of his dilapidated villa on the outskirts of Rome than let her in, and for no reason than it seemed to amuse him to be cruel. Meanwhile he hosted debauched parties, inviting all manner of dissolute reprobates into his home, and paid scant attention to his daughter by an earlier marriage—Anna's mother had died when she was a baby—and was indifferently negligent of her education. Milly was desperate to get Anna away from him, and five million euros would certainly help…

But she'd said no. She'd turned Alex Santos down, and right now, listening to her sister's voice wobble as she tried to be brave, Milly could not think why she had been so selfish.

'Why wouldn't he let you?' Milly protested as brightly as she could. 'It won't affect him, and he might like having the house to himself for a change.' But they both knew Carlos didn't care about that. 'How are things going, anyway?' Milly asked. She talked to Anna nearly every day, but, despite these daily conversations and reassurances that she was well, Anna was never able to allay her anxiety, a knot of tension that had lodged itself in her stomach six years ago, when they'd been separated.

'Okay,' Anna said on a sigh. 'He came back from the casino last night in a foul mood.'

'Oh, Anna…'

'I stayed out of his way, and he was gone again this morning.'

'But what do you *do*?' Milly protested. She hated the thought of her sister drifting around like a ghost in that crumbling villa all by herself, day after day, but Carlos had already refused to let Anna come to Naxos for the summer.

'I read. Play music.' Anna was an accomplished violinist, and Milly loved to hear her play. 'It's better when he's not here. Last week…' She stopped, and unease ran its chilly finger down Milly's spine.

'Last week…?'

'It doesn't matter, Milly.'

'It does. Tell me, Anna, please.'

'Why?' Anna's voice trembled. 'There's nothing you can do.'

'What happened?' Milly demanded. 'I need to know.'

'It's nothing, really.' Anna sounded subdued now, which made Milly feel even more alarmed. 'He had some friends over, and they got drunk. One of them came into my bedroom…'

'*What?*' Horror clogged in her throat and she tasted bile. The thought of some drunken lout in her little sister's bedroom made her want to run all the way to Rome, as fast as she could. 'Anna, what happened? Did he…did he try anything?'

'No, no, he went out again. He apologised, even…'

Milly felt herself breathe a little easier, but she still felt suspicious as well as deeply afraid. She didn't think Anna was telling her everything, and what if next time the drunken guest wasn't so accommodating? What if her sister was in more danger than Milly had ever realised or feared? With her honey-blonde hair and big blue eyes,

Anna was lovely, and just becoming a woman. She would be irresistible to some of Carlos' debauched friends.

'Do you have a lock on your door?' Milly asked. 'Because I think you should lock it. Every night.'

'I've put a chair under the knob since then. Really, it's okay, Milly.'

But it wasn't at all okay. Milly breathed in deeply, willing herself not to cry. She didn't want to make Anna feel worse. 'I'm so sorry this is happening to you, Anna,' she said softly. 'This isn't at all how I hoped your life would be like.' When she'd been little, Milly had promised to take care of her. Vowed to always protect her. And now she was powerless.

She sent money when she could, and she had a savings account in Anna's name, but there was so little she could do.

And yet with five million euros you could do so much more. You could bribe Carlos for custody, even...

'It's not your fault, Milly,' Anna said. 'And actually I was calling for another reason.' She paused, and Milly steeled herself, hoping there wasn't more to worry about. 'A space has opened up at the academy,' Anna continued hesitantly. 'I just got the email this morning.'

'The academy...' Milly's mind raced. She knew Anna had been dreaming of going to the prestigious music school in Rome for several years, but there had been no space, and, more importantly, no money. Carlos would never agree to pay for anything, and Milly couldn't afford the fees, even with her generous salary.

'That's wonderful, Anna, but—'

'I know it's a lot,' her stepsister continued in a quiet, intense voice. 'And you can't possibly pay it all, but I've arranged to give music lessons to some neighbours. It's not much, but it would help—'

'Oh, Anna.' Milly bit her lip. She doubted her sister could make nearly enough teaching violin to make up the difference, but she couldn't bear to disappoint her and put a stop to her dreams. 'What does Carlos say?'

'I haven't told him, and I don't plan to. He doesn't care where I go to school, and he might refuse just because he could. Besides, he doesn't have the money, and if he did, he certainly wouldn't spend it on me.'

'But...'

'I can forge his signature. I've had to before, when he's forgotten to sign forms and things. I'd leave and return home the same time every day, not that he notices. It could work, Milly. I'm sure of it. It's just the money...'

'I'll see what I can do.' Tears pricked Milly's eyes as she thought of her sister desperately trying to make this dream work, and all on her own strength. She was so young, and yet far too old for her years. Milly couldn't bear to think of the debauched scenes Anna must witness in her father's home, when Carlos had his horrible friends over. And when she thought of one of those amoral men looking at Anna, coming into her bedroom...

She had to do something.

'Thank you, Milly,' Anna said earnestly. 'I really appreciate it.'

'I can't make any promises,' Milly felt compelled to warn, even though she wanted to promise Anna everything. 'Send me an email with the details of the fees, okay? And I'll try to make the numbers work.' Although she doubted they would...*not unless she had five million euros.*

'All right.' Anna hesitated. 'The only thing is, the space won't be open for ever. The *principale* said I needed to send my deposit by the end of the week.'

'The end of the week—' Milly couldn't keep the words from coming out in a squeak of dismay.

'I'm sorry. I never dreamt a space would come up in time for me to start…'

'Send the email,' Milly repeated firmly. 'I'll look into it this afternoon, and if I can swing the fees, I'll wire the deposit as soon as possible.' Although it made her stomach sink to think of it. How would she be able to afford such a thing? And yet she knew she wanted to. Desperately.

How desperately?

That little voice continued with its sly whispers after Milly had ended the call. Desperately enough to marry Alex Santos? That would solve all of Anna's problems. *Do you really want to keep her safe?*

Milly scrunched her eyes shut, trying to block out that whisper, but it did no good.

Well, do you? the voice mocked. *Do you?*

'There is a woman here to see you, Kyrie Santos.'

Alex frowned as he listened to the disembodied voice of the receptionist on the intercom. 'A woman? I have no appointments. You know that.' His voice was sharp with recrimination. All the staff at his headquarters in Athens knew he didn't take unscheduled appointments. He didn't want prying eyes, ever. No one saw him while he was here; he had had a private entrance installed with a lift that went directly to his penthouse office. His door was always closed.

'Yes, I know, sir…' The woman sounded apologetic as well as uncertain. 'But this woman insists…'

'Insists on seeing me?' Alex repeated in disbelief. Who on earth could it be? It didn't matter. 'Then you can simply tell her I am not—'

'Insists that she is your fiancée,' the woman corrected in an embarrassed rush. 'I'm sorry, sir. I didn't know if…' She trailed off uncertainly while Alex frowned at his intercom, trying to process what he'd just heard. His *fiancée*?

Something far too like hope flared in his chest. *Milly.* It had to be her. She'd changed her mind...and she'd come all the way to Athens to tell him? He was surprised as well as both gratified and curious. 'Send her in,' he said gruffly, and then he rose from his chair and stalked to the window, trying to control his wayward emotions.

Since leaving the villa—and Milly— they'd been in a frustrating ferment. He didn't want to care about her refusal. He didn't want to feel the rejection, and yet he did. He'd been stewing over it for the better part of two days, telling himself it didn't matter even though he knew it did.

She was just a housekeeper, after all, and yet he'd wanted her. He'd wanted her to marry him, because rather surprisingly, considering how quick his decision to ask her had been, he realised he wanted her and no other. He desired her with a strength that surprised him; he'd spent the last few nights lying awake imagining his hands on her skin, his mouth... But of course their wedding night, if it happened, would be an exercise in endurance rather than an experience of passion.

With his gaze on the window and his back to his office, he heard the door open and then click softly shut, followed by a quick shudder of breath that made the hair on the nape of his neck stand up. She sounded as if she were steeling herself, and she probably was. He knew from experience it didn't get any easier to look at him. Every time he glanced in the mirror it was a shock.

'Kyrie Santos,' she said quietly.

'Alex,' he reminded her. He didn't turn from the window; no need to remind her of his scars. She was undoubtedly thinking of them already.

A heavy silence ticked on for several taut moments.

'I've…reconsidered your offer,' Milly finally said, her voice matter-of-fact and determined. 'If it's still open.'

Alex's gaze rested on the skyscrapers of Syntagma Square, his heart thudding hard even as he kept his voice measured, almost toneless. 'It is.'

'Then I'm here to say I will marry you… Alex.' Her voice held a tremor of emotion, perhaps fear. Was she scared of him? Or just repulsed by his scars? Maybe both, and for good reason. He hadn't given her any real reason to respond otherwise.

'Why have you changed your mind?' he asked. 'As a matter of interest?'

She took a quick, telling breath. 'I had more time to think about it.'

'And what did you conclude?' He couldn't keep a sardonic note of cynicism from entering his voice.

'That five million euros is a very good deal,' Milly answered after a moment, her voice ragged with honesty. 'And it will help my sister immeasurably.'

She sounded resigned—resigned to her fate, to him. She was signing her death warrant, and why? For the sake of her sister, of course. There was no other reason. He would be something she had to endure to get what she wanted. Had he ever expected anything else? Of course he hadn't. That was the deal he'd offered. That was what they were both getting. There was no reason to feel stung by it now. No reason at all.

'Very well,' Alex replied coolly. 'Then I will have the prenuptial contract drawn up immediately. Once you've signed it, we can be married immediately.'

'Immediately…' She sounded a little dazed by the prospect.

'There is no time to waste. I told you I wanted an heir. I'll arrange for you to have a medical examination tomorrow morning.' He heard her gasp but he didn't care. So what if he'd been blunt, even crude? It was the truth.

'But…but there's still so much to discuss…'

'Such as?'

He heard her swallow, and in his mind's eye he could picture the working of her pale, slender throat, see the widening of those pansy-brown eyes, the rise and fall of her chest. 'Lots of things. How it's going to *work*, mainly, and…and what precautions will be in place…?'

'Precautions?' The word came out sharp.

'I'm putting my life in your hands,' Milly retorted, her voice just as sharp as his. 'I need guarantees, Alex. Safeguards…'

'Very well. Then I'll put those in place.'

'Can't you turn and look at me?' she burst out, sounding both exasperated and emotional. 'I hate having a conversation with your back.'

He pressed his lips together, biting back the instinctive reply. *I didn't think you wanted to look at me.* He wouldn't lower himself by saying such a thing. Instead he turned around to face her, schooling his face into an expression of bored disdain.

'Here you are. And here I am.'

'Yes.' She gazed at him steadily, and he saw her gulp, her gaze darting to his scars and then back again. Her face was pale, her eyes huge. 'So now what?'

'Now we discuss the terms. The safeguards you mentioned.' He strode from the window and sat in one of the leather club chairs in front of his desk, gesturing for her to take a seat in the other. 'Shall we?'

'All right.' Milly walked over to the chair and sat in it.

Just two days ago they'd been in his study at the villa, talking about terms in theory. And here they were again, talking about them in reality. Everything had changed because she had agreed to become his wife. They *would* be married. He did not feel as triumphant as he'd thought he would…especially as Milly's gaze moved over his face, sliding away from the scarred side, and her fingers trembled before she knotted them together in her lap. 'So…?' Her tongue darted out to moisten her lips. 'Why don't you tell me what you suggest?'

'I suggest we marry immediately,' he answered with a shrug, purposely keeping his tone clipped, almost bored. 'As I said before. I can have the prenuptial contract drawn up by tomorrow, and we can be married the day after. I will have the marriage licence rushed.'

Milly squared her shoulders. 'And what would the prenuptial agreement state?'

'That you will receive five million euros, which will be repayable to me should we divorce.'

'Repayable?' She blinked. 'That's harsh. What if *you* divorce me?'

'I won't. But, to address any worries you might have on that score, I will have it put into the contract that you will be given an additional five million euros should I wish to divorce you.'

She shook her head as a shiver went through her. 'This is all sounding so cold.'

'Clinical, perhaps, but not cold. It's a business arrangement, Milly. We both know that.'

'Yes, but…are we ever going to get to know each other, even a little? Talk properly?'

Alex suppressed a shaft of impatience. 'We're talking now.'

'*Properly*, I said. Enjoying each other's company as… as friends, if not anything else. Have some sort of companionship, especially if we're going to be…to be *parents*.'

She choked on the word, her eyes huge. 'And what about that? What about how we raise our child?'

'We can discuss that in due course.'

'But don't you want to know me at all? Or have me know you? I mean, even just a *little*...' She trailed off, searching his face—and for what?

He stared at her for a long moment, wondering if she really wanted some kind of friendship—and why. Did she really want to get to know him, or was it just a salve to her conscience, because she felt guilty for agreeing to such a businesslike marriage? It was all pointless anyway, because he had no desire to get to know her. No wish whatsoever to make this more complicated than it needed to be. More emotional, more dangerous. Desiring her physically already felt like a step too far, a need he knew he shouldn't nurture.

And yet, despite all that, he could see the sense in a conversation, at least. Besides, he had a conference call in five minutes.

'Very well,' Alex said at last. 'I will arrange for you to stay at the Hotel Grande Bretagne for the next few days. Tonight we can meet for dinner and...talk.' His lips twisted, the scar pulling tight across his cheek. 'Get to know each other as you seem to wish...and agree on all the terms.'

CHAPTER FOUR

MILLY STARED AT her reflection in the gilt-framed mirror in wondering disbelief. Could this really be happening? Everything felt surreal, from the moment Alex had ushered her out of his office and an assistant had escorted her to the limousine waiting by the kerb.

It had been only a few minutes' drive to the luxurious hotel just off the other side of the square, and then up to the presidential suite, the most expensive and elegant accommodation in the hotel. Milly had wandered around the gracious rooms with their antiques and art—a dining room, living room, two bedrooms, both with en suite bathrooms nearly as big—wondering if this was what the rest of her life was going to be like. It seemed impossible.

Although her parents were both titled, they'd lived in shabby elegance, if that, barely scraping by on what was left of their inheritances; Milly was used to draughty mansion flats with leaky pipes and the heat cut off, or third-rate boarding schools in distant, remote locations with stern teachers and freezing showers.

Once she'd left home, she'd lived even more modestly—a cramped box room in a dilapidated student house in Edinburgh, and then a shoebox-sized studio in Paris. This was something else entirely, and it made her feel…strange. Was this what she would become used to?

But she hadn't been left alone to dwell on it for very long; she'd barely walked through the rooms before hotel staff were knocking on the door, ushering in a three-course lunch under silver domes and then, a short while later, a personal stylist from a nearby boutique wheeled in several suitcases of clothes, with instructions for her to pick whatever she wanted. Milly was overwhelmed.

And while it was rather fun to dine on lobster salad and caramel profiteroles, and even more so to pick out several simple and elegant outfits, it was also unsettling. What did Alex Santos want in return?

She knew the answer, of course. *An heir.* And that thought made her tremble, a shiver that started deep inside, in the core of her being, and spread out to the tips of her fingers and toes.

She could hardly believe she'd agreed to marry a man she barely knew, and yet she felt she'd had no choice. After ending the call with Anna, Milly had realised she would do whatever it took to make her sister safe and happy. And if marrying a stranger was the price she had to pay, so be it. It could be a lot worse.

She believed—or at least she hoped—that Alex Santos was a decent man. The knowledge that she had no real basis for that assumption settled heavily inside her.

At least she would have an opportunity to find out more about him before she signed any agreements or spoke any vows. Milly knew she was resting a lot on a single evening's conversation, but it was all she had. And hopefully, by the end of the night, she'd know more about the man she'd agreed to marry. Perhaps she'd even like him. That would be as solid a foundation for marriage as any she could hope for, and certainly better than what fools called love.

Her lips twisted grimly as she remembered how carelessly Philippe had used that word. *'Chérie, I love you. I fell in love with you the first time I saw you…'*

And like a besotted fool, she'd believed him. She'd wanted to believe him, because she'd wanted her life to be different from her mother's… Angelique Dubois, the ageing beauty who fell desperately in love, or seemed to, all the while having her eyes on the prize.

Her mother had married for money thrice over, and was now living in Los Angeles with her D-list celebrity husband, a man whose claim to fame seemed to be how many times he could check himself into rehab. Milly had never met him, and she hadn't seen her mother in years, except occasionally in the back of tawdry gossip magazines, usually in one of the smallest photos on the society pages.

She glanced in the mirror again, wishing she looked a little more…elegant. She'd taken a shower and spent an age styling her hair and doing her make-up with the high-end beauty products she'd been provided with, but in the end she'd wiped it all over and dragged a brush through her hair because she'd looked like she was trying too hard. She'd looked like her mother, painted with fake gloss, a shiny veneer that chipped all too easily. She never wanted to be like that.

And so here she was, dressed in a burgundy wrap dress of softest jersey, her hair in simple waves about her shoulders, not a lick of make-up on her face. She knew she wasn't beautiful, so there was no point even trying. Alex Santos was not marrying her for her looks, that much was sure.

From the front of the huge suite a door opened and then clicked shut, and Milly's heart stuttered. It was him, she knew it. She sensed it, even though staff had been going in and out all afternoon. It was as if the air around her had changed, and another shiver started in her core and radiated out.

'Milly?' His voice was terse, his footsteps echoing on the marble floor. Milly turned from the mirror, smoothing her palms down the sides of her dress as she took a steadying breath.

'Here,' she called, and stepped out of her bedroom into the hallway. Alex stilled just a few feet away, his gaze training on her, not a flicker of emotion on his face. It was still jarring to see his scars—half of him so very beautiful, and the other half pulled and twisted beyond recognition. She tried not to react, but she could tell she'd failed by the way his mouth tightened. She would get used to them eventually, she was sure. She wasn't *bothered* by them, by any means; they were just surprising, the contrast so stark.

'You look nice,' he said gruffly, and dropped his briefcase by the hall table.

'Thank you.' She let out a nervous little laugh. 'I've been ridiculously pampered since I arrived here. I feel like Cinderella.'

'And when will the clock strike midnight, do you think?' he asked sardonically as he tugged at his tic.

Milly watched him uncertainly, her gaze transfixed by the sight of his long, lean fingers pulling at the silken knot around his throat. He pulled it free with a snick of cloth and tossed it aside before undoing the top two buttons of his shirt. Again her gaze was helplessly drawn to his fingers, and the bit of bronzed skin he exposed—the hollow of his throat, the hint of his muscles. He was a beautiful man, and in a strange way the scars emphasised that. Her breath fluttered in her throat and she swallowed. Hard.

'What do you mean?' she finally asked when she'd managed to regather her senses. 'Do you think I'm going to change my mind?'

'I wouldn't be surprised if you did.'

'I won't.' She spoke firmly, determination firing her

words. 'I've made up my mind and I won't change it. But perhaps it is you who will change yours.' Although she hoped he wouldn't. She'd wired all her savings to pay for the deposit on Anna's school fees, and she needed the five million euros by next week to pay the rest.

'Hardly,' he scoffed, and then turned to stride into the living room. After an uneasy pause Milly followed him.

She stood in the doorway and watched as he unstoppered a decanter of whisky and poured himself a finger's worth. 'I've ordered our meal to come shortly.'

'All right.'

'So.' Alex walked to an elegant chair patterned in striped silk and sat down, the tumbler of whisky dangling from his fingers, his face angled away from her so she could only see his unmarked side. 'Tell me your terms.'

'I don't actually want to talk about terms. Not yet.' Carefully Milly crossed to the sofa perpendicular to him and sat down. 'I just want to talk.'

Alex lifted the glass of whisky to his lips and took a long swallow. 'Talk?' he repeated tonelessly. 'About what?'

'About each other. I want to get to know you, Alex, if just a little, and have you get to know me. I... I don't want to marry a stranger. Even business deals can be amicable.' She pleated her fingers in her lap, her heart jumping around in her chest. 'Can we do that?'

Alex took another sip of whisky as he considered Milly's question. Could she get to know him? Could he get to know her? It all sounded so innocuous, so sweetly innocent, and yet...

He was darkness inside, and if she saw that...if she *felt* it...she might change her mind. She almost certainly would. Never mind the scars on his face, there were worse things for her to discover, things he was able to hide. Yet refusing might make her reconsider. He had to walk a very fine line between friendliness and honesty, darkness and light.

'All right.' Alex forced a smile to his lips, and felt the familiar tug of his scar on the corner of his mouth. 'Let's talk.'

Silence pooled between them, stole the air. Alex waited it out, watching Milly as she struggled with what to say, where to look.

'Where did you grow up?' she asked at last.

'Here in Athens. Next?'

Her lips twitched, her eyes flashing with annoyance at his abrupt manner, but the truth was he didn't know how else to be. He'd long ago lost the ability to make small talk, if he'd ever had it. He'd learned to watch himself from an early age, and since the fire he'd become even more private and remote. He could not imagine changing. He had neither the desire nor the ability.

'Do you have any brothers and sisters?' Milly asked.

He clocked the present tense and answered it accordingly, already feeling far too raw, exposed by these seemingly innocent questions. 'Just the stepbrother, Ezio, from whom I'm trying to save the business.'

'You were close to your stepfather?' Milly recalled, and everything in Alex tightened. Already this was too difficult. Too much. His fingers clenched on his glass, knuckles aching.

'Yes. Now let me ask you some questions.'

'All right.' She settled herself back against the sofa, her slender hands resting on her knees. She looked lovely in the simple wrap dress, the burgundy colour picking up the dark honey strands in her hair, the gold glints in her eyes. Alex's gaze took in the simple tie at the waist that held the dress together and he imagined giving it one firm tug and seeing it come undone.

Heat flared inside him, dangerous and alarming. How could he desire her with such fierce need? He'd picked Milly James as a prospective wife because she was convenient, not beautiful. And she wasn't beautiful, in the conventional sense. If anything, she was exceedingly plain, with her brown eyes and hair, her slight figure. And yet right now he wanted her more than he'd ever expected—not just as a wife, but as a woman. That was unfortunate, because he doubted very much that she wanted him in the same way.

'Where did you grow up?' he asked, shifting to ease the ache that had started in his groin.

'All over. London, Paris, Buenos Aires for a bit.' She gave a small shrug. 'A few other places.'

'That sounds rather exotic.'

'If you like.'

She sounded guarded, which made him curious. 'Is there a particular place you'd call home?'

'Your villa on Naxos,' she replied, surprising him. 'It's an oasis of peace compared to some of the other places I've lived.'

'That's good to hear.'

'Yes.' She glanced away, something in her shuttering. It seemed she had secrets as well, or perhaps just pain. He felt a flicker of empathy, the last thing he'd expected to feel.

'And your stepsister?' he asked after a moment. 'Where does she live?'

'Rome.'

'Not too far, then. Do you see her often?' As far as he was aware, she hadn't taken off any time since being in his employ.

'As often as I can, but her father doesn't always allow it.'

Alex frowned. 'Why not?'

'Because he likes to be cruel?' Milly shrugged, glancing back at him with bitterness in her tone and pain in her eyes. 'He's a capricious wastrel, and he enjoys nothing more than being petty and cruel simply because he can. I've arranged a visit many times and at the last moment he slams the door in my face.'

Alex stiffened at the thought of a man being so wantonly wicked. He knew what capricious cruelty looked like, what it felt like, and he hated it with a fierce and deep-seated passion. 'Can't your sister get away to see you?'

'She's only fourteen, and she's afraid of him.' Milly's arms wrapped around herself, almost as if she were keeping herself together. 'Five million euros will help to protect her.'

'How, if your stepfather is as capricious as you say?' Making the point was hardly in his favour, yet he couldn't keep himself from it. The last thing he wanted was for her to regret their marriage more than she had to.

'I can pay for her school fees,' Milly said in a low voice. 'That will make a big difference. And if I offer Carlos a financial incentive, he might be willing to let Anna visit me more often.' Her gaze flew to his face. 'That would be all right, wouldn't it? To have her visit…'

'Of course,' he said tersely. 'I'll make sure to stay out of the way.'

She looked surprised, but then she nodded. Of course, she wouldn't want him there, scaring her sister.

'Who is this Carlos?' he asked. 'As a matter of interest?'

'Carlos Bentano. My mother's third husband, ex for the last six years.'

'Ah.' There was a wealth of meaning, a world of bitterness in her simple statement. He remembered her saying how she would never want to divorce. 'And what about your father?'

'He's on his third marriage. My mother has moved on

to her fourth, although I doubt they'll last very long.' She shook her head, her hands now clenched in her lap. 'I don't see either of them very much at all.'

'It sounds like it was a difficult way to grow up.'

'Not much fun,' she agreed, and then deliberately made herself relax. 'Not the way I'd choose to raise my own child, certainly.'

'Our child,' he reminded her, and watched her eyes flare—with alarm, no doubt. He needed to remind her of the purpose of their marriage—to produce an heir, and as soon as possible. Just in case she might forget that a wedding night was most certainly part of the deal, and as many nights thereafter as it took for her to become pregnant. After that he would leave her alone.

That persistent ache intensified, and his fingers itched to tug at that sash and watch the dress come undone. He pictured himself standing before her, spreading his hands to span her waist, feeling the warm, silky flesh come alive beneath his palms.

Then he pictured her flinching beneath his touch, averting her face. No, their wedding night, or any other encounter, wouldn't happen like that. It would be as businesslike as the rest of their marriage, because neither of them wished to suffer through anything more.

'Yes, our child,' she agreed softly as she lowered her gaze, her head bent.

'Should we talk about the terms now?' Alex asked curtly. They'd had enough of getting to know each other, it seemed.

She looked up, her momentary surprise replaced by stoic composure. He wished she didn't look as if she had to *endure* him quite so much, but he knew he couldn't expect anything else. 'All right.'

'So the terms of the contract will be simple. In exchange

for five million euros, you will marry me, stay faithful to me, and agree to share my bed until you become pregnant.'

She swallowed, the sound audible. 'And how often am I to share your bed?'

The way she said it made him think she wished to as little as possible. Alex hesitated, surprised by his own reticence to make this aspect of marriage as cold and clinical as the rest of it. And yet of course it had to be. 'Three times a week, unless it is during your monthly courses.'

'My…' Her face began to flush with colour. 'All right.'

'Do you wish to suggest something different?'

'No…' She swallowed again, and then let out a shuddery little breath. 'No.'

'I will endeavour to make it as pleasant as possible,' Alex said, his mouth twisting into a sardonic grimace. 'I appreciate the difficulties, of course.'

She didn't answer, which bizarrely annoyed and even hurt him. He had to stop *caring* so damn much. 'Is that all satisfactory?'

'And what about when I…when I am pregnant? If I am? What will happen then?'

'Then I'll leave you alone.'

'For…for good?' She looked startled. 'You're sure you don't want more children?'

For a second he imagined it, pictured a houseful of them—babies, toddlers, teens. Crowded around the table. Laughing in the garden. A fantasy. 'As I said before, one will suffice. After you have become pregnant and given birth, there won't be any need for us to continue the…arrangement, although of course we will still stay married.'

She nodded slowly, seeming to absorb that statement—and not to mind it. 'And I'll raise the child…our child… on Naxos?'

'Yes, until he or she is of an age to need more appropriate schooling. But those things can be negotiated at a later date. The important thing is to have the initial terms set down so we can move forward.'

'I can hardly believe we're doing this so quickly...' She shook her head, and Alex cut across her, determined not to give her the opportunity for second thoughts.

'It's how people have been doing it for centuries. There is no reason to think we won't both be happy.'

He'd meant to sound dismissive, but she cocked her head, her gaze moving over him slowly, taking him in, scars and all. 'Happy?' she repeated softly. 'Are you happy, Alex? *Will* you be happy?'

There was far too much sorrowful knowledge in her question and in her eyes, too much damned pity. 'I will be happy with the arrangement,' he told her shortly. 'That is enough.'

It wasn't until after he'd said it that he realised how revealing his answer was. A knock sounded on the door, and Alex called out in Greek for the member of staff to leave their meal in the hall, as they did not wish to be disturbed.

'Dinner is here,' he announced once the staff member had left, the door clicking shut behind him. He rose and strode towards the entrance hall of the suite. 'I hope you're hungry.'

'I am, even though I had an enormous lunch. I forgot to eat breakfast this morning, because I was in such a rush to get the ferry.'

'I didn't expect you to come to Athens,' Alex remarked as he wheeled in a trolley full of silver-domed dishes.

'I didn't know when you would be back in Naxos, and I wanted to see you as quickly as possible. Because of Anna.'

He glanced at her sharply. 'What is the urgency with your sister?'

'She's found a place at a prestigious music school in

Rome. She was on the waitlist, and a place has come up at the last moment. She's desperate to go—it will make a big difference to her, to attend.'

Alex frowned. 'Will her stepfather forbid it?'

'He won't even know. At least, that's how Anna is hoping it will all play out. But I needed to secure the deposit by the end of the week.'

'The end of the week...'

'Oh, don't worry,' Milly said quickly. 'I've paid it out of my savings. I'm not asking you to pay for anything...' She bit her lip 'I mean, I'll pay for her school fees out of, you know, the settlement.'

'I see.' She'd had even more reason to want that money—the only reason she would ever go through with something like this, clearly. She needed to provide for her sister, who, in a few days' time, would be as good as his sister-in-law. *Family.* He didn't want Milly to be scraping and saving in order to provide for what would be *his* family.

'I called her this afternoon,' Milly said quietly. 'To tell her I'd sorted the fees. She was so pleased.'

'And did you tell her you were to be married?'

'No.' Her lashes swept her cheeks as she lowered her gaze. 'I didn't want her to feel...'

A pause, and Alex filled it in grimly. 'Guilty? Because you've had to sell yourself in order to provide for your sister?' Milly stared at him uncertainly, clearly not knowing what to make of his comment, or why he'd made it in such a grim voice. And why had he? Everything was happening exactly as he'd intended it should. There was nothing to feel dissatisfied or unsettled about. Nothing at all.

CHAPTER FIVE

'Do you have any questions?'

Milly stared at the lawyer's bland face, her mind spinning. Did she have any *questions*? She glanced back down at the sheaf of papers spread on the desk in front of her, the typewritten text swimming before her eyes. She didn't even know where to begin.

'Miss James?' The slightest hint of impatience touched the lawyer's urbane voice.

'I think it should all be quite clear,' Alex interjected. He'd been sitting on the sofa in the lawyer's spacious office, silent and practically glowering, which Milly suspected was his usual look, at least when he had to appear in front of someone. The lawyer had seemed unsurprised by Alex's scars, but still kept sneaking looks at them, which Alex clearly noticed.

Milly took a deep breath as she tried to marshal her thoughts. She'd listened to the lawyer for the last hour as he'd outlined the terms of the prenuptial contract, but she'd hardly taken any of it in. She could still barely believe she was here, that she was thinking of doing this. She *was* doing this.

Last night, after their brief chat, she and Alex had eaten dinner mostly in silence. The food had been delicious, but it had begun to taste like ashes in Milly's mouth because she wanted conversation, not comfort. She wanted companionship, at least in a small degree, and as the evening had worn on she'd feared Alex would not be able to give it to her. Didn't *want* to give it to her, which was worse.

She'd made a few attempts, asking him why he chose to settle on Naxos—because it was convenient—and what his business was actually about—buying and selling property. She'd given up after a while, which she suspected was what Alex had wanted. Milly hadn't expected hearts and rainbows from him; of course she hadn't. But a little conversation wouldn't have gone amiss. She told herself it was better to know what to expect, and at least he wasn't attempting to flatter her the way Philippe had. Still, it felt like cold comfort indeed.

After dinner he'd returned to his apartment, curtly informing her that a limo would pick her up at nine for her medical exam, and then take her afterwards to his lawyer's office where they would go over the prenuptial agreement.

Then Milly had spent a restless night wondering what on earth was she doing even as she knew she wasn't going to change her mind. She couldn't, for Anna's sake. For Anna's happiness.

But this morning she was awfully tempted. First, she'd endured the most clinical medical exam she'd ever had at a private medical clinic, squirming in indignity and shame as the doctor had asked her questions about her period, her sexual history, her fertility.

When she'd left the office, her cheeks still scarlet with mortification, Alex had been waiting in the back of his limo. She'd blushed harder when he'd informed her that the doctor would email him the report. So now he would know her periods were regular, she'd never had an STD, and even that she was a virgin. Milly couldn't bear to meet his eye, but he didn't seem eager to meet hers, either.

He'd ushered her quickly into the limousine, and since then he'd seemed intent on ignoring her as much as possible. He looked devastatingly attractive in his steel-grey suit, his eyes piercing and blue, his dark hair the perfect foil to his crisp white shirt. The lawyer was obsequious in the way he studiously avoided looking at Alex's scars, and she could tell it annoyed Alex. It annoyed her as well.

She was already getting used to them, seeing the scars simply as part of who he was. Perhaps because she'd been around such superficial beauty for so long, she found she didn't mind them in a way he seemed to think people did. Her mother had chased physical perfection with spa days and surgery, expensive ointments and endless make-up, and in the end the beauty was nothing more than a glossy veneer. At least Alex's scars were real.

'Are you going to sign it, Milly?' Alex asked, his voice cutting through her jumbled thoughts. 'Or not?'

'Sorry…' She'd been simply staring into space for the last minutes, and she saw now that the lawyer was impatient, Alex annoyed. She reached for the heavy, expensive-looking fountain pen the lawyer had laid on the table next to the contract and uncapped it, her heart starting to thud.

She hadn't been able to take in all the terms the man had gone through, but she knew enough to understand the gist of what she was signing. Sort of.

She'd receive the five million euros as soon as they were wed. They were to have regular conjugal relations until she was confirmed pregnant. She would live on Naxos, but be free to travel to Alex's homes in London and Athens. Any other trips needed to be approved by him, although he'd assured her he would be reasonable. It felt a little bit like prison, a gilded cage, and yet, considering what she was getting, nothing seemed that unreasonable.

And yet…in the end, she was still selling herself for money. Did a wedding ring really make it respectable?

'Milly…' Alex said her name like a warning, and she closed her eyes.

She couldn't back out now. *For Anna.* She was doing this for Anna. Her mother had married various minor aristocrats so she could fund her extravagant lifestyle. Milly was doing it for the person—the only person—she loved. It was completely different. It had to be.

Wordlessly she bent her head, the contract's type swimming in front of her, and signed her name. Milly felt as if she'd just opened a vein and dripped blood onto the snowy white documents.

'There we are,' the lawyer said smoothly and picked up the contract, shuffling the papers into a neat pile. 'I believe that concludes our business for today.'

'Thank you.' Alex turned towards the door, and Milly followed him, her stomach churning.

What had she done?

For Anna. This is for Anna.

'That wasn't so bad, was it?' Alex asked her once they were safely ensconced in his limousine, the tinted windows hiding them from the world.

'I suppose not.' Milly's voice was shaky and she found she had to blink back tears. She hated feeling so raw and uncertain; she'd revelled in the quiet solitude of the last six months, the safety of them, and now she felt as if she'd just upended her entire life. She had no idea what to expect. Nothing felt certain or safe. Were they really going to be married *tomorrow*?

'Don't look so devastated, then,' Alex said, his voice a sardonic drawl. 'I promise I will make as few demands on your time as possible.' He turned away from her to look out of the window, and Milly tried to speak past the lump forming in her throat.

'Is that what you think I want?' He merely shrugged, and she made herself continue. 'I'm not expecting some sort of fairy tale, Alex. Of course I'm not. I wouldn't even want one, because I know they're not real.'

'Then we don't have a problem.'

'It would just be nice to be *friends*,' Milly persisted, her voice turning a little ragged. 'Right now it feels as if you can barely tolerate me.'

'I can tolerate you?' He let out a harsh laugh. 'Let's be honest with each other, Milly, if we can't be anything else.'

She gazed at him in confusion, wishing he would at least look at her. 'What do you mean?'

'You're the one who can't tolerate me,' Alex said flatly. 'And I don't blame you for it.'

She gaped, unable to frame a reply for several taut seconds. 'Is that really what you think?' she finally managed to gasp out. He'd always seemed so cold, she had trouble believing he could think that. Alex lifted one shoulder in a negligent shrug. *Look at me,'* Milly demanded. 'If we are to be married, at least look at me.'

He swung around to face her, his eyes glittering like blue fire—or maybe ice, because his expression was cold. Cold and furious. 'Are you sure you want to look at *me*?'

He held her gaze, and Milly did not look away. She didn't even blink. 'Is this about your scars?' she asked evenly, willing her voice not to tremble. She could feel the heat rolling off him, inhaled the citrusy scent of his aftershave that awakened her senses. 'Do you honestly think I'm so shallow? Why would you be willing to marry me if I was?'

'Shallow or not, I'm not very pleasant to look at,' Alex returned flatly. 'Fact.'

'Isn't beauty in the eye of the beholder?' Milly asked softly, and Alex rolled his eyes.

'How can you even say that with a straight face? You don't find me beautiful, Milly.'

She hesitated, sifting through her jumbled thoughts, and then chose honesty, painful as it was. 'No, I don't,' she agreed, and something flickered across Alex's face before his expression closed off completely. 'But not because of your scars. Because of how...how *cold* you're being. It feels as if you're choosing to distance yourself, and that's not how I want to start our marriage, even if it is one that is based on business.'

Alex was silent for a long moment, staring at her. Their faces were so close she could see the dark glint of stubble on his freshly shaven chin, the icy blue of his eyes piercing her like an arrow. She inhaled the musky smell of his aftershave again, and her heart tumbled in her chest.

Then Alex eased back, turning his head away from her in a deliberate movement. 'Too bad,' he said, and neither of them spoke again.

So she thought he was cold. Alex gazed dispassionately at his reflection in the mirror—full on, so he could see both the beauty and ugliness, the scars and the smooth skin. Dr Jekyll and Mr Hyde in the flesh—and in the soul. His face, he feared, was a reflection of who he truly was. Hiding the darkness. Pretending to the world that he was only half of who he was. That he didn't hurt the people he loved. That he didn't destroy them.

And she thought he was simply cold. Well, cold was better than cruel. Cold was fine—because it kept them both safe. And Milly would just have to learn to live with it, because he didn't know how to be anything else. From his childhood he'd learned to stay distant from other peo-

ple, out of self-preservation, and that had only been exac-
erbated since his accident. Eventually she would accept
how he was, and realise it was better this way. It had to be.

In any case, he saw the way she looked at his scars. She
might say they didn't matter, but of course they did. How
could they not? He'd seen the pity in her eyes, the way her
gaze darted away, and that told him all he needed to know.

He turned away from his reflection and glanced at his
watch; he was meeting Milly in a few minutes to take a
limousine to his private yacht docked at Piraeus. From
there they would travel to Naxos, where they would be
married.

Alex had been planning on a civil ceremony at the city
hall here in Athens, but yesterday, after they'd signed the
prenuptial agreement, after that taut confrontation in the
limo, Milly had asked if they could marry on the island,
in a church.

'I know it's a business deal,' she'd said with quiet dignity, her chin tilted at a proud angle, 'but it doesn't have
to be businesslike in every particular, and I would like to
marry in a church and say my vows before God.'

'Wouldn't you be saying them before God in any case?'
Alex had drawled, and she'd merely gazed at him steadily,
waiting for his answer, refusing to be baited. He'd felt
shamed by his seeming pettiness; the truth was the whole
ordeal of being with her, having her look at him, having
her want to *know* him, even in the smallest degree, left
him feeling raw and exposed, as if yet another layer of skin
had been peeled back to reveal the agonising nerve-endings underneath. He had enough scars already. He didn't
need any more.

'Please, Alex,' she'd said. 'This is a small request.'

Small to her, perhaps, but not to him. She had no idea
what awaited him on Naxos, why he'd been back only once

since the fire, and he was hardly going to tell her now. And so he'd agreed, even though he dreaded the thought of facing the villagers of Naxos, because he didn't want to have to explain and, in truth, something in him wanted to please her, which was absurd yet true. The small smile of thanks she'd given him when he had agreed had lightened his heart a ridiculous amount.

Milly was already waiting in the limousine when he left his flat; his driver had picked her up at the hotel before fetching him. Alex slid onto the leather seat, his thigh brushing hers before she inched away. He wondered if she would shrink away like that tomorrow night, when they were in bed. He thought it likely, but she would simply have to grit her teeth and bear it as she held up her end of the bargain.

'I didn't know you had a yacht,' she remarked as the limo pulled away from the kerb. 'You came to Naxos by helicopter.'

'I don't have time usually to travel by sea, but it does tend to be far more relaxing.' He paused, and then, somewhat to his surprise, decided to make the effort of conversing. 'Do you like sailing?'

'I don't know, I haven't been, really.' She smiled self-consciously. 'The only boat I've been on is the ferry to Naxos.'

'It is?' He frowned. From what she'd said of her parents, he'd surmised they were fairly well off, and she'd said she had lived in several cosmopolitan cities. 'I'm surprised.'

'Are you?' She shrugged. 'I never had the opportunity.'

'Yet you've lived in Paris, in London, in Buenos Aires.'

'What does that have to do with sailing?'

'I simply thought you would have had a variety of life experiences.'

She paused, her face drawn in reflective and even sorrowful lines. 'I suppose I've had certain experiences, but in their essence they've all been the same.'

'How?' The word came out abrupt, and she raised her eyebrows, a faint smile playing about her mouth even though her eyes still looked soft and sad.

'You want to get to know me now?'

'I'm curious.'

She shrugged. 'My mother found me to mainly be an inconvenience. She sent me to boarding school when she could afford it, and left me at home when she couldn't.'

Alex frowned. 'And what about your father?'

'They divorced when I was five. I rarely ever saw him.'

It sounded miserable—about as miserable as his childhood, and yet as far as he could tell she hadn't had the loving care of a stepfather the way he had been blessed to have. 'Were any of your step-parents decent people?' he asked. 'Besides Bentano?'

'I wouldn't call them parents, really,' Milly answered after a moment. 'They certainly didn't see themselves in that role.'

Which told him everything he needed to know, and left him feeling oddly unsettled, although he couldn't say why. They didn't speak again until the limousine pulled up to the dock at Piraeus, and Alex ushered her towards the gleaming white superyacht.

'This is yours?' Milly's eyes widened as she took in all fifty metres of the impressive structure.

'It belonged to my stepfather,' Alex answered as he took her hand to help her aboard. One of his staff, paid to be discreet and blank-faced, stepped back. 'He used to host parties on it, for business.'

'And you don't?'

'No.' Not any more.

She gazed at him uncertainly, their hands still clasped,

her slender fingers resting on his. 'Because of your scars?' she asked quietly, and he cringed at the pity he thought he heard in her tone.

'Yes, but also because I am not much of one for parties. Never have been.'

'You seem a very private man,' Milly acknowledged as he led her into the main living area, a luxurious, wood-panelled room with several leather sofas scattered about the plush, ankle-deep carpet. 'Were you always so?'

'Yes, I suppose.' He'd had to be. He turned away from her. 'Would you like something to drink? It will take about six hours to get to Naxos. We can be there by dinnertime, and then the wedding is scheduled for tomorrow at midday.'

'All right,' Milly said, her voice sounding quiet and a little sad. 'And yes, please, could I have some water?'

Alex snapped his fingers and one of his staff, one of the few he trusted to see him, stepped forward. 'Sparkling water and a whisky, please, Petros.'

'Very good, sir.'

Petros withdrew, leaving them alone. The yacht shuddered beneath them for a few seconds and then began to glide through the water.

'Are we going already?' Milly looked surprised, and a little excited. Alex recalled what she'd said about never having sailed.

'Yes, would you like to see?' He opened the French windows that led out onto one of the yacht's many decks, this one private, with a couple of rattan sofas and chairs. Ahead of them the Aegean Sea stretched out, a simmering, undulating blanket of blue-green.

Milly stood with her hands on the rail, her hair blowing back from her face, as she gazed out at the sea. She reminded Alex of the statue of winged Nike—courageous and proud. The thought made some forgotten ember flicker to life in him, something he thought had long ago crumbled to ash.

He imagined, for one piercing second, how things could be different. How they could talk, and laugh, and then go back inside and tumble into bed, spending the six hours to Naxos very pleasantly occupied. But of course none of it was going to happen like that. He was a fool even to dream of it, to let himself want it for so much as a moment. He'd *never* let himself want that kind of life.

'Are you looking forward to returning to Naxos?' he asked.

'Yes.' She turned to give him a small smile, her eyes crinkling at the corners. 'I really am.'

Alex watched her, noticing the glint of gold in her eyes, the dimple in her right cheek. For a second she looked happy, and it made him realise how worried and withdrawn she'd been before. It also made him realise that he liked seeing her happy, and the possibility that he might be able to be the person who made her so, even just for a brief moment, felt intoxicating. Impossible.

She was smiling because she was returning to Naxos, to the place she felt was home. It had nothing to do with him. It never would.

'Our drinks are here,' he said, and walked back inside.

CHAPTER SIX

MILLY STOOD AT the railing, watching as the smudge of grey-green came closer. Naxos. *Home.* She'd spent the six hours of their journey exploring the superyacht, prowling about its empty, opulent rooms feeling both anxious and dissatisfied. Alex had locked himself in his study as soon as they'd finished their drinks, claiming he had to work. Milly had a feeling he would be doing that a lot, and she told herself it was better that way. Better not to complicate things with anything so arbitrary as emotion.

That was what she'd agreed to. That was what she'd expected.

She breathed in the sultry, salty air, her heart lightening just a little as she imagined being back at the villa, among its familiar, comfortable rooms. *Safe.* And soon Anna would be too, God willing. Milly hoped Carlos would see reason and let her stepsister visit her on occasion, maybe even every holiday...

The thought of having Anna with her sent a smile spreading across her face and happiness blooming inside her chest. It would all be worth it then. The wedding, *the wedding night...*

Milly's heart juddered in her chest at the thought. She could not picture their wedding night beyond some hazy montage, like something out of a film, all soft focus and swelling violins. Of course, it couldn't exactly be romantic, and she would be a fool to expect or even want that. But would Alex become tender, once they were alone and intimate?

She had so little experience, and he knew that, thanks to the medical report. Would he be patient? Gentle? She hated the thought of being so vulnerable and exposed with a man who viewed that part of marriage in as businesslike a way as any other, and yet she feared that was exactly how it would play out…despite the way her heart somersaulted in her chest when she imagined him touching her. Kissing her…

Her whole body felt heated and she lifted her face to the sea breeze, willing the cool air to fade the telling flush from her cheeks. Never mind the wedding night, what about the wedding? She didn't even have a wedding dress, or a bouquet, or a veil. She had never been the kind of little girl to daydream of wedding dresses and fairy tales, but there were a few basics she thought she would have liked to have on the day, no matter how it had come about.

Now she told herself not to mind. She wasn't having that kind of wedding, that kind of marriage. It was still worth it, for Anna's sake. It had to be.

From behind her she heard the sliding door open and then Alex stepped out; his very presence sent a shiver skittering along her skin, a visceral reaction she could not suppress but hoped he didn't notice.

'We're almost there.'

'Do you moor the yacht at the villa?'

'Yes, have you never been down to the dock?'

'No, I haven't. I've seen it, but I've never had any reason to go down there.' Alex's island property encompassed over fifty acres. Milly had stayed in the villa and gardens mainly, with a few walks among the scrubby brush and olive groves that surrounded the place, but she hadn't ventured to the dock, which had been empty while Alex's yacht was moored in Piraeus.

'I'll give you a full tour, later,' he said, and she turned to him with a surprised smile.

'Will you?' She was pleased by the thought, but when she looked at Alex, he looked as if he regretted extending the invitation.

They were drawing closer to the dock, the villa rising above it on its clifftop, the dazzling white walls and blue-shuttered windows silhouetted against a lavender twilit sky, the sun a half-circle of burnt ember sinking behind the hills. Milly narrowed her eyes; someone was waiting on the dock.

'Who is that?' she asked, because she was always alone at the villa, save for Yiannis and his wife Marina, who came several times a week to do the gardening and maintenance around the place, and lived in Halki.

Alex didn't answer, and she glanced at him, wondering what was going on. His expression was suspiciously bland, as if he knew something but wasn't saying. 'Alex? Have you…have you hired another housekeeper?'

'Another housekeeper?' He looked surprised.

'I thought you might have…because…well, because…'

'Because you're going to be my wife?' he filled in. 'As it happens, I haven't hired someone else, but you can hardly continue in my employment, Milly, when you will be married to me.'

'I suppose not.' She saw the sense in it, but she liked her role at the villa.

'If you like, you can hire a housekeeper, when the time comes. You'll spend more time here than I will.'

'I'd rather just do it myself.'

He frowned, but then shrugged. 'Very well. It will be your choice.'

Which should have been a relief, but it also felt like a rejection. He didn't care what she did with her own time, in her own place; of course he didn't. She had to stop expecting something else, something deeper or kinder. She'd known what this was going in and she'd convinced herself she could live with it, even that it was what she wanted. Why was it so hard to accept? Why did some contrary part of her keep looking for more, even as she told herself she didn't want it?

'So who is that waiting on the dock?' she asked, and then her breath caught in her chest as they came close enough for her to glimpse the familiar dark blonde hair, the slender figure. 'It isn't...' But as the yacht drew closer to the shore, she knew it was. 'Anna,' she breathed, and then she shouted it, waving frantically. 'Anna... *Anna!*'

Tears sprang to Milly's eyes as her sister caught sight of her and started waving back just as frantically, jumping up and down in her excitement.

Milly turned to Alex, blinking back tears, overwhelmed with emotion. 'You did this,' she exclaimed as tears spilled over and she dashed at them. 'How...how on earth did you arrange it?'

He shrugged. 'Bentano can be a reasonable man when he has the right incentive.'

'But how...?'

Another shrug, the hint of a smile at the corner of his mouth that lightened Milly's heart even more. 'He's an ass, but he saw sense. Anna can stay here until she starts school in three weeks.'

'What...?' Milly breathed the word, hardly able to believe she had Anna for three whole weeks, and, even more

poignantly, that Alex had thought to arrange it. *How* had he managed it? And when? 'I don't know what to say.'

'There's no need to say anything.'

'But there is. This was so kind of you, Alex. I wasn't expecting…' She paused, unsure how to continue. She hadn't been expecting him to do nice things for her. It seemed to go beyond their business arrangement, and yet he had, and without any hint or hope from her. It overwhelmed her. It humbled her. And treacherously, it gave her hope that their marriage could be something just a little bit more than the cold and clinical deal he had first suggested. Not much more, of course, because neither of them wanted that. But a *little*. 'When did you arrange it?' she asked. 'How was there time?'

'I spoke to Bentano this morning, and fortunately for him he saw sense almost immediately. She flew on my private jet, and she arrived in Naxos just before us. Yiannis picked her up at the airstrip.'

What had Alex said or done to induce Bentano to agree? Milly couldn't even imagine it, but she knew it must have been something big. And he'd done it for Anna…and for her. 'Thank you, Alex,' she said, her voice throbbing with sincerity.

And then, because that didn't feel like enough, Milly stepped closer to him and put her arms around him in what was meant to be a simple hug, but immediately felt like something she shouldn't have done.

Alex stiffened in shock, but not before their bodies collided, Milly's breasts against the hard wall of his chest, her legs pressed to his so she could feel the outline of every powerful muscle. Heat flared within her, a white-hot pulse of sensation that jolted through her entire body and made her take a stumbling step back, shocked by the intensity of her feeling. *Her desire.* It ignited everything inside her, so she felt as if she were burning up. Had Alex registered her response, and was horrified by it? The thought was mortifying.

As Alex watched her step back, his expression closed right up, like the snapping shut of a fan. Milly realised she was already used to it, that emotional distancing he seemed to accomplish effortlessly. Clearly she'd stepped across a major line. 'Alex…' she began, but she had no idea how to explain what she'd been feeling, at least not without embarrassing herself. Her body still pulsed with a molten heat she'd never felt before, not even with Philippe. And Alex didn't seem to want it from her now.

'Milly!' She turned to see Anna calling to her from just a few metres away as the yacht was moored at the dock. *'Milly!'*

'I'm coming,' she called, and when she turned back, Alex had disappeared.

As soon as Milly left the yacht, Alex still nowhere in sight, Anna practically jumped on her. Laughing, she hugged her sister, so grateful to be with her once again. It had been far too long.

'I've missed you so much,' Milly exclaimed as they both wiped away tears. 'So, so much.' It had been nearly a year since she'd last seen her sister. 'I think you've grown a couple of inches, Anna.' Her sister definitely looked a little older, and even more beautiful with her honey-blonde hair and bright blue eyes. There could be no more men stumbling into her bedroom, of that Milly was certain.

'I can't believe I'm here.' Anna looked both emotional and thrilled. 'This place is amazing, Milly. And you have so much to tell me. You're getting *married*? How come you didn't mention that on the phone, huh? That's pretty big news.'

'Ah. Well.' Milly smiled weakly. 'It's hard to explain…'

'What's there to explain? Your fiancé sounds *so* nice. He insisted on flying me in his private jet.' Her blue eyes rounded comically. 'It was *incredible*. There were staff who just kept feeding me. I had the biggest ice-cream sundae I've ever seen.'

'Wow.' Milly let out a shaky laugh; her emotions were all over the place, from that sudden, surprising hug with Alex, to that terribly awkward moment afterwards, and now her sister with her for three whole weeks. Plus she had to explain her imminent wedding to her, and the reason for it. It all felt like too much. Her head and heart both ached, and, strangely, she wished Alex were here, helping her through this moment, although would he even be much help? Or would he just tersely tell her to get on with things, with that stony look on his face?

'Why don't we head back to the villa?' she suggested, taking Anna's arm.

'Where's Alex? I want to meet him.' Anna craned her head, looking for Milly's fiancé, but he still wasn't anywhere to be seen. Milly suspected he'd absented himself on purpose, and would continue to do so, a prospect that gave her a little pang of sorrow as well as one of relief. It was easier this way, but it still felt lonely.

'I think he's working,' she improvised. 'He's very busy with everything at the moment.'

'He must be.' Anna dropped her voice to a theatrical whisper. 'Milly, he's *mega*-rich!'

'Yes, I know.' Milly let out another little laugh. Like her, Anna had grown up on the fringes of an aristocratic world yet with no money. Like Milly, Anna was used to second-rate schools and draughty, crumbling buildings; neglect and genteel poverty were the standards by which she'd been raised. Milly had had six months to get used to the luxury of the villa; Anna was seeing it all for the first time.

'So how did you meet?' Anna asked as they walked up the winding, rocky path towards the house. 'Was it love at first sight?'

Milly thought of Alex's curt proposal in his shadowy study, and didn't know whether to laugh or cry. How on earth could she explain the business deal she'd made to her starry-eyed fourteen-year-old sister? She almost wished Alex had told her about Anna's arrival, so she could have prepared what she'd say. How she'd explain.

'It's a long story,' she said as they stepped inside the villa, the thick stone walls providing a blessed coolness. 'Have you eaten? Let me get you something…'

'I'm stuffed from all the food on the plane.' Anna flung herself on one of the squashy sofas in the living area off the kitchen. 'This place really is amazing. So, long story. Start from the beginning, because I want to hear everything.'

'I don't know if I can.' Milly tried for a light laugh as she poured them both glasses of water, handing one to Anna before pressing her own glass to her hot cheek. Anna looked at her, her eyes narrowing.

'What are you not telling me?'

'I haven't even started yet,' Milly protested. 'I haven't told you anything, Anna, obviously.'

'You know what I mean.'

Of course she couldn't fool her sister. Anna was ten years younger, but far too wise for her years, and she and Milly had always had a connection, even when they hadn't seen each other. It was like an invisible wire, drawing them together, binding them tightly even when they'd been hundreds or thousands of miles apart.

'You do love him, don't you?' Anna asked uncertainly, and now she sounded far too young. Milly looked away. '*Milly.* Why are you marrying this man if you don't love him?'

'He's a good man, Anna.' At least she hoped he was. Only a good man would arrange for her sister to visit, surely? It felt like evidence, proof, but hardly enough to build her life on…which was exactly what she was doing. Because she had to.

'How long have you known him?'

'Six months.' Which was more or less true, even if she'd only seen him for the first time a handful of days ago. 'He's my employer,' Milly explained. 'This villa is where I've been living as housekeeper.'

'That sounds like it could be romantic.' Anna's forehead crinkled. 'Falling for the boss…*is* it?'

What should she do? Say? Milly hated the thought of lying to her sister, but the truth felt too unpalatable to share. She couldn't burden Anna with the knowledge that she'd done this for her sake. It wouldn't be fair. 'It is, a bit,' she finally said. 'At least, it could be. The…the truth is, Anna, we're marrying as a sort of…business arrangement.'

'Business?' Anna sounded horrified. 'But, Milly—'

'But amicable too,' she continued quickly. 'Alex needs a wife, for, um, work reasons, and so…' She couldn't find a way to finish that sentence.

'*So?*' Now Anna looked horrified, as well. 'But what do you need, Milly? What do you get out of this?' She leaned forward, her eyes huge and swimming with tears, her expression beseeching. 'Please, *please* don't tell me you did this for my sake. For money. I couldn't bear it if you did.'

Milly stared at her helplessly and then did the only thing she felt she possibly could. She lied.

Today was his wedding day. Alex gazed at his reflection, wondering if anyone had heard he was on the island, that he was getting married. Would any of the villagers who had known him and Daphne be waiting at the remote chapel where the wedding was to take place? What would they think of his ravaged face, his presence here?

He'd avoided Naxos since the fire, unable to bear the place where he'd once been so happy, and when he had come here only a few of his staff had seen him. They were tight-lipped and loyal, and so no one from his past here knew what had happened to him. All they knew, he realised with a tightening in his gut, was that their darling Daphne had died. Daphne and Talos. And they would blame him, because it was his fault.

How would they react when they saw him? Would they sneer? Hiss? Spit? He wouldn't blame them for any of it. Nothing one of the villagers could say could be worse than what he'd said in his own mind. What he lived with every day. Two of the people he'd loved the most had died, and it was his fault entirely. The scars he bore were remarkably little punishment, considering.

And it seemed fitting, and somehow just, to walk among the people who had loved Daphne, to let them see his shame. To feel their hate…even on his wedding day. But perhaps no one would come to the chapel where they were to be married, a short distance from Halki. Perhaps the gossip hadn't spread of his marriage; perhaps they didn't care.

Squaring his shoulders, Alex turned away from the mirror.

He'd avoided Milly and Anna since their arrival yesterday, closeting himself in his study and missing meals. His fiancée and her sister would want some alone time, and he had no desire for Anna to flinch from his scars along with his bride-to-be.

Then yesterday evening Milly had slipped into his study and asked him to at least meet her sister before their wedding day. He'd said yes, because he realised it would be better for Anna to see his scars now and not in the church. But when he'd made an appearance on the terrace that evening, the setting sun turning the sea to a shimmering plate of gold, Anna greeted him without a flicker or quiver. Clearly Milly had prepared her for what he looked like, and he didn't know how to feel about that.

Upon examination, he realised he felt an irritating mixture of gratitude and hurt, which didn't make any sense. It was the same kind of ferment of emotion he'd experienced when Milly had hugged him and then stepped away so quickly—desire and disgust, hope and disappointment. He couldn't blame her for her reaction, and yet it still nagged at him, like a paper cut that wouldn't heal.

After trying to feel numb for so long, it all felt like too much. He didn't understand why he was responding to everything, why the simplest smile or gesture made him feel scraped raw. It wasn't supposed to be this way; he wanted, he *needed* to stay in control. Instead he felt edgy and irritable.

Even now he could remember the soft and pliant warmth of her body pressed against his for a few torturous seconds and his body ached with memory and desire. She'd jumped away from him as if she'd been scalded—or repulsed.

Well, tonight they would be closer still, but he would do his best to make it as brief as possible. That was the least he could do for his bride…perhaps the only thing.

Alex strode outside the villa, the bright summer sun hitting him in the face with a blast of unforgiving heat. Yiannis, acting as his driver, gave him a smile in the rear-view mirror as Alex climbed into the back of the car.

'You are ready, Kyrie Santos?'

'Yes. As ready as I'll ever be.'

'She is a good person, I think,' Yiannis ventured. Yiannis had been with Alex for over a decade; he'd been there at the fire, had helped to drag him out. He was one of the few people Alex trusted implicitly, and he knew Milly better than Alex knew her himself.

'Yes,' Alex answered tersely as he thought of Milly, her shy smile, those pansy-brown eyes. 'I think she is.' Unlike him.

They did not speak again as Yiannis drove him the few kilometres to Saint Panormitis, the tiny little red-roofed chapel set among the rocky hills outside Halki, the barren sweep of land meeting the bright blue horizon.

It was a lonely place, yet no less beautiful for it, the chapel huddled among the scrub and brush, its whitewashed walls dazzling under the azure sky. No one was waiting outside save the priest and the witnesses, two of Alex's staff in addition to Yiannis. He glanced around for Milly, but he couldn't see her anywhere, and with a lurch of panic he wondered if she hadn't turned up. What if she'd backed out at the last moment? He wouldn't even blame her, not really. Five million euros wasn't nearly the good deal she thought it was.

Yiannis touched his elbow. 'Miss James has gone into Halki,' he said quietly. 'For flowers.'

Relief pulsed through Alex even as he realised he hadn't considered any of the usual details involved in a wedding—flowers or a dress or the traditional party afterwards. Did Milly want those things? Should he have put some consideration into their business arrangement?

No, of course he shouldn't have. Realisation jolted through him, strangely unwelcome. Of course they wouldn't have those things. Why dress up what it was they had, put the plain truth in frills and lace? Milly had told him she was wary of love, cynical of romance, and he was the same. There was no need to pretend otherwise now, simply because they were making vows.

And then he turned and saw her. His heart seemed to stop in his chest as she crested the hill, her hair blowing loosely about her shoulders, a bouquet of tiny white star-like flowers and trailing ivy clasped in her hands. She wore a dress of ivory silk, the cut simple and lovely, with cap sleeves and an empire waist, the lace-edged hem brushing her ankles. Anna walked a little bit behind her, looking youthful and pretty in a pink sundress, and grinning with such obvious happiness that Alex felt jolted.

This almost felt like a *real* wedding. Which, of course, it was. And yet…he felt wrong-footed, *wrong-hearted*, as Milly walked towards him, a smile like a promise on her face, in her eyes. She was looking at him as if she *felt* something. She held out one slender hand, the other holding her bouquet.

'Shall we walk in together?'

Alex stared at her helplessly, so surprised by this moment, by her and even by himself. It felt far too important, as well as too sweet. The cold business deal he'd imagined was morphing into something else entirely, a couple on a hill, holding hands and making promises.

Anna, he saw, was still beaming at them as if she thought they were truly a man and woman in love. And for a single, blazing second, Alex could almost imagine that they were. That this was simple. 'All right,' he said, and he tucked Milly's hand into his, liking the feel of it there, snug and warm and safe.

Then together they walked into the little church.

CHAPTER SEVEN

SHE WAS MARRIED. Milly hadn't actually spoken any vows or made any promises, but the Orthodox priest had spoken for them, and they'd exchange crowns of laurel and shared a common cup, traditions in the church that Milly didn't completely understand but still seemed sacred.

She knew what they'd done was binding. She'd felt it in her soul, as if she'd just jumped off a cliff and now was soaring in the sky, unsure whether she'd continue to fly or plummet to the earth like Icarus with his waxen wings. How had Alex felt about the ceremony? When she'd looked into his eyes as they'd drunk from the same cup, she hadn't been able to tell a thing.

He hadn't spoken throughout the ceremony, and nor had she, but before they'd walked into the church, he'd almost looked…well, it was hard to know how he'd looked, considering how closed he was generally, but for a second he'd seemed…*moved*. And that had filled her with a sudden, buoyant hope that she was afraid to examine too closely. She wasn't going to fall in love with him or anything stupid like that, just because he'd been a little bit nice to her. She was going to keep this businesslike, because that worked for them both.

And yet…that moment had given her pause. Made her wonder if this odd agreement could turn into something else, something more like friendship. She would never wish for more than that. She wouldn't let herself.

Now they walked out of the church in silence, blinking in the bright sunlight, a married couple, although Milly still had no idea what their marriage was going to look like. *Or their wedding night.* The thought made her heart flutter with both anticipation and alarm.

As she stepped outside, it was so bright that she was blinded for a moment, but then she heard applause, and, when she finally blinked the world into focus, she saw a scattering of villagers on the rocky hillside, about two dozen men and women, all of them clapping, their gazes trained on Alex, their expressions strangely sober. She glanced back at Alex, and saw he looked as startled as she did.

Yiannis, his driver, said something to Alex in Greek, but Milly couldn't make it out. She had no idea what was going on. Who were these people?

Then Alex spoke. *'Efharisto,'* he said, a word Milly knew. *Thank you.* But then he said something else that she didn't understand, and the villagers all started shaking their heads. Anna glanced at Milly in confusion, but she just shrugged. She had no idea what was happening, or who these people were. Did they know Alex simply because he had a villa on the island? It seemed deeper than that, their silent stares both compassionate and convicting, as well as weirdly intense.

'Come on,' Alex muttered. 'Let's get in the car.'

'What about all these people…?'

'They've got what they came for.'

She frowned. 'And what was that?'

'To see me.'

'See you…' She shook her head. 'But why were they clapping for you?'

'They were clapping for us. For our marriage.' But Milly hadn't quite got that feeling. They had been looking at Alex, not her. It had felt more personal than mere congratulations. But her husband clearly was not in the mood for answering questions, for he took her by the hand and led her towards the waiting car. She climbed in, and Alex followed, then Anna. In silence Yiannis drove them away.

'So congratulations,' Anna said brightly once they'd left the chapel, the car hurtling down the hill towards home. 'That was a beautiful service.' She beamed at Alex, who looked entirely nonplussed, as well he should. Anna was acting far too cheerful. 'I hope you're going to celebrate today.'

He slid Milly a guarded look. 'I hadn't thought of it.'

'Well, I have,' Anna announced. Surprise flickered across Alex's face and then was gone, replaced by a cold, closed look Milly already knew well.

'Have you?' he remarked in a neutral tone.

'Yes. It's not much, but you are married and I think you should celebrate.' She gave him a challenging look, which Alex met, and Milly wondered how to intervene. How to keep her sister from spinning fairy tales, and annoying her husband.

Yesterday, when Anna had asked her if she loved Alex, Milly had spun a tissue of lies about how she'd fallen in love with him as soon as she'd been hired, gazing at him from afar until he'd asked her to marry him for business reasons.

She'd told Anna she'd said yes to his proposal because she wanted to be with him so badly, and she hoped he'd return her feelings in time, as he got to know her. Anna had bought the whole silly story from first to last, her eyes starry as she'd exclaimed how romantic it all was, while Milly had felt more and more wretched for lying to her sister.

'He must have some feelings for you already, Milly,' Anna had exclaimed. 'Why else would he ask you, you and not some socialite, to marry him?'

'I was convenient.' Already Milly had seriously regretted spinning the stupid story, but how could she tell Anna the truth? Her sister would feel horribly guilty that she'd forced Milly into a loveless marriage, even if Milly had been the one to make the choice. And it was her choice. She wouldn't let herself regret it.

'Still. He *will* fall in love with you, Milly, in time. Head over heels.' Anna's eyes had sparkled. 'I'll make sure of it.'

'Anna…' Milly had started in warning, but her sister had been on a romantic roll, determined to make the day special when Milly knew it wasn't—and her husband-to-be didn't want it to be. That morning Anna had insisted on going into Halki so Milly could buy a wedding dress and flowers.

Amazingly in the tiny village they'd found a wonderful dress in a dark and narrow little shop, one that fitted Milly perfectly, and felt like fate. When he'd heard about the wedding, the local grocer had picked flowers from his garden and given them to her for free, kissing her on both cheeks as he'd wished her health and happiness.

Milly had been torn between getting caught up in others' excitement, and a growing sense of dread that Alex wasn't going to like any of these romantic details. In fact, he'd probably hate them.

He'd seemed dangerously nonplussed by Anna's breathy sighs and approving smiles during the short ceremony, her sister clearly imagining a fairy tale where there so glaringly was none.

Now the truth of their marriage was being revealed, as

Alex stalked towards his study. He'd already plucked the laurel crown from his head and tossed it aside carelessly as Milly watched him, trying not to feel hurt even though she knew she'd save her crown, as well as her bouquet. No matter how businesslike their arrangement, it was still a wedding, and most likely the only one she'd ever have.

Alex disappeared into his study, closing the door behind him with a final click. So much for their celebrations. Anna gave her a sympathetic look, which only made her feel guilty.

'I think I should change,' she said as brightly as she could. 'And then we'll have something to eat.'

'But you've barely worn your wedding dress,' Anna protested. 'And you can't be acting as housekeeper on your wedding day of all days.'

'And who else will?' Milly answered with an attempt at a laugh. This felt like the least celebratory wedding day ever.

'I will,' Anna returned with spirit. 'You can't cook and clean today, Milly. I told you, we're having a celebration.'

'Anna, it's really not that kind of marriage,' Milly protested. 'Not yet,' she added, hating herself for continuing with the lie that she was madly in love with her boss—*and now her husband*. A tremor ran through her at the thought. What if Alex found out about the tale she'd been spinning? What if he believed it, and was horrified?

Anna's lower lip jutted out as she folded her arms. 'And what about tonight, Milly? Your honeymoon—'

'*Anna.*' Milly couldn't keep from blushing. The last thing she wanted to do was talk about *that* with her sister, or with anyone. She couldn't even *think* about tonight. Not yet.

'I'm *fourteen*, Milly,' Anna chided. 'And you're married. It needs to be special.'

'I really don't want to talk about this—'

'Fine. We won't.' Anna shooed her away. 'Go get changed. I'll take care of everything.'

'What?' Milly practically spluttered. She could not begin to imagine what Anna was thinking of doing, or what Alex's reaction would be. 'Anna, seriously, let's just relax, okay? There really doesn't need to be any fuss. Alex won't want there to be…'

'Don't worry,' Anna answered, half pushing her towards the stairs. 'You won't have to do a thing. I've got it all under control.'

Which worried her all the more. With mounting unease, Milly went upstairs to change. She took off her wedding dress slowly, her eyes on her reflection, noting the sorrow that had crept into them, casting shadows.

For a brief, painful moment, she imagined how different this day might have been. They'd have returned to the villa for a party, food and wine, laughter and dancing out on the terrace, until the sun set over the sea and Alex took her by the hand and led her back to the house, up to the bedroom.

He'd turn to her, his bright blue eyes turning sleepy and hooded as he tugged the zip down the back of her dress and the silky material fell away. Then he'd reach for her, and his lips would brush hers…

Goodness. Milly let out a shuddering breath as the effects of that image trickled through her like heated honey, making something both lazy and urgent unfurl deep inside. Such a different scenario had been all too easy to imagine, and yet she knew, she absolutely knew, it wasn't going to happen like that. She didn't even want it to happen like that. She'd told Alex the truth when she'd said she was wary of romance, cynical of love. Now that she was married, she most certainly could not go building castles in the air.

With a sigh, she turned away from her reflection, trying to banish the last remnants of that warm, sensuous feeling, and finished getting dressed. She needed to get back downstairs before her sister started festooning the villa with paper hearts and hiring someone to play the violin. Milly wouldn't put anything past her at this stage.

When Milly came downstairs, she saw that Anna had been busy getting things ready, although thankfully without any cringeworthy decorations or serenading violins. A table for two was set outside on the terrace, with the finest linens and crystal from the villa's cupboards. Yiannis must have been in on the plan because there was fresh food that had been brought from Halki—a mouth-watering Greek salad, crispy souvlaki and fresh pitta bread with several yogurt-based dips. Milly gazed at it in a mix of hope and apprehension; would Alex object to them sharing a meal together? She had no idea.

'This looks amazing,' she told Anna, grateful at least that her sister had only planned a meal, and not something more obviously romantic. 'But you should join us, Anna, and Yiannis, too. It is a celebration, after all—'

'Absolutely not,' Anna returned firmly. 'This is for the two of you. You need to get to know each other,' she added meaningfully, and Milly briefly closed her eyes. Alex would eventually twig to Anna's obvious attempts at creating romance, and then what would she say? He would no doubt be coldly scornful of such attempts, and Milly didn't think she could bear his contempt.

Yes, Anna was being young and sentimental, but she was a teenager and she'd had so little love in her life. Milly couldn't bear not to go along with it, even if the thought of Alex's reaction made her stomach cramp.

Anna ran to fetch Alex, and he strolled out onto the terrace with a bland look on his face, taking the table for two in his stride, although he didn't look particularly pleased about it. Anna had, of course, disappeared.

'I'm sorry about my sister,' Milly began awkwardly when they were both seated. 'She means well, really...'

'At least she's pleased,' he replied shortly.

'Yes...'

'She reminds me of my sister, how she used to be,' Alex said, then looked away, clearly wishing he hadn't shared so much.

'Your sister?' Milly searched his face, startled by this admission, just about the last thing she'd expected in this moment. 'I thought you only had your stepbrother, Ezio.'

Alex's mouth compressed. 'I do. Daphne died some time ago.' He began to dish out some salad on both of their plates, clearly unwilling to say anything more on that painful subject.

'I'm sorry,' Milly said quietly. 'That must have been very hard.'

'It was.' The two words were clipped, a hint of a warning in them. *Don't push it, Milly*, she told herself. At least Alex had offered something personal, even if he hadn't quite meant to. The door had cracked open just a little, and every so often she would push it a little further open. With time and patience, she might get to know him.

And is that all you want from your husband?

Milly chose not to pay attention to that mocking little voice. She wouldn't even know how to begin to answer that question.

Alex gazed out at the tranquil sea, the sun blazing down, and then turned back to the woman seated across from him. *His wife.* Milly had changed from her lovely wedding dress to a simple sundress in pale green, the skinny straps showing off her shoulders. She did have freckles there. Alex found his gaze skimming to them again and again, the dusting of gold urging him to press his lips to each one. Something, of course, he had no intention of actually doing. No doubt Milly would be horrified if he did.

It had been well-meaning of Anna to dress up their day a bit, although Alex could tell Milly was uncomfortable with it, something that irritated him even though he knew the reaction was unreasonable. Hell, he was uncomfortable, too. It was just a meal, but it wasn't what they'd agreed to. Nothing about this day felt the way he'd expected it to.

He'd viewed the ceremony as nothing more than a hurdle to get over, a hoop to jump through, and yet the words the priest had spoken had oddly moved him, as had the ancient rituals he and Milly had participated in—crowned with laurel, their eyes meeting over the common cup as they drank... He'd known marriage was binding, but he'd seen it as nothing more than a legal contract.

The ceremony in the tiny church had made him realise it was something sacred, and the thought humbled him. Scared him a little, too. What if he couldn't protect Milly? *What if he hurt her?*

'Alex?' Her voice, as well as the light touch of her fingers on his, startled him out of his dark thoughts. 'You suddenly started frowning rather ferociously.' Her lips trembled as she tried to smile. 'Is...is everything all right?'

'It's fine.' Alex forced a quick, tight smile to his lips, feeling his scar pull across his cheek, reminding him yet again of the limitations of their life together. The limitations Milly wanted as well as him. 'My mind was elsewhere. I'm sorry.'

'It's okay.' Her forehead was crinkled in concern, her gaze scanning his face. He looked away, angling his face so his scars were less visible. Even now, *especially* now, he didn't want her to see him like this.

'Well, I'm glad Anna isn't scaring you off,' Milly said with a light laugh. 'She's so excited about everything… and I think she's read too many romance novels.'

'She thinks our marriage is romantic?' Alex turned back to her, arching an eyebrow. 'Have you told her the truth?'

'Well…' He watched with dispassionate curiosity as Milly's face coloured. 'Sort of. She's…' She swallowed, and his gaze was drawn to the sinuous movement of her throat. 'She's hoping we fall desperately in love.'

He schooled his face into a bland expression even as her words blazed inside him, igniting what…? Hope? Horror? It was, of course, an impossibility. 'I hope you disabused her of that notion,' he remarked coolly.

'Of course I did.' The words came with such vehemence that Alex had to look away. He was an idiot to think for a moment that Milly might have been thinking or wanting something else—something he had no desire for, in any case.

'Right. That's settled, then.'

'Yes, I suppose it is.' Milly stared down at her plate, and Alex watched her, wondering what was going on in her head. Was she relieved? Or was she already regretting their impetuous marriage, realising the price she'd paid was too high? Tonight loomed in front of them, heavy with expectation.

He knew he shouldn't care about her feelings, and she certainly didn't care about his. And yet the ceremony circled in his head—the words of the priest, the common cup, their hands joined in a lover's knot of fingers. It had meant something, at least to him. Far more than he'd ever intended it to.

'All right, you two!' Anna called out gaily as she came

out on the terrace, brandishing a platter that held what looked alarmingly like a traditional wedding cake.

'Anna…' Milly half rose from her chair, her flush starting all over again, her eyes wide with dismay. 'Where did you get that…?'

'Halki is amazingly well supplied,' Anna answered blithely. 'And Yiannis helped me. It's been such fun.' She placed the platter with the cake on the table between them with a flourish. 'It's traditional wedding cake, with honey, sesame seed, and quince.' She made a face and Milly managed a little laugh although she still looked uneasy. 'I'd rather have chocolate.'

'How on earth did you get a wedding cake on such short notice?' Milly said. She slid Alex an apologetic glance, which he ignored. A cake wasn't going to make a difference to anything.

'The bakery had one in the window,' Yiannis supplied. 'It seemed ordained.'

Ordained. Fated. Words of romance rather than business. Yiannis was as much of a sentimental fool as Anna, both of them wanting to turn today into a fairy tale. It wasn't going to happen. The only fairy tale in which Alex had a role was *Beauty and the Beast*, and with him it wouldn't have a happy ending.

Still, for the sake of form, he managed a small, tight smile. 'You are both too kind,' he said, and he gave Yiannis a repressive look over the top of Anna's head. *Enough.* His driver gave a short nod.

'Cut the cake,' Anna instructed. 'Both of you at the same time. For good luck.'

'Is that a thing?' Milly said, narrowing her eyes in suspicion, and Anna just shrugged, innocence personified.

'Fine.' Alex rose, reaching for the knife Anna had brought along with the cake. He glanced at Milly, and then motioned to the knife. Hesitantly she took it, and then he wrapped his hand around hers, just as he had when they'd walked into church.

Together they cut into the cake, the knife sinking through the soft icing and sponge underneath, her hand slight and warm under his. As soon as they'd finished, Anna and Yiannis both clapped, and Milly yanked her hand away, and Alex stepped back.

'I have work to do,' he announced, watching Anna's eyes round with dismay. His wife, he noticed, looked relieved. Without another word he strode from the terrace. Milly had a short reprieve, he acknowledged grimly; they still had their wedding night to get through.

CHAPTER EIGHT

NIGHT HAD FALLEN. Milly stared out at the darkening sky, her belly a flutter of nerves. After Alex had retreated to his study Anna had insisted Milly have an at-home spa day, running her a bubble bath and doing her nails.

Considering she'd just had a host of treatments two days ago in Athens, Milly had hardly seen the need, but she hadn't wanted to disappoint Anna. She loved being with her, and, in any case, she'd needed a distraction as the wedding night had loomed closer.

As the sun had begun to set, Anna had announced that she was staying the night with Yiannis and his wife in the village, making Milly protest.

'Anna, you don't…'

'It's your *wedding* night, Milly. The last thing you need is a little sister in your space.' Anna had made a face. 'And truthfully, I kind of don't want to be here, you know?'

'It's not…' Milly had decided not to finish that sentence, mostly because she hadn't known how, and Anna had patted her shoulder.

'I'll be fine. I've been having so much fun these last two days, Milly, you have no idea.' Tears had filled her eyes and she'd blinked them away as she'd offered her a heartbreaking smile. 'Honestly, I feel like I have a life suddenly, instead of hiding away, just waiting for things to happen.'

'I'm glad you're here, Anna.' Milly had pulled her sister into a tight hug. 'Really glad.'

Anna had hugged her back before easing away with a bright smile. 'But I'm not going to be here tonight. So have *fun*.'

Fun didn't seem the right word, Milly thought as she paced the living room alone, dressed in a simple navy shift dress, yet another one of her outfits from those brought to her at the hotel.

She felt as if she were crackling with nervous energy, about to combust. *Where was Alex?* She hadn't seen him in hours, and yet she had no idea what she would say when she did see him. What she would do. And more importantly, more alarmingly and, yes, excitingly, what *he* would do.

Her mind blanked every time she started to think about it, even as her nerve-endings became hyper-aware and her heart began to thud, and that molten-honey feeling trickled through her, igniting aches she'd never felt before.

'Good evening, Milly.'

She whirled around to see Alex standing in the doorway, dressed in a white button-down shirt open at the throat and dark trousers. His hair was spiky and damp from a recent shower, his lean jaw freshly shaven. As always he angled his face so she couldn't see his scarred side, but, regardless, he was devastatingly handsome, and she felt herself go weak at the knees, swaying a little at the sight of him.

'H-hello.' Her voice came out breathy with nerves and inside her black flats her toes curled. Scars or no, he was so beautiful, and she was so plain. Did he desire her at all? She could tell nothing from his carefully bland expression. 'Anna has gone with Yiannis and his wife for the night,' she blurted, willing herself not to flush. 'To give us some privacy.'

'So Yiannis told me. That was very considerate of them.'

'Have you known Yiannis long?'

'Since I was a child.'

'You have roots here,' Milly observed. 'Yiannis, the villagers...'

'Yes.' He glanced away. 'We came here, as a family, when I was young. Holidays every summer, some of the happiest memories I possess.'

'And the villa...?'

'I've had it for ten years. Now come.' He spoke flatly as he held out one hand and Milly stared at him, trying not to tremble. This step felt as momentous as the one she'd taken before, into the church. There would be no going back.

His eyebrow lifted as he remained with his hand outstretched. 'Are you scared?' he asked, a hint of gentleness in his voice.

'A little,' she confessed.

His mouth tightened and he nodded. 'I will do my best to make this as quick and painless as possible.'

Which made it sound as if she was about to endure some awful medical procedure, and she hardly wanted *that*. Everything inside Milly shook.

'That's kind of you,' she said, because she was overcome with nerves and she didn't know what to say. She could hardly ask him to make love to her, could she? To kiss and touch her like the hazy images that kept flitting through her head and making her dizzy with desire?

Just the thought of admitting how she felt, opening herself up to such vulnerability, made her tremble in a whole other way. She couldn't do that. Now, more than ever, was a time to protect herself.

Alex's mouth twisted, tightening his scar. 'It's the least I can do, Milly. I'm sorry...' He paused, then shook his head. 'Never mind. This is the way it is.' He reached for her hand, his fingers sliding over hers and then tightening imperceptibly, drawing her to him. Milly's heart thudded in her chest.

They hadn't even *kissed*. They'd barely touched. And yet very soon they would be committing the most intimate act a man and woman could together, an act that would unite them for ever. She was terrified, and yet within that fear was a lick of excitement, an ember of need waiting only to be fanned into flame, if Alex would just show her some modicum of tenderness, of desire...

She knew she was attracted to Alex on a basic, physical level. Her body responded to his; even the expensive, woodsy scent of him enflamed her senses, stoking that ember. Yet Alex seemed completely unaffected by her as he led her away from the living room, up the stairs, towards his bedroom, striding along like a man intent on getting the job done.

But why should he desire her? In her head she heard Philippe's mocking voice. *'How could I want someone like you?'* And she tried to drown it out. She didn't want to think about Philippe now of all moments.

Alex opened the door to his bedroom and then sucked in a surprised breath. 'What...?'

Milly peered inside, her eyes widening as she caught sight of the creamy candles flickering on various surfaces, a bottle of champagne chilling in a silver bucket by the bed.

'I'm so sorry,' she mumbled, heat flooding her face as she thought of how this would look to Alex. 'This is Anna's work. Obviously.'

'Obviously?' he queried sardonically, and her blush intensified.

'I wouldn't do something like this.' Heaven forbid he think she was trying to make the mood romantic.

'Of course you wouldn't.' She couldn't gauge his tone as he strode into the room and began to snuff out the candles with the tips of his fingers, causing a sizzling sound with each one.

'Can't…can't you leave at least one?'

'I prefer the dark.'

'Please…just one. I don't want to trip over my own feet.'

He hesitated, his fingers hovering over the last candle. The air was full of the scent of acrid smoke. 'Fine,' he said shortly, and turned away. The room was lost in shadow now, the single candle barely piercing the darkness, the shutters closed against the starlit sky.

Milly stared at him through the gloom, her heart still thumping. 'What now?'

'What now indeed?' He let out a hard little laugh. 'Why don't we have a glass of champagne?' Alex reached for the bottle and popped the cork with quick efficiency; there was, Milly thought, nothing remotely celebratory about the sound. He poured a flute full and thrust it to her. 'This will help.'

'Help?' She took the flute and sipped at the crisp bubbles. 'You make it sound like medicine.'

'An anaesthetic, perhaps,' he drawled before draining his own glass.

'For what? Some *procedure*?' Her voice trembled. 'Is that how you see this?' She gestured to the empty bed, neatly made up and heaped with pillows.

'Don't you?' Alex challenged, his eyes piercing through the darkness.

'I… I don't know,' she admitted. She felt bound by her own fear. She wasn't brave enough to admit she wanted more, that she *felt* something for him, not when he was seeming so forbidding. 'Surely it's meant to be somewhat pleasurable.' She let out an uncertain laugh. 'You know more than I would, Alex.'

'It's been a long time since I've had that kind of pleasurable experience,' he told her sardonically, then he sighed. 'I'm only trying to make this easier for you, Milly.' He nodded towards her glass. 'Drink up.'

She did, gulping the champagne far too fast so her head started spinning even more. She'd never had much tolerance for alcohol, and she felt it now, her stomach seething both from the champagne and nerves. She watched, her eyes widening, as Alex began to unbutton his shirt.

'What…what are you doing?' she practically yelped.

'Undressing. The marital act requires a certain amount of disrobing.' His mouth twisted in something like a smile. 'Are you shocked?'

'Surprised,' she corrected, her gaze drawn to the sculpted muscles of his chest as he undid the buttons of his shirt with the same brisk efficiency with which he'd opened the champagne. He was beautifully proportioned, the candlelight burnishing his impressive physique in gold.

'Let's get this over with as quickly as possible, shall we?' he remarked. 'The sooner you become pregnant, the better it will be for both of us.'

She stared at him in dismay, her mind swirling from both his words and the champagne she'd just guzzled on an empty stomach. His hands went to his belt buckle and Milly couldn't keep from making a little sound of—something. She didn't even know what she felt. Her body responded to his, but her mind and heart were both in active rebellion. This had to be the most unromantic wedding night she could have ever conceived of…and yet that was why she was here, wasn't it? To conceive.

Alex nodded to her simple navy-blue shift dress. 'Do you need help with the zip?'

'No.' The word came out more vehement than she intended. She'd known Alex was businesslike, even cold, but she realised now she'd still hoped for some tenderness on their wedding night, some tiny hint of romance or affection. Instead he seemed more clinical than ever.

She turned away from him, fumbling with the zip. Maybe he was right, and they should just get this over with. Clearly he didn't respond to her the way she did to him, and that should be no surprise. She was plain; she knew that. She'd always known that. If he desired her at all, he surely would have handled this whole evening differently.

And, oh, she wished he had. Tears sprang to her eyes and she blinked them back furiously. *You agreed to this*, she reminded herself silently. *None of this should come as a surprise. This was part of the bargain.*

The zip snagged halfway down her back and she nearly wrenched her arm trying to pull it down further, letting out a little cry of frustration and despair as it continued to stick.

'Here.' Suddenly Alex was next to her, moving swiftly in the dark. She felt the heat of his bare chest, the brush of his arm, and she sucked in a breath as he gently removed her hand from the zipper and then slowly pulled it down himself. She sucked in a hard breath, her whole body hyper-aware as his fingers traced her spine, his breath fanning her neck, the moment spinning into something both taut and tender.

Heat bloomed inside her, unfurling like a precious flower, seeking sunlight. She swayed and he rested his hands on her shoulders; for a heart-stopping second his lips skimmed the nape of her neck and Milly couldn't keep from making a little mewl of desire. He stilled and she started to lean into him, longing for him to slide his hands from her shoulders to—where? *Anywhere.* She just wanted to be touched.

'*Milly...*' His voice was an ache, and it made unexpected tears sting her eyes. He pressed his lips against her neck again, this time in the curve of her shoulder, and she shuddered, arching her neck so he could have greater access.

For a second it seemed as if anything, everything were possible; as if a whole world of experience and emotion shimmered before them. His hands tightened on her shoulders and his lips moved on her skin. A shiver of longing rippled through her.

Then, all of a sudden, Alex lifted his head, dropped his hands, and stepped away. Milly half turned to him, conscious of her dress pooling about her waist, the longing that had rippled through her still licking at her senses.

'Alex…?'

'We should get this over with.' Alex walked towards the bed, slipping off his trousers while she watched uncertainly. Why had the mood changed, plunged suddenly from sweetness to sensibility, or something worse? Cold, clinical business. Again.

'Alex…' She stopped, because she had no idea what she would say. *'Please touch me?' 'Can't tonight be different?'* She couldn't make herself say the words. Despite the desire coursing through her, she still wasn't brave enough to risk what she felt.

'Come on,' he said, and nodded towards the bed.

Wordlessly Milly slipped out of her dress and underwear, not knowing what else to do, walked silently to the bed and lay down, longing only for him to touch her again the way he had before. Surely he would…? Why *wouldn't* he? She looked up at him appealingly, excitement stirring once more inside her just at the sight of him—his blazing blue eyes, his midnight-dark hair, his bronzed chest. She trembled with excitement as she licked her lips and whispered, 'I'm ready.'

Frustration bit deep as Alex stared at Milly lying on the bed like some virgin sacrifice, looking as if she had to brace herself for what lay ahead. She was actually *trembling*.

In any case, he supposed that was what she was—there could be no pretending she wanted to be here, that she was looking forward to being touched by him. She'd made her feelings plain enough, the way she'd gulped the champagne and insisted on unzipping her dress by herself.

For a moment, when he hadn't been able to resist touching her, he'd thought things might change. Then she'd shuddered and he'd realised what an utter fool he was making of himself. *And even if he wasn't*…even if she felt some small flicker of something…he couldn't risk it. He couldn't bear to be wrong. To be pitied…and by his wife.

Taking a short, sharp breath, his face angled away from her, he removed his boxers. Then he walked towards the bed and stretched out next to her, noticing the way she trembled even though he hadn't touched her yet.

She was tense as a bow, her toes pointed, her whole body rigid with expectation. Even so, she was lovely, her skin pale and golden, her body lithe and slender, her high, small breasts, small waist, and shapely legs all perfectly proportioned.

He ached to touch her, to explore every part of her body with his hands and mouth, and to have her do the same to him. Learning each other's bodies like living maps…but of course that was a nonsense. She didn't want to so much as *touch* him, much less explore.

Still Alex couldn't bring himself to climb on top of

her like some rutting stag. Gently he placed his hand on her hip, her skin cool and silky beneath his palm. She let out a shuddering breath. He slid his hand from her hip to her breast, unable to keep himself from the caress, longing for more.

Her breast filled his palm perfectly and he ran his thumb over the taut peak. Another shuddering breath and she bit her lip. Shame roiled in his stomach; clearly this was no more than an endurance test.

Alex removed his hand, his body already pulsing with need. It had been a long time since he'd been with a woman, and he knew it wouldn't take much to put him over the edge. Perhaps the kindest thing for him to do was, as he'd said before, simply to get it over with.

He rolled on top of her, bracing himself above on his forearms. Her eyes were still closed, her teeth sunk so deep into her lower lip she'd drawn blood. Self-hatred burned white and hot inside him. Was this really what it had come to? A woman who couldn't even look at him, who was tensing herself for his touch? Why had he ever thought marriage could be a good idea? Could *work*?

Her eyes fluttered open, her dazed gaze fixed on his face. 'Aren't you going to…?' she began, and Alex, hating himself even more, gave a terse nod.

'Yes.' He positioned himself at her entrance, nudging her thighs apart with his knee but they were rigid and unmoving. 'Milly, you have to relax at least a little bit,' he gritted. 'Otherwise…'

'I'm sorry.' Her voice was small, making him ache in an entirely different and more painful way. 'I just…' She took a hitching breath, making his guilt pierce even more deeply. 'I thought…' She stopped, and then she spread her thighs, inhaling sharply as he began to move inside her.

'Did I hurt you?' he asked in a low voice. He had barely *begun*.

'Not…not exactly…' She put her hands on his shoulders, clasping him to her, and even though he knew she was just bracing herself, the touch reached deep inside him. He couldn't remember the last time a woman had touched him, skin on skin, an intimacy he'd forgotten existed. It enflamed him even more, even as the shame of how he must be hurting her bit deeply.

He gritted his teeth as he slid slowly inside her, inch by precious inch, filling her tight warmth, pleasure flooding his senses as he sheathed himself fully. Her fingernails dug into his shoulders, her eyes clenched shut once more, her body still so very tense.

'Milly, relax.'

'I'm trying,' she gasped out with a nervous laugh that almost, improbably, made him smile. 'This is…very strange.'

'I know.' It was strange for him too, in an entirely different way. In the past, when he'd been with a woman, he'd been focused on her pleasure. It had been a source of both honour and pride, and yet this…

This was the opposite. Yet he couldn't imagine it happening any differently. Slowly Alex began to move, sweat beading his brow as he sought to make her as comfortable as possible, even though everything in him ached to find a faster and deeper rhythm.

After a few seconds, she began to match him, her hips moving jerkily. When Alex looked down at her, he saw how her face was screwed up, a drop of blood on her lip from where she'd bitten it. His vision was blurred at the edges, his mind dissolving as he came close to the peak.

'Alex…' Her voice was a plea, although for what he didn't know. Could it possibly be pleasure—could she be feeling even a little of what he was? At that thought, he came in an intoxicating rush, his body spending itself inside her, the pleasure crashing through him in intense waves.

They lay entangled for a few heart-thudding moments until Milly started to squirm beneath him.

'I'm sorry,' she said, her voice muffled. 'But I think I'm going to be sick.'

CHAPTER NINE

ALEX ROLLED OFF her in a lightning-quick movement and
Milly scrambled off the bed and raced to the bathroom,
barely managing to shut the door before she heaved into the
toilet. She should not have drunk that champagne. She'd
never had a head or, for that matter, a stomach for alcohol,
and the tension of the last hour had made it worse.

She knelt by the toilet, her cheek resting on the rim,
feeling more wretched than she'd ever thought it was possible to feel. She hadn't expected violins and roses as Anna
had wanted, of course she hadn't. She considered herself
a practical person. And yet that…*that*…

That had been her wedding night. She sat up slowly,
her body aching in strange places. She hadn't expected to
feel so *overwhelmed*. She understood why Alex had called
it the marital act. It had certainly felt binding. But she'd
wanted to be touched, and caressed, and kissed, and none
of that had happened, except for a few exquisite moments
at the beginning, moments that she now treasured because
she feared they would be so rare. Why had Alex stopped?
Should she have done something differently? Perhaps if
she had, he would have kept on with the lovely kisses and
caresses her heart and body both cried out for.

Instead, those tantalising flickers of pleasure she'd felt
when Alex had touched her had never had the opportu-

nity to fan into flame. She felt unsated, a restless ache at her centre that she knew only Alex could satisfy, and yet, despite those wonderful moments that had given her such hope as well as pleasure, it seemed as if he didn't want to. Didn't desire her, at least not enough to prolong what had happened between them. Should she really be surprised? He'd never indicated in any way that he responded to her physically, *little mouse* that she was.

Milly drew a ragged breath and then reached for the thick terrycloth robe hanging on the back of the bathroom door, grateful to swathe herself in its soft warmth. She dreaded leaving the bathroom and facing Alex again, but she knew she couldn't stay in here for ever.

She rinsed her mouth, combed her fingers through her hair, and gave her bleak reflection a wry look. Surely things could only get better. If they were able to get *worse*…but, no.

They'd talk, she decided. She'd tell him that she didn't care about romance, but the bedroom side of things could surely be better. What man wouldn't want to hear that?

One who doesn't desire you.

Flinching at the thought, she took a deep breath and then opened a door and stepped into the bedroom.

It was empty.

Milly gazed around the space, taking in the rumpled duvet, the single candle still burning. Alex was gone…and so were his clothes. Her stomach cramped at the thought. Was that *it*? She hadn't thought they were going to cuddle all night, of course, but…

She'd expected a little more than this. She had to keep giving herself reality checks, because, no matter what she told herself, she still came up against disappointment again and again. He didn't think of her with romance or even affection. He didn't desire her physically. When was she going to get it through her thick skull?

She sat on the edge of the bed, still unwilling to let go of the frail thread of hope. Perhaps he'd gone to get some food or drink, or…something. Surely he wouldn't just *disappear*.

Except he had. She waited for half an hour before she acknowledged he wasn't coming back. Feeling sick at heart, she ventured out of his bedroom. As she tiptoed down hallways and peeked in empty rooms, she realised he wasn't even in the villa. He hadn't just left the room, he'd left the whole house. Left *her*. Disconsolate, feeling more rejected than ever, Milly crept back to her own room and her own bed.

She woke some time after dawn, groggy from lack of sleep, her body still aching along with her heart. She hadn't heard Alex come back, and she had a leaden certainty weighing her down inside that he hadn't. She didn't know where he was, and he hadn't seen fit to tell her. Was that indicative of how their whole marriage was going to be?

By lunchtime Alex was still nowhere to be seen. Yiannis drove Anna back home, and she came into the house on a wave of enthusiasm, her bright eyes and ready smile making Milly realise afresh how much her sister wanted a fairy tale. And why shouldn't she? She'd had precious little happiness in her life.

'So?' Anna asked as she came into the kitchen where Milly was making a salad for lunch. 'How was it?' She held up a hand, pretending to shudder. 'Please don't give me any details. I just mean…was it romantic?'

That would be a big fat no, Milly thought sourly. After being on her own all morning she was starting to feel angry as well as incredibly hurt. Couldn't Alex at least have *said* where he was? What if he was hurt or lost, and she didn't even know it? And yet she doubted he was.

'It was fine,' she said as diplomatically as she could. 'It's going to take time, Anna. It's not a rom-com, okay?'

'I know.' Anna looked indignant, but it didn't last long. 'Did you like the candles? And the champagne?'

Milly thought of Alex snuffing them out with brusque precision. 'Very nice touches,' she murmured. 'Thank you.'

Alex did not make an appearance for the rest of the day—or that night. After her initial hurt, Milly decided she was relieved. It was easier to spend time with Anna without worrying that Alex was going to come frowning in on them. And if she kept telling herself that, she thought wryly, she might even start to believe it.

Anna, fortunately, had bought Milly's excuse that Alex had pressing work to do, and she didn't nag too much about where he was. Like Milly, she was enjoying the sister time they so rarely had.

After dinner, they piled on the sofa together and watched a rom-com, a big bowl of popcorn on their laps. Milly couldn't remember the last time they'd done something like that together—it had to have been before their parents had got divorced, when Anna was only seven or eight. Having her sister snuggling against her once again was a balm to her bruised heart. *This* was why she'd married Alexandro Santos. Not for whatever did or didn't happen in their relationship—or in their bedroom.

Still, both she and Anna felt the gap when the film had finished, and Anna was heading off to bed.

'Where's Alex?' she asked uncertainly as Milly took their dirty dishes to the kitchen.

'He's working,' she said as matter-of-factly as she could, trying to hide the hurt and confusion she felt. 'Don't worry,

Anna. Remember he's mega-rich?' Milly tried for a smile. 'He's got to make that money, you know. He'll be back soon.'

But the words felt hollow as she headed up to her own bedroom, wondering where her husband was—and when he would come back.

She found out the next day, from Yiannis.

'Alex went to *Athens*?' Milly stared at him in disbelief as he stood in the kitchen doorway, looking resolute but also a bit shamefaced at the news he had to deliver. Anna was still asleep; Milly had arisen at the crack of dawn, too restless to stay in bed. 'But why?'

'Work.'

Work. Of course. Still, she felt numbed by the news. He hadn't even said goodbye. The last time she'd seen him she'd been racing from his bed, about to be sick. 'When will he be back?' she asked, trying to sound practical rather than devastated.

Yiannis gave her a sorrowful look. 'I don't know, Kyria Santos.'

Kyria Santos. The name jolted her. She was Alex's wife, and yet she didn't feel like it. She felt even *less* important than she had as his housekeeper, having been utterly dismissed and ignored after giving so much of herself to him.

'I'm sure he'll be back soon,' she said, trying to sound matter-of-fact, and feeling she'd failed. But surely he would return in a day or two? He still needed an heir, presumably. What happened to three times a week?

But the days passed and Alex didn't return. He didn't even ring, and when Anna asked her why she didn't call him, Milly was too ashamed to admit she didn't have his mobile number, and she was too proud to call his office like some cold-calling supplicant.

She tried to ignore the hurt that needled her at inopportune moments, the memory of his touch that had been so sweet, and then how awfully it had all ended. She wished she knew what was going on in his head, never mind his heart, but she felt as if she had no clue about him at all. He was as much a stranger as ever—even more so, because now she was married to him.

As the days passed Milly did her best to relax into time spent with her sister, whether it was curled up on the sofa watching films, or strolling along the beach, or having a coffee in the village. The time was precious and fleeting, for all too soon three weeks had passed and Anna needed to return home to get ready for school.

'I'm going to miss you so much,' Milly said, her voice choking as she watched Anna pack her bag. Yiannis had given her the message from Alex that Anna would return to Rome via his private jet, and Milly tried not to feel stung that he hadn't deigned to tell her himself.

'Perhaps I'll be able to visit for a weekend some time,' Anna suggested. 'Or for Christmas…'

But Christmas felt like an age away. 'I'll make sure of it,' Milly said firmly. She intended to use a chunk of her five million euros to give Carlos an incentive to let Anna consider Naxos her home. She was just working up the courage to confront him.

And what about Alex? More and more she felt the need to talk to him, to confront him about the nature of their marriage. It had been over two weeks since their wedding day, and she'd not had one word from him save for the message from Yiannis. It was more than an insult; it was cruel. She hadn't thought him capable of such unkindness, and the fact that he was unsettled her. What kind of man had she married after all?

'He'll come back, Milly,' Anna said softly, as if she

could read her unhappy thoughts. Perhaps she could. 'I'm sure he will.'

'Yes, I know he will,' Milly returned with false cheer. She wasn't sure of any such thing, but she wasn't going to let her sister worry. 'Ring me as soon as you get back, all right? And I want to hear everything about your new school…'

'Of course.' Anna threw her arms around her and Milly held on tight. 'You'll get bored of me prattling on about it, I'm sure.'

'Never,' Milly returned. 'Never, ever.'

The house felt even emptier after Anna had gone; Yiannis had driven her to the airstrip, with Milly accompanying, waving her off onto Alex's luxurious jet that she'd never even seen before. Back at the villa, Milly wandered around the empty rooms, battling a swamping sense of loneliness she'd never experienced before, at least not in the villa.

She loved it here. It was the first place she'd really been able to think of as home. And yet now the rooms held memories that taunted her at every turn. The study, where Alex had asked her to marry him. The pool area, where they'd spoken in the dark and she'd seen his scars. The bedroom, where she'd felt both the sweetest, briefest pleasure and the most heart-rending pain.

Where she'd once been cheerfully productive, tidying rooms, weeding the garden, shopping in the village, now she felt adrift, restless and bored. Waiting…and she had no idea how long she would have to wait for, or what would happen when Alex finally returned. *If* he would return.

His marriage was a mistake. Two and a half weeks had not shaken that certainty from his core. Every time he closed his eyes, Alex pictured Milly's terrified face, heard her whimpered words. *I think I'm going to be sick.'*

What had he been thinking, believing he could marry a woman? That either of them could endure it? He'd left Naxos immediately; he knew Milly would be relieved and he hadn't been able to bear the thought of seeing the revulsion on her face yet another time.

No, better to stay away. And now it had been over two weeks, and any chance of a pregnancy—although Alex could hardly credit that such an awkward act could result in something so fortuitous—could be dismissed. All he had to do was call Milly and ask her. Assuming she wasn't pregnant, he would have the marriage annulled. His mistake would be rectified. They could both go on with their lives.

Autumn crisped the air, a few leaves fluttering down outside his office window, when Alex steeled himself to make the call. He listened to the house phone in Naxos ring, wondering if Milly would pick up. What had she been doing these last few weeks? Anna, he knew, had gone back to school. He'd made all the arrangements himself, and even now he allowed himself the barest flicker of pleasure that he might grant Milly some small happiness in that regard.

'Hello?' She sounded tired, he noted, and even dispirited.

'Milly, it's Alex.'

He heard her suck a breath in sharply. '*Now* you call.'

'It's been over two weeks.'

'So? Is that some deadline?' She let out a harsh laugh that sounded like despair. 'Where have you *been*, Alex?'

'Working.' He could feel himself prickle defensively; she sounded accusing but he'd been offering her a kindness.

'I know you've been working, but…why did you leave so suddenly? I came out of the bathroom…' She stopped, her voice choking before she drew a steadying breath. 'I thought you wanted an heir. You're not going about the most effective way to get one.'

'Are you pregnant?' he asked bluntly.

'Pregnant?' Another one of those awful laughs. 'Are you serious?'

'I know it is unlikely, but I need to ask. It's been two weeks, so I believe you could take a pregnancy test if necessary?' He'd looked it up online, but he was by no means an expert in these matters.

'No, I'm not pregnant,' she said after a moment, her voice sounding suffocated. 'I don't need to take a test.'

'Then we can have the marriage annulled.'

'What...?' Her breath came out in a rush. 'Why?'

'I realised it was a mistake,' Alex said flatly. 'And I'm sure you've come to the same conclusion.'

'But why?' She sounded bewildered rather than the relief he'd expected, and it unsettled him. This was really not the way he'd expected the conversation to go.

'I don't think we need to go into details, do we, Milly? Our wedding night spoke for itself.'

'About that—'

'I don't wish to discuss it. The pertinent facts remain unchanged. You may keep the five million euros. If you wish to remain as housekeeper, you may. Nothing need change for you.'

'Except, of course, the fact that I would no longer be married.'

'I hardly think that would bring you distress.'

'What is that supposed to mean?' Now she sounded angry, and he didn't understand it. He'd expected a sigh of relief, a stammered apology perhaps. Not this indignation, almost as if she were hurt. Or was it just her pride that was dented?

'Let's not quibble—' he began, only to be cut off.

'Quibble!'

'Regarding your sister, I've arranged for her to board

at the music academy, so she does not need to reside with Carlos Bentano. Holidays she can spend with you.'

'What…?' Milly's breath came out in a sudden rush. 'How did you manage to arrange that?'

'Bentano is a reasonable man, when his comforts are put in jeopardy. His house is heavily mortgaged and he faces foreclosure. I had the mortgages transferred to me.'

'Alex, you didn't have to—'

'Anna is my family now,' he cut across her. 'Of course I will take care of her.'

'But she's not your family, if our marriage is annulled,' Milly pointed out sharply. 'You have no responsibility for her then.'

Alex was silent, unsettled by her reasoning. He'd felt strongly about making sure Anna was provided and cared for. He'd failed his own sister, but he wouldn't fail Milly's. But of course she was right; once their marriage was annulled, he would have no relation to or responsibility for Anna. In all likelihood, he'd never see either Anna or Milly again. Why did that prospect give him a sudden, keen sense of loss, like a punch in the gut? He barely knew either of them.

'Even so,' he said. 'It is done.'

'Why are you doing this, Alex?' Milly asked softly. 'How can you be so kind and so cold at the same time? Can't we just…talk?'

'There's no point.'

'What about your heir? Your business?'

'It will go to Ezio eventually.' He hated the thought, but he would learn to live with it. 'I will put as many safeguards in place to keep him from running it into the ground.'

'I don't understand you,' she burst out. 'Why—?'

'I didn't ask you to,' he cut across her swiftly. He didn't

want to do a post-mortem on their failed marriage. It would serve no purpose, and every word, every memory, was agony.

'I know you didn't,' Milly said with quiet dignity. 'You've made that very, very clear.' And with that she hung up the phone, the slam of the receiver into the cradle blasting in Alex's ear.

He tossed his mobile on his desk, turning towards the window. She was angry, which he didn't entirely understand. He'd made the call expecting her to be relieved, bracing himself for the whoosh of breath she'd release, the burden lifted from her slight shoulders. Instead she'd sounded bewildered. Disappointed. Even hurt.

Or was he just projecting his own feelings onto her? Because the agony of their wedding night was a scar he'd have to bear, worse than any on his face. Her revulsion. Her fear. Her utter disgust...

He needed to stop thinking about it. His brief association with Milly James had opened up a part of himself he'd thought had been locked away for ever. She'd peeled back a protective layer without even trying to and he needed to find it again. Rebuild his defences, so no one could ever get close again. That, Alex knew, was the only way forward.

CHAPTER TEN

MILLY WALKED AROUND the villa in a daze of shock for two days, Alex's awful conversation running through her mind, before she galvanised herself into action. She couldn't leave it like that. She certainly couldn't let *him* leave like that, not least of all because Alex's brusque rejection of her reminded her too much of her past. Her entire childhood, and, really, her whole life, she'd been tidied out of the way when her parents couldn't be bothered to deal with her.

It reminded her of Philippe's cruel rejection as well, except Alex was so unlike Philippe. He was honest, or at least she'd believed him to be, and for that reason alone she needed to have a face-to-face conversation. She deserved one.

So, Milly decided, she was going to go to Athens and beard the lion in his twenty-second-floor den. She told Yiannis first, betting on the fact that Alex hadn't told anyone about the proposed annulment yet, and because she knew she needed his help to get there, just as she had before.

'I fancy a shopping trip to Athens,' she said as casually as she could one sunny morning in early September. 'Could you drive me to the ferry?'

Yiannis looked conflicted. 'Kyrie Santos won't like you taking the public ferry—'

'I took it before,' Milly objected. 'Thousands of people

take it all the time.' And she was quite sure *Kyrie Santos* didn't care what she did, or how she did it.

Yiannis started to shake his head. 'Yes, but that was before you were married. Kyrie Santos is very protective of his own. If you wait a day or two, he can have the yacht back here—'

'But that would be such a waste,' Milly protested. 'And actually...' she lowered her voice conspiratorially '... I want to surprise Alex with my visit.' Which was true enough, if not in the way Yiannis might think or hope, judging by the light sparking in his eyes. She knew Yiannis and Marina, just like Anna, were desperate to see a happily-ever-after. And while Milly had no illusion that *that* was going to happen, she still wanted answers, if nothing else.

Yiannis still looked torn. 'I don't know, Kyria—'

'Milly. You called me Milly before I was married. And you're not my keeper, Yiannis.' She gentled her words with a smile. 'I'm a grown woman, and I've lived on three different continents in my lifetime. I can do this. All I'm asking is for you to make it a little more convenient.'

He finally agreed, even giving her the key to Alex's flat, and Milly wasted no time in packing a bag. She still didn't really have a plan besides getting to Athens and confronting Alex, but that was enough to go on. She could think about it on the ferry, or make it up as she went along. The important thing was that she be able to see him face to face. If he'd even let her.

The trip across the Aegean was choppy this time of year, and Milly spent most of the six hours being sick over the railing, so by the time she arrived in Athens she was wrung out like a dish cloth. Not the most auspicious start to her visit, but she was still determined, at least.

Even though the key to Alex's flat felt as if it were burning a hole in her pocket, she chose instead to rent a room at a modest hotel, not wanting to run into him by accident when she was unprepared.

She showered and changed, regarding her rather wan appearance in the mirror with a wry grimace. She certainly did not look her best, but she doubted there was much point in making herself up anyway. It wasn't as if she was about to seduce him. He'd made his physical feelings for her very clear.

She had just stepped into Syntagma Square, where Alex had his offices, when she saw the flashing sign for a chemist's. She paused, because, despite having told Alex on the phone that she wasn't pregnant, she hadn't actually had a period since their wedding and she knew she probably should have. The irregularity was undoubtedly down to stress—what else could it be?—but just to be sure she went into the chemist's and, in halting Greek, asked for a pregnancy test. The chemist was all beaming smiles as he fetched her one, and Milly paid for it and shoved it to the bottom of her bag. She'd deal with that potential complication later. It was just a precaution, anyway. It seemed hard to believe that a single brief and loveless act could have resulted in a baby.

'Kyrie Santos is very busy,' the receptionist in the lobby of the gleaming skyscraper informed her repressively when Milly asked for him. It was a different woman from the one she'd dealt with before, when she'd said she was Alex's fiancée, and far snootier. 'And,' she added with something like relish, 'he never receives visitors.'

'He'll receive me,' Milly informed her shortly, although she wasn't at all sure. 'I'm his wife.'

The receptionist's mouth dropped open as she took in Milly's rather rumpled appearance with barely masked derision. 'His *wife*?'

'Yes, his wife. Now, why don't you ring him and tell him I'm here, before you embarrass yourself any further?' Milly had never talked to anyone like that in her life, and yet she couldn't deny it felt good. After a lifetime of being stepped on or pushed aside, she was finally sticking up for herself. Alex's rejection had pushed her into it, made her strong. She only hoped it did some good.

The receptionist picked up her phone, muttering into it in Greek, while Milly waited, trying to look calm and assured instead of terrified. After what felt like an endless moment, the woman put the phone down and nodded. 'You may go up.'

Her heart felt as if it were climbing into her throat as she soared upwards to the office that covered most of the twenty-second floor. What would Alex say when he saw her? What would *she* say? She hadn't thought this out carefully, simply running on pure adrenaline and emotion.

The doors pinged open and Alex stood there, glowering. 'What are you doing here?'

'Seeing my husband,' Milly fired back as she stepped out of the lift. 'Or was that not part of your *terms*?'

'The terms are moot,' Alex returned evenly. 'Considering our marriage is about to be annulled.'

'Yes, about that. Does annulment count the same as divorce?'

'What?' Alex looked nonplussed as Milly strolled into his office, trying to hide how she trembled. Where had she got this courage? And what was she going to do with it? 'What does that matter?'

'Because the prenuptial contract stated that you owe me another five million euros if you divorce me.'

Alex closed the door behind him, looking incredulous. 'Is that why you came here? To demand more money?'

'No,' Milly cried with ragged emphasis. 'I came here for

a straight answer, Alex. How do you think it feels, to have your husband walk out of your wedding night and then disappear for three *weeks*? And then the next communication is that he is intending to annul your marriage?' Tears started in her eyes but she blinked them back furiously, determined to stay strong. 'How could you be so cruel?'

'Cruel?' If anything her husband looked even more incredulous. 'I wasn't being cruel, Milly. I was being kind.'

She let out a harsh laugh, just as disbelieving as he was. 'Then you have a very twisted idea of kindness. Do you know how awful I felt? How…how rejected?' She sniffed, folding her arms and tilting her chin in a pointless effort to hide the worst of her pain.

Alex shook his head slowly. 'Milly, if anyone felt… rejected…' He took a swift breath. 'Look, there's no getting around the plain fact that our wedding night was a disaster. I tried to make it as—as endurable as possible, but I know you still found it difficult to…' He blew out a breath, colour slashing his cheekbones, his scars mottled red. 'To touch me. Or even look at me.'

Milly stared at him in confusion. 'What…?'

'Come now, Milly, let's not prevaricate. It was obvious.' He strode to his desk and sat behind it, as if he could turn their fraught conversation into a business meeting, as usual. 'I was trying to spare either of us any further discomfort. Marriage was a foolish choice for someone like me.'

Milly stepped closer to him, her mind racing with all he'd said—and hadn't said. Could this really be about his *scars*?

'Someone like you? Who is that, exactly?'

Impatiently Alex gestured to the scarred side of his face. 'Do I have to spell it out for you?'

'Yes, I actually think you do.'

His mouth compressed, his nostrils flaring. Milly forced herself to stare him down. 'I disgusted you, Milly. That much was clear. I disgusted you so much you were sick.' The words fell like lashes on her back, on her heart.

'Alex, I was sick because I'd guzzled too much champagne.'

'One glass—'

'On an empty stomach, and far too many nerves. I was terrified, Alex. I was a virgin.' Her voice wobbled. 'You knew that, didn't you?'

Colour slashed his high cheekbones. 'Yes—'

'And did you ever think that maybe that's why I was scared, not because of some scars on your face?' Fury boiled through her, surprising her with its force. 'Could you stop thinking about yourself for one moment to think about how *I* felt? A virgin who had barely been kissed, on her wedding night with a man who was practically a stranger—'

'A man who repulsed you—'

'Oh, stop talking like that! I don't care about your scars. And if you had bothered to pay attention, you would have realised I wasn't repulsed at all. I *desired* you, you…you ninny!'

Alex stared at her in disbelief. Why was she pursuing this complete fabrication? 'Your actions said otherwise, Milly.'

'You're not listening to me,' Milly snapped. 'I was a virgin. I was nervous. I drank too much champagne on an empty stomach. *You didn't even kiss me.*'

Her words fell like hammer blows, shattering his illusions, and yet he still couldn't believe it. 'You didn't want me to kiss you.'

'How on earth do you know that?' she demanded, looking entirely fed up. Still Alex couldn't let it go.

'Everything you said and did told me so. You didn't want help with your zip…'

'Because I was nervous and you seemed so cold—'

'And when I did help you, you shuddered—'

'With desire, not disgust. When you touched me… Alex, I wanted you to touch me more. I was desperate for it, but you stopped.' Milly tilted her chin, colour flaming her face. 'What is it going to take to make you believe me, Alex? Do you think this is easy? How much do I have to humiliate myself?'

'The humiliation was mine—'

'No. I desired you.' Her voice trembled. 'You're the one who—who seemed not to want me.'

His mouth fell open as he stared at her, utterly shocked by this admission. 'I think I gave evidence of my feelings, Milly,' he said evenly.

'You mean because you could—you could complete the act?' She shrugged scornfully, her chin tilted at a haughty angle, her face the colour of a tomato. 'Most men can do that, as far as I can tell. It doesn't…it doesn't actually mean anything.'

Alex turned away abruptly, rubbing his hands over his face. Was it possible that he'd got this so terribly wrong? Had he let his own fears and weaknesses distort his perception that much?

'Why do you think I wouldn't desire you?' he asked finally, his voice low, his back still to her. Milly didn't respond for a long moment, and when she did her voice was small, suffocated.

'Because…because I'm plain. I know that. I'm a…a little mouse.'

'A little mouse?' He whirled around, furious on her behalf. 'Did someone say that to you once?'

'Yes—a man. Philippe.' Her throat worked convulsively

as she swallowed. 'I thought I loved him, but it was just a mirage. A fantasy.'

Jealousy boiled through him, surprising him with its force. 'And what happened?'

'He didn't feel the same way. Well.' She let out a sad little laugh, her shoulders hunched as her gaze slid away. 'The truth is, he was a cruel and dishonest man. Charming, but it was nothing more than a veneer, and, after living with my mother, I thought I would recognise that, but I didn't. I fell for his lines.'

Alex's fists clenched. He hated this man already. 'What happened between you?'

'Nothing, really.' Her lips trembled as she tried to smile. 'I made a fool of myself, basically, following him around, listening to his lies. He told me he'd fallen in love with me, but then I…' She paused, swallowing hard, and he realised how difficult this was for her.

He was both humbled and shamed to realise she had her own painful memories, her own insecurities. Of course she did. How could he have been so selfish, so arrogant, as to think he was the only one?

'You don't have to tell me, Milly.'

'No, I want to.' Her chin lifted another notch. 'Because then maybe you'll understand where I'm coming from, for once.' *Ouch*. He waited while she fought for her composure to continue. 'He was one of my mother's cronies, from when she lived in Paris. The circuit of impoverished aristocrats and D-list celebrities. Really, a stellar group.'

'How did you meet him?'

'He sought me out, because he knew my mother. That should have sent the warning bells ringing, but he seemed so sincere, and I wanted to believe him. No one had ever shown that kind of interest in me before.'

'No one—'

'I'm plain, Alex. I know that.'

'You're not—'

'Anyway.' She shook her head, refusing to believe him, just as he'd refused to believe her. 'We started dating. He told me he loved me. He…' Her voice faltered. 'He wanted us to spend the night together, at a hotel. All very romantic, but I was hesitant. It felt too fast.'

'Tell me,' Alex said in a low, deadly voice, 'that he didn't hurt you.'

'No, not like that. Just my feelings. We were at a party and I'd gone to the ladies'. I wasn't very comfortable there—it was his crowd, not mine. Anyway, as I came back I overheard him talking to his friends.' She bit her lip, sinking her teeth into it just as she had on their wedding night, her face shadowed with remembered pain. 'They were joking, taking bets as to when he would—when he would deflower me. I stood there, hardly able to believe it, and then he joked about how he'd have to grin and bear it, because he found me so…' She stopped, and Alex took a step towards her.

'Milly, don't. The man sounds like an utter bastard.'

'Well, I'm sure you can imagine what he said. And then one of his friends saw me, and nudged him, and he turned around and laughed in my face. He didn't even try to deny it. He told me he'd been given a dare, to seduce the plainest girl he could find. That's when he said it— *"Do you honestly think I could fall for a little mouse like you?"*' She bowed her head. 'Look, I know he was a jerk. I realise in that moment he was trying to save face in front of his friends. I know his words aren't some gospel truth. I'm… I'm over that.'

'Are you?' Alex asked in a raw voice. She'd faced the kind of rejection he hadn't let himself face, because he'd hidden himself away. She was, he realised, far braver than he'd ever been.

'Yes,' Milly said firmly. She lifted her head to look at him, blinking back tears, her jaw set. *So brave.* 'Yes, I am. But perhaps now you understand, Alex, why I acted the way I did on our wedding night. I had painful memories, too.'

His jaw clenched with self-recrimination. 'I wish I'd known.'

'You never gave me the chance to tell you. And I admit, I didn't really want to lay myself bare like that.' Despite everything, she managed a wry smile. 'I was bare enough.'

'I'm sorry,' Alex managed, the words feeling both strange and sincere. 'I didn't realise that. I didn't...' He shook his head. 'I suppose I was only thinking about myself.' Even though he'd convinced himself he was thinking about her, being kind when in reality he'd just been protecting himself. Again.

'So here we are.' Milly flung her arms out. 'Two people who got it all badly wrong, because they were both so scared.'

He opened his mouth to deny it, but how could he? As much as it shamed him, he had been scared. Scared of being rejected. Of being hurt. And so he'd hurt her instead.

'I'm sorry,' he said again.

They stared at each other for a long moment, the air tautening between them. 'So now what?' Milly finally asked softly. 'Are you still determined to annul our marriage?'

'I thought I was doing you a kindness.'

'And I'm telling you now you aren't.'

He took a deep breath, forced himself to ask the question. 'Do you really want to be married to me, Milly? Anna can stay in school. You can keep the five million euros—'

'I honour my commitments, Alex. My *vows*.' Her voice

shook. 'And the truth is, I don't want to be rejected again. I'm not looking for love, but I thought—I hoped—we could have some kind of affection between us. But perhaps now I need to ask you the same question—do you really want to be married to me? Do you—do you desire me?' Her voice trembled and broke on the words.

For a moment Alex couldn't speak. He couldn't believe she'd suffered from as much doubt as he had—*and he hadn't even realised*. And now she was asking him point-blank to admit the truth, and he knew he would, he had to, no matter what it cost him. Even if she turned away. 'Yes,' he said in a low voice. 'I do. Truly, I do. You're lovely, Milly. The freckles on your shoulders…'

She let out an incredulous laugh. 'Of all the things… the freckles on my *shoulders*?'

'I dreamed about kissing them,' he admitted, heat unfurling through his body at the thought. He wanted to kiss them now. 'Kissing all of you…'

Her eyes smoked and blazed as she met his gaze boldly. 'Then do it,' she said.

CHAPTER ELEVEN

HEAT BLOOMED AND rushed through Milly as she stared at Alex, daring him to prove his desire. Needing him to desperately, because if he didn't do something, she would. Or else she would combust.

'You mean…' he began, looking startled, and she wondered how such a powerful and beautiful man could have become so uncertain. The scars were deeper than they looked.

'Yes. Now.' Her voice turned ragged with her need. 'Please.'

He took a step towards her, and then another. Milly held her breath. Then he was standing in front of her, looking at her in wonder. 'Are you sure…?'

'How many times do I have to say it?' Milly demanded.

Gently he touched his fingers to her lips, and even that sent need arrowing to her core. 'I haven't kissed a woman since before the accident. I haven't so much as *touched*…'

'Touch me.'

And then he did. He bent his head, one hand anchored to her waist as his lips skimmed hers. Her mouth opened hungrily, already wanting more. She reached up and put her hands on his strong shoulders, drawing herself to him. As their bodies collided she sucked in a hard breath. Everything in her felt as if it were on fire.

And amazingly, wonderfully, Alex seemed to feel the same, for his brush of a kiss turned into something hungry and demanding, something wonderful. His mouth plundered hers as he pulled her tight against him.

'Now do you doubt me?' he demanded in a growl against her mouth, and she let out an incredulous laugh, intoxicated by the need she felt in both him and herself.

'Show me more.'

And he did, hoisting her by the hips and seating her on his desk as he swept papers away with one commanding hand. He parted her thighs, standing between them, as he kissed her with both thoroughness and urgency. She drove her hands through his hair, careful even now to avoid his scars, unsure if they might pain him. Not wanting anything to break this moment.

'Touch me, Alex,' she half whimpered. 'Touch me more, *please.*'

He slid his hand along her thigh, making her squirm as his fingers found her bare flesh. And then higher still, and she let out a moan of both pleasure and frustration. *More.* She still wanted more.

And then he was at her centre, touching her with such intimacy and expertise that she felt as if she were flying apart. Still it wasn't enough.

Emboldened by her desire, she reached for his zip. Alex tore his mouth from hers. 'Milly…'

'You don't receive visitors, remember?' she said, feeling reckless, and his little smile made her want to sing.

Then his face darkened with passion as he tugged at his zip and pulled her even closer, settling himself between her thighs.

Milly braced herself against him as he began to slide inside her, the invasion both sweet and strange and *so much*.

'Tell me if I'm hurting you,' he gasped, and she shook

her head, her head pressed against his shoulder as her body adjusted and together they found their rhythm.

'You're not. You're not at all.'

And then she lost the power to speak, to think; all she could do was feel the exquisite pleasure of his body inside hers, the overwhelming intimacy of it, this act that would bind them together for ever. Nothing could split this asunder. *Nothing.*

And when she came, it was like the splintering of stars, the word dissolving and then coming together again with a new, crystalline brightness as he cradled her in his arms, holding her as if he'd never let her go. And in that moment, she knew she didn't want him to.

Yet he did, easing back slowly, looking stunned by their explosive interaction. 'Did I hurt you?' he asked in a low voice, and Milly nearly laughed aloud.

'No.' She regarded him closely, trying to figure out what was going on behind those shadowed eyes. 'Did you think you did?'

'I lost control.'

'So did I.' She paused, the confidence that their love-making had given her starting to seep away. She was cold and sticky and her skirt was rucked up to her hips. She wriggled to try to get it down and give herself a modicum of modesty. 'Does that have to be a bad thing?' she asked cautiously.

'No, I...' Alex shook his head, raking his hand through his hair as he turned away to do up his trousers. 'I never expected this.'

He didn't sound particularly pleased, and Milly had no idea why. Surely a physical attraction between them was a good thing, especially if he wanted a child? Briefly she thought of the pregnancy test in her bag, and then pushed the image away. She couldn't be pregnant. She couldn't deal with being pregnant, not now, so soon. Surely it had just been stress.

'Expected what, exactly?' she asked as she eased herself off his desk and straightened her skirt. Her lips felt swollen from his kisses, her body aching in a rather lovely way. Still, she felt the need for caution; Alex certainly seemed guarded. No matter how uninhibited they had been moments before, in the throes of passion, things clearly were different now.

'Expected us to have…a physical attraction.' He turned back to her. 'It wasn't in my planning.'

'Well, surely you can make room for it?' Milly suggested, trying to smile. 'It will make trying for a baby more pleasant, at least.'

'Yes, I suppose.' He still didn't look happy about it, though, and Milly wasn't brave enough any more to try to tease him out of it. In truth she had no idea what to do now.

'So you're not going to annul the marriage,' she said at last, because that felt like the most important thing.

Alex hesitated, making her freeze. Surely after what they'd just experienced, what they'd shared, he wouldn't…?

'No,' he said at last, sounding reluctant. 'I won't.'

Alex had no idea how to feel. What had just happened… what he'd just felt…what *Milly* had felt…

It had blown his mind. Destroyed all his preconceptions. And left him spinning in a void of unknowing, because nothing about their business arrangement had made him expect *that*. And *that* had been amazing. Incredible. The best sex he'd ever had, because it hadn't just been sex.

And therein lay the problem. They were treading on thin ice, moving into dangerous waters. Emotional ones.

'Alex?' Milly straightened her skirt, looking uncertain. 'Why do you look as if you're not happy about this?'

'It's fine,' he said, which was no real answer at all. 'I just didn't expect…' he shook his head '…any of this.'

'Right.' She smiled shyly. 'Can't we just…consider this a bonus?'

A bonus. He stared at her as if seeing her for the first time. Her hair was tumbled about her shoulders, her face still rosy, her lips still swollen from his kisses. Looking at her now, he wanted her all over again, with a deep and abiding need that shocked him.

Of course Milly didn't know, and he wasn't about to tell her, that he hadn't physically desired a woman like this in nearly two years. He hadn't desired a woman at *all* in that time; he'd never thought to feel that need again—and now it was overpowering him. It was thrilling, but it was also alarming. It made him vulnerable. It made him weak.

'Alex…?'

He retrained his distant gaze on her. He was being irrational. *Emotional*, which was something he tried never to be, because he knew where it led. A physical relationship didn't have to mean anything. It hadn't before. Yes, they were married now, and *that* meant something, but this didn't have to. This could be just what Milly had said…a bonus. A very nice bonus.

'Sorry.' He gave her a quick smile. 'I like your thinking.'

Her face lit up as she smiled shyly. 'You do?'

'Yes, I most certainly do. It's just taken me a little while to catch up.' She scanned his face, waiting for more. Alex reached for her and she came willingly into his arms, something else that felt strange. He could get used to this, he realised, and then where would he be?

'This is an unexpected perk,' he murmured, and then brushed a kiss across her lips. She responded instantly, fitting her body to his, wrapping her arms around his neck, tempting him to take it further. A lot further.

But now was neither the time nor the place, despite what had just happened right on his desk. He needed to regroup, regain control, and figure out exactly how he was going to handle this unforeseen complication. *This bonus.*

'Why don't you go back to my flat?' he suggested. 'Make yourself comfortable, order in food. I'll join you as soon as I've finished up here.' He turned to reach for his phone. 'The doorman will give you the key. I'll call a limo…'

'I already have a key,' Milly confessed. 'Yiannis gave it to me when I told him I was coming to Athens.'

'He did?'

'I told him I was coming to surprise you. I made it sound like…well, exactly like it happened, as it turns out.' Laughter bubbled up inside her and spilled out. 'I just didn't realise that was going to be the case.'

She sounded so happy, and Alex could hardly credit he had made her that way. And yet it made him wary too, because what happened when he inevitably disappointed or hurt her? When she found out the truth?

'That's easily dealt with, then,' he said with a smile. 'I won't even have to ring the doorman.'

'All right.' She hesitated, and he simply stood there, hands in his pockets, waiting for her to go. Half of him wanted to snatch her up in his arms and bury his head in her hair, bury himself inside her again and again and again. Because he could. Because she wanted him to. Because he'd never, ever expected this much and it scared the hell out of him.

'I'll see you soon?' she asked, a gentle query, and he nodded.

'Yes. Soon.'

'All right,' she said again, and then she was gone, the door clicking shut softly behind her, the only thing remaining of her presence the faint lemony scent of her perfume—and the detritus of his papers scattered on the floor from when he'd swept them away in a moment of pure, blazing passion.

What was happening to him? What had happened to *them*? Alex walked slowly to his desk and sank into the chair, still dazed by the whole surreal encounter. Less than an hour ago he'd been intending to annul the marriage. He'd already called his lawyer to draw up the documents. And now…and now…

And now his marriage was going to look very different. Feel very different.

But not that different.

Alex let out a shuddering breath and reached for his papers. He still had work to do, a property deal in Sicily to look over, but he felt as if he couldn't concentrate on anything. His mind kept going back to the moments he'd had with Milly, when she'd stared him straight in the face and said, *'I desired you.'* When she'd thrown back her head, her voice a throaty growl as she'd pleaded with him. *'Touch me, Alex. Touch me more, please.'*

He rose abruptly, his blood heated simply from the memories. He was half inclined to take off after her now, spend the rest of the day and the whole night in bed.

But, no. He needed to think. He needed to remember to stay in control, because Milly might have, incredibly, accepted the scars on his face, but she had no idea about the ones on his soul. She had no idea what he was capable of, how he'd failed the people he'd loved. And if she learned any of that, she wouldn't be able to look him in the eye. She wouldn't be able to stand being touched by him. He was sure of it, and he knew already it would hurt more because of what they'd shared.

He had to find a way to keep his distance…and enjoy this *bonus*.

Which, Alex acknowledged, he should be able to do without a problem. He was a man, after all, a man who had once had an active sex life, who had managed to separate sex and love with absolute ease. This shouldn't be a problem, he told himself grimly. He would make sure it wasn't.

CHAPTER TWELVE

MILLY STEPPED INTO Alex's penthouse apartment in one of Athens' best neighbourhoods with a rush of released breath. Her body still tingled from their lovemaking, her mind still reeled. So much had happened. So much had changed. She hoped.

She put her bag down by the door as she took in her minimalistic but clearly luxurious surroundings. The penthouse was open-plan, with a soaring glass ceiling and floor-to-ceiling views of the Acropolis. White and grey leather sofas were scattered over the gleaming black marble floor, and a huge canvas of white with a few artful black splotches and lines took pride of place over the fireplace.

Milly stepped closer and realised the painting wasn't the stereotypical abstract modern art; it was a child's drawing that had been magnified, stick figures with lopsided heads and wide smiles. Her heart constricted. Why would Alex have such a picture in his flat? What did it mean to him?

She studied it for a few more minutes noting there were three people in the picture, two adults and a child. Who had drawn it? Or did it mean nothing—it was some interior designer's attempt at modern art?

She turned away to explore the rest of Alex's domain: a large kitchen of gleaming chrome and granite led off the main living area, and down a corridor were two sumptuous bedrooms, one done in navy, one done in cream, each with its own luxurious bathroom. Spiral stairs at the end of the corridor led up to a private gym and a study, as well as an enormous roof terrace with an outdoor pool, the water sparkling under the midday sun.

It was every bit as luxurious as the villa on Naxos, and yet besides the child's drawing over the fireplace, it felt strangely impersonal. Just like the villa, there were no photographs, no knick-knacks, no books or mementoes. It was a blank canvas, a clean slate, almost as if Alex had tidied away evidence of himself on purpose.

Back downstairs, Milly wondered what would happen when Alex returned home. She recalled his remoteness with a prickle of unease; no matter how explosive their lovemaking had been, he'd still kept a certain emotional distance that she supposed was second nature to him. He was a guarded, private man, and his scars had made him even more so.

Which she'd known going into this marriage, and still had to accept now. The trouble was, Milly acknowledged, what had happened between them today had changed things for her. She knew it wasn't supposed to, and sex was meant to be just sex, but it hadn't felt like that at all. It had felt intimate. Incredible. *Important*. And she was going to have to keep reminding herself that Alex definitely did not feel the same way…which was a good thing, because, no matter what their physical chemistry was like, Alex Santos was not a man to give your heart away to. He certainly didn't want to take it, and she didn't want to be hurt. Again. Keeping things on a physical-only level was better for both of them.

With hours before Alex was due to return, Milly decided to take advantage of the decadent bathroom, and filled the sunken marble tub right to the brim with hot water and plenty of luxury bubble bath. As she reached for a fresh change of clothes from her bag, her hand closed around the slim cardboard box she'd bought this morning. The pregnancy test.

For a second she hesitated; now would be a perfect time to take the test, to make sure she wasn't pregnant. But without fully thinking about what she was doing, Milly shoved the box deeper into her bag. She was almost sure her missed period was down to nothing more than stress… there was no need to take the test right now. She could wait a little while.

But as she sank into the heavenly hot and fragrant water, Milly had to acknowledge her reluctance to take the test was more than the prospect of wasting it. She didn't want to be pregnant yet. She didn't want to upend things, not when she and Alex were starting to get to know each other. When their marriage could be just a little bit more than the business arrangement they'd both agreed on. She could wait a few days, or even a few weeks. In all likelihood her period would arrive by then anyway.

As evening approached, nerves started to flutter in Milly's belly, of both trepidation and excitement. Since there was no food in the house, she ordered a meal to be delivered, and then she spent an age redoing her make-up before wiping it all off. This was ridiculous. It was too late to try to impress Alex, and yet she wanted to do something to show things had changed between them.

When the door to the flat finally opened, she was speechless with nerves, only able to stare at him across the darkened room, moonlight spilling in through the windows. Alex stood still for a moment, framed by the light from the hallway, the electric blaze of his blue eyes visible even in the dim lighting, and sending spirals of excitement and desire coursing through Milly. All she could do was stare—and want.

Alex's briefcase fell from his hand with a *thunk*. In one fluid movement he closed the door behind him.

'I've been waiting for you,' Milly said breathlessly, half wondering if Alex felt the same taut need that she felt, running through her like a wire, pulling her to him.

Except she wasn't being pulled; he was coming towards her, shedding his jacket and tie as he walked. Her breath bottled in her chest, her heart thumping double time as Alex discarded his tie and then pulled her into his arms. His mouth came down on hers and that was all she needed for the excitement to burst out of her in a frenzy of response; she kissed him back with all the urgency and passion she felt, her hands clawing at his shirt, longing to feel his bare skin on hers.

Shedding clothes, they tripped and stumbled their way towards the bedroom, and then fell on the bed in a tangle of limbs. Milly gasped and arched as Alex's mouth roved over her, branding her skin with his hot touch. She came alive under his hands in a way she'd never experienced, never expected, and when he finally began to move inside her she cried out in both pleasure and surprise, that again it could be so incredible between them. So important.

They were lying on the twisted sheets, their hearts both still thudding, neither of them having said a word, when the doorbell rang. Alex tensed and Milly laid her palm flat on his chest, revelling in the feel of him.

'That will be the food I ordered,' she said.

'Ah.' Alex relaxed, a smile teasing his mouth.

'I'll get it,' she said, and she rose from the bed, flinging on a dressing gown before hurrying to the door.

As she signed for the food and took the order, her body feeling sated and sleepy and yet also achingly alive, she realised she was buzzing in places she didn't even know she had. She was also happier than she'd been in a long while.

This was definitely some bonus, she thought, a smile curving her lips as she returned to the bedroom with several containers of takeaway.

'Why do you look like the cat who got the cream?' Alex asked, stretching in bed, his voice holding a teasing note that was entirely new—and wonderful.

'I did get the cream,' she dared to tease, and he laughed, another sound that was both strange and wonderful. She felt as if she were chipping away at Alex's icy exterior, and the glimpses of both the heat and heart underneath thrilled her.

She shed her dressing gown and got back in bed, and together they relaxed, eating Chinese food amidst the tangle of the duvet. Milly felt buoyant with happiness, as if she could float right up to the ceiling.

'So did you close any property deals today?' she asked, and Alex looked surprised by the question.

'Do you really want to know?'

'Of course I do.'

He shrugged. 'I'm working on a low-income housing development in Piraeus. It's an area of the country that has suffered from the economic crisis, and the housing stock is shockingly substandard in places.'

'That sounds like a worthwhile project.' For some reason Milly had imagined that Alex's property deals were for top-end resorts and hotels, not housing for people in need. 'Do you make money from that?' she asked curiously.

'Yes, assuming you do the thing properly. The houses are environmentally friendly and made of locally sourced building materials, and everyone employed to work on the project will be local. It's meant to revitalise the community, not just provide housing.'

'That's amazing, Alex.'

He shook his head. 'Not really, it's smart. There is a profit in it for me.' He looked at her seriously, the light-hearted expression dropping from his face. 'Don't start seeing me as some white knight, Milly, just because we're good together in bed.'

She felt her face warm because that was exactly what she'd been doing. Every little thing he did or said that was kind or good helped her construct a picture of him—the picture she realised she was desperate to see.

'I wouldn't say white knight exactly,' she said as lightly as she could. 'But why dismiss it when it's clearly some-thing good?'

'I'm not dismissing it,' Alex said shortly. 'I'm just warn-ing you.'

Stung now, she stared down at her half-eaten noodles. 'Of what, exactly?'

He touched her chin with his fingers, tilting it so she had no choice but to gaze up at him—his smile strangely compassionate. 'What we have is good, Milly. It's a bonus, like you said. An amazing bonus. But that's all it is.'

'I know that.' She spoke stiffly, embarrassed that he felt the need to give her such a warning. He could see right through her, and she felt as if she couldn't see him at all.

'I just don't want to disappoint you.'

'You won't, Alex.' She eased back so his hand fell away from her face. 'I'm going into this with my eyes wide open, trust me. I won't let myself be disappointed.'

He certainly knew how to ruin a mood. Alex watched Milly broodingly, half wishing he hadn't issued such a bleak warning, yet knowing he'd had to. He'd seen the stars forming in her eyes, and he even understood why. Their incredible physical intimacy made her want a deeper,

emotional one. It was natural, expected. They both needed
to guard against it.

The smart thing, he knew, would be to send her back
to Naxos and get on with his work. Yet despite the words
he'd just spoken, he was reluctant to do just that. They
were married; they enjoyed each other's bodies. This could
be simple.

'Why don't you stay in Athens for a few days?' he suggested. 'You could do some shopping, if you like.'

Milly wrinkled her nose. 'I've done enough shopping,
thanks to the assistants you had come to the hotel before.
But I would like to take in some of the sights. I've never
seen the Acropolis, or any of the museums.'

'Then you must do so.' He gave her a wolfish smile.
'Tour Athens by day, and then we can entertain ourselves
at night.'

She smiled back, but he saw the remnants of shadows
in her eyes, and he knew she took his words as he meant
them—another warning as well as a promise.

The next few days were some of the most pleasant Alex
had ever known—and not just pleasant, but truly happy.
He thought back to when Milly had asked him if he was
happy, if he would be happy, and he'd told her being happy
with their business arrangement was enough. But now that
didn't feel like nearly enough, and he was far happier than
he'd ever expected or hoped to be. It made him feel uneasy, because he knew all too well how happiness could
be taken away. How he could destroy it.

But he pushed those thoughts away, determined to enjoy
this brief respite. In a few days Milly would go back to
Naxos; this was a moment in time, nothing more. They
could both afford to enjoy each other.

And they did…both in bed and out of it. Alex was surprised at how much he enjoyed the out of it part, because when they were in bed, everything was explosive. But out of it, he found he liked chatting over a meal, or watching something inane on TV. He especially liked coming back to a warm and lit flat, to a *home*. As the days progressed, Milly filled the kitchen with food and started preparing their evening meals. Alex had told her they could order in, but she was insistent, saying how she liked to cook.

And he liked her cooking—liked the fragrant smells that filled the rooms, the simple but delicious meals they ate together. It felt like a family.

Which reminded him of their true purpose. 'Do you think you might be pregnant?' he asked matter-of-factly one evening as they lay amidst the tangle of his sheets, their hearts still thudding from the intensity of their lovemaking.

'Pregnant?' She tensed, and he didn't miss the flash of something that looked almost like fear streak across her face before she schooled her expression into something far more innocuous. 'It's a bit early, don't you think?'

'You're young and healthy, and the doctor said there were no medical issues.'

'Yes, but we've only been married a month, and we've been apart for most of that.' She let out a little, uncertain laugh. 'We don't have to rush things, do we?'

'Rush things?' He stared at her, trying to discern what was clearly making her uneasy. 'It's not a matter of rushing things. Nature will take its course, and we're certainly doing as much as we can in that regard.'

'Yes...' She looked relieved, and unease trailed along his spine. Was she hiding something—some fear, some feeling? What was she not telling him?

'I just wondered. You will tell me, of course, if you think you might be?'

'Of course.' She spoke quickly. 'Of course I'll tell you.'

Alex told himself to banish that faint unease as the days moved on, and it was easy enough to do so. And somehow the few days in Athens turned into weeks, and neither of them spoke about her going back to Naxos.

And then one day, when he came home from work, the flat as lovely and welcoming as ever, she sprang something on him.

'Anna rang.'

'Oh?' As usual Alex dropped his briefcase and shed his jacket and tie. 'How are things at school?'

'They're really good.' She sounded hesitant, which made him wonder.

'And?'

'And she's been selected to play at a charity gala next week, a black-tie event. It's a huge honour, and she asked if we could go.'

'To Rome?'

'Yes.'

He stared at her for a moment, registering the nervous, beseeching look in her eyes. 'That's not a problem. You're not a prisoner, Milly. You're free to go. I have a suite on standby at the Hotel de Russie.' One he had not needed to use since his accident, but still. 'I'll make arrangements for you to stay there.'

'I don't want to go alone.' She spoke softly, imploringly, her eyes huge. Alex stilled.

'What are you saying?'

'Why don't you go with me? Anna asked specifically for us both to go. She wants us both there.'

'At a charity gala? With hundreds of people present?'

Milly tilted her chin, a gesture Alex recognised for when she was settling in for a fight. 'Yes.'

'Milly…' He blew out a breath, resenting that she'd put him in this position. 'Do I really have to explain…?'

'I know you don't like to go out in public, Alex, because of your scars.' Milly spoke softly, but with determination. 'I understand that.'

'Do you?' he burst out. 'Do you really?'

'How long has it been?' The words were little more than a whisper. 'Since the fire?'

He felt his hands clench and forced himself to relax them. 'Twenty-three months.'

'And in all that time you haven't gone out in public?'

She made him sound like some sort of pathetic hermit, which infuriated him all the more. 'I go to work, I travel as needed, I am perfectly content as I am. Don't try to *re-habilitate* me, Milly. That's the last thing I need, trust me.' Because it wouldn't happen, no matter how hard she tried, and in the meantime she'd ruin what was between them, between her pity and his pride.

'And what about what I need?' she countered. 'A husband who can accompany me to public events, be by my side? You can't live this way for ever, Alex—'

'I can live how I choose.'

'What about if—when—we have a child?' Milly cried, her voice wavering. 'Will you still hide away then? Will you never take him or her out? Never show up for his concert or sports matches—?'

'I'm not *hiding away*.'

'That's exactly what you're doing,' she shot back.

He glared at her, fury coursing through him. He took several steadying breaths, determined to remain calm. 'You don't understand.'

'Then help me to understand,' she implored. 'Tell me what's really going on, beneath this over-the-top aversion to being seen in public.'

Yet he knew he could never do that. Tell her about the fire, about how it was his fault? Reveal to her the man he truly was, the man he was afraid he always would be? It would end everything, but perhaps that was what they needed. These last few weeks had been nothing more than a mirage anyway. The realisation was painful but necessary.

'Is this just about how people see you in public, Alex?' Milly asked quietly. 'Or is it something more?'

He stared at her for a long moment, his jaw clenched. 'I don't like to be reminded,' he finally said, the words dredged up from deep inside him.

'Of what? The accident?'

'Yes. And…' He paused, unwilling to say more, yet knowing Milly would not let it go. 'I hate people looking at me with pity. It's even worse than disgust.'

'Have you given anyone a chance?' Milly asked softly. 'Perhaps they wouldn't.'

'Don't be naïve, Milly.'

'I'm not saying everyone would be understanding or accepting. I know the world doesn't work that way, Alex. But I didn't see you the way you thought I did. I still don't, and I never will. What if you gave others the chance? What if you freed yourself from this prison of your own making?'

'It's not that simple—'

'It *is* simple, but that doesn't mean it's easy. I know that.' She gazed at him steadily, her heart in her eyes. *Her heart.* 'I know I'm asking for a great deal. I do realise that, and I *will* understand if you refuse me. But for my sake, for Anna's sake, for the family we might have one day together…will you try this once? If it all goes terribly wrong, I won't ask again.' She gave him a small, wry smile. 'At least not for a long time.'

Improbably, his mouth twitched in the smallest of smiles. 'At least you're honest.'

'I try to be. But will you do this one thing for me, Alex? Come to Rome? Go to the gala? I want to be there with you, and Anna wants it, as well. She reminded you of your sister, you said…' She trailed off uncertainly, and he knew he hadn't hid the flash of anguish he felt at the mention of his sister.

To bring Daphne into it…but Milly didn't even know what she was saying. What memories she was dredging up like old, painful ghosts, haunting him. Always haunting him.

'Please,' Milly whispered.

And even though everything in him resisted, even though he knew it would be hard and no doubt humiliating, he did the one thing he'd never expected to do. He said yes.

CHAPTER THIRTEEN

OUTSIDE THE PENTHOUSE suite stars twinkled in a darkening sky as the lights of Rome glittered below. They'd arrived in the Eternal City this morning, and the charity gala was in less than an hour.

After lunch together in their luxurious suite, Alex had insisted on Milly pampering herself at the hotel's beauty spa, as well as arranging for a stylist to come in with several incredible evening gowns for her to choose from. She'd selected a column-style gown of burgundy lace, with heels dyed to match, and had her hair swept back into a loose chignon, a few wisps framing her expertly made-up face.

Looking in the mirror, Milly hardly recognised herself, and excitement along with nerves fizzed in her stomach. She was going out for the evening...*with her husband*.

Milly had been both humbled and gratified by Alex's willingness to do this for her. They hadn't spoken again of the evening or what to expect, and now, with it looming closer, she couldn't help but worry. What if it all went horribly wrong? What if people stared and whispered, or made Alex retreat even further into himself?

She wanted to believe it wouldn't happen that way; she desperately hoped this evening could be the beginning of a new life for them both.

A new life... The words caused a fluttering of panic

inside her. They had now been married for nearly two months and the pregnancy test had remained in the bottom of Milly's bag, tucked away out of sight. With each passing day, she was realising she had no need to take it; her body told its own story.

Her breasts felt fuller, and she still hadn't got her period. Even more tellingly, in the last few days she'd started feeling nauseous in the mornings. She might have been innocent but she knew enough to recognise the signs. She was almost certainly pregnant.

But if you don't take the test, you can't say for sure.

She wasn't ready to tell Alex that she was having his child. She wasn't ready for things to change between them, as she knew they would, and the fear that lodged behind her breastbone like a cold, hard stone was that once he found out she was expecting, he would send her back to Naxos and be done with her…just as he'd said he would before they'd married. One child was all he needed. He'd promised he wouldn't touch her after that.

Milly knew things had changed since they'd made that businesslike agreement…*but how much*? Despite the passion and intimacy they enjoyed in bed, in many ways Alex still felt like a stranger, cloaking himself with an emotional remoteness she was starting to hate…because he was a stranger she was falling in love with.

She certainly hadn't meant to. She'd been determined to guard her heart, had convinced herself after all the bad examples and experiences she had that she wasn't interested in love. But now Milly knew that for the fantasy it had always been. She wasn't just interested in love…she was desperate for it. Why else would she have fallen so easily for the far too glib lies of Philippe?

Because after a lifetime of living on the sidelines, being nothing more than an inconvenience to the people who were meant to love and cherish her, she longed for the kind of love that she'd read about in fairy tales, the kind of consuming, overwhelming, passionate and tender love that she wanted to believe could exist between a man and a woman.

Perhaps she'd never seen it in real life and hadn't experienced it herself—yet—but she still believed it existed. She still hoped for it.

And she couldn't risk telling Alex that she was pregnant and having it all change. Having him shut down and push her away, out of self-protection or convenience or fear. Just a few more weeks…a little more time for their relationship to grow and flourish, for Alex to realise he needed her.

Do you really think he's going to fall in love with you?

Milly turned from the view of Rome to gaze at her reflection in a gilt mirror. No matter the hairstyle, the make-up or the gown, she was still a plain little mouse. She always would be. If her own parents hadn't been able to love her, how could a man as handsome, complex, and kind as Alex? Because he *was* kind. He hid it well, but she'd seen it time and time again, the thoughtful touches, the surprising sensitivity, the tenderness. He was a good man, a wonderful, man…but how could he love her?

'Milly.' The way he spoke her name, like a caress, made a shudder of longing run through her. She would never get tired of him saying it, of him touching her, of anything about their life together. But would he? She didn't trust her own powers of persuasion. She still felt incredulous that he could desire her physically, never mind feel something deeper and more important. It was all so fragile, and she wasn't brave enough to risk it yet, even though she knew she should.

'I have something for you.' She half turned, catching her breath at the sight of him in a tuxedo, looking devastatingly as handsome as always. His dark hair was brushed back from his face, his eyes electric blue, his skin like bronze. The scars made absolutely no difference to her; he was the most handsome man she'd ever met, and he made her heart beat double-time by just looking at him.

'Turn back around,' he instructed and she did so, letting out a soft gasp as he clasped a diamond and sapphire necklace around her neck, the heavy stones cool against her skin. 'There are earrings to match.'

'Alex, it's amazing…' In the mirror the necklace, made of several large sapphire-encrusted diamonds, glittered and winked. It was the most extravagant and beautiful piece of jewellery she'd ever seen. She caught his gaze and managed a trembling smile. 'I don't know what to say…'

'They belonged to my mother,' he told her as he fastened the earrings in her ears, the gentle touch of his fingers making her shiver. 'My stepfather gave them to her on their tenth anniversary.'

The fact that they were an heirloom, part of his history, made them even more special. 'I don't even know anything about your mother,' she remarked as she touched the diamonds, watched them sparkle. 'Is she…was she…?'

'She died ten years ago. Cancer.' His tone was matter-of-fact, but his eyes were bleak, and empathy twisted inside her. 'It was better that way. Better she didn't see…'

He trailed off, his expression closing, and Milly reached up to clasp his hand resting on her shoulder. He might not want to say anything more, but she could give him that much, at least. They remained that way for a few precious seconds, with no need for words.

Then Alex stepped away. He was always the first one to do so, Milly acknowledged with a pang. Always the first to close down a conversation, to turn away, to keep it about sex. She tried not to mind, but it hurt. Every single time, it hurt. 'The limo is waiting.'

Milly reached for the matching burgundy silk wrap to cover her shoulders. Now that it was autumn, the nights were becoming chilly.

As she slid into the limo, her nerves started up again, along with the excitement. What would this evening hold? What did it promise? Maybe, just maybe, it really could be the beginning of something wonderful.

She slid a glance at Alex; he looked preoccupied, a bit stoical. She knew how hard this was for him, and she wanted to say something to encourage him, but she feared anything she said would just be a painful reminder of the challenges that lay ahead.

'Anna is so looking forward to this,' she said instead. They hadn't been able to see Anna before the gala, because of her rehearsals. 'It really is a huge honour for someone in her year to be chosen.'

'I look forward to hearing her play.'

He looked so tense that Milly ached to do something to help him relax. The limo pulled up in front of the private villa where the event was being held, an impressive eighteenth-century home just off the Piazza di Trevi. A throng of people was ascending the steps, and Milly's insides twisted with anxiety as she saw a handful of paparazzi on hand to photograph the event, something she hadn't expected. Photographs were the last thing Alex would want, and she saw his mouth tighten as he caught sight of them.

'I didn't realise…' she began, an apology, and he shook his head.

'Shall we?' His voice was toneless yet resolute. A valet opened the door of their limousine and Milly slid out, blinking as the cameras began to snap, as the paparazzi called to her in rapid-fire Italian.

'Is that Alexandro Santos?'

'Why hasn't he been seen in public in months?'

She hadn't anticipated this level of interest and specu-
lation. Alex would hate it. She ignored the questions as
Alex got out of the car, and it was as if everyone around
them drew in a collective breath. A hushed silence fell,
and then the cameras began to click and snap as the questions increased in volume and urgency.

'What happened, Alex? Tell us your story.'

'Is this why you haven't been seen in public?'

'Who is accompanying you?'

Milly struggled to hold her head high, keep the smile
on her face. She would not let these wretched photogra-
phers capture anything other than the pride and love she
felt for her husband.

She reached for his hand, twining her fingers with his
as she gave his fingers a squeeze. To her relief and joy,
he squeezed back as they made their way into the villa.

This was a living hell as well as a surprising, unexpected
heaven. Alex had anticipated some paparazzi to skulk
around the villa, even though he knew Milly hadn't. No
society event in Rome would occur without some jaded
journo or other covering it. He'd known people would be
shocked; he'd kept his secret well, along with his loyal staff.

He'd also known it was time to reveal it. Over the last
few days he'd come to realise Milly had been right when
she'd said he couldn't stay hidden away for ever, and the
most surprising thing was, as painful as this felt, he didn't
even *want* to hide any more.

He was married, and hoped to have a child. He couldn't
live the way he had been, hiding not just from staring
crowds but from life itself. This was the first important
and challenging step, and he had Milly to thank for it.

No one spoke to them as they entered the villa, although
Alex recognised many of the other guests. No one knew

what to say. He'd kept a low profile, and so of course there had been rumours. Nervous breakdown, rehab, a top-secret deal, a consuming love affair. He'd always been a private man, and so the rumours had faded after a while as people assumed he was just keeping to himself. Now they would know the truth.

And the truth will set you free.

That, he acknowledged grimly, would be asking for too much. Still, he was here, and Milly was by his side, looking magnificent and fiercely proud, as if she would take on anyone who dared to say something amiss. At the sight of her something unfurled in Alex, something far more tender and important than the overwhelming physical chemistry they shared. Something he craved, even as he reminded himself to keep his distance. Keep both of them safe.

Yet he could hardly keep his distance now, as they debuted in society as a married couple. Now was the time for solidarity, for togetherness, or at least its illusion.

'Alex…' A hand clapped on his shoulder, and he turned to see an old business acquaintance, Lukas Petrakis, smiling at him with a mixture of warmth and sympathy. 'I heard rumours of an accident, but they were so vague…' he said in a low voice, his gaze flicking to the left side of his face.

'Fire.' Alex kept it succinct, and Lukas nodded with a grimace.

'I'm so sorry…'

'No matter.'

'And this…?' He turned to Milly.

'This is Milly.' Alex paused. 'My wife.'

Lukas' eyebrows rose briefly but otherwise his expression remained friendly and pleasant. 'I'm so pleased to meet you. I didn't realise Alex had married.'

'Only recently,' Milly answered with a smile. 'We're newly-weds.'

'You've kept a lot quiet,' Lukas remarked, 'but then you always played your cards close to your chest.'

'Indeed.' Alex inclined his head, and they continued to move through the crowd.

It wasn't, he came to realise as the evening progressed, as agonising as he'd expected. In fact, it was more than tolerable. Yes, some people looked at him with pity, others with horrified fascination, but for the most part people were kind, sympathetic, friendly.

With Milly by his side he felt stronger, able to face anything, even as he acknowledged that some part of him had always known it wouldn't be so bad. It had been his pride along with his shame that had kept him hidden, unwilling to face people's pity as well as the reality of his own guilt every time another stranger caught sight of his scars.

It seemed his pride had now been dealt with, but as for his shame...

'Anna's playing now!' Milly whispered excitedly, and Alex retrained his focus on the small stage set up at one end of the private ballroom. As a hush fell over the crowd, Anna entered, looking young and lovely in a black velvet evening gown. She searched the crowd for a moment, her face lighting up as she caught sight of Alex and Milly. And then she began to play.

The hauntingly sad and beautiful notes of *Chaconne* by Tomaso Vitali soared through the space and wrapped around Alex's heart, each stroke of the bow on the violin seeming to reach right inside him. His fingers tightened on Milly's as he let the music breathe through him, awakening longings and hopes he could no longer keep buried, at least not in this moment.

He wanted more for his life than the cold, lonely existence he'd been trudging through day by day for the last two years, and even for his whole life. Always keeping himself apart, first from safety from his father's fists, and then from his own shame and guilt.

And he still felt the shame and guilt over failing Daphne, but he felt something else too. *Hope.* Fragile, faint, but there. Definitely there. He glanced at Milly, and saw tears sparkling in her eyes, and with a thrill of longing he wondered if she was as affected as he was. *Felt* the way he did…

It was all so much…the music, the evening, *Milly.* His life had broken open along with his heart, and he couldn't control either any more. He didn't even want to. He clung to Milly's hand, or perhaps she clung to his. Either way they remained together, joined by their hands, the music, everything. Tonight he would tell her how he felt…

Then the piece ended, and the room was completely silent for a few taut seconds before the applause broke out, and Anna beamed.

Milly slid her hand from his as she began to clap. 'I'm so proud of her,' she murmured. 'So proud. I never thought to have a moment like this…sorry, I'm turning into an emotional wreck, aren't I?' She smiled wryly as she dashed the tears from her cheeks, and Alex came back to reality with an almighty crash.

Milly had been emotional because of *Anna*, not him. How could he have dreamed otherwise even for a moment? She didn't feel what he did, not even a little bit, and he felt biting disappointment along with an awful relief that he hadn't got to the point of declaring, and embarrassing, himself. 'Shall we go say congratulations?' he enquired, and Milly nodded.

As soon as Anna saw them, she pushed her way through the crowds, throwing her arms around Milly and then, to Alex's surprise, around him.

'I'm so glad you came!'

'Anna, you were amazing.'

'Oh, no, I flubbed a note in the second movement—'

'Truly you were,' Alex said. 'I was very touched by the music.' That was all it had been—an emotional reaction to such a sad and evocative piece.

'Yes.' Anna studied him with bright eyes, and then glanced at Milly. 'You seem happy,' she said, sounding both satisfied and hopeful.

'We're happy to be here, and to see you,' Milly said quickly. 'Of course we are.'

'Yes, we are,' Alex added swiftly. Yet another reminder. Milly seemed intent on showing him that they were there for Anna, and Anna only. 'We must take you out for some celebratory cake and champagne.'

Anna's cheeks pinked. 'I'd love that!'

'Then it's decided.'

They celebrated in the private dining room of a nearby exclusive restaurant, with Alex ordering tiramisu and a bottle of the best champagne.

'No champagne for me,' Milly said with a little smile. 'I've had enough to drink already. But Anna can have a sip.'

Alex frowned, because as far as he recalled Milly had stuck to sparkling water at the gala, but perhaps she was remembering the last time they'd had champagne—when she'd been sick on their wedding night. A reminder he hardly wanted now. In any case, he didn't press the point, but poured Anna a small glass.

'To Anna and her stunning performance,' he said, and everyone raised their glasses. It was, Alex reflected broodingly, a reminder to him as well as a toast. Tonight had been about Anna...*only* Anna.

Both he and Milly were quiet on the way back to the hotel, having dropped Anna off at her school's boarding house. Neither of them spoke as they entered their suite, and then Milly put a hand on Alex's shoulder. He stilled.

'Alex.' She spoke his name softly.

'What is it?' His voice came out harshly; he felt too raw, after all the emotions of the evening, the impossible-to-ignore realisation that he felt something for Milly. How much, he couldn't bear to think about. Whatever it was, he could quash it down. He would have to.

'Thank you,' Milly said softly. 'Thank you for going out with me tonight. Thank you for standing by my side.' She gazed at him trustingly, her eyes wide and guileless, her expression full of sincerity and empathy.

'I should say the same,' Alex said gruffly. 'You had the harder role, undoubtedly.'

'I did not,' Milly asserted.

'Being seen with me—'

'Alex.' She pressed her finger against his lips, a whisper of skin. 'Don't say such a thing. Don't even think it. You were the handsomest man there tonight, as far as I was concerned.'

'Milly…' It came out as a warning. He did not want her pity, the useless stroking of his ego for sympathy's sake. Not now, when he'd been on the verge of feeling so much more for her.

'I mean it…' She took a step closer to him, so her hips brushed his and need, as ever, flared inside him, white-hot. 'What will it take for you to believe me?' She searched his face, looking for an answer he couldn't give because the truth was he didn't know. Then she lifted her hand and traced the deep ridges of his scars with her fingers. Alex sucked in a hard gasp, the damaged skin oversensitive, her touch achingly tender. In all the times they'd made love, she'd never touched his scars before. It felt as if she were touching his soul.

'These scars are part of who you are,' she said softly. 'They tell the story of you, and I only know part of it, but I know this: I know they show you are a survivor, and that you are strong.'

'You don't know…'

'Tell me, Alex.' She cupped his scarred cheek with her hand, and he closed his eyes, both savouring and reviling her touch. 'Tell me about the fire.'

He didn't speak for a long moment. *He couldn't.* Yet he felt the memories rising like a tide within him, and he knew he would speak. He would tell her about that terrible night. And maybe it would make her walk away from him, or at least stop trying so much, making him care whether she wanted him to or not. Perhaps telling her was the answer, the way to keep them both safe—and separate.

'It was at my house,' he finally said, the words seeming to come from far away. 'Here in Athens. I had a villa in Kolonaki.' Milly simply waited, her hand still on his cheek, touching him so tenderly. 'My sister, Daphne,' he said, knowing it was all disjointed, fragments of memory lodged in his throat— in his heart—like broken shards of glass. 'And…and her son, Talos.'

Milly's breath came out in a soft gasp of sorrow. 'Oh, Alex…'

'They both died.' He shook his head. 'I should have been able to save them.'

'How?'

Could he really tell her all of it? The terrible truth? Yes. He had to. For both of their sakes.

He took a ragged breath and opened his eyes. 'Let me start at the beginning,' he said.

CHAPTER FOURTEEN

MILLY WATCHED AS Alex walked away from her, loosening his bow tie and shedding his jacket and cummerbund. Even now, *especially* now, he looked devastatingly attractive—his body one of leashed power and innate authority, his face drawn in stark lines of remembered pain. She wanted to put her arms around him. *She wanted to tell him she loved him.*

But she didn't dare, and she knew now was not the time anyway. Now was the time for Alex's story, at last. And perhaps it would draw them closer together. She prayed it would.

'The beginning,' Alex stated flatly, 'is that my father was a terrible man. Abusive to my mother as well as to my sister Daphne and me.' Milly opened her mouth to express her horror and sorrow, but Alex cut across her before she could frame a word. 'He was clever about it, so no one knew outside the family. He always made it feel as if it were our fault—we'd done something to provoke him.' A pause as Alex stared out of the window, lost in memory. 'He would fly into terrible rages.'

'I'm sorry…'

'On the outside, we looked like the perfect family. My father was successful, my mother beautiful, Daphne and I were model children. We were too scared to be anything else. As a family we were private, because we had to be. We didn't make friends, we kept everyone as an acquaintance. It was easier that way.'

Which explained so much about Alex's need for privacy and distance now, Milly thought with an ache. He shoved his hands in his trouser pockets as he stared out at the night.

'But then my father went too far. He broke my mother's arm, and that was something she couldn't hide.' Another pause, and Milly wished he'd turn and look at her. 'I confronted him. I was fifteen by then, practically a man. And I beat him within an inch of his life. Broken nose, broken jaw, broken wrist. Internal bleeding. He was in the hospital for weeks, thanks to my fists.'

Milly couldn't keep from gasping at the awful image. She suspected he'd meant to shock her, and he had. But she still wanted to hear the rest of it.

'What happened then?' she asked softly.

'He pressed charges. My father thought he was above the law, but he wanted to make sure I wasn't.' Alex let out a rush of breath as he shrugged. 'I ended up spending a few months in juvenile detention. Not the high point of my life. But by the time I came out, my father was long gone—he'd taken a corporate job in the Middle East. And my mother was married to my stepfather, Christos.'

Milly waited, knowing there had to be more. Much more. After a long moment, Alex resumed his story. 'I was angry and impossible, but Christos took me under his wing. Treated me like his own. And I learned self-control.' He paused. 'Christos was tough on me, but in a good way. But we all had scars from my father's treatment, and that showed itself in different ways.' He paused, and Milly waited, her heart in her mouth. How much more could there be to this awful story? And yet she knew there was worse to come. He hadn't even spoken about his sister yet, not really.

'Daphne married an abusive man when she was just twenty,' Alex resumed. 'Nikolaos Aganos. We didn't realise what was going on at first. She hid it well, but we'd all become experts at hiding. And perhaps we didn't want to realise. Perhaps we closed our eyes, because we were experts at that too. But then it got worse—it always does. And two years ago, she finally left him, running to me, bringing her four-year-old son Talos with her.' He fell silent, his expression bleak, his body taut. 'I'll never forget how she looked, coming to my door. A black eye. Bruises…bruises on her *throat*.' His voice caught, and Milly reached out a hand, desperate to comfort him even as a sense of dread seeped into her stomach. She knew Daphne was dead, and that there had been a fire…

'Oh, Alex…'

'And Talos was so terrified, he had become mute. He wouldn't say a word, just clung to her and hid his face.'

'That must have been so terrible,' Milly said quietly. Any words felt utterly inadequate. 'I'm so, so sorry.'

'You know what my reaction was?' Alex asked in that flat tone she had come to hate, except now she knew how much pain that toneless delivery could hide. 'Anger. Just like before, with my father, I felt rage—a consuming, overwhelming fury, one I could not control. And I let that guide me. I let it *drive* me. I never learn, do I?'

Milly stared at him uncertainly. 'What…what do you mean?'

'I left them there, Daphne and Talos. I left them alone in my house even though I knew they were hurting and terrified. And I went in search of Aganos. I think if I'd found him, I might have killed him.' He gave her a cold smile, the coldest she'd ever seen. 'In fact, I'm quite sure I would have.'

Milly's heart lurched as that persistent dread swirled inside her, the most corrosive of acids. 'But you didn't find him…'

'No, because while I was out in the city baying for his blood, he'd gone to my house…and set fire to it.'

Milly's hand covered her mouth. 'No…'

'Yes. Daphne and Talos were sleeping. The doors were locked. When I came back, the whole place was in flames.'

So why was he the one with the scars? Milly studied him, the clenched fists, the heaving chest, the eyes full of pain. 'You went in,' she said softly. 'Didn't you? To rescue them?'

'I didn't do much good, did I? I found them, curled up together, unconscious from the smoke. I carried them both outside, and a burning beam fell across my face as I came out of the door. But none of it mattered. They both died from smoke inhalation within the hour.'

'Oh, Alex…'

'If I'd been there—'

'But how could you have known?' Milly burst out. Realisation crashed through her, at what Alex had endured, what he had blamed himself for, for so many years. 'That fire was *not* your fault.'

'I might not have lit the match,' Alex returned staunchly, 'but I'm still to blame. I chose anger over empathy. I chose to seek personal revenge rather than to be there for my sister and her son, and as a result they both died.'

'They might have died anyway,' Milly argued, and Alex let out a harsh laugh.

'You don't really believe that.'

'You might have died as well—'

'No. The only reason Aganos came to my house was

because he knew I wasn't there. He said as much in court, when he was on trial. He'd been watching the house, watching me.'

'Even so,' Milly began shakily, but then stopped. She knew whatever she said right now was crucial; she felt their relationship might turn on the words that came out of her mouth, and that thought was terrifying, because the truth was she had no idea what to say, or even what to feel.

Perhaps Alex was right, and his sister and her son *wouldn't* have died if he'd been there. Perhaps he'd let anger get the better of him more than once, but it had been a righteous anger, an anger fuelled by love and pain and the desire for justice. 'You can't torture yourself over this, Alex,' she said finally. 'Don't live your life in the past…'

'My sister and her son are *dead*.' The words came out savagely as he turned to face her. 'Because of me. And you say I should let it go? Give myself a break? Do you really think that, Milly? Or are you finally realising that I'm not the man you thought I was, have been *hoping* I was? Because that's what's been going on, isn't it?' His mouth twisted in a sneer, his scars pulling tight, his face a mask of derision. You've been starting to care for me, haven't you, no matter what you've told yourself? You've been painting rainbows in your head and now you know that you shouldn't have.' Milly blinked, his words like hammer blows to her heart, shattering it like the fragile thing she knew it had always been.

'You can't say I didn't warn you,' he continued. 'All I wanted out of this marriage was an heir, but perhaps it's better that I don't reproduce.' He lifted his chin, his eyes glittering fiercely. 'I'm not the man you've been wishing I was, Milly. Well, at least now you know. Before it's too late.'

'Too late for what?' Milly asked, her voice and body

trembling. He was pushing her away on purpose, she knew it, and it hurt more than she thought possible. Her illusions were shattered...not by what Alex had admitted to, but *why* he was admitting it. Because he didn't want her to care for him. 'Do you want me to walk away from you?' she asked, her voice wobbling on the words. 'Is that what this is about, Alex?'

He shrugged a shoulder, coldly indifferent to her plea. 'You can do what you like.'

Milly swallowed hard, trying not to feel hurt. He *wanted* to hurt her, she knew that much, and that was painful enough, never mind the words he said. She was tempted to do just what he said—walk away. Save herself from any further pain. Except she knew she couldn't make that choice. Wouldn't. And yet she was so very afraid that what had been hoped to be a beginning was going to be an awful end.

'I can't walk away from you, Alex,' she said, one hand pressed to her still-flat stomach. 'Whether I want to or not.'

His mouth twisted. 'Bound by our vows?' he stated sardonically. 'How quaint, Milly—'

'No,' Milly said, and now she really was shaking, both inside and out. How had it descended to this, so quickly? She pressed her hand flat against her belly, imagining the flutter of life she knew was inside her. 'I can't, because I'm pregnant.'

Alex stared at her for a full minute, the words taking that long to penetrate his dazed mind. He took in her terrified expression, her trembling hand on her belly.

'Pregnant,' he repeated tonelessly. 'You're sure?'

'Yes. Very.'

He continued to study her, noticing how her lips trembled along with her hand; her gaze slid away from his.

She couldn't even look him in the eye. 'How far along are you?' he asked, suspicion creeping down his spine with cold fingers. 'How long have you known?'

'A…a little while.' She still wouldn't look at him.

'Milly.' His eyes narrowed as he took in other details of her appearance he hadn't realised until now: her fuller face and breasts, the slight roundness of her belly. 'How long?' he demanded harshly.

'A…a few weeks. I think we conceived on our wedding night.' She spoke softly and Alex swung around, stalking to the window as he fought a sweeping sense of betrayal—and hurt. That had been nearly two *months* ago. Why had she kept it from him? Why had she *lied*?

'Were you ever going to tell me?' he asked, his voice low and furious. 'Or were you just going to hope for the best?'

'What is that supposed to mean?' Milly sounded near tears. 'Alex, I was going to tell you. Of course I was. It's just… I was scared.'

He swung back around. *'Scared?'*

'Yes. Scared.' She nibbled her lip, reminding him of her fear on their wedding night. The fear, it seemed, she'd always had of him, and now he'd given her even greater reason to be afraid. How could he have ever thought this would have worked? That a man like him, scarred inside and out, could love someone—and more importantly, more laughably, be loved himself?

'We can still divorce,' he heard himself saying.

'What?' Milly's eyes rounded, her jaw dropping. 'You don't mean that.'

He didn't know what he meant. He felt dazed, over-whelmed by the emotions that had spiralled through him in the course of a single evening. Realising he cared for Milly, telling her the truth, realising she didn't care about him. And now a baby. A child, the very thing he'd wanted all along…

'I don't know,' he admitted rawly. 'But at this moment it seems sensible.' He breathed out slowly, remembering what he'd told her back when they'd been ironing out all the details, how he wouldn't touch her once she was pregnant. No matter how amazing their chemistry had been, it was clear a real relationship was not possible. He was a fool to think, even for a moment, that it could have been.

'In any case,' he told her, 'now that you are carrying my child there is no reason for you to stay in Athens. You can return to Naxos tomorrow.'

Milly stared at him for a long moment, her expression impossible to read. 'Is that what you want?' she asked finally, and Alex made himself nod. It was better this way. It had to be.

'Yes,' he said. 'It is.' He paused, searching her face, trying to see if there was any affection or hope there, but she wasn't giving anything away, her face closed up, her eyes shadowed. 'I assume it is what you want, as well. You said Naxos was your home.'

Her gaze slid away from his. 'Yes…'

'So there is no difficulty.' He didn't quite make it a question, but he waited, willing her to say something. *Anything.* One word from her, he thought, and he'd take it all back. He'd demand or even beg that she stay.

But he'd put himself out there too much already tonight. He'd told her everything; he'd made himself more vulnerable than he could bear, and he didn't think he had it in him to do it again, not without a word, something from her to give him hope. Help him to believe.

And so he waited for a full heart-stopping minute, and she didn't say anything. Not one word. She just nodded slowly, and, filled with equal parts anger and pain, Alex walked out of the room.

Milly slept in the second bedroom that night; Alex heard the click of the door, and then, to his further grief and pain, the turn of the lock. Did she think he was going to invade her bedroom, demand his rights?

It took him hours to fall into an uneasy doze, and in the morning, when Alex woke, gritty-eyed after a restless night, he found that she had already gone.

'She called a taxi,' the concierge informed him apologetically when Alex confronted the man downstairs. 'Quite early...she said she was catching a morning flight back to Athens.'

'Of course.' He turned away, not willing to show a stranger how those words felled him. Clearly Milly couldn't wait to leave him. He'd expected to have her accompany him back to Athens, and then take his yacht to Naxos. But, no. She'd gone her own way, without even saying goodbye. She'd wanted quit of him as soon as she could.

It was better this way.

The words felt meaningless to him now, because it didn't feel better at all. He felt hurt and angry, filled with a grief that was deeper than he'd even imagined it could be. Yet could he really blame Milly for taking the out he'd offered?

No, he couldn't. Alex took a deep breath as he cloaked himself in a cold, icy calm. He wouldn't be angry, not this time, and he wouldn't be hurt. Neither would he care.

Yet Milly's absence ate at him all the way back to Athens, and then for the next two weeks as he heard nothing from her, and refused to reach out himself, out of both pride and hurt. He did satisfy himself that she'd got back to Naxos safely, having spoken to Yiannis, but with Milly he did not share a single word.

It was better this way.

Maybe if he kept repeating it to himself, he'd believe it one day. Believe that he could live alone and be, if not happy, then at least satisfied. But he felt neither, and every day that passed was a solitary torture.

Several times a day Alex found himself picking up the phone, starting to dial. He'd just call to see if she was all right. To check on her pregnancy. But every time he started to press her number, he stopped. He would not do it. He couldn't.

And then, three weeks after that awful night in Rome, both the beginning and end of everything, Yiannis called, his voice sounding far too grim.

'Alex,' he said. 'It's Milly.'

CHAPTER FIFTEEN

IT ALL HAPPENED SO QUICKLY. One minute Milly was walking along the dusty road to Halki, trying to enjoy the crisp autumn day and not feel the swamping of misery that had accompanied her most days since leaving Alex in Rome, and the next she was sprawled belly-down on the road, grit embedded in her hands and knees and chin, everything stinging and smarting.

Too dazed to realise what had happened, Milly simply lay there for a moment, shocked by how quickly she had fallen. Painfully she got to her hands and knees, one hand cupping her belly protectively; at fourteen weeks, she had a small, neat bump. Then she felt a trickle of hot wetness between her thighs, and everything in her clanged with panic.

Somehow she managed to get to her feet; her body ached all over and her hands, knees, and face were smeared with blood and pebbled with grit. But worse, far worse, was the fear that she was bleeding. That she might be losing this baby.

The next hour was a blur; she stumbled back to the villa, terror clutching at her as she felt a band of pain start in her lower back and radiate out. Contractions. She was having contractions, and she was so early in her pregnancy still.

'Please, no,' she gasped, and then she rang Yiannis. He was there in minutes, bundling her in his truck and taking her to the hospital in Naxos' main town.

'I must call Kyrie Santos,' Yiannis told her as she sat in a plastic chair in the hospital's crowded waiting room. Although Milly hadn't spoken of it, she knew Yiannis suspected there had been an acrimonious separation between her and Alex. 'He will want to know.'

Would he? Three weeks and there had not been one word. *Not one word.*

Milly had talked herself round and round in circles, first cursing herself for not being brave enough to tell Alex she'd fallen in love with him, and then trying to convince herself she'd done the right thing in leaving, when it had been so painfully obvious he was pushing her away. He didn't want what she wanted. He wasn't willing to take the risk. And in any case, this was what they'd agreed on, when they'd discussed those cold, clinical terms. This was what she'd expected all along.

But now all she could think about was her baby. Her precious baby, so tiny and fragile inside her. *Stay safe, baby, please...*

Yiannis left her to make the call, and when he returned his face was grim. 'Kyrie Santos is sending an air ambulance immediately to take you to Athens.'

'What? But—'

'The facilities here are not adequate for emergency maternity care,' Yiannis continued. 'Many women go to Athens for such care.' He squeezed her hand. 'It is going to be all right, Kyria Santos.'

But Milly feared it wouldn't be. And ridiculously, perhaps, it hurt that Alex was sending an ambulance rather than coming himself. He didn't care about her; it was only his precious heir that mattered. *Stay safe, baby...*

The short flight to the hospital in Athens was the lone-liest and most terrifying experience of Milly's life. The contractions and bleeding had continued, making her dread the worst. As the helicopter could only hold one patient, Yiannis had not been allowed to accompany her. She was completely on her own, and she felt it every second of the hour-long flight.

The sense of fearful loneliness continued when she arrived at the hospital in Athens, and after some initial checks, she was scheduled for an ultrasound to check on her baby. Although some of the consultants and techni-cians spoke English, it wasn't enough for Milly to under-stand whether they were reassuring or warning her, and her Greek wasn't up to the standard to ask the questions she desperately needed to.

As she waited for her scan, still not knowing what was going on or whether her baby was alive or dead, all she wanted was Alex. She'd been so stupid, so stubborn and foolish and afraid. She'd gone back over that night in Rome and rewritten it a thousand times in her head, but now, facing this alone, she knew exactly what she should have done.

She should have been brave. She should have told him she loved him, no matter how much he was trying to keep his distance, and that the regrets of his past made no dif-ference to her. She should have held him in his arms and kissed his scars and promised him that their love could heal him. If she'd done all that, all the things that had been in her heart, perhaps she wouldn't be alone here now. Per-haps Alex would have admitted he felt something for her; perhaps he would have been brave enough to say what was in his heart.

But she hadn't done any of it, Milly acknowledged in

the cold, sterile loneliness of an anonymous waiting room. She'd looked at Alex's furious face, heard his cold tone, and she'd taken him at his word and retreated. Every insecurity she'd ever had had begun to blare in her brain.

No one has ever loved you. No one has ever fought for you, or stood by you, or cared enough to take a risk. Why did you dare think this man would?

And so she'd stayed silent. And she'd let her heart break.

Worst of all, she feared now it was too late. Alex wasn't even coming to see if she was all right; in three weeks, he hadn't contacted her at all, not even to ask about their own child. If there had been a moment when he'd cared, or *could* have cared at least, it was gone. She hadn't risked her own heart, just as she'd told Alex three months ago. She'd said she hadn't seen the point, but unfortunately now she very much did. The trouble was, it was just too late.

'Where is my wife?' The words came out in a low growl of both menace and authority. The receptionist's eyes widened as she took in the full force of him, six feet three of powerful male on a mission.

'Your name, *kyrie*…?'

'Alexandro Santos,' Alex bit out. The nurse glanced at his scars but he barely noticed, hardly cared. 'And my wife is Milly Santos. She was brought here by air ambulance twenty minutes ago for a suspected miscarriage.' The words felt like a punch in the gut, leaving him breathless with pain. 'And I want to see her *immediately*.'

It had been just over an hour since Yiannis had rung him with the news that Milly had fallen and her pregnancy was threatened. An hour of raking himself over the coals, again and again, because it would *never* be enough.

How could he be failing someone he loved *again*? Having walked away *again*, instead of staying where he was needed, if not wanted? He never should have let Milly return to Naxos alone. He should have never stayed silent, too proud and ashamed to reach out to her. If something happened to the baby…*their child*…he would never forgive himself.

'Kyria Santos is in the ultrasound department,' the receptionist told him. 'If you go to the left—'

Alex went to the left. He strode down the hall, fists clenched, heart pumping. This time it *had* to work out. This time it couldn't end in tragedy and despair, not like before…

But he, more than anyone, knew there were no guarantees. No fairy promising a happy ending, waving her pointless wand. Life didn't work that way, and as he turned the corner he steeled himself for the worst.

'Alex.' Milly's voice sounded as if it were torn from her chest, a ragged cry that reached in and wrapped around Alex's heart.

He dropped to his knees in front of her, wrapping his arms around her slight frame as she pressed her face against his shoulder, her body shaking with the force of her sobs.

'Milly…*agapi mou*…' My love. The words had slipped out, spoken from the heart, and he was glad. He put his hands on her shoulders, easing back so he could look into her face. 'Are you all right in yourself? You are not hurt…?' Her chin was smeared with blood, a bruise on one cheekbone. It made Alex ache.

'Just scraped.' Milly sniffed. 'But, Alex, the baby, our baby…'

A fist closed over his heart. 'You have had the scan?'

'Not yet. But I've…' She dropped her voice along with

her eyes. 'I've had bleeding and contractions…oh, Alex, I'm so scared.'

He pulled her to him again, stroking her hair as he offered her words of comfort. *Agapi mou. Kardia mou.* My love. My heart. He didn't know if she understood what they meant, but he couldn't keep himself from saying them. From meaning them. Now that she was in his arms again, the life of their child in danger, he knew he meant them more than anything he'd ever said in his life.

He loved her. And he would tell her, whether she loved him or not. She deserved to know. He wanted her to know. He needed it.

'Milly Santos?'

They both tensed at the sound of her name on the nurse's lips. Alex helped her rise shakily to her feet and then he accompanied her into a darkened room for the scan.

'Please make yourself comfortable,' the nurse instructed. 'The technician will be with you shortly.'

Moments later the technician came in, a kindly-looking woman with a sympathetic smile. Alex watched, his heart caught in his throat, as Milly lifted her shirt, revealing the slight swell of her baby bump. *Their child*, right there. Tears clogged his throat and he swallowed hard. *Their child.*

'Let's see how baby is doing,' the technician murmured in Greek, and they both waited breathlessly as she squirted the cold, clear gel on Milly's stomach and then began to swipe and probe with the wand. Within seconds an image appeared on the screen, black and white and blurry. Their baby.

And it wasn't moving.

'*Alex…*' Milly's hand grabbed hold of his hand, and he held on tightly, wanting to imbue her with his strength. His hope. *Please, God. Please, not this time…*

And then, like the miracle it truly was, the tiny form

on the screen flung out an arm. The technician turned up the volume on the ultrasound machine and the room was suddenly filled with a loud whooshing noise.

'Baby's heartbeat,' the technician explained. 'Sounds a bit like a galloping horse.'

'You mean…the baby is okay?' Milly asked tremulously, in halting Greek. She turned to Alex. 'Can you ask her…? I don't understand enough Greek…'

'Of course.'

He spoke swiftly to the technician, and then turned back to Milly, unable to keep the emotion from his voice, his eyes. 'The baby is all right. Perfectly healthy. They want to keep you in hospital for a few days, and then bed-rest for a while after that, because the contractions are a concern. But everything looks okay, Milly.' He broke off, finding it hard to speak. 'Our baby is going to be all right.'

They didn't talk as Milly was taken in a wheelchair to a hospital room, the best Alex could procure. She looked exhausted, her face pale and grey with fatigue, and Alex knew she needed to sleep.

'Alex…' she began, sounding uncertain, and gently he pressed his fingers against her lips.

'Shh. You need to sleep. We can talk later, Milly.' He settled himself into a chair by the bed. 'I'm not going anywhere.'

She nodded slowly, her eyelids already fluttering, and within minutes she was asleep.

Milly woke slowly, blinking the hospital room into focus as memories rushed through her. The fall. The ambulance. *Alex.*

She turned her head, her heart leaping into her throat at the thought that he might have left, but he was there, just as he'd promised he would be. His unmarked cheek was resting on his hand, his scarred cheek turned to her, his eyelids drooping in sleep. He looked wonderful.

Alex's eyes fluttered open and then his electric-blue gaze trained on her and he straightened. 'You're awake.'

'Yes.'

He leaned forward, scanning her face. 'How do you feel?'

'Aching all over. And still so tired.' Tremulously, wanting to be brave, she reached for his hand. He took it, twining his fingers with hers. 'Alex…'

'Wait.' His voice was rough. 'Don't say anything, Milly.'

Her heart felt like a bird fluttering in her chest. 'Why not?' she whispered.

'Because I want to say something first.'

She swallowed hard. She had no idea what he was going to say, but she feared it. He looked so serious, so intent. 'All right,' she finally managed.

Alex bowed his head. Several moments passed before he looked up again, and when he did Milly saw the sheen of tears in his eyes. 'Milly, I'm sorry. So, so sorry.'

'For…what?'

'For letting you down. I never should have…there are so many things I shouldn't have done.' He drew a shuddering breath. 'I shouldn't have assumed things on our wedding night that made it such a disaster. I shouldn't have asked to have the marriage annulled. I shouldn't have pushed you away, time and time again, because…because I was a coward. An emotional coward.'

'Alex…'

'And most of all, I shouldn't have kept myself from telling you that I love you.'

Milly felt as if her heart had somersaulted in her chest.

For a few seconds she couldn't make sense of the words, was afraid to trust them. 'You…'

'Love you. Yes. I think I fell in love with you right from the beginning, although I convinced myself I felt nothing. And over these last few weeks…the time we've spent to-gether…the courage and kindness you've shown…'

'Courage!' Milly let out a trembling laugh. 'I was as much a coward as you, Alex. Why do you think I said nothing that night in Rome?'

He winced, shaking his head. 'That was my fault…'

'It was mine, as well. After so many years of feeling pushed aside and unloved, I let those fears govern my head and heart. I wanted to tell you I'd fallen in love with you, but I didn't because I was scared.' She shook her head, regret turning her voice ragged. 'It was the same reason I didn't tell you I was pregnant. I was afraid that once you found out I was, you'd send me away. Tell me you didn't need or want me any more.'

Alex grimaced. 'And that's just what I did, because I thought it was for the best…except I didn't, really. I didn't at *all*. The last three weeks have been hell for me, Milly. I've picked up the phone a dozen times a day to ring you, but I never did, because I was too proud. Too afraid.' He shook his head. 'And I left you alone while you were preg-nant…if something had happened to our child…'

She reached over to take his hand between both of her own. 'Alex, you have carried the weight of the world on your shoulders for too long. You can't blame yourself for everything.'

'But if I'd been there—'

'I still would have walked into Halki on my own. Do you really think you could have stopped me? And if it hadn't been a walk into the village, it might have been on the stairs, or going down to the beach… You're not God,

Alex. You can't control everything, and you can't blame yourself every time something goes wrong.'

He was silent for a long moment, staring down at their clasped hands. 'But it was my anger, my pride and my shame that kept us apart, just as before. I was too proud to admit I was wrong, and too ashamed to risk telling you how I felt.'

'But you are now,' Milly said softly. Her heart was filling up to overflowing with hope and happiness. 'And that's what matters. What we say *now*. The past is in the past, Alex…all the pain and hurt and regret. It's shaped who we are, but it doesn't have to shape our future. It can't be changed, but it can be redeemed.'

'Do you really believe that?' he asked hoarsely.

'Yes, with all my heart.'

Alex looked at her, his hand still clasped between hers, his expression utterly serious. 'Did you mean what you said, Milly? About having fallen in love with me?'

Her mouth was dry, tears brimming in her eyes, as she answered. 'With all my heart.'

'Why?'

He sounded so incredulous, she couldn't help but laugh. 'Because you're wonderful, Alexandro Santos. You're kind and thoughtful and courageous and honest. And you're quite handsome, as well.'

'Handsome—' he scoffed, but she shook her head, pressing her palm against his scarred cheek.

'Devastatingly handsome and sexy to boot. I love you, Alex. I've fallen in love with you over the last few months, and I want to spend the rest of my life loving you, if you'll let me.' It felt so good to say the words, so freeing and wonderful. Not scary after all, in the end, and definitely worth the risk.

'If I'll let you? I'll count myself blessed to do so. All I

want to do is make up for lost time, Milly, and love you for the rest of my days.'

'Starting now?' Milly said softly.

Alex placed his hand on her slight bump, a look of wonder on his face. 'And lasting for ever.'

EPILOGUE

Six months later

'IT'S A GIRL!'

Alex let out an incredulous laugh as the doctor lifted the squalling, red-faced baby onto Milly's chest. Tears streamed down her cheeks as she touched the damp, dark ringlets of their infant daughter. 'She's perfect.'

'She looks like you,' Alex said as he dropped a kiss onto her forehead. It had been an intense twenty hours of labour, and Milly had been amazing throughout, as brave as he'd ever seen her be.

'Like me?' Milly scoffed as the nurse placed her daughter in her arms. 'She looks like you. Dark hair and blue eyes. Beautiful.'

'Her eye colour might change,' the nurse said with a smile.

'Either way, she's perfect,' Alex stated definitively. 'Because she's ours.'

'Yes.' Milly cooed down at her daughter. They hadn't talked too much about names, not daring to hope so much. It had been a difficult pregnancy, and Milly had gone into preterm labour several times before the doctors had been able to stop it. She'd been on bed-rest for four months, and their daughter had finally been born at a healthy thirty-eight weeks, to both of their relief. They'd both been afraid they might never reach this moment, but they had. And while the last six months had been scary, they'd also been wonderful, for the uncertainty of their situation had brought them together, stronger and more in love than ever.

They'd learned to turn *towards* each other when they were frightened or worried, rather than away. They'd come to depend on each other utterly, and for that they were both thankful, as well as for the miracle lying in Milly's arms.

'Have you thought of a name?' Alex asked softly as he gazed down at the Madonna-like picture of his wife holding their child.

'I have,' Milly admitted, her gaze on their daughter. 'If it was all right with you, I was thinking of Daphne.'

Alex blinked rapidly, moved by her suggestion. 'If you really mean it…'

'Of course I do.' Milly looked up at him, her beautiful face suffused with love and tenderness. 'Would you like to hold her, Alex? Would you like to hold your daughter?'

Wordlessly, unable to frame the words, he nodded. Gently Milly transferred their daughter to him and Alex cradled her tiny form, amazed and humbled by the slight and yet overwhelming weight of her. His daughter. Daphne.

As Milly had told him all those months ago, the past could not be changed, but it could be redeemed. *He* could be redeemed, and the proof of it was here in his arms, by his side. His daughter. His wife. *His family.* For ever.

Turning back to Milly, Alex reached for her hand. In that moment, they needed no words, nothing but the joining of their fingers, their hearts. Together. Always. Her eyes full of love, Milly smiled at him, and with his heart overflowing, everything in him singing with joy, Alex smiled back.

* * * * *

COMING SOON!

We really hope you enjoyed reading this book. If you're looking for more romance, be sure to head to the shops when new books are available on

Thursday 13th June

To see which titles are coming soon, please visit

millsandboon.co.uk/nextmonth